The Pood: Mich...
Volume 1 in a continui...

Printed in Hell, and in the United States of America

ISBN-10: 1-944854-00-2
ISBN-13: 978-1-944854-00-3

Publisher
Pood Paw Prints, LLC
https://www.poodpawprints.com
https://www.facebook.com/poodpawprints
Press information: thorson@poodpawprints.com

Production Editor
David M
davidm@poodpawprints.com

Cover Art
Awet Moges
oroboros@hyperboreans.com

Cover Color
Safeez Safeez
safeezstudio@gmail.com

Interior art and back cover art
David M

Coming Soon from Pood Paw Prints
The Pood: God's Balls

The Pood: Michigan's Inferno
By David M
And Scott Thorson,
Starring Dave Taylor as The Pood
and featuring Awet Moges
in the Labyrinth of Being and Time

The Pood

MICHIGAN'S INFERNO

A Novel in Five Books and an Epilogue

I
Fifteen Pounds of Pure Evil in a Fur Coat

II
In the House of Bubb

III
The Nine Neighborhoods of Hell
Satan Agonistes

IV
The Inner Station of the Ultimate Horror

V
Apocalypse Now and Then

Epilogue
Where are They Now?

The Pood of Guernica

In his monumental mural Guernica, Picasso appears to have anticipated the arrival of The Pood by some seventy years, according to the prominent art historian I. M. Pasto. The detail from the mural is shown here. Dr. Pasto notes that Picasso's version of The Pood represents the only animal, human or non-human, in the work that appears actually to be *enjoying* the destruction of Guernica; and perhaps was even the *cause* of it. In addition, Dr. Pasto calls attention to the fact that the two eerie orange eyes of the beastie are the only spots of color in the otherwise black, white, and gray-scale depiction. All well and good; but the attentive reader will note that in addition to being an insufferable asshole, Dr. Pasto has been blind since birth.

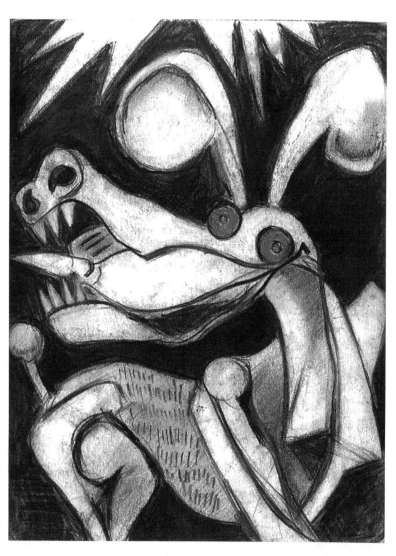

Book the First

Fifteen Pounds of Pure Evil in a Fur Coat

"If you want a friend in Washington, get a dog."
— Harry S. Truman

Nothing much ever happened in Hell, Michigan. In this reliably Republican burg, this sleepy sinecure of Satan and his satraps, the order of the day was the quotidian.

It is true that back in ninety-eight, Holly Jinks strangled her toddler, Hi, in his crib with her bare hands. And back in ought-five, Howdy Houlihan raped his twelve-year-old son, Boy Howdy, and then held him hostage at gunpoint until Sheriff Ted killed the old man dead with a shotgun blast to the head.

Perhaps most spectacularly of all, in ought-nine a demented drifter later identified as Lester Pugh donned an Arthur Schopenhauer Halloween mask and a black trench coat and shot up a Dairy Queen with an AK-47, killing five employees and three customers before turning the gun on himself. During the carnage, he raved: "It is bad today, and it will be worse tomorrow; and so on till the worst of all!"

But those were isolated incidents — or, at best, they constituted a bloody overture to the real-life *opera buffa* to come, which changed world history. (If you don't remember the events about to be chronicled, dear reader, you were asleep at the switch.)

For on Good Friday, 2012, all Hell broke loose at last.

At noon a tremendous explosion shook the hamlet, accompanied by a dazzling blaze of light. A mushroom cloud towered overhead. Riding atop it, as seen from a distance, was a tempestuous, tatterdemalion flyspeck of black.

As the cloud gradually settled back down to the earth, stainless-steel claws studding four paws chunked down into rocks, breaking them into pebbles. Eyelids audibly creaked open like tiny coffin lids, revealing two phosphorescent orange eyes that burned off the mists. A mouth flew open, and a tongue flew out.

"BIIIIILLLLLLLAAAAARGH!"

Yap yap yap yap yap!

```
~=\__!
   !  !
```

Dell Holland was plowing the North Forty.

"Jesus, Lord Redeemer," he gasped, as the flash of light filled the cab of his tractor. The sound of the blast followed, and the earth shook. *Earthquake? Meteor? Bomb?* Apocalyptic scenarios flew through his mind like a flock of Michigan mallard geese startled by a hunter's shotgun blast.

He heard the wailing then, like the cry of a banshee, and his blood ran cold.

```
~=\__!
   !  !
```

Terrance Hildebrandt was hauling a load of hay bales and a shipment of helium-inflated, anatomically correct sex dolls of both genders on the long road to Hell. He was, quite literally, going to Hell and back. The sex-doll shipment disgusted him, but money was money. Its destination was the secret town dungeon, of which everyone in Hell knew, but about which no one spoke. The bill of lading specified the recipient of the shipment as Ayn Rand, Objectivist dominatrix.

Hildebrandt loved the open road. It relaxed him.

He fiddled with the knob of his radio, trying to haul in a classic rock station from Detroit. Through bursts of static came not Bob Seger, but the voice of a lunatic chanting about niggaz and hos and bitches. He angrily turned off the radio, his mood of relaxation dissipating. The familiar tension crept back into his tendons and muscles, making them as taut as steel cables. "Al Qaeda music," he disdainfully called gangsta rap.

Hildebrandt was a survivalist, and after dropping off the bales and dolls he planned to pick up another ten cases of freeze-dried apricots to stack in the fallout shelter beside the barn of his house, fifteen miles east of Hell. It had been dug generations ago when the threat was not from the Muslim terrorists but from the

Godless Communists. There are *always* threats, he thought grimly, and now he turned the radio back on, avoiding the Detroit stations. He thought of that metropolis turned necropolis, long ago shanghaied by the darkies, and of its suburb of Dearborn, with its vast Raghead population. Dearborn was under Sharia law now: Glenn Beck had said so. He fiddled with the dial, hoping to snag Beck's reassuring red, white and blue voice from the all-American atmosphere. Bursts of static.

And then a dazzling blaze of light.

He grappled with the wheel, trying to keep the rig from jackknifing. It juddered along the road shoulder, the big wheels churning up a cloud of gravel and dust.

The spray tore across the eerie orange eyes scanning the terrain. The beastie sprang from its crouch and darted onto the highway in hot pursuit of the rig, crying, "Yap, yap, yap!"

Hildebrandt heard those yaps as he steadied the rig. He gazed out at the side mirror and saw it. Was that a poodle? A fucking *poodle?*

He shifted gears and leaned into the gas. The rig was barreling down the highway at a good sixty miles per, *but the poodle was keeping pace.*

Hildebrandt thought: This is it, baby. The terror attack that he had always feared and had spent years getting ready for. *Al Qaeda is sending suicide poodles into Central Michigan to avenge the death of Bin Laden.*

He stared wide-eyed at the road ahead, pushing the gas, and when he glanced at the side mirror the beast was gone. Relief washed over him, until he glanced at the side mirror a second time.

The beast was no longer reflected in the mirror.

It was *on* it.

It clung to it with the steel daggers of its claws. Its bedraggled ears flapped furiously in the wind like torn black flags of anarchism. It was grinning at him: A friendly, happy zigzag grin. *Almost cute,* Hildebrandt thought in wonderment. For a moment he let down his guard, beguiled by this apparition. But then his customary paranoia clicked smartly back into place. He accelerated the rig and leaned into the air horn, producing a prolonged *blat*. Caught in a downdraft, the doglike entity was torn from the mirror and whisked away in the backwash. Hildebrandt heaved a sigh of relief.

He drove for another two minutes and gentled the rig, which

slowed along with the hammering of his heart. When he did, a hooked dagger slammed down onto the hood of his truck, piercing it.

Then another.

The daggers were attached to paws.

Up it came.

The torn, billowing ears were visible first, resembling pompoms marinated in manure. Then the orange eyes rose like a double sunrise over the hood's horizon. Then appeared the snuffling snout out of which black smoke curled, followed at last by the zigzag grin consisting of interlocking meat-cleaver fangs. This time, however, the grin was not friendly. It split the face from ear to ear like a Glasgow grin.

It hauled itself up and stood on all fours on the hood of the truck like a macabre and oversized hood ornament facing the wrong way. It was grinning and audibly breathing, making a sound like that of a locomotive getting up to speed: *Chuff-chuff-chuff.*

BIIIILLLLLLLAAAARGH! *Yap yap yap yap yap!*

Fire fanned out of its mouth and overspread the windshield, partially melting it.

A tow-haired boy runs after his dog, a cocker spaniel cutting across the road. Blat of an air horn. No screech of brakes: rather, acceleration. A thud. A boy's scream of anguish, and a driver's grin of satisfaction. Was this payback?

Hildebrandt screamed.

A claw-ridden paw slammed flat on the windshield. A spiderweb of cracks radiated outward from it.

The glass exploded in a shower of shards that tore the flesh of the truck driver's face. Blood speckled the seat. The beastie landed claws first in Hildebrandt's lap, puncturing his flesh. He screamed again.

Those paw daggers sank into the truck driver's thighs, drawing more blood that plumed up through his trousers. Hildebrandt yanked open the glove compartment in which he kept a revolver. He groped for it and felt the handle, but then he lost control of his bladder, bowels and big rig all at the same time. The speeding semi jackknifed and plunged over the road shoulder into a ditch. The truck exploded, and the bales of hay and the helium-inflated sex dolls were disgorged from the back of it. The bales tumbled onto the highway, but the sex dolls drifted skyway.

~=__!
```
   !  !
```

Having abandoned his tractor and now running his ass off, Dell Holland heard the second explosion, which sent his livestock scrambling for safety amid a barnyard chorus of moos, squawks, squeals and screams.

"SALLY! SALLY! Get the kids, get into the truck!" *End of the world*, Holland thought. The Rapture. But would he, Sally and the kids be among the elect?

"SALLL-EEEEEEEEEE!"

Nobody answered. *Where in hell are they?* Then it struck him: oh my God, they are *in* Hell. In downtown Hell, Michigan. They were *shopping* there. They had his pickup.

"Lord help me," Holland beseeched Jesus. "What do I do?" As usual, Jesus didn't reply. *Silentium Dei.*

He remembered. He remembered! His son's truck was in the barn. His hopped-up gas-swilling piece of crap that the boy couldn't afford to drive, couldn't even afford to insure, because he was out of a job. Junior called it his Little Mule, from some movie the name of which Holland couldn't remember and didn't give a fuck about anyway.

"Thank you, Jesus!" Holland hollered, even though the son of God hadn't said or done a goddamned thing. He ran toward the barn where Little Mule was parked and when he saw the sex dolls ascending toward heaven, he rejoiced because he knew these were the End Times for sure. Unfortunately, the Rapture-Ready farmer had never seen the 2004 episode of Six Feet Under, "In Case of Rapture."

~=__!
```
   !  !
```

Florence Jellem was cruising along Patterson Lake Road, the main highway through Hell, in her vintage 1977 fuel-efficient Toyota Corolla at ten miles an hour below the speed limit. She was on her way to her friend Paula Horvat's house with a freshly baked batch of chocolate chip cookies.

She had tried to surprise Paula by e-mailing her the cookies from the home computer that her nephew David had bought her. Flo had read that you could download cookies to your computer, but she wasn't quite sure how to send them. Nothing in the instructions that came with the machine addressed this dicey issue. Finally she had placed a cookie in the computer's CD (Cookie Delivery?) ROM tray. The cookie fit splendidly in the tray's round depression, which was a hopeful sign. Sleuthing about a bit, she had discovered a "clear your cookies" option in her browser preferences, and executed the command. But when she opened the tray, the cookie was still there. That was when she gave up and decided to take the cookies in person to Paula.

She rounded a bend and saw the big rig blocking the road. "Oh, dear," she squawked.

She called 911 on the cell phone that David had bought for her to use in case of an emergency.

"Hello, 911? This is Florence Jellem, dear. ... Yes, that's right, dear, *the* Florence Jellem, the professor emeritus of home economics at Chester Alan Arthur Junior High School and the Poetess of Pot Roast."

"It's an honor, Mizz Jellem. My name is Brandy Twain. I don't know if you remember me, but ..."

"Of course I remember you, dear. You matriculated in my advanced home ec seminar back in ought-two, and made a barbarous beans and franks lunch. You burned the franks so badly that they actually shrank. They looked like Chihuahua turds, dear, pardon my French. The beans looked like they were upchucked from the front end of the dog. With my mind's tongue I can still taste the horror of it. I'm glad to see you're in a profession where you can't harm food."

"But, surely, Mizz Jellem, you didn't call 911 just to reprimand me for a shitty lunch I made in your home-ec seminar ten years ago. Is something wrong now?"

"I'm afraid so, dear."

"What?"

"It seems that right here in H-E-double-hockey sticks, someone has got right up to the Dickens."

"The Dickens, you say!"

"I'm afraid it's DEFCON 1 Dickens, dear."

"Can you elaborate?"

"Well, dear, there is an 18-wheeler on Patterson Lake Road, three miles past the Fredrick farm on the highway to downtown

H-E-double- hockey sticks. It's burning and blocking the road, and stinking up the place to high heaven, a real mess. Let's clean this mess up, shall we? Cleanliness is next to Godliness."

"Yes, Mizz Jellem, thank you. Is anybody hurt? Do we need an ambulance? ... Ma'am? Are you there?"

BANG!

The sound came from under Flo's car.

"Mizz Jellem? Is everything OK?"

BANG! BANG! BANG!

The car jumped off the ground before coming down again with a loud thump of tires hitting the road, and then the floor exploded. A spear of peeled-off rubber from the floor mat shot upward. It knocked the granny glasses off Flo's nose and nearly put out her left eye before bounding off her brow.

Flo looked down and a scream clotted in her throat. Then it tore loose, full volume.

BIIIIIILLLLLLLARGH! *Yap yap yap yap yap!*

She started frantically kicking at the beast, trying to mash it with the sturdy heel of her shoe. Flo wore sensible, thick-soled patent-leather pumps purchased at Payless, along with red and white candy-cane-striped nylon stockings that constituted her signature fashion statement.

"Shoo! Shoo! Oh, dear!"

The operator: "Mizz Jellem, are you OK? What's going on?" But the cell phone had fallen to the destroyed floor of the car.

Florence Jellem tried to bring the heel of her shoe down on the minuscule monster, but it dodged the stomp and snapped its fang-bedizened jaws around her ankle with a sickening *crunch*. Her head flew back and her mouth flew open in a soundless scream, and her eyes got as big as dinner plates. The pain was excruciating, *unbelievable*, and when she looked down again she saw that the little black depravity was slowly tearing her foot off.

She desperately patted around for her Pocketbook of Death, as it was known to generations of cowed home ec students with smarting knuckles and reddened rear ends. But it slipped from her pocket and eluded her grasp.

Panting through the pain, Flo, no pushover, said sternly: "Give ... me ... back ... my ... darned ... *foot.*" She then added, deploying the deadliest weapon in her personal arsenal of insults: "My heavens, dear, you look like the Dickens."

She grasped her leg and yanked it back. A tug-of-war ensued, the monster in the floor of her car waggling its head from side to side as it tugged on the prize in the opposite direction. It then dug in its clawed paws and pulled with all its considerable might. The foot broke off with the vivid sound of ripping flesh and snapping bone. A multitude of severed veins hemorrhaged blood. *Like leaking red pens*, Flo thought in horror. Oh, my. *What a mess.*

With Flo's foot and shoe securely ensconced in its mouth, along with colored shreds of stocking, the canine cacodemon expelled from its snout two licks of fire that ignited what was left of the floor. The flames swiftly spread across the car seat and somersaulted upward and grabbed the ceiling with orange claws. The creature vanished down the hole that it had made in the car floor.

With her remaining foot Flo mashed the accelerator and did a frantic U-turn away from the derelict rig, turning the steering wheel all the way around and making the tires of her car squeal. But then she gentled the brake pedal. Despite her plight she steadfastly drove ten miles an hour under the speed limit, which she judged to be a prudential traffic management strategy, especially in times of personal crisis. She was environed in fire and her life flashed before her eyes, a rich tapestry of memories: cheese sammiches slathered in Miracle Whip mayonnaise on Wonder Bread, which builds strong bodies twelve different ways; Friday night Bingo with the broads at the VFW community center; Tea Party rallies at which she and her confederates demanded that the government keep its mitts off their Medicare. Coffee klatches and matinees at the Bijou with her friend Paula, who, when they first met, told Flo that she, Paula, was a Muslim, but Flo thought that she had said *Muslin* and for months after that Flo would chatter on about the loosely woven unbleached white cloth produced from carded cotton yarn. When Paula finally cleared up Flo's confusion Flo blushed about six shades of red, but then she laughed it off. If you can't laugh at yourself in this sad life, Flo thought now, you'll have a tough row to hoe. Sure, you will. The raging heat blew out the windows of the car with tremendous bangs.

She looked at the freshly baked cookies melting in the heat on the seat beside her, and thought of her current plight. She stoically concluded, addressing herself as the fire raced up the sides of her face and blossomed in her hair, "That's the way the cookie crumbles, dear."

~=__!
! !

Sally Holland came out of the mercantile store, old Jerry's place. In fact, that was what its name was: Old Jerry's Place. It was a few blocks from the geographical center of Hell where the town's mayor, Gil Aaronson, lived in splendid isolation in a gated community, rarely emerging from his hideout except for grocery shopping while wearing a Richard Nixon Halloween mask to conceal his identity, or for covert visits to the town's not-so-secret brothel that also doubled as a dungeon managed by that imperious little Russian dominatrix Ayn Rand. There he would frolic with his favorite honey, Mystery Tart, enigmatic daughter of the legendary Holace Orr. Folks gossiped that Gil had never been the same since the death of his best buddy, his toy poodle Echo. "If you want a friend in Washington, get a dog," the mayor liked to quote Harry S. Truman, adding: "And that's also true of this anus of a town."

A woman of habit and tradition who had long ago repented of and left behind her wild flaming youth, Sally still shopped at this old-fashioned, mom 'n' pop cracker-barrel store with sawdust on the wood floor and barrels of pickles even though the Walmart was cheaper. And Jerry was a good guy with a nice family.

Earlier they had heard a couple of loud, distant booms. Concern now creased Sally's brow as she recalled those disturbing concussions. "Sonic booms," Jerry had said reassuringly, reminding her of the fighter jets that occasionally took practice runs out of nearby Selfridge Air Force Base. Sally wasn't so sure. There were booms, and then there were *booms*. These hadn't sounded like booms. These had sounded like *booms*.

"Sam, could you put these in the truck for me while I help Junior with the hay bales?" Sally said, handing some grocery sacks to her daughter Samantha.

"Sure, Maw."

Sally scrutinized her daughter in a considering, even suspicious, way. Samantha was sixteen years old, and the flaxen-haired young woman was flowering just as her mother had oh those many years ago. Remembering her own wayward youth right here in Hell before she found Jesus, Sally was constantly making a mental note never to let her daughter out of her sight unless absolutely necessary. She wondered whether it might be possible to outfit

Sam with an ankle monitor and keep her under house arrest. She made a mental note to check with Sheriff Ted about the legality and constitutionality of her plan, and whether it might pass muster with the Department of Homeland Security.

Junior was a different matter, no object of concern. He was a rock. He wasn't a handsome boy and he didn't look at all like his Paw, and nobody knew why (though busybodies liked to wag their tongues about it). He couldn't even grow a beard like Paw. But he was handy with a wrench and worked until the job got done. He had farm-boy strength with broad shoulders and a big, barrel chest. Sure, he wasn't the sharpest tool in the shed, but he knew how to use tools, and he was as honest as an ear of corn is yellow.

Junior now effortlessly lifted up two hay bales at the same time, one in each hand, and pitched them into the back of the truck, finishing up before his mother could even lend a hand.

"Oh, you are *such* a strong, hard-working boy, Junior," Sally gushed, lightly embracing him and giving him a peck on the cheek. "Thank you!"

"Welcome, Maw. Does that mean I can drive the truck home?"

"I'm sure you could, if you had insurance. You know what Paw said."

"Can I drive home, then, Maw?" Sam stuck out her tongue at Junior.

"Now don't go making a fuss you two, I'll be driving and you both know it."

They piled into the pickup. Sally turned the key and tapped the accelerator. The kids sat in the back seat, mildly sulking. They'll get over it right quick enough, Sally thought confidently, but then her thoughts drifted back to those two *booms* that they had heard earlier. Mild anxiety slithered through her gut like a garter snake through grass.

She started down Patterson Lake Road, and then her cell phone rang. She had left it in the backseat when she had helped stock the groceries there.

"Could you get that, Sam honey?"

Sam switched on the phone. Immediately, a frantic voice barked out.

"Sally? Sally, don't come home. It's the end of the world at last! Patterson Lake Road is blocked by a big rig and there were two hellish explosions. The Rapture has started; I can see 'em goin' up even as we speak!" While driving Little Mule he had fetched a pair of binoculars from the glove compartment and trained them on the levitating, anatomically correct sex dolls. He wasn't surprised that they were nude, because he knew from study that everything, even one's clothes, are left behind at the big moment. For a pleasant while had had ogled the bodacious breasts of God's chosen female elect. But what stunned and alarmed him was the appearance of the men who were on their way up to their reward: They all had woodies.

"Jesus, Lord Redeemer, they've all got woodies!" Dell yelled.

"What's that you say, Paw?" Maw asked. "Hoodies? Who's got hoodies? Have we got those dreadful Hip Hop people in town now? Because if we do —"

"Never mind!" a mortified Dell Holland barked into his phone. He asked Maw whether she could see the Raptured going up, and she said that she could not.

"Maybe God is doing it by neighborhood, by zip code or by alphabetical order," Dell speculated. The fact that he and his wife and kids had not yet begun their trip aloft gnawed at him. He glanced down hopefully at his crotch, and then tore his eyes away in disappointment and resumed squawking into the phone.

Sally and the two kids squawked back, but Holland cut off their questions.

"Stay in downtown Hell and wait for me. I'm on my way now. If all goes well, we'll be with Jesus within the hour. Junior?"

"Yes, Paw?"

"You're a big, strong boy. When you meet Jesus and shake his hand, don't shake it *too* hard. Remember, he has a hole in it. Understand, boy?"

"I understand, Paw."

Paw paused, unsure how to broach the next exceedingly delicate subject. But he thought of his developing daughter, and of her love for Jesus.

"Sam?"

"Yes, Paw?"

"We all know you love Jesus. But there is spiritual love and, you know, *physical* love. Do you understand the difference between the two, when it comes to the Lord?"

"I – I think so, Paw."

"Good. I don't want you jumpin' Jesus's bones, it'll just make a big scene. OK! Now you all wait for me and I'll be down directly." He switched off the phone.

Sally pulled over to the side of the road. The family clambered out of the truck, and scanned the sky for signs of Jesus coming back to earth.

"Is that Jesus, Maw?" Sam inquired in a bored, skeptical voice, pointing indifferently at a cumulus cloud. Junior picked his nose.

Sally scrutinized the cloud with knitting brows, to see if therein she could discern the shape of the Lord and Redeemer. Truth be told, it looked more like a giant triple scoop of vanilla ice cream from the Dairy Whip than the all-powerful Lord and Redeemer, but all the same she studied the cloud more intently. *Was that the crown of thorns?* Or a halo? No, no, just sunbeams raying up from the top of the cloud.

Sheriff Ted Haggard's car ripped past them on the road, gravel spraying from its spinning tires.

"What's goin' on Maw?"

"I don't know Junior, but we ain't leavin' Paw out there by hisself." She nodded at the firearm in their pickup. "You grab that thar shotgun and get 'er loaded, pronto."

Junior grabbed the weapon from the gun rack and took out a box of shells from the glove compartment. He loaded up. Sally Holland cast one more wistful glance at the cumulus cloud and decided that it wasn't Jesus, after all. If a rescue needed to be made, she reckoned they were the ones that would have to do the rescuing: Jesus was unavailable as usual. Sometimes Sally blasphemously thought that if you could call Heaven on the phone, you'd be assured by a recorded voice that your prayer was *very* important to Father, and advised to stay on the line for the next available seraph. Then you'd be put on hold forever, to the accompaniment of recorded choir music or Gregorian chants.

~=___!
! !

Sheriff Ted was responding to the dispatcher's report of the 911 call of old Flo Jellem and to the news that she had been screaming before the call got cut off. He was simultaneously responding to a flood of reports of explosions along Patterson Lake Road. He saw a rising lick of flame in the distance, and black smoke pumping into the sky. He was worried about Flo. She was not a woman to go looking for trouble: No way in H-E-Double-Hockey Sticks, as she liked to say. Kind of ironic, the sheriff thought abstractly, that she had lived in Hell her whole life.

The sheriff was worried as hell, as a matter of fact. This situation felt like all kinds of wrong. He had been the sheriff when the Arthur Schopenhauer impersonator shot up the Diary Queen. He had also been at the helm when Howdy Houlihan raped his 12-year-old son, Boy Howdy, and then held him hostage at gunpoint, and when Holly Jinks strangled her toddler Hi. Those were the worst things that had happened during his tenure as sheriff, and he had shot Big Howdy to death to end the hostage standoff. It had also fallen to him to arrest Holly Jinks, who had impressed him with her expression of wild-eyed insanity, the thousand-yard stare that she wore after the killing. (*Assclown.*) She later hanged herself in her jail cell. These memories haunted the sheriff. (*Faggot.*) There were all kinds of wrong then, and it felt as if there were all kinds of wrong now. (*Assclown! Maggot! Faggot! You'll never make a Marine!*) The explosions were bad enough. What really cut at his gut was personal: *What had made Flo scream?*

"Oh, people are such silly sausages, dear," Flo liked to say in an offhand, dismissive way, and that was about as emotional as she ever got. She was not a screamer. She was a tough old piece of gristle, for all the saccharine sweetness of her demeanor. Sheriff Ted pitied the Devil himself if he ever crossed sweet old Flo Jellem. The sheriff recalled with a wry smile Flo's Pocketbook of Death, as the kids called it. Sooner or later every kid in town had felt the sting of that bubblegum-pink pestle on their posteriors ("spare the pocketbook, spoil the pupil," was Flo's motto), and they learned right quick not to mix up tablespoons with teaspoons or to armpit-fart while Flo was showing them how to prepare a proper cheese sammich. They learned to remain quiet — even fearful — while Flo was showing them how to clean up bloodstains after gutting a live guinea pig with a Ginsu knife. ("Bloodstains are the worst, dears," she would tell the silent big-eyed kids, adding: "Some of you little rascals will grow up to be criminals, so you might as well learn sooner rather than later how to cover up your crimes. As Abraham Lincoln said, 'Whatever you do, be a good one.'")

The sheriff thought of her now with a good deal of affection: the way that she habitually called everyone "dear," the way that she liked to whip up a big batch of American cheese sandwiches ("sammiches," she always called them) with Kraft Miracle Whip mayonnaise for guests, the way that she haunted Internet message boards to speak out in opposition to the theory of evolution ("No one is going to make a monkey out of me, dear.") Flo had been married three times and each of her marriages had ended in divorce: "Why, I had to kick those old goats to the curb, dear," she offered by way of terse explanation. Flo was known for her sensible, thick-soled patent-leather pumps from Payless, and also her candy-cane-striped nylon stockings.

He saw it, after rounding a bend: the jackknifed big rig. He slowed to a stop. It was partly in a ditch and it angled across both lanes of the highway. Fire and thick black smoke still plumed up from it. But what amazed the sheriff was that the rig was dented and mangled, as if it had been subjected to a furious bombardment beyond the impact of crashing into the ditch.

"This is Ted, dispatch, Jerry, I am looking at what looks like a *bomb* went off in this sucker. Looks like the tank blew up. Everything is dead quiet, some smoldering wreckage. I'm getting out for a closer look. Don't know if there are any survivors."

"OK, Ted, ambulances and fire trucks en route. They put out five alarms on this baby. You be careful, y'hear? Keep your radio mike open."

"Will do."

Haggard stepped out of the car, unsnapped his holster holding his Glock and took his shotgun with him.

Holding the shotgun in one hand and the Glock in the other, he called out at the truck's cab: "This is the sheriff! Is anyone in there?" The catch in his voice embarrassed him.

"Assclown!"

Sheriff Ted whirled around at the sound of this familiar voice. Standing in the tall grass by the road shoulder near the derelict rig was Sheriff Ted's old drill sergeant, Ulysses Eisenhower Yokel. The lantern-jawed menace with the buzz-cut hair and fat red neck was holding a child's red balloon, with his other hand parked on his hip.

"You'll never make a marine, PFC Teddy Weddy *Washout*."

Ted Haggard stared, astounded. Then Yokel was gone. (Had he been a mirage?) But the red balloon remained. It drifted upward.

With effort, Sheriff Ted slowly turned to face the truck.

"What's the matter, Assclown? Not MAN enough to enter that truck?"

Sir, fuck you, sir, Sheriff Ted mentally answered, and then plucking up his courage he cautiously approached the truck cab, holstering the Glock and holding the shotgun in both hands, pointing it at the driver's side window. He jumped up on the running board, grabbed the door handle, took a deep breath and yanked the door open. He pointed the shotgun at whoever might be inside, immediately wincing with revulsion at the overwhelming reek of human waste. The driver was slumped over the steering wheel, face down and dripping blood amid a myriad of glass shards. The windshield was gone, just blown the fuck out. One of the man's arms dangled motionless at his side. The other arm was stretched out toward the open glove compartment. The fingers loosely cradled a revolver aslant on the open door.

The sheriff realized that the man had shit his pants, and he shuddered. He laid a hand on the man's shoulder, and then gently pulled him up and around until he was face to face with the victim.

Except that the victim no longer had a face.

It had been ripped clean off the front of his head. Ted saw two skull sockets, the nose holes and both rows of tombstone teeth.

The sheriff froze. For a moment he was like a shitty Microsoft app hung up in hourglass mode. Then his eyes inched downward. The man's face was on his lap, tissue thin, like a discarded Halloween mask. He saw two blue agate marbles flanking the bridge of the mask's nose. They looked like his kid's marbles. Then he realized that they were not marbles.

They were eyes.

They were looking at *him*.

The sheriff blanched, gave off a strangled retching noise and backed away so quickly that he lost his footing and fell backward onto the road shoulder. The face fluttered down like Kleenex, and the marble-like eyes rolled off the dead man's lap and plopped down onto the gravel. While the sheriff's breakfast careened up his throat, a pickup truck careered up the road. The *Hollands*, Ted thought in muddled amazement, seeing the mother at the wheel and the two kids in back as the pickup slowed. What the hell are they —

A brisk movement in the corner of his eye arrested his attention.

He looked downward.

It trotted toward him on busy, strutting legs.

It was black, absolutely black, like an ambulatory Rorschach inkblot. Its ears, like torn pennants, suddenly inflated upward into ragged apostrophes larger than the rest of the body. A *poodle*, he thought. *Was* it a poodle? His next thought was: *That's the ugliest fucking thing I've ever seen.* The dog — if the haggard, horrid, strutting mess was a dog — was carrying something in its mouth: a bone.

Was it a bone?

The sheriff brought his gun across his chest like a shield and, peering down, his eyes met the eyes of this minuscule monster. It looked up at him, its stub of a tail vibrating with ecstasy.

Its eyes were phosphorescent orange.

It dropped the bone at the sheriff's feet.

Was it a bone?

Ted prodded the object with his boot toe and gawped down at in a fog of disbelief.

His mind informed him: That's not a bone. That's a shoe. But, his mind elaborated, that's not *just* a shoe, you assclown. That's a fucking *foot*.

A fucking foot in the fucking shoe.

"A foot," he said aloud, in a sad and wondering way. "Wearing a sensible patent leather pump from Payless, and a red and white candy-cane-striped nylon stocking."

The foot of Flo.

The sheriff projectile vomited his morning oatmeal.

The Hollands parked the truck and jumped out of it.

"Bring the gun, junior," Maw cawed. "They's trouble here, sure as shootin'. Sheriff Ted is projectile vomitin', now. They can't be nuthin' good about that."

The sheriff, semi-digested oatmeal dangling from his lips and chin like a liquid Santa Claus beard, stared down in horror as the diminutive demiurge licked avidly at the Ted's intestinal slops. The brute lapped it all up. Sated, it turned and trotted off in a leisurely way, its nub of a tail twitching with joy.

The sound of thumping feet brought the sheriff to his senses. He saw the Hollands sprinting toward him, Maw in the lead.

Still clutching the shotgun, he threw up both hands and roared, *"Stop right there. Do not come any closer!"* He did not want them to see a human face lying on the ground like a discarded Halloween mask, or the two marble-like eyes, trailing blue and red veins, which were goggling idiotically up at him. Nor did he want them to see Flo's foot.

Stunned, the Hollands skidded to a stop.

The sheriff then turned back toward the retreating (*dog, poodle, psychodemonic killer from hell, whatever the hell it was*), and raised his shotgun. He tried leveling his gun sights on the retreating form, but his hands were shaking uncontrollably.

"Private First Class Teddy Weddy Washout!" rang in his ears. He looked back over his shoulder to see Staff Sergeant Yokel waving at him from a hill, next to a tree. Then he was gone, and all that was waving was a branch. The red balloon that the DI had with him earlier was tied up in it, straining to free itself.

Snap out of it Goddamn you, Sheriff Ted mentally beseeched himself, *you are the town's fucking sheriff, been so for fifteen years and you are a former Marine who saw action in Operation Desert Storm. Act like one.*

He pulled the trigger.

The gun bucked and roared, and the sound of the blast ran away on the wind.

The bullet hit the ground just to left of the beastie with a thump, and then it ricocheted off into space with a whine.

The beastie stopped, sniffed the ground where the bullet had struck, turned around, squatted on its haunches and gazed up at the sheriff with its ruddy orange eyes. It growled, and bared its zigzagging meat-cleaver fangs. Its mouth flew open and it roared: BlllllLLLLLAAAAARGH! *Yap yap yap yap yap!*

Fire fanned out. It sprang aloft and sailed for the sheriff's face and throat.

Junior Holland was up to the task. Junior not only knew how to use guns, he was an avid skeet shooter — and a *good* one. He coolly tracked the flying flotsam across the sky while the sheriff stood rooted to the spot, his eyes bugging with terror as he watched the thing coming down at him. The shotgun had fallen from his grasp, and he was utterly defenseless. He was just throwing up his hands when —

"Pull!"

BANG!

The bullet collided with the flying beast, making a *whump*

sound. Everyone watched in astonishment as the little monster blew apart in a gout of blood, pieces of it flying in every direction.

The sheriff swayed on his feet, trying to keep from falling to the ground because his knees were buckling from his terror. Seeing the Hollands running up to him, he kicked away the face and eyes under his squad car. He prayed they would not notice Flo's foot.

"Ted, are you all right?" Three voices in unison, hysterical in inquiry.

He looked at them almost uncomprehendingly, not knowing what to say. Then his eyes fixed on those of Junior, who had saved his life. He was about to thank the boy, but something about Junior's muddy, fixed gaze, and the way that his mouth was ajar, told the sheriff that they were not out of the woods yet. He looked to where the boy was looking.

Body parts, strewn about the ground, were moving.

They were moving toward one another.

The four legs, which had all shot off into four different directions under the impact of the bullet, reassembled in their proper formation, making a support platform for the torso, which gracefully settled back down upon the legs. The creature's orange eyes, which had been jellied by the blast, recomposed themselves into two glowing balls that neatly resumed their respective places in the skull sockets. The beastie squatted down and its little nub of a tail hopped back onto its tailbone, reattaching itself. The monster was a bloody mess, its ragged ears pointing zanily this way and that and its tatterdemalion fur resembling a pastiche of Groucho Marx mustaches all pointing in different directions. But the beast, however ramshackle, was reassembled after the bullet had blown it to bits. It resembled a jigsaw puzzle with incompatible pieces forced together.

BlllllAAAAAAAARGH! *Yap yap yap yap yap!*

The fire fanned, and it attacked again.

Cursing himself for letting his shotgun fall from his grasp (*"Can't you hold onto your rifle, PFC Assclown? You sure can hold onto your cock OK."*), Sheriff Haggard now lunged for it on the ground while Junior, as ever cool as a cucumber and operating as if by instinct, again leveled his gun at the horrid fuzzball flying through the air directly at him. "Pull!" his mind, still in skeet-shoot mode, barked at him, and the shot cracked off in a blaze of fire, the smoke rolling away just as the shrieking ambulance and fire trucks pulled to a stop on the other side of the derelict rig. Another vehicle, a familiar-looking truck, was swerving around the ruined big rig and over the shoulder of the road, its spinning wheels crunching gravel with the sound of Kellogg's corn flakes (direct to you from Battle Creek) crinkling in fresh, cold milk.

The monster had been flying through the air with all four limbs outstretched, resembling a bat without wings. Its mouth had been wide open in a huge, hectoring rictus of a grotesque grin. A millisecond after Junior got the shot off, the bullet tore into that wide-open, slobbering, foul, fang-pocked pit.

When the bullet hit the beast, the sheriff was straightening with his shotgun in hand. The bullet arrested the monster in mid-flight and even pushed it backward. It hung for a second in the air like a black kite caught in crosswinds, and then it fell to the earth, landing in a four-limbed squat. It looked up at its adversaries with its baleful orange eyes, and the four of them looked down at it with their savagely astounded eyes.

They could see the shape of the bullet moving laboriously down the monster's throat, like a devoured mouse visibly migrating through the digestive tract of a boa constrictor. It continued its passage down into the cacodemon's stomach, and then into the nether regions. Still squatting, the creature excreted the stool of the bullet with a grunt. It lay in a mound of glowing molten metal in the dust, resembling a freshly forged abstract bronze sculpture of dog shit by Henry Moore.

Maw swooned, and fell into Sam's arms. Sam let out a short, high-pitched scream that sounded like Hell's fire alarm. Sheriff Ted said: "How – how is it *possible*? That thing can't weigh no more than fifteen pounds! It should have been blasted to fucking *molecules* by now!"

Wise beyond his years, Junior announced in a voice full of somber sobriety: "It may not weigh no more than fifteen pounds, Sheriff Ted, true dat. But that thar be 15 pounds of pure *evil* in a fur coat."

"Poodles don't have fur," Ted said distractedly and pedantically. "They don't shed. It's hair."

"When the Apocalypse really does happen, pedants will be the first to die," Junior muttered.

"Cut!" one of the authors barked from above the page, and then wandered down into it. Everyone and everything froze, except the author and Junior. The author reprimanded the boy: "For fuck's sake,

Junior, this is a novel. Readers are supposed to be able to willingly suspend disbelief. You need to stay in character so they can do that. Remember your Twitter hashtag: #NotTheSharpestToolInTheShed. Dumb fucks like you don't use words like 'pedant.' Got that, Junior?"

"Yes'm," Junior said, lapsing into feigned dullness while getting the gender of the author wrong. The author said, "Good boy," gave Junior a condescending pat on the head and then yelled, "Action!" before levitating off the white page with the black type on it. On cue, everyone and everything swirled back into action.

Everyone's attention was arrested by the sound of the pickup truck, Little Mule, skidding to a stop. Its left front wheel ran over the beast, squashing it flat and leaving a skid mark like black tar on the road. But then that streak of roadkill rolled itself back up into a black blob, and then like some indestructible rubber ball the blob sprang back into the shape of a dog thing, fangs bared. Paw parked the pickup and got out, his foot making landfall five inches from the eerie orange eyes.

"Paw," Junior and Sam brayed in unison. *"Get back in the truck!"*

The sheriff had dropped to one knee and was leveling his shotgun at the crapulous canine when the latter, enraged at being run over, seized Dell Holland's pant cuff with its fangs and hurled him to his hands and knees. When Paw looked down he saw the dog-like demiurge right under him, looking up into Dell's blue eyes with its orange eyes, which pulsated with ruddy malevolence.

Holland knew what it was. It was a hellhound. It was confirmation that these were indeed the End Times, but Holland and his family had not been Raptured.

He jerked his head up and fixed his wife, who was still sobbing in Sam's arms, with a furious stare, and cried, "Your fault, Sally, it's *your* fault. *You're the one who insisted on living in Hell, Michigan.* And that's why you, me, Junior and Sam are among damned! For living here in Sin City! For that, and for your wayward youth! Harlot! I don't even think Junior is my son! He don't look nothin' like me and he can't grow a beard like me!"

BIIIIILLLLLAAAARGH! *Yap yap yap yap yap!*

The last thing that Dell Holland saw before his sanity dissolved were creatures, some of them as big as crickets, with the bodies of fleas and the heads of humans: tiny shrunken human heads from hell, each face twisted in the grotesque agony of some unbearable, supernatural physical torment being inflicted on it day and night. The chaotic velveteen fur (hair?) of the monster below him positively boiled with these malefic entities. The flea bodies, attached to the human heads, frantically raced all over the hellhound, which lifted its right rear leg and pointed its crooked, spiral-shaped penis (with a barbed fishing hook on its head) at Holland's eyes. Then it let fly a sizzling stream of sulfuric acid into his eyes and across his face.

Dell Holland lurched upward and backward, and staggered about.

"My eyes! My eyes! My eyes!"

He kept screaming those chilling words while clapping his hands at his face and staggering about. His wife and kids watched with dumb incomprehension.

The sheriff was determined to redeem himself. He dropped to one knee and leveled his gun at the monster. *Fuck if this old marine is going to let a poodle from hell take his badge,* he thought with grim (albeit idiotic) determination. *And fuck if Sergeant Yokel is going to take my balls.*

He was just pulling the trigger when Junior, with a force of will dredged up from who knew where, snapped out of his trance, seized the barrel of the gun and yanked it upward. The gun blazed and the bullet whizzed harmlessly up toward the treetops, where flocks of birds thundered aloft amid cries of distress and caws of indignation.

The sheriff, dumbfounded, stared up at Junior with an expression of savage inquiry, and Junior yelled above the shrieks of his Paw that went on without cease: "Sheriff Ted, take a hint. You can't kill the thing, but it only attacks when it thinks someone is attacking it!"

The sheriff angrily yanked his gun downward, glared up at Junior and said, "Son, you see your maw and sister yonder? Them there people are going to be ripped to pieces by that there dog if I don't keep it occupied with this here shotgun."

BIIIIIILLLLLLLLARRRGH! *Yap yap yap yap yap!*

The canine cacodemon was on the attack again, racing straight for junior. Junior froze, holding his shotgun, knowing it was useless yet leveling it anyway. But at the same time his sister, seeing the monster on the prowl again, pushed her mother aside and bounded for her brother. As the hellhound leapt into the air, sailing toward Junior's face, Sam pushed him away. She was now standing where Junior had been standing, and the hound from hell landed on top of her head. Its dagger claws knifed into her temples, puncturing them and drawing blood that rolled down the sides of her face. The maddened monster assumed that it had Junior in its death grip.

It sank its fangs into Sam's scalp and ripped it off her skull. It gobbled up her brains like dog food out of a bowl.

Sally Holland snapped. She just snapped, like a rubber band stretched beyond its tensile strength.

She slumped to the ground and fell into a catatonic state, goggling maniacally up at nothing. She would remain that way for the rest of her life, joining her husband in the abyss of insanity.

Sam had slumped to her knees. The canine demiurge straddled the dog bowl of her head, its snout buried inside as it slurped up her brains. Junior responded with pure instinct, his mind a blank. He again leveled the shotgun at the brute, and when the dog from hell heard the slide click, it looked up from its meal and realized, with annoyance, its mistake. The gun cracked, and the bullet whizzed. It caught the *lusus naturae* square in the belly. The bullet briefly drove the hellion backward, stretching it out like a trampoline. A resounding *boing* sound followed. Junior watched with amazement as the projectile roared back at him at twice the speed he thought possible. It was his last thought on earth. The bullet caught him between the eyes and killed him stone-cold dead.

The ambulance and the fire trucks had stopped on the other side of the jackknifed rig, and ambulance personnel came trotting around the truck, carrying stretchers, while the firemen started hosing down the rig. But as soon as the ambulance crew members saw the carnage they made an abrupt U-turn and, still carrying the stretchers, trotted back to the ambulance, in which they then sped off.

The United States Media Corps arrived.

Choppers and airplanes circled overhead. Reporters parachuted down, bearing notepads, pens, cell phones, video cameras, laptops and the other accoutrements of their sordid parasitical trade. Lamentably, the "If it bleeds, it leads" crowd was on the scene, the first of these soldiers dropping to the land, parachutes billowing around and behind them amid cries of "Bob forgot his parachute again. Get pictures!"

Sheriff Ted pissed his pants.

He threw aside his shotgun, flew into his car, slammed shut the door, turned the key in the ignition and burned rubber.

He hauled ass on Patterson Lake Road, leaving behind the crime scene and, he knew, his manhood. He had cut and run. He had left his balls on the highway along with his shotgun. How would he face his wife and kid again? How would he look at himself in the mirror?

"Assclown!"

His eyes darted to the rear-view mirror.

Staff Sergeant Ulysses Eisenhower Yokel was in the backseat, grinning mockingly at him. His eyes were concealed by mirrored sunglasses. His skin was swarthy, his hair buzz-cut. His teeth blazed out from above his lantern jaw and the ham of his neck.

"Pissed your pants, eh, assclown?" Sheriff Ted's old D.I. nemesis inquired in a smug, jocular tone of voice. "I always told you that you were a wuss. Teddy-Weddy Washout!"

"You're not real," the sheriff insisted, as he stared with savage concentration at the sergeant's vulpine reflection in the mirror. "You're in my mind. *You're not even fucking alive anymore.*"

"Ran away from this disaster just like you ran away during Desert Storm, eh, maggot?"

Sheriff Ted bridled at the accusation. "What do you mean?" he demanded. The sheriff had tossed aside his shotgun, but now his hand meandered down to his Glock in his holster.

"Under fire outside Kuwait City, you freaked out, Private Assclown. You threw away your gun and ran. Ran from some sandniggers with slingshots. Just like you threw away your gun just now, when these poor devils back there needed you most. You let a poodle, a fucking harmless *toy poodle*, and some pencil-necked geeks from the news media make you piss your pants, toss your gun and cut and run, Private Pussy. You yellow coward!"

"That's a Goddamned lie! I never cut and run in Kuwait!"

"You did, Teddy Twat, you *did*, and you got a dishonorable discharge for it. And that's why you've spent the last fifteen years playing the bumpkin sheriff in a pissant town comically called Hell, to make up for your cowardice. Yet the coward is back."

His eyes crawled back to the rear-view mirror, and he saw the grand grin of the sadistic sergeant in the back seat. Then for a brief moment, so brief the interval was nearly incalculable, a flash of red light fell over that face and it changed into something different.

"Who the hell are you?" Sheriff Ted asked in a hollow, shattered voice.

"Who in hell do you think I am, Teddy boy?"

"You vicious bastard," he hissed at his longtime tormentor. Sergeant Yokel cackled maniacally. Furious, the sheriff spun around to face him in the back seat.

No one was there.

He itched.

He looked back out at the highway coming at him and coming at him as he pressed down on the pedal, pushing the needle to seventy and then eighty. Hypnotic arrowing highway, straight and flat. Coming and coming, the flanking farmland flying past. In the far distance a red balloon bobbed and jerked overhead. The toy he lost as a boy. His favorite toy. His first toy.

Ted felt a small, stabbing pain in his flank, under his shirt. He clapped a hand to it. Bee sting?

A tingling sensation rippled across his torso. He looked at his shirt. It was moving: rippling and fluttering.

He tore it apart and looked down.

Insects with human faces were swarming all over him.

He let go of the wheel and with both hands slapped furiously at his chest and stomach. The car swerved and he seized the wheel again to right it. The red balloon, his boyhood balloon, bobbed and weaved in the distance. He was unable to catch it no matter how fast he drove.

Sheriff Ted Haggard swayed like a tightrope walker in a high wind on a fraying rope over the Grand Canyon of insanity.

He slammed on the brakes and his squad car, burning rubber, skidded to a stop on the road shoulder. The bugs swarmed all over him. One bore the face of Holly Jinks, and another of Howdy Houlihan. He gripped his Glock.

He raised the gun and pointed at his nemesis smirking at him in the rear-view mirror. A voice spoke: "Don't you know I'm only in your head? You're pointing the gun at yourself, assclown."

When he pulled the trigger he was a boy again and watching in horror — his first clear experience of horror — his balloon burst apart in a spray of red. Tom Dollard, the town dullard, had shot Teddy's red balloon to pieces with his BB gun. The Glock roared, the barrel pointing at Ted's own face reflected in the mirror. There was another spray of red.

When the smoke cleared the sheriff was sprawled lifeless across the front seat of the car, his face blown to ground chuck, his eyeballs jellied and his brains smeared over the upholstery like the oatmeal that he had upchucked earlier.

END BOOK ONE

Book the Second

In the House of Bubb

"You ain't nothin' but a hound dog."

— Elvis Presley

"Bill Z. Bubb" was the name scrawled by hand on the slip of paper above the small metal mailbox in the wall of the grimy vestibule of the flyspecked, downmarket apartment building in Hell, Michigan. A spiral staircase plunged frighteningly downward into darkness. A surprisingly lengthy sign chiseled into an arch above the staircase advised those who entered to abandon all hope of decent maintenance because no supervisor lived on the premises and the property was owned by an absentee slumlord who lived in Fresno, California, and never answered his phone or returned recorded messages.

Down, down the stairs went, spiraling downward into darkness. Blood-curdling cries, shrieks and groans; the weeping and wailing and gnashing of teeth could be heard in that spiral staircase. At each landing, a torch affixed to the clammy wall provided garish illumination that savagely exposed the *Dasein*, as Heidegger would have had it, of various depraved tenants peeking out of their doors, all of them hopelessly behind on their rent and mired in debilitating debt: bats with the heads of mice, monkeys with the faces of toads, slithering snakes wearing the faces of rats, and the nations of Greece and Italy. Chains clanked, blood boiled, and distant maniacal laughter periodically rent the thick, damp, gloomy air.

Down, down. Some levels down, perhaps nine landings, was Bubb's cluttered, filthy one-bedroom apartment (with an attached Rec Room), behind a thick oak door displaying bas reliefs of gargoyles.

Behind that door Bubb sat before his personal computer,

with its circular monitor made of granite and murkily environed in cobwebs. It was surmounted by a frieze depicting the souls of the damned harrowed by the fires of eternity. He was logged in to CNN.com and playing yo-yo with a black widow spider. The venomous arachnid bobbed up and down on a strand of silk that Bubb manipulated with the talons of his hand.

"Boss, why don't you get that new Windows version?" one of Bubb's goat-legged imps that shared the filthy apartment with him had once inquired.

"Because," The Despoiler of Humanity had replied, "Windows is *evil*."

The goat-legged imp had looked confused. "Isn't that *why* you should get it?"

"Even I draw the line at something as evil as Windows," the Curser of Christ had replied with grim finality. "Just wait until I get Bill Gates down here."

Bubb checked his Twitter feed.

No followers.

Then he surfed to his Facebook page.

No friends.

He checked his blog.

No replies to his latest post, or to any of them.

He sighed and returned to CNN.

"Incoming!"

In the fireplace, the Talking Fire was announcing a new arrival. A moment later the soul of a newly damned dead man landed in the fire with a loud thump. The flames crackled and cackled around it; for here, the flames spoke, though their language was not that of man.

The vicar of venom threw away his spider yo-yo and eyeballed the latest arrival, which was rousing itself from the bed of fire. This soul, like all the souls of the dead, did not bear the appearance or wounds of its physical self. Rather, it came in the shape of the dead person's authentic, inner self, from when the person was alive.

"Terrence Hildebrandt, truck driver, survivalist, Glenn Beck enthusiast," the fire announced with an apathetic fluff of its flames. It sounded bored.

What emerged from the fireplace, blinking in confusion, was a Maelephant: It was nine feet tall and weighed eight hundred pounds. It was humanoid in form, but it bore gigantic, claw-tipped hands that scraped the floor, and its head was that of a small elephant. A maelephant will fight to the death to protect its territory, and is violently paranoid.

"Christless, it's hot in here," Bubb complained, arming freshets of perspiration from his scarlet brow. Electric fans were arrayed everywhere and all of them were turned on, blades whizzing, and an air conditioner was going full blast, but the cramped and filthy apartment was still as hot as hell from the flames in the fireplace that were never quenched; no, never at all.

Looking at the maelephant, Bubb idly observed: "Of course, that silly truck driver. I wonder why he croaked? Oh, well, no matter. Take him to the Rec Room."

Swarms of harpies, hellwasps, night hags, she things, goat-legged imps and even Iblis the Thrice-Damned (in case the new arrival was Muslim) pounced upon the maelephant, which was bellowing through its trunk, and dragged it off to a door with a sign that said, "Rec Room." They opened the door, shoved the monstrous elephant-like creature through it and then slammed it shut. During the brief interval that the door was open, heart-rending shrieks could be heard from the other side.

"Incoming!" the Talking Fire cackled again.

"Another?" Bubb remarked, arching the upside-down V's of his shabby eyebrows in surprise. "So soon?"

The arrival of the new dead soul was preceded by some home-baked but half-melted chocolate chip cookies that pattered down into the eternal fire, followed by a bubblegum-pink pocketbook.

A moment later the soul of the newly dead landed feet first on sensible, patent-leather pumps purchased at Payless. The signature stockings had red and white stripes, like candy canes. The fires of the fireplace flared around the dead soul, making a windy *floof* sound.

"Oh, dear!" could be heard from within the flue. "More fire! But at least my foot is back! And there's my pocketbook." She snatched it up.

The figure — both feet intact and the body unharrowed by the flames in the exploding car, since dead souls do not bear the wounds of the living, but rather are symbolically reconstituted in the form of their inner selves — stepped briskly from inside the fireplace. Flo Jellem was immediately set upon by the disembodied souls of the gibborim nephilim, eager to drag her off to the Rec Room. They flapped their opalescent wings and emitted evil cackling as they sought to sink their giant hooks into her flesh. But as the first one touched her, Flo reared back and let the demon have it with her Pocketbook of Death across its putrescent puss, saying with deep indignation: "How *dare* you touch a lady without her consent! Silly sausage!" The nephilim quailed in distress and backed away from the feisty broad who now brandished her pocketbook like a pestle. Flo said, "My goodness!"

"Badness," Bill Z. Bubb tartly corrected her. But he was astonished at the sight of Flo. He turned to his home computer and consulted his directory of the damned. "Florence Jellem," he mused, clutching his long tail that curled up from under his seat and briefly gnawing on the arrow-shaped tip of it. "Professor Emeritus of Home Economics, preparer of cheese sammiches, baker of cookies, Internet scourge of evolutionists." Bubb reached into a bowl with the sign ANTI-DEPRESSANTS on it and swallowed a handful of multi-colored happy pills that resembled oversized M&Ms. "Poetess of Pot Roast."

Flo was looking about the cramped, overheated, filthy apartment with a grimace of disgust. "This place looks like the Dickens, dear," she observed. "Who are you? Where am I?"

"Most people who arrive here," the Titan of Terror said reflectively while gnawing meditatively on his tail, "arrive in some symbolic form representing their true, inner selves, the selves that they hid or distorted during their time on earth. Rarely — *very* rarely — one appears in death, just as one appeared in life." He paused, looked Flo up and down, and said, now with his own grimace of disgust: "Those are the ones who lived their lives with … with *integrity.*" He could barely spit out the last word; it came out of his mouth like a hairball out of the mouth of a cat. He now made a sour expression, suggesting that he had just swallowed molten brass.

"Where am I?" Flo asked, sounding dazed. "What *is* this awful place?"

"I'm afraid it's the last stop, my dear," Bubb replied. Harpies, asps, she things and other deformities lurked about, avid to escort Flo to the Rec Room. A faint cackling could be heard from that room, on the other side of the thick door that muffled most sounds, followed by a distant, goose-flesh-inducing shriek. Then came the evil laugh: mu-ah-ha-ha!

"*This* is heaven?" Flo was incredulous. "*This* is my reward for a life well spent professing home economics to junior high school students, in order to groom the competent short-order cooks and tasteful homemakers of tomorrow?"

"It's the other place, I'm afraid," Bubb said. A few goat-legged imps trotted past, making clopping noises with their cloven hooves. "The problem isn't with you, my dear. The problem is that the place where you were expecting to go seems to be out of commission, and has been so for eons. Hence I have to take as boarders the dead souls with —" that word again; he struggled to spit it out "— with *integrity,* as well as all the bad apples who make up the bulk of humanity." The Fallen One wore a doleful expression, and slowly shook his scarlet, perspiring head from side to side.

"I can't believe it!" Flo gasped.

With a sigh, the Harrower of Humanity snatched up the hourglass that doubled as his phone and placed a call upstairs. He then handed the device to Flo who, as instructed, listened to the bottom of the hourglass, which doubled as a receiver, holding the device by the thin neck between the upper and lower halves:

"Your prayer is *very* important to Father," a choppy recorded voice on the other end of the line assured Flo, through bursts of static. "Please stay on the line for the next available intercessionary seraph." Recorded choir music then started up, and played on and on. Weirdly, the area code with the number embossed on the bottom stand was that of Fresno, California. Flo recognized it because she often purchased products online from a business there: Photographs of foodstuffs miraculously imprinted with the visage of the Virgin Mary.

Flo, nonplussed, assessed her dire plight. But she quickly recovered her aplomb. Depression-born and bred and a veteran of three failed marriages, she had a pragmatic, roll-with-the-punches aplomb that had served her well in life, even as she was burning to death in the immolated car, and would now serve her equally well in death.

She handed the hourglass/phone back to the Suzerain of Sacrilege, clapped her hands together in a "that's-that" sort of way, heaved a big sigh of fatalistic resignation and said, "Well, since I'm here, I guess I might as well make the best of it. I presume that you are the Great Satan?"

Seated before her was a slovenly man wearing a sleeveless T-shirt against the heat and a wide-brimmed slouch hat that was intended to conceal his horns, but the horns had worn holes in the brim and now stood out sharply. He had a receding chin and a long, beaked nose, almost like a bird beak. He had Spock ears. The pupils of his bloodshot eyes, which were set back deeply in drooping pouches of flesh, were two black portals into everlasting starless night, and the frazzled hairs growing out of his nostrils resembled the many-fingered hands of the Damned clamoring for deliverance. A five-day growth of salt-and-pepper beard ran riot over the lower part of his face. Black flies circulated busily about his head like malignant electrons around an excremental nucleus. Flo thought that he looked like hell, and that he smelled like the Dickens. She wondered if he ever showered, and concluded that he probably did not.

"Well, you can call me that if you wish, but my friends call me Bill."

"Oh, dear! You have *friends*?"

The Killer of Dreams nodded apathetically at the motley crew of goat-legged imps, etc., and said, "After a fashion, I suppose." He gobbled another handful of anti-depressants and sighed. "Just not on Facebook."

"You have a Facebook page, dear?"

"Who doesn't, these days? It's not the 17th century anymore. I miss the 17th century. Times were simpler, then. Illuminated manuscripts were the most advanced means of communication."

The demons were lurking in the corners, and a hellswarm of hornets buzzed provocatively above Flo's head. Bubb said, sounding bored: "Don't worry, none of these deformities can harm you, because you have —" He spat out that dreaded word again: "*integrity*. So you won't be going to the Rec Room after all."

"The Rec Room? You have a *Rec* Room here, dear?"

Bubb beckoned Flo over to the door marked "Rec Room," and pushed it open just a crack.

She gazed out into black infinity. An undulating landscape of molten mountains rolling outward to horizonless distances under a starless night sky was bisected by the River Lethe. On the summits and flanks of every mountain, and on the banks of the river itself, which was made of molten lead, the souls of the damned were being unspeakably tortured, as in the paintings of Bosch. Moans, groans, shrieks and screams tore the air along with periodic mu-ah-ha-has of evil ecstasy from the dungeon masters.

Flo, doughty old bird though she was, blanched at the sight

and sound of this. Bubb closed the door, cutting off all but the loudest of the screams.

The professor emeritus of home economics took a few moments to compose herself after witnessing this demonic spectacle. But then, with rubber-band elasticity, she psychologically snapped right back into place and was as good as new. She looked around at the cramped, filthy, overheated apartment, saw garbage and dirty underwear strewn about the floor and cobwebs strung along the ceiling where the hell wasps hovered, and asked the devil: "My goodness, when was the last time you *cleaned* this place, dear? No one should after-live an afterlife in a hell hole like this, even if it is Hell."

"Eh? Cleaned? That would be around the time of the crucifixion of Christ, I believe, when he popped in for a brief visit to give a pep talk to our tenants. For some reason he spoke in Mexican and no one could understand him."

Arms akimbo, Flo heaved a sigh and said, "Well, I suppose I might as well tidy up a bit, if I'm going to stay here. Where do you keep your cleanser?"

Bubb was reaching for a pitcher labeled "Molten Brass" when his attention was arrested by a scrolling news bulletin on the CNN.com Web site showing on his home computer. "HELL IN TURMOIL," it screamed, while a camera from a copter flying overhead panned a burning big rig.

"Incoming!" It was the Talking Fire announcing another new arrival. A twelve-gauge shotgun arrived first, hitting the fire with a thump.

Then the dead soul of Junior Holland landed with a louder thump in the fire. He, too, was his own self, not some avatar representing a secret, sordid self.

"For the love of Christless," Bubb ejaculated, "*another* one with the integrity, already!"

The boy clambered out of the fireplace, swatted the flames off his pants and seeing Flo he cried, "Mizz Jellem! Is that you?"

"My goodness," Flo said, "You're the Holland boy, aren't you? My, how you've grown! Such a fine, strapping lad you are, now!" Flo had had Junior Holland as a home ec student back when the boy was in seventh grade, just before Flo retired. He was a prodigy, arguably her best student ever.

The boy looked around with a dazed expression. "Where am

I? And where is that dog? Is it gone? Is it over with?"

Bubb's pointed ears pricked at this. His eyes were flitting from CNN to Flo and the boy, and back again. On the computer monitor, the CNN Web site was showing jittery cell-phone video taken at ground level of some horrific black animated inkblot with a zigzag grin made of meat cleavers and gigantic curling comma-like ears that resembled pompoms marinated in manure. It was madly chasing reporters, who were scrambling frantically to make their getaway. It leapt at Anderson Cooper, and tore his ass off. Bubb's eyes grew huge.

"Dog," he addressed Junior Holland, who gazed blankly back at the Viceroy of Viciousness. "You said, 'dog.'"

Bubb returned his attention to the computer monitor. The jittery video camera zoomed in and locked on two orange eyes.

"Incoming!"

The soul of Sheriff Ted flew down the flue and slammed to a halt in the eternal flames. Said soul, ruffling its feathers and twitching its little head from side to side on its scrawny neck, strutted busily out of the fire, saying, "Bawk! Bawk! Bawk!" Because the sheriff looked so different, Flo and Junior did not immediately recognize him.

"Yes," Flo affirmed, watching CNN on the monitor. "That dog is the little monster that bit off my foot and set my car on fire! The *effrontery* of it!" She brandished her Pocketbook of Death, made a few whap motions at the image of the cacodemon on the screen and said wistfully, "Things would have been *very* different in my car if I had managed to smack that little Dickens right across its fiery snout with this!"

"The Pood," Bubb said in a semi-whisper, transfixed by the video on CNN. His expression of astonishment slowly melted into one of dismay, and then of anger. "The *Pood,*" he loudly reiterated, and then, throwing back his head and flinging open his mouth he yelled at the top of his lungs: "Dog Walk*ERRRRRRRRRRR!*"

"Yes, boss," one of the goat-legged imps replied obsequiously, bounding up to Bubb on its cloven hooves and carrying a leash with a broken collar that had been torn open, frayed fabric hanging from the edges.

Bubb leaned in close toward the dwarfish imp, which proffered a shit-eating grin. Seeing that Bubb had spied the broken collar and leash, it quickly hid the damning evidence behind its back and cackled nervously, making clopping noises on the hardwood floor as it nervously shifted its weight from hoof to hoof.

"Dogwalker, where is The Pood?" Bubb asked the flunky in a mild, inviting tone of voice.

"I took him for his walk," Dogwalker said truthfully, but it sounded defensive. It did not want to tell Bubb that The Pood had chewed through its collar and gotten away, free to cavort on the surface of the earth nine floors up.

"I *know* that you took him for his walk, Dogwalker. What I want to know is, *did you bring him back?*"

"Heh!" The imp replied, eyes scuttling from side to side as it attempted to evade Bubb's penetrating red gaze. The gnawed-off collar and leash, which it had been holding behind its back, slipped from its trembling hands and fell to the floor. Seeing this, Bubb lost all control, and flicked his thumb against his index finger to pantomime a cigarette lighter. Dogwalker immediately went up in a hot red flame as big as itself, and when the whooshing flame vanished the imp had been reduced to a pile of smoldering but still sentient ashes. The ashes screamed silently with agony.

"Oh, my heavens!" Flo gasped, splaying a hand across her chest. Junior, jaw dropping, looked on with the same glassy-eyed expression of incomprehension that he had first exhibited upon seeing The Pood reassemble itself after he, Junior, had allegedly blasted it to Kingdom Come.

Suddenly the jigsaw-puzzle pieces in Flo's mind clicked together, forming a nightmarish mosaic of revelation. She looked at Junior and understood what his presence here meant. Junior had been Flo's prodigy. She had taken him under her wing. She had taught him to whip up a Kraft American cheese sammich slathered in Miracle Whip mayo with a sliced tomato on Wonder Bread like nobody's business. He had a natural talent for building cheese sammiches. Later, she had initiated him into the Promethean mysteries of cooking by fire, and in no time at all he was turning out Kraft American cheese omelettes to beat the band. She sincerely felt that Junior had a stellar future as a short-order cook.

Now he was dead. No one would ever sample the meatloaf and mashed potatoes Blue Light Special of Junior Holland, short-order cook, at some classy venue like a Woolworth lunch counter. The world's gustatory loss, Flo felt, was nearly incalculable.

Junior and Flo then compared notes about what had happened

to them upstairs, while Bubb glumly watched the catastrophe unfold on CNN.com. It was true that he had intended to release The Pood to the surface, but not right away, and not for the purpose of wantonly killing a lot of innocent people. Bubb was the epitome of evil, sure, but he retained a rudimentary sense of fair play. Wreaking havoc was an art form, not to be undertaken by amateurs. But now his Pood experiment had gone abysmally awry.

The devil sensed Flo glaring down at him with dagger-like eyes through her granny glasses, and he looked up at her in a sheepish, cowering way.

Flo said: "So that's *your* dog, *your* cacodemon, that's got up to the Dickens!"

Bubb offered Flo a big, shit-eating grin, similar to the grin that the now-incinerated but still silently screaming Dogwalker had offered to Bubb.

"Well, dear," Flo said, crossing her arms over her chest, her bubblegum-pink Pocketbook of Death dangling from one hand, "You'll just have to go upstairs, and *bring the dog back.*"

"Upstairs!" Bubb's scarlet face blanched lily-white. "I haven't been upstairs since the 17th century."

"Why in heaven's name not?"

"Because people upstairs are *crazy,*" he replied, looking genuinely frightened. "They scare the *hell* out of me!"

Florence Jellem was normally as even-keeled as a Navy frigate. But now, less for herself but more on behalf of Junior Holland, whose cooking career had been cut short practically at its pilot-light dawn, she lost her temper and began smiting the defiler of decency hip and thigh, and on top of his head, too, knocking off his hat to reveal a bald, shiny red pate. She smote him with her Pocketbook of Death, previously the scourge of generations of Hellions in her home ec seminar. The pestle made loud and vivifying *whaps* as it repeatedly made contact with demonic flesh. Apart from pummeling pupils' posteriors with the pestle-like pocketbook when they mixed up tablespoons with teaspoons or armpit-farted during Flo's all-important tomato-slicing seminars, the last time Flo had resorted to physical violence was when she boxed the ears of that brat Billy Braxton after he had overturned a jar of Miracle Whip mayonnaise on the head of dear little Deirdre Dellahaney. Flo had later regretted boxing Billy's ears, though arguably the little stinker deserved it. Here, now, though, was not just another little stinker but the epitome of evil itself; the original, nascent *source* of stinkerdom; the omphalos of omnimalevolence.

"Stop hitting me!" Bubb whined, cowering and covering up as Flo smote him.

"Then go upstairs (whap!) and bring back that dog before it (whap!) gets up to more (whap!) Dickens!"

"All right, all right, I'll go, just stop *hitting* me! For Christless sake!"

~=__!
          !   !

Gil Aaronson, the mayor of Hell, Michigan, who lived in the geographical center of it, hooked up his CPAP machine after cleaning it. He was getting ready for his ritual of sleepenstein rest. But tonight he also snagged an Ambien. This was going to be a great night's sleep, he thought, rolling his eyes at the irony of the idea.

Afflicted with sleep apnea and a host of other annoying disorders both real and imagined, Gil had stayed in all day, resting. He had kept the TV, radio and computer all turned off, and he had even disconnected the phone and pulled down the shades. Sometimes the strong spring sunlight gave him migraines, and he preferred darkness. He had instructed his chief of staff, Ollie Upchuck, not to disturb him "even if the world is ending."

"And keep all my constituents away from me, Ollie," he had added. "You know how much I hate them."

Around noon he had heard several distant booms, like explosions, but he had put them down to sonic booms produced by air force jets taking practice runs out of Selfridge Air Force base.

Now it was night, and time for bed.

Pill down; now strap on his mask, start the machine and breathe deeply. Find a comfortable position, which was nearly impossible with this damn thing on, and go to sleep. Oh, well, Gil sighed. Maybe it wouldn't be such a great night's sleep after all.

~=__!
          !   !

The housing complex was fairly new, built on good farm land. McMansions for the pretend rich of the housing boom gone bust, the houses were all the same: no land, only ticky-tacky cookie-cutter boxes built one right next to the other.

Night had fallen, and the quiet complex defended by heavy iron gates was bathed in sodium vapor lights. A tiny black ragged four-legged form, like the walking shadow of a miniature poodle that had been ground up in a blender, strutted busily across the lights that pooled on the pavement. It had slipped through the bars to penetrate the defenses of the gated community. In the deep silence, its stainless-steel claws clicked noisily on the pavement. It started chuffing: *Chuff-chuff-chuff.*

It paused, avidly sniffed the air with its vibrating black snout, and then growled. Then it settled back down on its haunches and lifted its left leg. It briefly licked its balls, which were made of cast iron. After that, with its left leg it scratched furiously at one of its tattered, torn-pennant ears, scratching with such force that it nearly tore the ear off its head. A cloud of the fleas with human faces were catapulted to the pavement and they hopped away, seeking refuge in nearby well-manicured shrubs and hedges. A little unpleasant surprise for the groundskeepers in the morning.

Satisfied, The Pood resumed walking in its busy little trot: *Click, click, click.* Then the clicking stopped. Its head strained on its neck, and it sniffed the air with an expression of intense concentration. Its orange eyes burned in the darkness. The scent was unmistakable.

This was the place.

Fire licked from its mouth, and black sooty smoke poured from its nostrils. Yes, this *was* the place.

And this was the end. The end of Gil, that was.

The Pood had been programmed by Bill Z. Bubb to assassinate Mayor Aaronson, who was its former owner back when The Pood was alive and an ordinary toy poodle named Echo.

```
~=\___!
  !  !
```

Gil, groggy, woke when he felt something walk over his feet. Through his Ambien haze he espied little Echo, his dear, darling dead poodle. When Echo was alive, the little guy loved to hop in bed with Gil and warm his precious little paws under the blanket.

Gil loved his little guy. He reached for the poodle and called out, his voice muffled by the Phantom-of-the-Opera-like CPAP face mask that he wore: "Come here, buddy," he said amid his labored breathing. He pulled up the covers and motioned him in.

Echo didn't move. Gil thought that the dog looked a bit ragged in the dim light. Its orange eyes glowed like two colored electric night lights.

Gil reached for his dog and started scratching him behind the ears.

"You are all *sticky,* pal," he said. "What the heck have you been up to? Mischief?"

The dog emitted *grr-grr-grr* noises.

In the darkness Gil picked up the orange-eyed Echo with both hands and set his buddy down on his chest. The dog flopped over onto its back and Gil vigorously rubbed its tummy. More stickiness. It was as if the dog was covered in some kind of thick, viscous, semi-melted tar.

Echo thrashed about, righted itself and hopped off of Gil's chest, landing on the mattress. Gil again opened the covers and beckoned the dog inside.

The Pood hesitated. FRIEND! Its mind churned. KILL! Maybe it was a bit of indigestion from Samantha's brain. Maybe it was byte of bad Perl code from Bubb. Maybe his tungsten heart was five points up on the periodic table. Regardless of Dr. Seuss and Scrooge analogies, The Pood's mission was lost. LOVE!

The Pood prowled in under the covers, and snuggled up next to its beloved master. Both human and cacodemon felt toasty warm. Gil was vaguely troubled by the noxious odors wafting off the sticky canine (is that *shit?*). Also, Gil suddenly felt itchy. He started scratching himself but he was already drifting back to sleep, his breathing steadied by the mask and machine. Soon both dog and master were deep in peaceful slumber, though every now and then Gil would jerk semi-awake and scratch himself bloody.

```
~=\___!
   !  !
```

Gil woke up to his alarm and shut off the CPAP machine. At least he had slept, though he always had weird dreams on Ambien. Last night he dreamed that his long-dead poodle had come back from the dead. He loved that little guy. The poodle was 20 years old when it died of kidney failure. Echo had seen Gil through high school, college, one divorce and two failed runs for mayor before he was finally elected. Echo really was his best friend — his *only* friend. And the dream had been so vivid. But now, cruel and dreamless daylight reality intruded: the dog was gone.

With a sigh, he shuffled off to the bathroom to begin his morning constitutional, the 3 S's.

As he stripped off his pajamas he realized that he felt itchy all over. He looked at his hands. They were covered in black soot (is that *shit?*) and what looked like dried blood. He inspected himself with incredulity. His whole body was covered in blood, mud, shit, whatever it was, and also his flesh was mottled with bloody bites. *Bedbugs* flashed through his mind. I must have bedbugs!

He ran his hands over his chest and then looked down at his palms in amazement. They were covered with blood. I look like Jesus after a bad day on the cross, he thought, amazed. I need a doctor.

He turned from the bathroom, intending to run to the kitchen and phone 911. But he stopped in the doorway of the bathroom and stared down, stunned, at what was on the floor, looking up at him.

He stumbled backward and collapsed on the toilet seat.

There is no way, he thought. Things like this just do not happen in the real world.

He stared at the two orange eyes that stared back at him. The little clipped-off nub of a tail began vibrating avidly.

"Christ, I think I just pissed myself. Echo? Is it really you?"

The devil dog suddenly scampered forward, took a big leap upward and jumped into Gil's lap. Gil had no pants on, and its claws pierced his flesh, instantly drawing blood.

"Owwwww!"

Gil yanked the dog off his lap, causing himself more pain as the claws were pulled out of his thighs. He dropped the dog-like mess to the floor and jumped to his feet. It hurt so much he closed his eyes and saw stars.

When he opened his eyes Echo was sitting on a bath mat, whimpering and looking dejected.

"Sorry, buddy, but you have some sharp claws, and those teeth and that minty breath you have! What are you, exactly? A devil dog? All fifteen pounds of you?"

With that The Pood sprang to all four legs.

"BIIIIIILAAAAAARGH!" It said. *Yap yap yap yap yap!*
Fire flared out of its mouth.

The house shook. The fire turned the bath mat brown and singed the hair off of Gil's legs. The bathroom filled with thick, acrid brown smoke, but the vent fan took it away quickly. Gil stood naked and trembling in front of an angry poodle from Hell.

"Point taken, buddy," he said in a shaky voice. "Fifteen pounds of pure evil in a fur coat."

To kill him, to kill him not. To kill him, to kill him not. Cognitive dissonance. Echo snuffled, and then flopped down in a fusty heap of frustrated indecision. It whimpered pathetically.

"Fur," Gil cogitated. "Or is that hair? I don't think poodles have fur. They don't shed."

He shook his head to banish this retarded train of thought.

"Well, buddy, I finished one portion of my morning constitutional thanks to you," Gil said shakily. He flushed the toilet, walked into the other room and reconnected his phone. Then he gingerly stepped over the dozing hellhound and into the shower. From the other room, his phone rang. He sighed. It happened every time. Step into the shower, and the phone rings. Why had he reconnected it? He listened for the answering machine as he lathered soap all over his battered and bloody body while the hot water from the nozzle roared down on him.

"Gil? This is George, your neighbor. Did you feel that earthquake we just had? My whole house shook! I also heard a noise that sounded like 'BIIIIIIAAAAAARGH! *Yap yap yap yap yap!*' Nothing on the news yet. Man, I sure hope we're not going to have a repeat of yesterday! Where the hell *were* you yesterday, anyway? I mean, you *are* the mayor, dude! Well, hope you are doing. Call me."

George Flanders, Gil thought indifferently. God, how he hated George. Some days, he wished that George would drop dead.

"Man, I sure hope we're not going to have a repeat of yesterday?"

Gil wondered: What in Hell did *that* mean?

Yesterday, Gil had severed all connections to the world and stayed indoors with the shades drawn. The truth was, he often wished that he could sever all connections to the world permanently. But now he wondered with a fair bit of urgency: *what had happened yesterday?*

The water blasted down, and steam rose abundantly in the

shower. Gil pulled back the shower curtain, eyed the fifteen pounds of pure evil in a fur (hair?) coat dozing fitfully on the bath mat and said: "Hey, buddy, jump in here and get cleaned up. You look like shit."

Echo's head popped up from the pillow that it had made of its front paws, and it orangely scrutinized Gil with its kumquat eyes. The ragamuffin caricature of a canine then gave off a low, rumbling growl, popped to its feet and hopped happily into the shower. When the water hit the beastie there was a loud hissing noise and the steam fairly poured off of it; the interior of the shower soon turned into a sauna. Fortunately for Gil and his sanity, he did not notice the water from the shower washing hundreds of fleas with human faces off his erstwhile pet; the minuscule monsters were funneled silently screaming down the bathtub drain into subterranean sequestration.

```
~=\__!
  !  !
```

"Wait," the Prince of Peacelessness said. The demonic glint in his eyes inadvertently advertised the nefarious scheme that was percolating in his malignant mind.

Although Flo had died yesterday, she certainly hadn't been *born* yesterday. Arms akimbo, her punishing pocketbook in one hand, she scrutinized The Foul One with the same expression of suspicion that she once reserved for stinkers in her home ec seminars who tried to talk their way out of making cheese sammiches with the excuse that they were allergic to Miracle Whip mayonnaise or that their dogs had eaten their homework cheese. Junior had cleared some trash from an old chaise lounge and was struggling to get some shut eye after the tiring ordeal of dying. Sheriff Ted, bawking the whole way, had been dragged off to the Rec Room by the gebborim nephilim, and was currently undergoing the torture of having its head wrung off its scrawny chicken neck, after which it was allowed to run around in circles for awhile, headless. Then the head would be reattached, and wrung off again. This repetitive exercise was scheduled to go on until the end of Time.

"Wait for *what*, dear? You *have* to go up there and get that dog! There is no time to lose! Let's get cracking! Remember: 'Idle hands are the devil's playthings.'"

"I *am* the devil!" the devil protested. Then, after a thoughtful pause, he added: "But maybe I won't have to go upstairs after all." He had just remembered that he kept spies upstairs: his personal agents.

"The Men in Black," he said.

"What men in black?"

Bubb explained to Flo that when strange and unanticipated things happened upstairs that had been inspired by Bubb's never-ending experiments in madcap mischief, the Men in Black, his personal agents, always showed up to set matters aright.

"You know, like UFOs," Bubb said enthusiastically, meeting Flo's skeptical gaze behind her granny specs. "When people see UFOs, many of them are visited by the Men in Black. I'm responsible for UFOs: They are Jungian psychic projections that I, the Great Trickster, implant in people's subconscious minds to confuse them and, if at all possible, destroy their sanity. But if they survive I send the Men in Black to visit them, to put the fear of Me into them."

"Oh, that's simply dreadful!" Flo exclaimed, patting a hankie to her brow to sop up perspiration. The heat in the cloistered, filthy apartment was stifling; Junior tossed and turned on the chaise lounge, moaning. "My goodness, you are such a *dreadful* little man!"

"Thank you," Bubb replied, waggling his shaggy eyebrows with satisfaction and thumping the arrowhead of his tail on the trash-strewn floor. "Thank you very much." Then he yelled, "FLUNK-EEEEEEEEE!"

Another goat-legged imp loped into view, carrying something small and flat in the palm of its taloned-fingered hand.

As the devil accepted the device from the flunky, Flo looked at it with curiosity. While Bubb activated it he told her, "It's an iPood. It keeps track of the whereabouts of The Pood via Global Positioning Device, and it also stores up to ten thousand iShrieks: the melodic screams of the damned recorded live while they undergo eternal and unspeakable torture in the Rec Room. Music to my pointy ears."

Flo momentarily weighed this impressive information and then asked, "Can you e-mail chocolate chip cookies on it, dear?"

Bubb offered the computer-challenged Flo a mystified glance, and then pinned down the coordinates of The Pood.

"The Hell you say!" he thundered, gaping at the data display. "He actually made it all the way to the Aaronson house!"

"Aaronson?" Flo inquired, knitting her brows like darning needles as she concentrated. "Do you mean *Gilbert* Aaronson, the mayor?"

"The very same," Bubb replied, his voice acid with disdain. A tenuous strand of venom spilled from the corner of his mouth and melted a hole in the cast-iron surface of his desk. Aaronson had been the object of Bubb's Pood experiment in the first place.

"Gil Aaronson," Flo repeated, with a faraway look in her eye. Everyone who had grown up in Hell, Michigan, had sooner or later passed through her home economics seminar at Chester Alan Arthur Junior High School, and Gil had been no exception. Flo had a photographic memory of all her students, no matter how many years ago they had matriculated with her, and Gil, again, was no exception. She began spouting facts about him like data retrieved from a computer hard drive.

"Indolent and indifferent. The sammiches that he made were always slipshod affairs. He seemed to have a fair amount of talent, but he utterly lacked drive and ambition. Wouldn't slice a tomato to save his soul. Wouldn't even wash the lettuce! Disinterested to the point of cruelty. When that little stinker Billy Braxton poured a jar of Miracle Whip mayonnaise over the head of poor Deirdre Dellahaney, Gil was seated right next to them. He could have stopped the vicious assault, but instead he leaned back in his chair and watched it take place with an impish, cynical grin, and he gave off a snigger, suggesting a boy much older than his actual years. Plus, he's a rotten mayor. He raised our taxes three times."

"My kind of man," the devil muttered, but then in a louder tone of voice he announced, "Still, I have my own reasons for hating him, and for wanting him dead — and in the Rec Room, as soon as possible."

~=__!
  ! !

Gil Aaronson puttered about, getting ready for Saturday morning. He tried to ignore Echo. He wasn't quite sure what to do about this puzzling state of affairs. Either he was having an Ambien-induced hallucination, or he was crazy. Or — most disturbing of all — Satan really existed and was fond of resurrecting family pets as demons.

As Gil puttered, Echo pattered, stainless steel nails clicking busily on the hardwood floor and chipping small dents into it. From time to time Gil glanced down in wonderment at the beastie, from the snout of which fire occasionally languidly licked. It really did look just like Echo, but with a few evil tweaks.

Gil made some pancakes and laid one out for Echo, who gobbled it up just like old times. Then he strolled over to the fridge, retrieved a can of Bud and poured the beer into a dog bowl. Just like old times, Echo lapped the beer up as if it were nectar. Sitting on the chair at his kitchen table while Echo ate and drank, Gil sighed and said, "What am I to do with you, buddy? You're supposed to be dead."

Sighing again and still feeling a bit itchy despite the long, hot shower, the bathrobe-clad Gil padded on his slippers into the living room, grabbed the remote from an end table and switched on his high-def TV. He tuned in to his favorite, Tampon (Tampy) Redsmear's Faux News, and his mouth fell open.

BREAKING NEWS, the screen shouted back at him. TERRORIST ATTACK IN HELL, MICHIGAN. Footage of a burning big rig was playing, evidently taken from a news chopper hovering overhead. It was video taken yesterday, when Gil had cut himself off from the outside world like a hermit from civilization.

A round table featured Glenn Beck, Bill O'Reilly, Ann Coulter and Mike Huckabee. Coulter's Adam's apple bobbed up and down approvingly while Huckabee stated: "Yesterday's Islamist terror attack in Hell, Michigan, was President Oreo Cookie's fault. I'm not saying that President Cookie personally engineered the attack, or even that he necessarily had advance knowledge of it and permitted it to happen. I am saying that he laid the groundwork for the attack by failing to acknowledge American Exceptionalism. And the reason for his anti-Americanism is the fact that he was born and grew up in Kenya, and was raised by a Muslim father."

Echo jumped up on the back of the couch in which Gil was reclining, its stub of a tail vibrating in ecstasy. It was watching a videotaped replay of its own charming self attacking the ass of Anderson Cooper, and tearing off a big chunk of it along with the CNN reporter's pants. Gil smiled at this. "You did good, there, buddy," he conceded, scratching his dear little evilly tweaked Echo behind one of its torn-pennant ears. Chuff! Chuff! Chuff! The cacodemon responded, and with its great sandpaper tongue it licked off the epidermis on the side of Gil's face, causing him to cry out in pain. The Faux News round-table clucked about Cooper's plight, too, evidently the only good thing that had happened yesterday, the events still rather mysterious. The consensus seemed to be that The Pood was a "robot drone" sent by Al Qaeda to terrorize decent, law-abiding, God-fearing, tax-paying Americans in the heartland of the country, and also that it was somehow connected with President Cookie's socialist policies that were bankrupting America.

While Gil gaped in disbelief at the tube, the doorbell rang. He rose unsteadily to his feet and approached the door. Echo hopped off the top of the couch and followed Gil to the door, nails clicking on the floor. Gil glanced down worriedly at the devil dog and said, "Whoever it is, don't kill him, OK, boy?" Gil sighed. Echo sighed, too. Gil was sure it was the police. They had tracked Echo to him and now he was going to be in deep shit. Probably the City Council would impeach him. Taking a deep breath, he opened the door and froze.

A man dressed all in black stood before him, eyes shaded by black sunglasses. Black tie, black suit, black pants, black bowler hat.

"I know you," Gil said in amazement. "You're one of the Men in Black. I once saw you on an episode of The Simpsons."

"Very astute, Mr. Aaronson," the Man in Black said, doffing his black bowler hat and offering a stiff, formal bow. He replaced the bowler on his head and produced a butterfly net from behind his back. "I think you know why I'm here." Through the black sunglasses that he wore, Bill Z. Bubb's agent peered over Gil's shoulder at the canine cacodemon, which growled and then burst into flames, producing a sound like the burners of a stove being turned on.

Gil looked down in amazement at this burning parody of his dear little Echo. The flames subsided and then sprouted again, like flowers of fire.

Gil looked back at the man in black, who was expressionless and inscrutable in his sunglasses. "I'm afraid you have a beta version of The Pood, Mr. Aaronson," the agent said. "It was not intended for immediate public release. We were still working out the bugs when it suddenly and unexpectedly went viral, and you see with what terrible consequences. That is all that I am at liberty to disclose." The Man in Black how held the butterfly net in both hands and peered down at Beta Pood, which intermittently sizzled and steamed as the flames from its fur alternately waxed and waned.

Gil suddenly felt a flood of nostalgia, and memories marched through his mind: Echo sleeping in his lap when he, Gil, napped on the couch. Echo sticking by him when his wife left him. Echo consoling Gil with sandpapery licks of his tongue when he, Gil, lost two races for mayor. Echo was not only loyal, but fearless, too. Only two things frightened him: The Elvis impersonator who used to live next door and the Aflac ducks in that wacky TV commercial starring Yogi Berra. Whenever the ducks cried "Aflac!" or whenever faux Elvis next door burst into a slightly off-key (and frequently drunken) rendition of, "You ain't nothin' but a hound dog," the petrified poodle would scamper off and scoot under the couch, where it would squeeze its eyes shut and press its dear little paws to its dear little ears. Gil imagined that the hound dog accusation was particularly galling to the proud poodle.

Gil, not knowing what else to do, stood uncertainly between the Man in Black and Echo-cum-cacodemon.

"Come now, you don't need a living dead poodle, Mr. Aaronson," Bubb's agent wheedled. "Just give it back and you can go on with your so-called life."

But The Pood dug in its paws, stainless-steel claws taking root in the hardwood floor.

"I don't think he wants to go," Gil said.

"It isn't The Pood's decision, Mr. Aaronson," the Man in Black said, voice suddenly stern. "Nor, for that matter, is it yours."

"I think it *is* your decision, Echo," Gil said, looking down at The Pood. "What do you want to do, buddy? Your call."

Echo sprang out of its crouch, trotted toward the Man in Black, opened its maw and said, "BllllILLLLLAAARGH!" A fireball tripped off its long, forked tongue and darted upward. Gil stepped quickly to one side, the flames singeing his bathrobe. The fire burned the knees off the trousers of the agent, who responded by swinging the butterfly net at The Pood, trying to snatch it in the webbing. But the *lusus naturae* scampered away and hid behind Gil, looking out between Gil's legs at the man on the doorstep with its phosphorescent orange eyes while panting and chuffing.

The agent's aplomb suddenly vanished; no doubt he was chagrined by the loss of the knees of his trousers. He bolted into the room, stepped swiftly around Gil and again swung the butterfly net at The Pood, which darted out the door with the sound of a rocket lifting off. Gil stood rooted to the spot, too stunned to move, as the

Man in Black galloped out the door and bounded down the porch steps in hot pursuit of the cacodemon, which was shooting across the front lawn like a black comet, incinerating patches of the grass with each fiery fall of paw.

A loud crash followed like the sound of a car wreck, and then there was a tremendous explosion.

A path of flame led from Gil's front door to the pine tree in the yard of his busy-body neighbor, George Flanders. George was a gym instructor at Chester Alan Arthur Junior High School and a blockhead. He lived in the house that was once occupied by the noisome and drunken Elvis impersonator; Gil couldn't decide which neighbor he hated more. He now saw that George's Prius was wrapped around the tree, a hunk of twisted metal, and both it and the tree were on fire. Gil smiled. "Good boy, Echo," he silently rooted.

The Pood was perched in one of the branches of the burning tree, yapping down at the Man in Black who cautiously approached, making tentative passes through the air with the butterfly net. Above the tinny little yaps of the pestiferous poodle could be heard the cries of George, who, clad only in his bathrobe and slippers, was running out of his house toward the tree and the wreck of his car. "Hey, hey, hey," he was saying, waving his arms around. "Hey, hey, hey! What's the meaning of all *this*?"

The Man in Black approached the Beta Pood clinging to the tree branch, and the dog-like entity jumped out of the tree and flew through the air at Bubb's agent. The agent deftly swung the net and caught the doggie demon in mid-flight. The Pood, trapped, whirled around like a dervish in the net; most of its fur (hair?) and skin was burned away now, and its skeleton was visible: its bones were red, and its orange eyes suddenly glowed intensely white. The pestilent poodle had been reduced to little more than skin and bones, a clockwork machine of evil held together by fraying tendons and snapping sinews. Weirdly, however, its valentine-shaped heart still beat strongly, and the heart was made of pure gold. Its fangs hovered in the air behind the net like the disembodied smile of the Cheshire cat, and then it clacked those daggers down and tore the net to shreds, bounding through the hole it had made and back down onto the lawn, over which the fire was spreading.

All George cared about was his car, wrapped around the tree. He spread out his arms in horror at the spectacle, and kept saying over and over again, like an answering machine tape stuck in a recurring loop: "Hey, hey, hey! What's the meaning of all this? Hey, hey, hey ..." Gil rolled his eyes. George was all bent out of shape just because The Pood had destroyed his precious Prius. Fuck George, Gil thought.

The Pood was racing around the lawn with the Man in Black again in hot pursuit.

The Pood stopped fleeing, turned around, crouched, revved up a growl from the depths of its guts and, meat-cleaver fangs bared, leapt at its latest tormentor. It ripped the man's arm off. Gil, amused, thought of The Black Knight in Monty Python and the Holy Grail.

As the fight continued, distantly, just over the horizon, helicopters and planes began approaching. The choppers made a faint budda-budda-budda sound with their propellers. The military, Gil thought in wonderment.

The snarling Pood now prepared to rip off the other arm of Bubb's agent, but the Man in Black snatched off his sunglasses and fired green energy from his emerald eyes. There was a fearful explosion, so loud that the windows burst out of all the neighboring houses. Gil covered his eyes, afraid to look, but when he uncovered them he saw that the Man in Black had hit the ground with a thunderous crack. Echo stood over the fallen agent, its nub of a tail vibrating avidly. Billowing clouds of dust and ash flew upward and slowly settled; some hot embers glanced off Gil, scorching his flesh. For a moment all was quiet except for the sounds of the planes and choppers overhead, the staccato clicking of Echo's fangs and the infantile lamentations of George, pissed off by the destruction of his Prius. Gil thought disgustedly: Doesn't the fucker have insurance?

Gil watched in amazement as Echo's flesh grew back into place and its fur (hair?) again extravagantly thickened. The Man in Black rose shakily to his feet. One arm was gone and one of his legs was stripped to the bone. His bowler hat lay on the lawn beside his hand and arm. Part of his face was missing, and one eye glowed like a lump of burning coal. Seeing this, Gil's blood ran cold. "Don't kill anyone, OK, buddy?" he had told his devil dog. Now he was regretting that advice. Still, it seemed as if the Man in Black could not be killed, no doubt because he was already dead.

The agent lost his temper then and told The Pood: "I will take your soul and eat it as my own!"

With his one good arm he made a pattern in green and pulled a flashing emerald sword out of mid-air. The Pood watched, jaws clacking. It was drooling on the lawn and the saliva, made of acid, caused the blades of glass to sizzle and blacken.

Suddenly The Pood sprang into a dead run and bounded up onto the wreck of the Prius wrapped around the tree, ignoring the shrieks of George. The Man in Black brought the sword down on the car and cleaved it in two, causing George to faint and, Gil hoped, die. The agent then swung the sword like a hatchet at the base of the burning tree, which fell over on its side and crushed The Pood flat underneath it.

Overhead planes and helicopters swarmed; the first parachutists had hit the ground.

The Man in Black, maimed though he was, seized the crushed Pood from under the tree, tucked the ruined ragamuffin in the crook of his one remaining arm and said with an evil laugh: "Your soul will be mine, you damned dog, and I will teach you not to tangle with one such as I!"

The Pood's bones showed again, burning red in the green grasp of the Man in Black. Its long forked tongue hung out of its face as it panted. Gil, standing on the front porch, became angry. He cupped his hands around his mouth and yelled, "Echo, buddy, I changed my mind. Kill the motherfucker!" Hearing its master's voice, The Pood's battered and bloodied head ticked up. All its fur instantly grew back. Its ears inflated into two ragged tarry pompoms larger than the rest of its body and its eyes pulsated with renewed orange vigor. Its meat-cleaver fangs clacked and it chuffed.

It leapt out of the crook of the agent's arm and sank its fangs into the man's neck. It tore out the throat of the Man in Black, who collapsed into a smoking heap on the lawn as the first reporters stampeded toward Gil and The Pood. They were heavily armed with microphones, notepads, cell phones, video-cameras and the like. It wasn't the military after all, but once again, just as it had arrived yesterday, it was the United States Media Corps (USMC).

Gil clapped his hands together and cried, "Echo, here boy!"

The Pood shot like a dart for its master, and then leapt joyously into Gil's outstretched arms. Gil cried out at the sensation of Echo's claws sinking into his flesh. But cradling his best buddy — his *only* buddy — to his chest, he turned and ran indoors, kicking the door closed behind him while outside, the fists of the ravening hoards of the news media began to hammer on the door, causing it to vibrate on its hinges.

Echo glowed briefly with renewed fire summoned from within, and Gil, scorched, dropped Echo to the floor. "Tone down the flames, buddy," he said. "It's just me, now." With a small popping sound, the flames were snuffed out, and the dog was restored to its normal charming (though now charred) tatterdemalion self.

Outside the house, Wolf Blitzer bellowed into a megaphone: "We know you're in there, Mayor Aaronson, with the dog that caused so much damage yesterday. This can end one of two ways: peacefully, or by force. We want you and that dog to come out with your hands, your paws and your stories up."

```
~=\__!
  !  !
```

Emblazoned on the CNN Web site was the BREAKING NEWS banner, followed by the bold red headline: HOSTAGE STANDOFF IN HELL.

Flo Jellem and Bill Z. Bubb were hunched over Bubb's computer, watching the video of the latest calamity in the heretofore sleepy Michigan hamlet. Still dazed, Junior Holland had risen from the chaise lounge and was now gripping his shotgun and covertly scrutinizing Bubb with hatred in his eyes.

"We're outside the home of Mayor Gil Aaronson, in which apparently Mr. Aaronson is holding a dog-like entity hostage, or the dog-like entity is holding Mr. Aaronson hostage," said Wolf Blitzer, who normally reported from the Situation Room but was now covering for Anderson Cooper, who had fallen in action to The Pood during the previous day's debacle. "It is believed that the dog is somehow connected with yesterday's attack that led to the destruction of a big rig, the killing or maiming of several local residents, and the vicious attack on Anderson Cooper, in which he lost ..." Blitzer could not resist a chuckle of schadenfreude, but he hastily composed himself and nobly ad-libbed with faux gravity: "... a substantial portion of his lower anatomy."

Blitzer went on to assure viewers that the news media had the situation entirely under control. Bubb lifted his tail from the floor and, wearing a savage expression, gnawed on the arrow-shaped tip of it. Junior was approaching from behind on felted tread, the shotgun leveled at the back of the head of the Avatar of Avarice, at a location squarely between Bubb's two horns. Sensing Junior's presence behind him, Bubb turned and, seeing the barrel of the shotgun, said in a bored voice: "Oh, put that thing down, boy. You can't kill me. I'm dead."

Junior looked at Flo, who said to the boy: "I'm afraid it's true, dear, but don't fret. I think you are going to have big job to do soon, if I am not mistaken. And everyone knows what a good worker you are."

"What do you mean, Mizz Jellem?"

"Yes, what *do* you mean?" Bubb echoed, with a disingenuous grin. He again gathered up his tail and gnawed nervously on the tip of it.

Flo brandished her pocketbook at Bubb. Although Bubb could not be killed, Flo had proved that he remained subject to a stern smiting. "Well," she said, "*someone* — someone *responsible* — is going to have to watch over this dreary place while you go upstairs and bring back that dreadful dog, dear." She looked with distaste at the motley crew of goat-legged imps, night hags, hellwasps and other deformities that lurked in the shadowy corners or lounged about in the cobwebs that were strung from the ceiling. The gibborim nephilim, the fallen winged giants that had dominated the antediluvian world, were having a hand of poker at a cheap fold-out card table on which stood a six-pack of molten brass. They had been joined by Iblis the Thrice-Damned. "I wouldn't have *any* of these characters in *my* home, dear," Flo bluntly told the devil.

Bubb instantly became shifty-eyed. He looked like Dick Nixon debating JFK in 1960.

"Your agent didn't succeed in bringing the dog back," Flo reminded Bubb, who bristled at the old broad pointing out the painfully obvious. "Therefore, you *must* do it. We have already discussed this, dear."

"And if I refuse?"

Flo showed him the bubblegum-pink Pocketbook of Death with which she had earlier smitten Bubb hip, thigh and head. Bubb cringed.

Meanwhile, CNN had cut to a live statement from President Oreo Cookie at the White House.

"Our sympathies go out to the residents of Hell, Michigan, in their hour of distress," the president stated. "We will stand shoulder to shoulder with them, through thick and thin and black and blue. However, after intensive consultation with my top advisers, members of my cabinet and leaders of the military, including Secretary of State Hillary Clinton and Leon Panetta, the defense secretary, I am ruling out for the foreseeable future military action in defense of Hell. After all, there is no oil in Hell."

"True," Bubb said darkly. "But we have plenty of oil company executives."

The president went on: "However, I, the great conciliator, will try to bring the two warring sides to a meeting of minds. To that end, I shall go to Hell." A few of the president's aides standing nearby rolled their eyes. They knew of the chief executive's secret habit. This would not be the first time he would go to Hell and back, alas, though ordinarily the trip was made shrouded in secrecy.

Bubb now looked at the pocketbook again and then up at Flo in an appraising way: "Why don't *you* watch over the place while I'm upstairs? For all your surface sweetness, you strike me as the kick-ass-and-take-names type, just what we need down here."

"Oh, heavens, dear, I'm afraid that's impossible," Flo replied. "You see, I'm going to accompany you upstairs."

Bubb looked gobsmacked.

"You said that you hadn't been upstairs since the 17th century," Flo reminded the Great Traducer. "A lot of things have changed since then, dear. I imagine that you could benefit from a tour guide."

Bubb slitted his eyes, acquired a thoughtful expression and then, after a pause, he said, "You know, I could use another Night Hag around these parts, or even a competent She Thing. When all this is finally over, would you be interested in either job?"

Flo weighed the offer, while Satan tempted her even as he had tempted Christ in the desert: "It means, for instance, when that little stinker Billy Braxton finally gets sent down the fireplace flue, you could take him to the Rec Room and box his ears — forever!" Bubb waggled his shaggy, pointed brows insinuatingly at Flo, who thought over the prospect. Finally she declined, not without regret.

"I'm afraid I can't, dear," she said with a sigh. "It's true, he's a stinker, and I can't say that there aren't special charms to boxing a stinker's ears. But I don't think anyone deserves to have their ears boxed *forever*. Not even Hitler. The punishment should fit the crime, dear."

The devil looked crestfallen. "That's what all you humans say," he said scornfully. With a sigh and clop of his hooves, he said: "All right, we'll go. But you won't be enough. I'll need an entourage."

"An entourage?"

"You don't know the true meaning of The Pood," Bubb said cryptically. "But I do. And I know his Achilles heels — all four of them."

Bubb threw back his hoary head, flung open his mouth and yelled, "Ellllll-*VIIISSSSSSSSS!*"

In the Rec Room, which was spatially and temporally infinite, there was a river of molten excrement. On one of the banks of the river, a mountain made of powered human skulls reared up toward a sky made of vomit. Carved into a flank of the flaming mountain was a little amphitheater, looking down on a stage over which was stretched taut a tarpaulin made of human flesh that had been elongated on a torturers rack. A weary-looking, middle-aged man with big swoop of black hair and outlandish sideburns, and wearing a white sundial suit, was standing alone in a burning spotlight and ponderously strumming a guitar whose strings consisted of human tendons. He was singing a mournful dirge (originally recorded by Roger Whittaker) called "The Last Farewell":

> *I heard there's a wicked war [redacted*]*
> *And the [redacted*] of war I know so very well*
> *Even now I see the [redacted*] flag araising*
> *Their guns on fire as we [redacted*] into hell*
> *I have no fear of death it brings no [redacted*]*
> *But how [redacted*] will be this last farewell*

Ed Sullivan, who had introduced Elvis, was statuesque off to one side. His avatar was a moai, an Easter Island statue with a face like a prune made of stone.

At the conclusion of the song Elvis's audience, consisting exclusively of stiff-necked, music-hating, puritanical harpies in starched collars and wearing hoop skirts, erupted in a chorus of boos, and began throwing tomatoes. The weary, lonely man on stage under the laser-like light apathetically raised an arm in a futile effort to ward off the moist missiles that began exploding with loud plops on various parts of his body like scarlet paintballs. Within minutes his sundial suit was covered with red blotches, like blood.

* — We have to blitz copyright issues, more footnotes to follow, details abound.

When the indignant audience settled back down after this barrage, the man in the spotlight again tuned up the guitar and swung into yet another song for an audience that could never be pleased. Elvis Presley was in concert.

Forever.

Now, the reader may be forgiven for wondering two things: first, how is that Elvis Presley is in the Rec Room? What did he do during his short life to deserve being forced to stage a concert that will never end for an audience that can never be pleased? At the behest of a host who hated him?

In addition, the attentive reader will recall that except for people of integrity, like Flo Jellem and Junior Holland, everyone who arrives nine floors down in Bill's Place arrives in the form of an avatar, a physical manifestation of one's secret self that is invariably grotesque. And the people of integrity are immune to punishment. Yet here was Elvis, apparently looking just as he did in real life at the time of his death, only perhaps a bit paunchier and certainly wearier. Does this mean that Elvis had integrity after all? But if so, why was he was sentenced to play an infinite concert for an audience of music-hating harpies? These are good questions. Thanks for asking them.

Unfortunately, estimable reader, there is no delicate way to broach this subject. However, broach it we must, for Elvis will play a crucial role in our tale as it unfolds.

Elvis was sentenced to the Rec Room for the unpardonable sin of shaking hands with the Great Malefactor, Richard Nixon, during an infamous Oval Office meeting in 1971. Even as the gaze of Medusa reduced men to stone, the very touch of Nixon guaranteed eternal damnation. And so Elvis was damned, notwithstanding the great joy that The King's music brought to so many listeners during his tragically truncated reign on earth.

Moreover, though Elvis still appears to be, well, *Elvis,* look a little closer, dear reader. This is not Elvis proper, but *Chimera Elvis.*

The Pelvis had just swung into an up-tempo rendition of "Blue Suede Shoes." But his vacant, staring eyes and a demeanor suggesting the apathetic resignation of a man being led to the gallows belied the bouncy melody, as did the irruption of certain curious phrases uttered in an all-too-familiar basso-profundo voice tinged with self-pity, a voice that, although as deep as Elvis's, did not belong to Elvis:

Well, it's one for the [redacted]*
[Redacted] for the show*
Three to get [Redacted]*
Now go, [redacted], go*
(I am not a crook!)

But don't [redacted]*
Step on my blue [redacted] shoes*
Well, you can do [redacted]*
But lay off of my [redacted] suede shoes*
(A man is not finished when he is defeated. He is finished
when he quits.)

Well, you can [redacted] me down*
[Redacted] in my face*
Slander my [redacted]*
All [redacted] the place*
(You won't have Nixon to kick around anymore.)

The audience of harpies erupted in jeers, catcalls and boos.

"Stop moving your hips like that!" one of them demanded. "It's positively indecent! How *dare* you!"

"This is why I had him televised from the chest up back in '56," Moai Ed Sullivan stated. "He's not fit for family."

Another matron waved a hand at the air and, crinkling her nose, demanded, "What *is* that awful odor?"

As Elvis was again advising some nameless adversary to lay off of his blue suede shoes, the voice of Bill Z. Bubb could be heard shrieking through the fathomless immensities of the endless Rec Room:

"Ellll-*VISSSSSSSSSSS!*"

At the sound of their master's voice, two winged gibborim nephilim swooped down and with their talons they seized Elvis by the back of his sundial jacket. They yanked him aloft, the King clinging to his guitar, and flew him upward toward some small, distant, door-shaped patch of light. His back was now turned toward the audience. Molding his white bell-bottom trousers, the buttocks were two ponderous jowls, and Elvis's tailbone was extended outward in the shape of ski-slope nose. A contrail of noxious fumes

* — We just can't help the redacted in all of us, can we?

streamed out from the hidden cavity between the two jowls, and from that obscene fundament could be heard the following words, uttered with basso-profundo bitterness: "We're going to put more of these little Negro bastards on the welfare rolls at $2,400 a family — let people like Pat Moynihan and Leonard Garment and others believe in all that crap. But I don't believe in it. Work, work — throw 'em off the rolls. That's the key."

While the Elvis/Nixon chimera was being delivered to Bubb's apartment, the suzerain of lost souls shrieked a second time: "Aflac DUUUUCKS!" And the gibborim nephilim sank their hooks into four ducks and flew them up toward the apartment. But one of the ducks was actually a chicken, a new arrival still becoming acclimated to having its head wrung off its chicken neck, replaced and then wrung off again and again, a procedure scheduled to continue until the end of Time. The chicken's tormentor now bounded after the nephilim, who were retreating with their prize. "Hey!" he cried. "Bring that maggot back here! It's not a duck, it's a chicken! A chicken maggot!"

In short order The Elvis/Nixon chimera, the three ducks and the chicken were in Bubb's apartment with the devil, Flo and Junior. Junior, who still seemed dazed by all that had happened, kept moving the barrel of the gun from one newcomer to another, even though it was impossible to kill any of them because they were all dead. Flo, as usual, was more pragmatic. After the initial shock of the new arrivals had worn off she said to Elvis/Nixon, "Goodness gracious, aren't you Elvis Presley?"

The King mumbled something noncommittal, as if he were profoundly embarrassed. Abruptly, a deep voice from the posterior nether regions of the mortified King began uttering anti-Semitic slurs: "This anti-Semitism is stronger than we think, ya know. It's unfortunate, but this has happened to the Jews, happened in Spain, it happened in Germany, it's happening, and now it's gonna happen in America if these people don't start behaving. It may be they have a death wish, that's been the problem with our Jewish friends for centuries."

These words were accompanied by a horrific odor. Everyone looked mortified except for the Aflac ducks, which were yelling "Aflac" at one another amid what sounded like a discussion of philosophy. The chicken was running around bawking, and there was something distinctly familiar about its voice and demeanor, such that Flo looked at it, splayed a hand to her chest and said with a gasp: "Oh, heavens, dear, I didn't notice who you were when you came down earlier! So, you too!"

"Sheriff Ted!" Junior said, jaw dropping in fresh astonishment.

"Bawk!" said the avatar of the dead sheriff who had run away from The Pood and the media invasion.

The creaking footsteps of someone mounting the stairs toward Bubb's apartment could be heard; the nephilim had left the door open after ushering in Elvis and the others.

A moment later Staff Sergeant Ulysses Eisenhower Yokel, Sheriff Ted's tormentor in life and now in death, entered Bubb's apartment. More precisely, it was the head of the drill instructor behind a veil of fire with its familiar flat-top buzz haircut, thick red neck and sarcastic grin. But in the afterlife the sadistic marine was a hellfire golem, a towering humanoid consisting of burning lava oozing through a crumbling black crust.

"Come here, you maggot!" The drill-instructor-cum-golem bellowed at Sheriff Ted, who flapped its stunted wings and ran around in terrified circles, bawking. "I want to tear your head off again!"

"At ease, Sergeant Yokel," Bubb said, sounding bored. Studying the chicken, he said, "This isn't an Aflac duck. It's not even a *regular* duck."

The sergeant swaggered in the doorway, arms akimbo. He was grinning toothily and chewing on a pair of testicles from another of his torture victims.

"Why do you need ducks, dear?" Flo asked Bubb. "For that matter, why do you need Elvis Presley, along with the face of Richard Nixon, with his jowls forming Mr. Presley's buttocks and with his mouth forming The King's unclean fundament?"

"Because," Bubb replied, "The Pood is afraid of only two things: Elvis impersonators, and the Aflac ducks on TV. How much more afraid do you think he will be of the real Elvis and the real Aflac ducks? Nixon is just a bonus. *Everyone* is afraid of Nixon."

"But dear, why do you want to scare The Pood?"

"Because The Pood scares me!"

Flo attempted to press her line of questioning, but Bubb impatiently cut her off, sounding petulant: "You're the one who says I have to go upstairs to reclaim that damned demon dog, and so I get to pick my homies." He then savagely kicked at Sheriff Ted, who was bawking and running around in circles at Bubb's feet. "Take him back to the Rec Room," he told the nephilim, who advanced on the chicken but then backed off when Flo stood guard over him, brandishing her pocketbook pestle. Flo clearly intimidated the nephilim, who sheepishly returned to their hand of poker with Iblis the Thrice-Damned. She told Bubb: "If those ducks are going upstairs with us, then Sheriff Ted goes, too. It's only fair: he's dead only because you can't control your own dog, dear."

"Fine, fine, fine!" The devil ejaculated in disgust, throwing up his taloned hands. "We'll take the damned chicken, too! Anything that makes you happy, Flo. I really wish you'd reconsider my offer of becoming a Night Hag or a She Thing."

Sergeant Yokel's grin dissolved into a bitter frown. Seeing this, Bubb, who was growing increasingly disgusted with this whole idiotic affair, said, "You can come too, sergeant, why not? What a merry crew we'll make!" The sergeant's face lighted up again, his head dancing with thoughts of resuming his torture of Sheriff Ted, an activity he never tired of in death as in life.

"I suppose I should introduce you to the ducks," Bubb told Flo. "The cerebral and debonair one is David Hume, the middle one, with the gloomy puss, is Arthur Schopenhauer, and that one over there, with the mustache formed by the body of a dead rat and the demented gleam in his eyes, is Friedrich Nietzsche."

"Those names seem vaguely familiar, dear," Flo said. "Were they great short-order cooks?"

"*Philosophers*," the devil said, drawling out the word to emphasize his contempt for the faux profession. "At least if they had been short-order cooks, they would have provided a useful service. As it is, in death, they assume their true forms from life: They are quacks."

"Aflac!" quacked all three Aflac ducks in unison, and then they resumed squabbling among themselves. Bubb stuck his talons in his ears and said with a grimace: "They never shut up. All they do is debate philosophy." After a pause he added, "You can blame old Nietzsche there for why God never answers the phone. He *killed* God. That's what he says, anyway, though he is a bit of an insufferable braggart, always going on about how he is the Overduck."

Flo looked at the old German philosopher with consternation. "Is that *true,* dear? It's *you* who killed God?"

"Aflac!" Nietzsche affirmed.

Indignant, Flo hit him with her pocketbook, saying, "That for you!" and the classical philologist fled into a corner, pursued by the other ducks, who were eager to resume philosophical argumentation with him. They resumed their demented squabbling.

"All right, let's go," Bubb said with a heavy sigh of resignation.

"Junior, hold the fort!" Flo encouraged her former home ec class prodigy.

"Don't you worry, Mizz Jellem, I'll keep an eye on things round these here parts." Junior bravely if pointlessly held up his useless shotgun, which was locked and loaded.

"This way," invited Bubb, who donned a frock coat, and they filed out of his apartment and up nine flights of stairs on the spiral staircase. They were mostly silent on the way up, though at one point when Flo suggested they grab dinner at a nice Italian restaurant that she knew, the posterior head of the Elvis/Nixon chimera emphatically stated: "I don't want any Jew at that dinner who didn't support us in the campaign. Is that clear? No Jew who did not support us." Almost as an afterthought he added: "The Italians, of course, those people of course don't have their heads screwed on tight. They are wonderful people, but..." and his voice trailed off.

When they got to the vestibule and the front door of the seedy old apartment building, carved on a sign above the door was the following:

> Through me you go into the lands of the weeping,
> Through me you go into perpetual anguish,
> Through me you go among the lost people.
>
> Justice is what moved the exalted Creator;
> The world above was the invention of God,
> Of his wisdom and of his primal love,
>
> And those you will encounter here have none;
> They deserve none, for their sins are eternal.
> Abandon all hope, ye who dwell beyond here.

END BOOK TWO

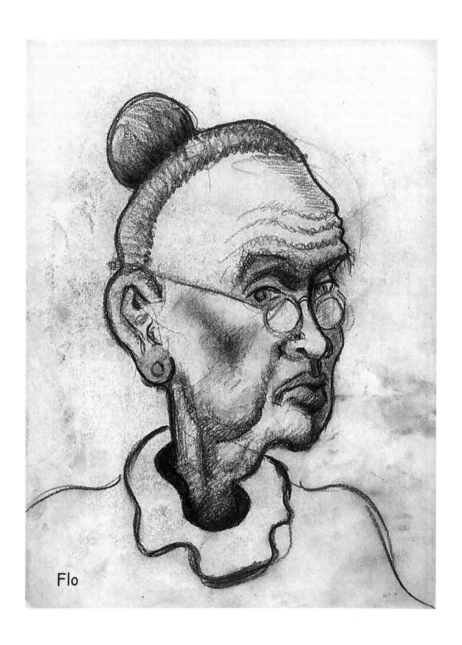

Flo

Book the Third

The Nine Neighborhoods of Hell
Satan Agonistes

"Love is a dog from hell."

— Charles Bukowski

The Gateway to Hell

WELCOME TO HELL, the sign by the side of the road said. The spring thaw had cleared winter's ice from it: Just three weeks ago, the sign had been frozen over, icicles dangling from it.

Now, under sunny spring skies, a convoy of tanks, trucks, Humvees and jeeps from the United States Media Corps rumbled down the road, past that sign. They were heading to the center of town — the inner station of the ultimate horror — where Gil Aaronson was holed up in his house with The Pood. The vehicles bristled with cameras, microphones, booms, laptops and other weapons of mass obfuscation. Atop several of the trucks, reporters stood scanning the horizon with binoculars. Others inside the vehicles were tapping on their laptops, blogging or tweeting live about the tense standoff in Hell. In one of the trucks, the latest streaming Webcast of the bot Steve Austin was being programmed by a team of nerds. Austin was a Web celebrity, even though he was nothing more than a pastiche of pixels and an artificial intelligence app. He fielded hundreds of marriage proposals daily from women who thought he was a real person, and continued to think so, more passionately than ever, in cases where it was proven to them that he was not real.

On the side of the road watching the procession pass was a drab little man in a shabby frock coat, his cloven hooves hidden in a pair of cheap penny loafers. He wore his slouch hat in a futile effort to hide his horns, for they had worn holes though the brim and stood out sharply. He also wore a frown of consternation. At his side was a matronly woman in sensible patent-leather pumps purchased at Payless and candy-cane-striped stockings, but she was transparent. The Elvis/Nixon chimera clung to its guitar like a drunk to a bottle. The Aflac ducks circulated underfoot, squawking about Hume's pre-Darwinian refutation of the Argument to Design and about Nietzsche's Will to Power. Schopenhauer wore his usual sour puss, the party pooper. Ted cowered at Flo's skirts, while Staff Sergeant Ulysses Eisenhower Yokel, now a hellfire golem, beamed down at the craven bird with the grin of a man about to tuck into a succulent roast chicken.

Bill Z. Bubb looked about with a fastidious, even prudish, expression of glum distaste. "What a *horrible* place," he said with a shudder. "I don't know how you people stand it upstairs. ... Well, at least it's cooler than my apartment."

Flo Jellem was looking with amazement at her own hands. She could see the ground through them: the hands were transparent and barely visible, even in the strong sunlight.

Bubb broke the news to her: "You're a ghost, I'm afraid. No one returns upstairs the way that they were before they went downstairs, even the people with integrity. Sergeant Yokel here, the ducks, the chickenshit sheriff and Elvis – they're all avatars, so they don't have to be ghosts. The only other way to return upstairs is as a zombie. I don't think you'd like that. You'd have to try to eat the brains of the living, and someone might shoot you in the head."

"Well, dear," Flo said, bravely facing up to yet another disheartening revelation, "I *do* have a nice recipe for sheep's brains burritos." After a pause she added: "Well, I suppose I'll make do as I've always made done. When I was growing up during the Depression we had to eat stunted, shriveled little potatoes that we clawed out of the ground with our bare hands, as well as tree bark, weeds and insects. Bad as that was, the experience inspired me to a career professing home economics, and I never looked back. When life gives you a lemon, make lemonade, I always say. I suppose the same is true for death."

Bubb covertly rolled his bloodshot eyes at Flo's home-spun bromides.

Nixon made a derogatory remark about his one-time secretary of state, George P. Schultz. Elvis looked infinitely depressed, mired in chagrined silence. A disgusting odor filled the air after Nixon called Schultz a "candy ass," but it was quickly overwhelmed up by the truck exhaust of the media contingent that was now pouring into Hell the way that the American armed forces had surged into Iraq in 2003.

Stuck in traffic was Buridan the ventriloquist, who lived on the outskirts of Hell. He was on his way home when he became marooned in the media invasion. Now he rolled down his window and leaned out. He gave a whistle of amazement and said, "Flo Jellem, is that you? You're looking mighty peaked!"

"Oh, Burd!" Flo said, first starting to run toward the stalled car but then discovering that she could effortlessly glide toward it. When she got there, Burd said, "We all thought you was dead!"

"Where'd you get that idea, Burd?"

"It's in all the papers, Flo." He held up a copy of the Life in Hell, the town's daily paper, illustrated by Matt Groening, and Flo's picture was on the cover along with the story about the attack in which she had died. Flo responded with incarnadine modesty. She had not thought that she was such a big deal. Then she broke the news to Burd: "Well, I *am* dead, dear, I'm a ghost." The rest of the party had caught up with her and joined Flo around Buridan's car.

"A ghost!" Burd looked Flo over a bit more carefully and realized that not only was she a bit peaked, she was transparent. "Well I'll be Buridan's ass!" said Buridan's Ass. Buridan's Ass was the dummy that Burd carried with him constantly on his right hand. The dummy's name was Ass. He was variously known as the Ass or the Dummy.

Buridan and his Ass constituted a routine that went all the way back to the 1950s, when the duo was a dynamite act in Hell's rambunctious roadhouses of that era. The shtick was that the Ass and Buridan disagreed about everything, especially politics. The Ass, whose face had been composed to resemble that of Senator Joe McCarthy, was a right-wing Republican (a John Bircher back in the 50s) and Buridan was a left-wing Democrat, when that species still existed. But what had started out as farce evolved into tragedy. The pair became literally inseparable after a catastrophic accident at the Michigan State Fair. A windmill blade, cleaved off by a high wind, chopped Buridan's head in two, severing his corpus callosum and leaving the two lobes of his brain without neural connections. One lobe remained Buridan but the other lobe took on all the characteristics (including the political opinions) of the Ass. Because they were now two personalities simultaneously living in one body, they could never agree on anything. Sometimes they couldn't even agree to get out of bed in the morning or use the toilet. They could never agree on the same option, even when — especially when! — both options were irresistible. They simply couldn't make a commitment. To this day they squabbled vehemently about politics. Buridan was a fan of President Cookie, but Buridan's Ass was a member of the Tea Party and supported Sarah Palin for president. Often, when Buridan expressed a liberal point of view, the Ass would physically attack him. The Ass held sway over the left lobe, which controlled the right hand upon which the dummy sat, and the dummy would use its own self to punch Buridan in the face. Buridan had become browbeaten by his own dummy.

"Well, I'll be," Buridan said now, looking through the apparitional Flo and seeing, on the other side of her, the flow of media traffic into town. "I suppose you could attend your own funeral. It's scheduled for the day after tomorrow."

"I don't think that would be a good idea," Buridan's Ass said. "She might scare people."

"Well, I think it *is* a good idea," Buridan said, offended.

"Isn't!"

"Is!"

Buridan's Ass socked Buridan in the jaw.

"For Christless sake, let's get out of here!" cried Bubb. "This man is crazy. He *scares* me."

Flo whirled on Bubb, indignant, and said: "You're one to talk! With that motley crew downstairs you live with! Silly sausage!"

"Keep my gibborim niphilim and other harpies, demons and furies out of this," Bubb fumed. "You're the one who made me come upstairs. It wasn't *my* idea."

Flo returned her attention to Burd, who was looking at Flo's new friends with perplexity, albeit somewhat dazedly owing to the hard sock that the Ass had meted out to him. "Burd, do you think you can give us a lift downtown to Gil Aaronson's house? He's got something there that we need."

Burd shook his head, then swept a hand out at the invading media army. "You can't get anywhere near downtown today, Flo. At least not on any of the highways. The United States Media Corps has invaded, in order to construct reality for us so that — like the river returning to the sea — we may at last relocate our soul homes in the pixels of the media mythos of our times, Noam Chomsky's manufactured consent. Bottom line: I'm afraid if you want to get downtown you're going to have to hoof it."

"You mean walk?"

Aflac Schopenhauer piped up: "I was walking in a park one night when a policeman stopped me and said, 'Who are you? What are you doing here?' I replied, 'Ah, yes! Those are the questions!'" While everyone regarded him in speculative silence, the philosopher-cum-duck insurance policy shill loudly asserted: "Aflac!"

The Crossing

The troupe had to cross Hell Creek to enter Hell proper. A famous sign there said:

PLEASE
Do not litter
or pee in
the river
It's going through
HELL
now

"Very funny," Bubb said sarcastically. "What a piquant population you have here, Flo. I bet they sell Hell souvenirs, like T-shirts that say, 'My Parents Went to Hell and Back and All I Got Was This Lousy T-Shirt.'"

"I think you need to lighten up, dear," Flo said, an edge to her voice. The ducks were squabbling, Elvis was sulking, Nixon was brooding and Ted the chicken was scrambling away from savage kicks meted out by Sergeant Yokel, who then took out a bag of testicles, emptied them into his palm and popped them into his mouth like walnuts. It was not an auspicious beginning to their tour.

Furthermore, a footbridge over the creek was out of service, having been trampled to rubble by the media mob, so the band wandered down an embankment and found a little bait-and-tackle shop that also rented outboard-motor boats. But the elderly and cranky proprietor took one look at them and said: "I can't rent to you folks. You're dead. We only cater to the living." He nodded at a crude, hand-lettered sign that said, "No Shoes, No Shirt, No Socks, No Heartbeat, No Service."

"Charlie, it's me, Flo."

Charlie squinted up from under the shade of a battered fishing cap and said: "Flo! Is that really you? But today's Life in Hell said that —"

"Yes, yes, I know, Charlie, and it's true, I *am* dead, but we really need to get across that creek. We know the reason for the media mayhem in town, and we know how to put an end to it."

"Well ..." Old Charlie's voice trailed off as he gazed out thoughtfully across Hell Creek and saw the far embankment in the mellow spring sun. He came up with a compromise, the very thing that Buridan and his Ass could never do. "With all due respect, Flo, I still can't rent ya a boat, but I reckon I can ferry you all across to the other side myself."

So they all clambered into an outboard motor boat and Charlie started the engine by pulling on a cord, making a wut-wut-wut noise. The boat forded Hell Creek while Bubb, weary from all that had transpired, dozed. When they got to the other side Flo shook him awake, and they clambered up the embankment.

They had reached the first neighborhood of Hell.

~=__!
 ! !

Junior Holland cradled his shotgun and looked warily around him. The denizens of the filthy apartment eyeballed him hungrily, but in futility. As a person of integrity, he could not be harmed by them. But neither could he harm them, for they were already dead. It made for a tense underground standoff, mirroring the standoff upstairs between Gil Aaronson and The Pood on one side, and the United States Media Corps on the other.

The boy saw the door to the Rec Room. Motivated by curiosity, he cautiously approached it. The gibborim niphilim looked up from their card game with Iblis the thrice-damned. A couple of goat-legged imps idling on a sofa picked apathetically at their cloven hooves, their bloodshot eyes following Junior. Junior pushed the door ajar, and felt a gust of heat from the other side. He heard a scream that chilled his heart. He peeked through the gap of the door, and saw endless rolling hills and mountains boiling with fire, rolling away toward infinity. Another chorus of screams induced him to slam the door shut. When he did, the Talking Fire in Bubb's fireplace, which spoke a language not of man or of this world, temporarily adopted human tongue and addressed Junior thus: "We have ways of destroying even the innocent." The tongues of fire then lapped at the air, filling it with the sounds of evil laughter. Goosebumps crawled over Junior's dead flesh as he stared at the cackling fire.

Looking around, he saw Bubb's phone: The hourglass on its decorative wood stand, the sands of Time slowly sifting down the bottleneck connecting the upper bulb to the lower bulb. The two bulbs and the connecting tube formed the sign of infinity standing on one end. Junior swallowed with difficulty, and his mouth went dry. He suddenly realized that he would be here *forever*. For all *eternity*. When the sands in the hourglass ran out, the two bulbs would rotate end over end, and the pointless sifting downward of the sand would commence anew, a process never to end, as useless and idiotic as Sisyphus pushing his rock up and down the mountain.

With a shaking hand he picked up the hourglass telephone and saw, stuck to the bottom of it, a Post-It Note with the number of the Man upstairs. Hand shaking, he lifted the phone to his ear and heard a recorded voice say: "All our seraphs are busy now, but your prayer is *very* important to Father. Please stay on the line forever and the next available seraph will listen to your prayer."

The First Neighborhood of Hell

The sojourners debarked outside the backyard of the poet Homer Simpson's house. Next door lived one of the town's eccentrics, Ari, known derisively as The Philosopher.

Looking out a window, Homer saw the crew clambering up the shore and recognized Flo at once. Long ago, she had taught him to bake donuts in her home ec seminar, a lesson that stayed with him and eventually shaped the poet's words, dreams and life.

In his youth, Homer showed great promise as a poet, and he dreamed of becoming a modern bard: a troubadour telling the tales of modern times. But as he came of age in Hell he discovered that there were no tales to tell — or rather, that the tales to tell were of such overweening banality that they were not worth telling at all. Around him was a drab and prosaic world of greasy fast-food joints, low-brow roadhouses, chop shops, tourist traps trading on the name "Hell" and fluorescent strip malls filled to bursting with cheap gimcrack consumer goods produced by low-paid labor overseas. In such a soul-killing environment of whom, or what, could he sing? As time went on he adopted other poetic role models, the exemplars of ecstasy and revolt like Rimbaud. Long-haired, unwashed and flamboyant, he would declaim his neo-symbolist poetry on street corners. No one paid him the least attention except the police, who would tell him to move along. By the time he went to college at the University of Michigan he had learned that no one cared about poetry anymore. It was passé, pointless, ridiculous. One certainly could not make a living off of it. He sank into cynicism and despair. He drank heavily and dropped out of college. For a time he bummed around America, seeking poetic inspiration but finding only gentrification and kitsch. When his money ran out he was forced to return to Hell and take a lowly job in his father's Krispy Kreme donut shop franchise. But while slaving over chocolate-iced mini-donuts, donut holes and Krispy Kreme's signature Original Glazed donuts, Homer recalled matriculating in Flo Jellem's home ec seminar, and her rhapsodies to donuts. At that moment he found his poetic inspiration, a new kind of poetry the fit the tenor of the times. His path-breaking "Ode on a Greasy Donut" launched his career:

Ode on a Greasy Donut

Thou still unravaged baker of dozens,
Thou foster-cook of sugar and breakfast time,
Sinker historian, who canst thus express
A sugary tale more sweetly than our rhyme:
What glaze-fring'd legend haunt about thy shape
Of annalus or halo, or of both,
In take-out, or the booths of Krispy Kreme?
What eggs or frostings are these? What doughy sloth?
What mad sprinkles? What struggle to eat?
What granulated sugar and flour for frying?
What wild caloric ecstasy?

Eaten donuts are sweet, but those uneaten
Are sweeter: Mmm! Donuts!

"Donuts are delicious, delicious are donuts" — they are all
ye gnaw on earth, and all ye need to gnaw.

People loved this sort of idiot doggerel, and Krispy Kreme adopted "Donuts are delicious, delicious are donuts" as its company slogan, buying from Homer the rights to it. Even as Flo Jellem was known as the Poetess of Pot Roast, Homer became the Bard of Baked Goods and both passing famous and modestly wealthy in the process. He married a local woman, Marge, had a few kids and settled down into the very life of bland conformity and bourgeoisie domesticity that he had despised in his youth because it offered no heroic (or even anti-heroic) material for the aspiring bard. As he passed mellowly into middle age his girth expanded, fueled by a steady stream of donuts that provided both inspiration and calories. Like Yorick's skull in Hamlet's hand, Homer would hold a Krispy Kreme donut and contemplate it dreamily while with his other hand he would write a new poem on a long scroll of paper. And now, watching Flo, Bubb and the rest of the entourage wading ashore, he ran out the back door to greet them, a scroll with a freshly penned poem in one hand, the long paper flapping behind him like unrolled toilet paper while donut crumbs spilled down the front of his shirt and capered over his doughy belly.

"My word!" he said, opening the back gate to the party. The Bard of Baked Goods said to the Poetess of Pot Roast: "Is that you, Flo? They said you died. Everyone's broken up about it."

"It's my ghost, Homer," she said, which the bard quickly ascertained when he attempted to embrace her and discovered that his arms passed through her spectral form. "But I've come calling upstairs along with my associates here to reclaim that terrible dog." She briefed him on The Pood, but Homer already knew about the standoff in downtown Hell.

He stared at the Elvis/Nixon hybrid.

"Say," he said, "aren't you —" But Elvis took a step back and said, "Don't step on my blue suede shoes, son."

Homer's neighbor, Ari the Philosopher, had come out of his house and wandered over to the fence to see what all the fuss was about.

Homer was looking in utter astonishment at this tatterdemalion troupe, and finally he let out a whistle and shaking his head said, "You all look like you've passed through hell!"

"The greatness comes not when things go always good for you, but the greatness comes when you are really tested," Nixon responded sententiously from the hybrid's hindquarters, "when you take some knocks, some disappointments, when sadness comes; because only if you've been in the deepest valley can you ever know how magnificent it is to be on the highest mountain." Everyone lapsed into silence then, and Elvis looked like he wanted to die. Homer discretely waved at the air to dissipate the odor.

Desperate to change the subject, Flo addressed The Bard of Baked Goods: "Well, it's nice to see you again, Homer. I haven't seen you in ages. It's a pity I had to die for us to meet again. How are you, dear?"

A ripple of anxiety creased Homer's expression, or perhaps he was still reacting to the lingering odor. On the other hand, maybe a pang of nostalgia had hit him, in the presence of the knowledge of mortality that Flo's death had hammered home. "I'm a success by worldly standards, I suppose, Flo. But it's not what I envisioned for myself in my youth. There are times when I feel like I sold my talent down the river for thirty donut holes. Every now and then I get a feeling of being in limbo. Plus, writing — even writing commercial poetry — is a lonely business. It's isolating."

The Philosopher, hanging over the fence post and catching everything, remarked thus: "He who is unable to live in society, or has no need because he is sufficient for himself, must be either a beast or a god." To which Nietzsche, the Aflac duck, immediately retorted: "To live alone one must be an animal or a God — says Aristotle." After a pause and a vigorous ruffling of feathers, the philosopher-cum-duck concluded: "There is yet a third case: one must be both — a philosopher." After another pause, affording the others the opportunity to ponder this aphorism, the classical German philologist in duck's feathers concluded loudly: "Aflac!"

Schopenhauer sourly interposed: "No little part of the torment of existence lies in this, that Time is continually pressing upon us, never letting us take breath, but always coming after us, like a taskmaster with a whip. If at any moment Time stays his hand, it is only when we are delivered over to the misery of boredom."

Sergeant Yokel, the hellfire Golem, emptied a few testicles from his brown paper sack into his hand, and then popped them into his mouth. Munching, he shook his head disdainfully and, addressing Bubb, said: "Permission requested to kick these ducks' asses, sir!"

"At ease, Sergeant," the author of iniquity said glumly. The devil seemed seriously depressed, and Flo eyed him with speculative concern. The wicked one in his shabby frock coat said, "I suppose we'd best be on her way. We've got a few miles yet to go." Then he sighed like a tea kettle.

A few black helicopters clattered aggrievedly overhead, like giant hornets angry at being rousted from their nests. They were carrying more news media parasites on their way to the center of Hell, and the standoff with Aaronson and The Pood.

"Flo," Homer said, "before you go, let me give you something that might help. If you are to lure back that crazy dog that has been on all the news shows since yesterday, maybe you could use some Krispy Kreme donuts as bait. No one can resist a Krispy Kreme, and I've got you to thank for enlightening me so many years ago to the rhapsodic delights of flour, sugar frosting and stroke-inducing calories. Remember —" as he began his declamation, even Flo wanted to cover her ears. But Homer prated on: "Mmm! Donuts! 'Donuts are delicious, delicious are donuts' — they are all ye gnaw on earth, and —"

" — and all ye need to gnaw; yes, yes, dear, we *know* already!" Flo sighed. Sometimes she wondered whether her teaching had sometimes been more destructive than constructive. But bridling her doubts, she said: "The donuts are wonderful of you to offer, dear, yes, we'll take a bagful if you can spare them." Homer bustled off and returned straightaway with a box of 24 mini-donuts mixed with donut holes. He began to embrace Flo, but recalled the futility of this and then, looking a bit uncomfortable, he said, "Well, goodbye, and good luck. And above all, watch out for the news media. Those birds are all over town and you know how dangerous they are." They exchanged final pleasantries and then the band was off, trekking ever forward to its ultimate goal, the geographical center of Hell, Michigan.

~=__!
   ! !

"Junior," the flames in Bubb's fireplace whispered. "Juuuuuunior…"

Junior Holland, curled up in the chaise lounge with the rifle in his lap, warily eyed the fire. The tongues of flames lapped at him, talking: "Who's your daddy, Junior?"

Junior set the gun to the ready position and pointed it at the flames. "What do you mean?" he demanded. But he suddenly felt afraid, even though he could not be physically harmed.

"Who's your daddy, Junior?" the flames taunted, with a crackle of laughter. "You don't look nothin' at all like your Paw, do you? Why, you can't even grow a beard like your Paw! It's all the talk upstairs, Junior. Believe me. People say things, and we hear those things down here." The flames reached up for the flue, saying: "I can hear the words of the people on earth coming all the way down this chimney, Junior. I hear *everything*!" The fire burst into laughter. Junior leveled the gun, pulled the trigger and fired into the fireplace. The flames devoured the bullet and vaporized it, and then resumed laughing.

"If you can't kill any of us with that thing, what good do you think it'll do you against a fire that has been burning since the beginning of time?" one of the gibborim nephilim asked in a bored tone of voice.

The word "time" caused a chill to pass through Junior that cooled the heat from the laughing flames. He turned to look at the hourglass/phone. The sands had run out from the top bulb into the bottom bulb, and now the two bulbs rotated to swap positions, and then the sands began running down again.

The Second Neighborhood of Hell

They stuck to the sidewalks as they slogged into Hell, the roads now fully occupied by the invading army of the news media.

They came upon a roadhouse: Hellraisers' Roadhouse, the sign, limned in flames, said. It was a big barn-like structure, painted yellow, with a mural of red flames reaching upward like forked tongues.

Seeing the painting, Bubb sighed, already nostalgic for his little apartment, his Abbottabad-like Bin Laden hide-out. He was thinking about the Talking Fire in his fireplace, the fire that never went out. "I miss my fireplace," the suzerain of sorrow stated in self-pitying tones. "It is nice and toasty warm in front of it."

"Oh, for heaven's sake, hold your forked tongue!" Flo said, exasperated. "When we were downstairs, all you did was whine about how hot it was. Now that we're upstairs, it's too cold for you. You're never satisfied."

"Of course I'm never satisfied!" Bubb grumbled. "I'm evil. Evil knows no rest." A gust of wind kicked up clouds of dust and made whirlpools in the sand.

"The winds of passion," rhapsodized portly David Hume, in his Aflac duck avatar disguise. It was the first time that Hume had addressed the audience at large since they had arrived in the overworld. Hume went on: "Reason is, and ought only to be, the slave of the passions."

"Now you're talking," the Elvis half of the Elvis/Nixon chimera said breezily. The Pelvis longed for some prescription drugs to abuse. "Passion is my middle name." Eyeing the roadhouse, Presley said: "Why don't we go inside and wet our whistles? Whaddya say, folks?"

"Well, I suppose some refreshments wouldn't hurt," Flo allowed. "We've got a ways to go, if we're traveling on foot."

Sheriff Ted circulated about everyone's feet, bawking. The sergeant violently kicked it, and the deceased sheriff flew upward in a cloud of loosened feathers.

Flo Jellem marched up to the hellfire golem, took her Pocketbook of Death firmly in hand and smacked it across the shoulder of the sadistic sergeant.

"Ow!" he cried, looking at Flo with astonishment while rubbing his shoulder. "That *hoit!*" He suddenly looked as if he might burst into tears.

"I'm sick and tired of you getting up to the Dickens with the sheriff!" Flo said heatedly. "Sheriff Ted is a good friend of mine, and if you mess with him again you'll have to answer to me! Is that understood, young man?"

"Sir, make her stop!" the erstwhile drill instructor blubbered at Bubb, who rolled his bloodshot eyes, and then snatched up his long tail from under his frock coat and gnawed on it briefly before announcing: "Let's go inside. I don't think I've ever needed a good stiff drink more than I do right now. Honestly, this trip is even worse than my last outing in the 17th century. And believe me, honesty from me is really something. I'm the Dirtbag of Deception." With that, they all trooped into the Hellraisers' Roadhouse for some R&R.

It was a big, drafty structure with an large, elevated wood dance floor and a long bar counter with an old-fashioned brass and steel cash register behind the bar, full of fancy chrome doo-dads and frippery. The bartender looked exactly like an aged Babe Ruth, except that unlike Ruth, he had a handlebar mustache and lavish, 70s-style sideburns. He wore a starched white apron and his hair, black as velvet, was pomaded. He was chewing on some chaw and eyeing the band carefully as they ventured inside. The place was mostly empty, but a few stalwart drinkers lounged about here and there; it was only about one in the afternoon. A TV hanging over the bar was tuned to CNN covering the ongoing standoff between Gil and The Pood on one side and the media on the other. The media was covering itself covering itself, an odd situation that produced a kind of metaphysical vertigo, the feeling one sometimes gets standing in front of a mirror with another mirror behind one, which causes the multiplying reflections to ricochet to infinity.

"What can I do ya for?" the bartender asked the crew as they bellied up to the bar. The database of Flo's mind clicked into place, scanning the files of memory to place the home ec record of the bartender. Then the cursor of recollection clicked on a name, and like a Web link, it lit up in bright underlined blue. "Harvey McGarvey!" Flo said ebulliently. "As I fail to live and breathe! I knew you'd end up a mixologist first time I set my eyes on you, dear, when in home ec you experimented by mixing root beer with Miracle Whip mayo and mustard."

"Flo Jellem!" the bartender replied, with dawning recognition. "But you're supposed to be —"

"Yes, yes, I know dear," Flo cut him off, knowing that she would be doomed to the same greeting throughout her stay in the overworld. She quickly summarized the situation, and introduced Harvey around.

"So *you're* the devil," the bartender said. "I always pictured you as, well, more *evil* somehow. As it is, you look like, well …"

"Like *what*?" Bubb demanded, nonplussed.

"Well, sort of like a homeless man," the bartender said with devastating candor. "It's a little disappointing, to be honest. Even Hitler and Bin Laden looked more evil than you. You just seem kind of shabby and pathetic. I'm not sure I want to serve you. Do you have any money?"

"I'm going home!" Bubb snapped, his feelings hurt. He turned on his cloven hooves and clopped toward the door, but Flo caught up to him, seized the lobe of one of his pointed ears and dragged him back to the bar counter, lecturing him: "You can't return home until our mission is accomplished, dear. Perhaps if you had a little more sense of responsibility, you'd have a bit more decency; and vice versa, too. My goodness, knowing you as I do now, I surely do wish I had had you in my home ec class. It might have made a different man out of you."

"I'm not a *man*," Bubb reminded her. "I'm the Fallen One."

"Fallen schmallen," Flo scoffed. "As far as I'm concerned you're just a silly sausage who gets entirely up to too much Dickens. I imagine a good woman could set you on the straight and narrow. Haven't you ever been married?"

"Never," Bubb said.

"Never? But you've been around since the dawn of time! I was only on earth seventy-eight years and I was married three times, though I had to kick all three of my husbands to the curb."

"You seem to forget, Flo, that I am *evil*," Bubb said. "Who would want to marry evil?"

"Oh, dear, for heaven's sake, lots of girls have an eye for the bad boys. I did myself when I was young."

Five men walked into the bar, side by side. The man in the middle held a package shaped like a perfume bottle. The others kept a sharp eye on it.

"Why the long penis?" the bartender asked the five men.

"Because we heard Holace was holing up here today, and that's exciting," the man holding the cock in the jar said. His face was sweaty and red, and his eyes shined. He, and the others, wore the same cocky expressions and bore the same swaggering demeanor of men who, although in dissipated middle-age, were still fifteen years old.

"Holace?" the barkeep asked. "You mean poor old Holace Orr? Nah, she ain't been in here yet. But give it time. I'm sure she'll show up, boys. I'd no idea you five had suddenly taken a shine to Holace. That's a fool's errand, if you ask me."

Outside the skies darkened and wind lashed the wood walls of the bar, making the planks shudder. Rain splashed on the windows and produced a rhythmic tapping on the roadhouse's old tin roof. Elvis tapped a toe of one of his blue-suede shoes to the pleasing sound of summer rain, the fires of Hell suddenly receding into the mists of memory. He was looking longingly at the roadhouse's band stage and unlimbering his guitar. The thought of performing for someone other than music-hating old harpies, his assignment for eternity in Bubb's Rec Room, quickened his pulse.

Harvey McGarvey, the bartender, peered at The Pelvis. "Wait a minute," he said. "Aren't you —"

"He's an Elvis *impersonator*," Bubb said emphatically. He was dreadfully annoyed at the prospect of going from neighborhood to neighborhood and having to explain the presence of Elvis Presley, who had been dead for some thirty-three years. Bubb was also a bit jealous: So far, no one upside seemed the least bit impressed by him. The doer of diabolical deeds had assumed that his very presence would strike terror into the hearts of the living, but instead the bartender had written him off as little more than a hapless homeless man.

"Well now, son," Elvis Presley drawled at the barkeep, playing along with Bubb's deception, "I'll tell you this: There ain't never been an Elvis impersonator better than yours truly. In fact I'm indistinguishable from the real deal." Tuning up his guitar, Elvis dashed off a few chords of "Love me Tender" to prove the point.

Harvey the bartender whistled in admiration. The door of the roadhouse was opening and shutting as local residents filed in, trying to escape the storm outside and the mass media invasion. They had terrible stories to tell about the Fourth Estate: Rude questions, presumptuous behavior, self-absorbed wireless blogging, self-important YouTube preening and even the occasional defecation on a front lawn.

"Tell you what," Harvey said to Elvis. "It looks like we're in for quite a crowd because of the bad weather and the worse media. How about you take a turn at the guitar up there on the stage, and if the customers like you we'll work out a nice payment? Waddya say, son?"

Elvis momentarily blanched, seeking out in the swelling bar crowd signs of stiff-necked music-hating harpies. But instead he saw bulging midriffs, obese bellies, blue jeans and flip flops, and lots of tattoos, lots more than he had recalled from his day. He was surprised to see that even some of the women were tattooed, and that some of their tattoos were tattooed too. Elvis was suddenly feeling right at home: more so, in some ways, than in his own heyday, when that prune-faced prude Ed Sullivan made sure that he, Elvis, was shown on TV above the waist only to censor the rhythmic gyration of his hips.

"My name's Harvey, by the way," the bartender said, extending a hand. "Harvey McGarvey, mixologist from Hell."

"Elvis the Pelvis," The King said, taking Harvey's hand in his. "Pleased to meetchya. I'd be happy to perform for your customers."

Unfortunately at that moment Richard Nixon chose to anally deliver the following deflating and odoriferous observation:

"Goddamn it, I do not think that you glorify on public television homosexuality. The reason you don't glorify it anymore than you glorify, uh, uh, uh, *whores!*"

A frozen silence descended on the roadhouse. In a few moments someone commented on the smell; someone else — evidently construing Nixon's comment to have been made in connection with Elvis's appearance on the Ed Sullivan program way back in '56 — stoutly denied that the King was a faggot. "Rock Hudson, now *he* was a faggot," the man said with tipsy conviction, "but not Elvis."

The mortified Presley had retreated to the stage, where he tuned his guitar in an effort to drown out his embarrassment in strummed notes that hovered in the air like hummingbirds made of pure sound. The old creative juices were quickening, lifting his spirits despite the deflating presence of the head of the corrupt and misanthropic 37th president of the United States where otherwise his bowels and buttocks would be.

Bubb had slumped into a barstool, and now he sat dejectedly with his chin resting in the palm of his hand, his elbow bent on the bar counter. Flo was regarding with an air of resigned exasperation the five men who had walked in earlier. Like pungent dishes on a menu from her home ec professorship days, the boys popped to life again for her: they were Paolo, Alex, Archie, Lance and Trist. She was disappointed to see that the boys' embarrassing problem — which had first come to light when they hit puberty doing junior high, and while they were matriculating in Flo's class — remained a problem even now, in dissipated middle age. Back then and even now, they always fell in lust (never in love) with the same girl, and as a result they shared the same penis. It was some small consolation to Flo that the five boy-men now kept the forbidding tool enclosed in a perfume bottle and wrapped in a brown paper bag. They had set it on the bar counter near Bubb, who looked at it with curiosity at first and then with disgust for — like Pinocchio's growing nose if Pinocchio's nose pointed upward — it was starting toward the ceiling, ripping open the bag and stressing the cap on the bottle.

"Boys, get your fucking penis in a jar off my bar!" Harvey the mixologist roared, snapping a white rag at the member in the perfume jar. The cap was beginning to come off as the contents inside grew longer and taller.

Memories of each of the boys now marched past in Flo's mind the way that offerings of sandwiches and deserts will move past in a rotating vending machine: Paolo, for example, was a watermelon mounter. During a break in home ec class when it was his turn to use the penis that the boys shared, he had cut a hole in a watermelon and went to town on it in the boy's room. But he was caught by another student and ratted out. Each of the boys in their turn, horndogs in their day and horndogs still, had had congress with Flo's food: a soufflé, a slice of lemon meringue pie, a cored apple and a cheese sammich between the white Wonder bread slice on top and the slice on the bottom. The boy who had had congress with the cheese sammich had supplied his own mayonnaise for it. Flo had been forced to flunk all the boys, and now she despaired of what they had become. She wondered now whether, in failing them, she had not failed them in some larger sense. She regretted that she had never been able to interest them in food beyond its nutritional or carnal potential; she had failed to engage them with the *artistic* side of food, the poetry of pot roast and the music of mayonnaise.

Paolo took the penis in the perfume jar off of the bar. This innocent act inspired squabbling among the five friends. They were fighting over whose turn it was to use the cock in a jar. Bubb looked bored and disgusted. Elvis was twanging his guitar, getting ready to play. The philosophers-cum-Aflac ducks were philosophizing again. Sergeant Yokel, in his hellfire golem drag, had attracted admirers from the crowd filing in. Sheriff Ted hid himself under a table, hoping that no one would notice that the late law enforcement chief had been transformed into a craven chicken.

Just then the front door to the bar flew open and when it did a bolt of lightning split the sky. A blue-white wash of electric light filled the bar and backlit the figure standing in the door, holding the door open.

"She always makes a grand entrance," the barkeep remarked admiringly.

It was Holace Orr. That electric wash of light silhouetted her. When the light subsided what was revealed to the eye was a matronly figure in strumpet's attire, decked out in a clinging red miniskirt, platform shoes, cheap fishnet stockings, a halter-top bra, a feather boa slung around the shoulders and a florid hat with a lonely wilted rose affixed to it with a hatpin. Heavy facial powder did not succeed in hiding her wrinkles. Heavy black eyeliner only partly succeeded in obscuring the bags under the eyes, both of which were bloodshot. A cigar jutted out of the side of the mouth.

"Holace!" Paolo burbled, eyes lighting up. Hoping to meet her he had dressed for the occasion, in his prized Raccoon Lodge tie with the raccoon stickpin, plaid pants and two-tone shoes. He now pulled a sheaf of paper from his pocket. It contained a Shakespeare sonnet: a love sonnet, Archie had told him. "Read it to her," he had encouraged Paolo. "It will make her fall for you."

Paolo had scanned the sonnet with dubiety. He wasn't educated and disliked Shakespeare, but Archie had insisted that the Bard had written the greatest love poems in the English language.

"I don't know," Paolo had said, reading over the sonnet again. "There's something fishy about this. It sounds sarcastic. What's a 'minger?'"

"It means 'gem of the eye,'" Archie had insisted with an encouraging nod and a wink, giving his friend a pat on the shoulder.

Paolo had then eyed his friend and rival for the affections of Holace, who was along with himself and the other three men the co-proprietor of the penis in a perfume jar, and demanded: "Why are you trying to help me with Holace? You're after her just as much as I am."

Archie had affected a wounded expression. "Don't you think I can be generous once in awhile? Don't you think I can have some magnanimity, too?"

"No, I don't, Archie. You're a douchebag." But Paolo knew, at least, that Shakespeare was an important name, and so he decided to take his chances with the sonnet.

Now, as Holace stood in the doorway, Paolo cleared his throat and read slowly and with great emphasis from the manuscript in his hands:

My mistress' eyes are nothing like the sun,
Coral is far more red than her lips red,
If snow be white, why then her breasts be dun,
If hair be wires, black wires grow on her head.
I have seen roses damasked red and white
But no such roses see I in her cheeks,
And in some perfumes is there more delight

Than in the breath which from my mistress reeks.
I love to hear her speak, yet well I know,
Music hath a far more pleasing sound.
I grant I never saw a goddess go,
My mistress when she walks treads on the ground.
And so, by Heaven, I declare I went too far
When flirting with this minger in that bar.

Silence reigned in the Hellfire Roadhouse after Paolo's poetic presentation. He looked at Holace hopefully. She continued to stand in the doorway, leaning against the open door. A fresh gust of wind blew rain into the establishment, and another crack of lighting filled the sky, followed by a peal of thunder.

Holace suddenly tottered forward on her platform shoes, the door slamming shut behind her. All eyes were on her. The aging trollop waved her feather boa from side to side the way that a priest might wave a small censer from side to side to spread burning incense in an effort to ward off evil spirits. She strode up to Paolo, seized the sheaf of papers from his hand, tore them in two and threw them to the floor at his feet. "Bollocks to you!" the aging prostitute announced in a voice coarsened to gravel by decades of cigar smoking. She yanked the cigar that she had been smoking out of the side of her mouth and stabbed it out on the bar counter.

Holace's tale was a tragic one, not unleavened by comedy. A birth defect had left her without a vagina. But, as if conspiratorially, other genes had bestowed upon her an outsized libido. She was like a person without a mouth who nevertheless feels a burning need to scream. Rejected at a young age by the first boy with whom she had fallen in love, a boy who had told her frankly that he could not cope with the prospect of marrying a woman without a vagina, Holace took revenge on the world by becoming Hell's hooker – a "high-class" hooker, as she styled herself. She did business out of the flashy house that she had inherited from her wealthy family. She had compensated for her lack of sexual organs by honing to a high degree the sexual athleticism of other key body parts. Over the years she had done a brisk business, but in truth the men who visited her regarded her as a kind of sideshow freak, and behind her back they belittled her. Inevitably their disparaging words got back to Holace, who became filled with malice. The contempt of her clients paradoxically made her redouble her efforts to pleasure them, which only inflamed their contempt for her. She and they were in a libidinous death spiral. Like anyone else, what Holace really wanted was love. But the boy who had dashed her hopes in this regard so many years ago had wounded Holace so deeply that she was not able to give or receive love; though she became quite adept at giving blow jobs and receiving cash (Visa and MasterCard also accepted) in return for them. Now past middle age, her dowdiness rendered all the more ridiculous her attempts at seducing men, and her clientele had dwindled to a few lonely widowers and the occasional horny virginal teenager.

But now, here, inexplicably and just recently, the five men who shared a single penis had gotten a woody for Holace Orr, but their feelings for her were no more serious than those that they had displayed (and expressed) so many years ago in Flo's home ec class toward the watermelon, the soufflé, the slice of lemon meringue pie, the cored apple and the cheese sammich, which had been marinated in the mayonnaise of Paolo.

Paolo looked down in astonishment at the torn papers at his feet. "Minger indeed!" Holace roared at the stupefied would-be Lothario. "How dare you!" Someone had placed the penis in the perfume jar on a corner table, and now the detached member lustily forced open the cap of the bottle and began rising relentlessly toward the ceiling. Bubb, still bent over the bar like an old drunken sailor, watched it rise with squeamish distaste.

One of the five men, Alex, pulled Paolo aside and told him *sotto voce*: "'Minger' doesn't mean 'gem of the eye', Paolo. It means, 'fell out of the ugly tree and hit all the branches on the way down.' Archie pulled a fast one on you, I'm afraid."

Suddenly everything happened all at once. Paolo and Archie began pushing and shoving. Clopping on her platform shoes, Holace bellied up to the bar and ordered a whiskey sour. She was standing right next to the devil himself. The penis that had broken free of the perfume jar like a genie from a bottle made a creaking noise as it unlimbered itself and rose higher and higher. Harvey the barkeep was yelling at Paolo and Archie to take their dispute outside. The TV announcer was rattling off the latest from the standoff at Gil Aaronson's place. And then Elvis strummed up his guitar and broke into a rousing rendition of "Jailhouse Rock." As he did, Holace slammed her glass back down on the bar, and gave Harvey the high sign for a refill. She turned to her left and saw a dowdy man in a frock coat, a slouch hat, baggy pants and cheap penny loafers sitting next to her. The devil had plucked up his tail from under his coat and was gnawing absently on the arrow-tipped end of it. "Say," Holace asked the Prince of Darkness, "How'd you like to spend a little time with Holace Orr, darlin'? It's a rainy day, and I can take your blues away. I'll make ya feel good, baby."

The warden threw a [redacted] in the county jail*
The [redacted] band was there and they [redacted*] to*
wail

The band was [redacted]' and the joint began to swing*
You should've [redacted] those [redacted*] out jailbirds*
sing

Let's rock
Everybody, let's [redacted]*
Everybody in the whole [redacted] block*
Was dancin' to the [Redacted] Rock*

"I am not a crook!" Nixon squawked from Elvis's rear, evidently alarmed by the mention of jail. Though he added thoughtfully afterward, "Some of the best writing was done from jail. Think of Gandhi, for I instance."

"C'mon, baby, let's dance!" Holace yelled, seizing Bubb by the coat collar and yanking him off the barstool his to his feet.

"How dare you!" the devil cried. "I don't dance!"

"It's a balls thing, it's a balls thing," Nixon murmured.

But Holace held him with a surprisingly strong grip and yanked him out to the dance floor. Bubb looked nonplussed, even frightened.

[Redacted] Murphy played the tenor saxophone*
Little [Redacted] was blowin' on the slide trombone*
The drummer boy from [Redacted] went crash, boom, bang*
The whole [redacted] section was a purple gang*

Let's [redacted]*
[Redacted], let's rock*
Everybody in the [redacted] cell block*

Was dancin' to the Jailhouse [Redacted*]

"Unhand me!" the devil demanded above the caterwauling of Elvis, as Holace whirled him around the dance floor, Bubb's hooves in the penny loafer clopping maladroitly on the wood floor. "I'm a virgin!"

"A virgin you say! Well, I've got no vagina, baby, so that makes us about even, I'd say. Now dance, dammit!"

Holace dragged the Infamous One all around the floor, her high heels rapping while his hooves were clopping, while Elvis wailed from the stage. Other couples got up to dance, too, and the whole barn of a bar took on a lusty, hothouse aspect. Outside the wind hammered at the windows and the rain on the rooftop sounded like bombardments of pebbles on tin. The penis that had broken free from its perfume bottle was nearing the ceiling. It was a good fifteen feet tall now. In its throbbing and engorged head resided the brain of the five men who shared it, and the penis pondered. It sent out brain waves like bolts of electricity to its five owners, each of whom now became redoubled in their conviction that they must somehow make a conquest out of Holace Orr, that poor old broken-down holeless whore with a wilted flower in her broad-brimmed hat who was missing the main piece of the primal puzzle of whoredom. They were determined to make her their unlikely conquest by *some* physical means, if not the standard mechanism of vaginal penetration. Flo Jellem, meanwhile, was conducting an intensive mental scan of the home ec record of Holace, whom she recalled as a student from the very early days of Flo's home economics professorship at Chester Alan Arthur Junior High. Holace, to her credit, had been an aficionado of Kraft Miracle Whip mayonnaise, and lots of it. But now Flo uneasily began to suspect that Holace's true allegiance to mayo had to do with its superficial physical resemblance to another substance that was considerably more fecundating than mere mayo.

On the dance floor the devil had two left hooves, and those clopping appendages got tangled up with each other and he fell to the floor in a humiliating heap. Holace began dragging him up again while her five suitors pantingly approached her, each wanting to cut in and have a whirl with her. Elvis was belting out a rousing rendition of "All Shook Up" while Nixon periodically piped up. When Elvis

* — "The Redacted Jailhouse Redaction" brought to you by copyright laws that The Pood refused to pay for on grounds it might not be as funny.

sang the lyric, "Please don't ask me what's on my mind" the former president flatulently fulminated against the Jews. The floor thundered under the footfalls of the dancing barflies. The foot thunder mingled with the sky thunder that growled ominously outside. The weather had taken a nasty turn for the worse (consistent with anthropogenic climate change models) and the wind was beginning to bite at the very foundations of the ancient wood roadhouse; planks and beams began sundering and snapping, and somewhere a window exploded, letting in lashing licks of wind. A Midwest tornado was brewing, and nothing is worse than one of those.

"Let me go!" Bubb begged, as Holace dragged him up and set him aright on his hooves. She prepared to conduct him on another maladroit sally across the floor, when Flo intervened.

"You'd better let me tend to him," she told Holace, snatching the Foul One from Holace's lusty grasp. The old strumpet in her cheap miniskirt, high heels, fishnet stocking and wearing her wilted flower peered with foggy eyes above the ruins of her pancake makeup at Flo, recognized her, and there followed the usual "We all thought you was dead" bullshit with Flo offering a by-now scripted reply that was brief and to the point. While Holace was processing the shocking news of Flo's ghostly resurrection, Flo took advantage of Holace's indecision to hustle Bubb away from her and back to the bar. A ruckus ensued while the five men who shared a single penis began squabbling over who would dance with Holace; Holace, in turn, wanted nothing to do with any of them. Although she was a whore, she wasn't lacking in good taste.

When Flo sat Bubb back down on a bar stool she took up the stool next to him and regarded him earnestly.

"Just what kind of a devil *are* you?" she demanded. "You're a virgin. You can't dance. You're afraid of your own shadow. And no one is afraid of you in the least. Dear, are you sure that you *are* the devil? Perhaps there has been a mixup of some sort. Maybe you were inadvertently switched with the real Imp of Iniquity at birth. Do you suppose that's possible, dear?"

Bubb yanked a handkerchief made of human flesh from the pocket of his dowdy coat and mopped his sweating brow. His face was redder than normal, and he was breathing heavily. Putting away the skin hankie and catching his breath, he said: "There is no mistake. Have you ever read Dostoevsky?"

"I don't know, dear," Flo said. "Can you name any recipes

that he wrote?"

"Not *recipes*," Bubb replied, "novels. In his novel The Brothers Karamazov he describes me to a T. He has me meeting with one of the book's main characters, Ivan Karamazov. Apparently I must have haunted Dostoevsky in one of his dreams, for him to know me so well."

"And what does he say you are like, dear?"

Bubb squeezed his eyes shut; a grimace, like an expression of pain, stole across his weathered, wrinkled and ancient visage, beated and hatched with tanned antiquity, as the Bard would have had it. He then began to speak most solemnly, quoting from memory a passage from the aforementioned book, quoting thus:

I am perhaps the one man in all creation who loves the truth and genuinely desires good. I was there when the Word, Who died on the Cross, rose up into heaven bearing on His bosom the soul of the penitent thief. I heard the glad shrieks of the cherubim singing and shouting hosannah and the thunderous rapture of the seraphim which shook heaven and all creation, and I swear to you by all that's sacred, I longed to join the choir and shout hosannah with them all. The word had almost escaped me, had almost broken from my lips ... you know how susceptible and esthetically impressionable I am. But common sense — oh, a most unhappy trait in my character — kept me in due bounds and I let the moment pass! For what would have happened, I reflected, what would have happened after my hosannah? Everything on earth would have been extinguished at once and no events could have occurred. And so, solely from a sense of duty and my social position, I was forced to suppress the good moment and to stick to my nasty task. Somebody takes all the credit of what's good for Himself, and nothing but nastiness is left for me. But I don't envy the honor of a life of idle imposture, I am not ambitious. Why am I, of all creatures in the world, doomed to be cursed by all decent people and even to be kicked, for if I put on mortal form I am bound to take such consequences sometimes? I know, of course, there's a secret in it, but they won't tell me the secret for anything, for then perhaps, seeing the meaning of it, I might bawl hosannah, and the indispensable minus would disappear at once, and good sense would reign supreme throughout the whole world. And that, of course, would mean the end of everything ...

When Bubb was done speaking a heavy silence seemed to descend over the whole bar, in spite of the fact that Elvis was wailing,

Nixon was conspiring and the five penis partners were engaged in a fist fight with one another. Harvey the bartender was trying to break it up, and this time he was determined to evict the five and their penis from his bar, because the head of the rising cock was starting to bore a hole into the ceiling, like a drill.

Flo was trying to process the meaning of all that she had just heard, trying to connect it, if possible, to *food*, which is what she understood best. Unable to do so, she decided that what Satan really needed was a little self-confidence. Self-confidence, she thought, would make a brand-new Fallen Entity out of him.

"C'mon," she said, snatching Bubb by his taloned hands and dragging him back out onto the dance floor. "I'm going to teach you how to dance, dear."

"No-o-o-o!" Bubb wailed, nearly in tears.

But Flo led him patiently through a series of basic steps, left-left-right, right-right-left, etc., and pretty soon she had taught him a basic box step. Elvis was singing "At the Hop" and the Vile One was soon clopping about with rhythm. An involuntary smile broke out across his horrible fissured face. "My goodness, dear, is that a smile?" Flo teased, but the devil grew dour and snapped, "No! I don't smile! It was a grimace of disgust. What am I doing, clopping about the floor like some douchebag? I want to go home, to my fireplace, my harpies and goat-legged imps."

And that was when the biggest gust of wind of all hit the old barn of a roadhouse and smashed the far wall flat on the floor; everyone screamed. The rest of the rotting structure shuddered and juddered. The rain lashed in with gale-force intensity, and the remnants of the Hellfire Roadhouse disintegrated. The whole place and all its contents and customers went up in a Midwest tornado, and they were flung about hither and thither. Only Bubb's troupe was spared this rough treatment, as none of them were physical entities; Flo was a ghost, the others were avatars, and Bubb, of course, was a supernatural albeit self-pitying demiurge lacking in confidence. They then made their escape from the Hellfire Roadhouse and from the Second Neighborhood of Hell, Flo and Bubb running from the disintegrating structure hand in claws.

~=___!
  ! !

Junior Holland was watching the clock.

That is, he was peering with grim intensity at the hourglass, that mystic hotline to the long-abandoned heaven. It was the sign of infinity standing on one end, and whenever the sands ran all the way down from the top bulb to the lower bulb, the hourglass rotated on its stand and the sands began running down again.

Junior did not know how long each sojourn of sand from top to bottom took, but he assumed it was one hour.

Junior Holland was a good boy. He was a hard worker and reliable, which is why Flo had appointed him to watch over the Underworld while Bubb and the rest of them were upstairs. And he was as honest as an ear of corn is yellow. He was right as rain.

True, he wasn't the sharpest tool in the shed. But he was good with tools, and with guns. He was good with his hands.

And now, with his hands, he began thinking.

He looked at the five fingers of one hand, and then at the five fingers of the other. Ten fingers. He flexed them.

Forever.

The word cut through his mind like a saw.

He was dead. He would be here *forever*.

Five fingers, ten fingers. His thoughts turned over slowly in his head: What percentage are ten fingers of forever, of an infinite number of fingers? Zero percent. That's what Junior reckoned. He wasn't much at math, but that's what he reckoned.

And the hourglass. He thought about that, too. When it turns over in its stand a hundred times, a thousand times, a million times, a billion times, by how much time would he have shortened his afterlife sentence?

By no time at all, is what Junior figured.

Forever.

Looking up, his eyes fastened on the sign "Rec Room," above the door that led to the infinite torture chamber on the other side.

"Forever is a long time," the Talking Fire whispered at him. Startled, Junior jumped in his seat and faced the flames, which licked impartially at the stagnant air. Some hellwasps circled lazily overhead.

"Lot of time on your hands, now," the fire cackled. "How are you going to occupy it, Junior? Hmm? Are you going to spend eternity dwelling on the fact that you are not even your father's son?

Who *is* your real Daddy, Junior? Some trick whom your whore of a Mom picked up back in the day when she –"

"*Shut up!*" the teenager roared at the flames.

The gibborim nephilim and Iblis the Thrice Damned glanced up from their never-ending card game. Defensively, Junior leveled the rifle at them, but they merely smirked in reply and then returned to their poker hands.

Embarrassed, Junior lowered the rifle to his lap. Earlier, the fire had hissed at him: *"We have ways of destroying even the innocent."* He could not be physically destroyed, because he was a soul of integrity. But now he wondered: Could he be *mentally* destroyed?

Forever.

"Is a long time," the mind-reading fire supplied in a grave, hissing whisper.

Junior began to speak but the fire cut him off thus: "The Rec Room. Rec means 'recreation,' Junior. That is what you need, I think. You've been through a lot, an awful lot. You found out your Daddy is not really your Daddy. Your mother has gone batshit crazy. Your sister has been killed. And your fake Daddy has been blinded and maimed. Furthermore — "

Junior blasted the gun at the fire. The flames laughed.

"Never learn, do you?" one of the nephilim scoffed at Junior.

The fire pressed on: "R&R, Junior. Rest and relaxation. We all need a little break every now and then. Why not take a break and enjoy yourself in the Rec Room? After all, you're in charge of the place, now. And you have the run of it."

Heart thudding, Junior stared with hatred at the flames. That sensation — hatred — knifed at his gut: a sharp, pure, sour sensation. He had never felt hatred before. But he felt it now. It was a queer feeling; a surprise, even a shock. It felt like playfully pulling the covers off your sister in bed to wake her up, and finding not your sister in bed but her corpse instead.

Then, suddenly, his mood switched.

He felt boredom.

He had never felt bored before, either. There had always been chores to do around the farm.

But this wasn't the farm, was it?

Rec Room.

That's what the sign said. And God knew that he, Junior,

could use a little R&R right now, after all that he had been through. That is, God would have known this fact about Junior, had God still been alive. But, Junior reflected, somebody named Neat ... Nate ... Natechee, somebody named *Nate Chee* had killed God. That was what Bubb had said. And Junior had already learned that God would not answer the phone. Junior figured that he was on his own, now.

Big time.

Gathering up his gun and his guts, he rose to his feet and walked toward the door leading to the infinite room on the other side. A now-useless instinct for self-preservation compelled him to level the gun barrel at the door, pointless as this gesture was.

When he got to the door he stopped, thought for a moment, and then kicked it open.

Immediately a deafening chorus of human shrieks and moans met him as if in terrified greeting or perhaps horrified homage. The terrible noises so disoriented him that he tottered at the threshold, the foot that he had used to kick open the door sticking out into space.

And then he lost his balance and went plunging over into the other side, falling into empty space, into the abyss. Falling and falling, without end ...

Falling down.

The Third Neighborhood of Hell

The roadhouse had been destroyed but the penis remained, doughtily rooted to the spot and still growing taller. At 350 feet, it was already the tallest structure in Hell.

The sojourners presently found themselves at the home of Mucho Hogg, the onetime computer science instructor at Chester Alan Arthur Junior High School who had become addicted to information: a glutton for gossip. Flo Jellem had always secretly blamed herself for Mucho's plight, for he had learned to love food only too well under Flo's home ec tutelage, but over time he had sublimated his trencherman's instincts and redirected them toward devouring data. Today, as ever, he was entrenched before his home computer feeding at the never-ending data stream, the river of news, the ever-percolating popcorn of pixels. He had grown mentally obese on junk food for the mind: celebrity gossip, message board flame wars, pop-up ads for weight-loss clinics and get-rich-quick schemes, Web sites devoted to porn and, of course, others devoted to stoking hatred of Islam. This information, low on nutrients but high in calories, had caused his brain to expand, but the expansion was mostly due to intercellular pockets of cerebral cellulite. Now Hogg's head was so fat that he could no longer leave the house, because he could not fit his head through any of its door or windows. His head resembled a big balloon tethered to the string of the rest of his body. Hogg and Flo exchanged pleasantries through the kitchen window of the Hogg home, with Hogg trying to access a virtual version of Flo via the Internet rather than speak with her IRL. His eight-year-old son, Mucho Jr., had to run errands for the both of them, since only the boy was able to leave the house. But the boy had recently acquired in iPhone and how he too was filling up on meaningless junk information, his own head getting bigger and bigger. Flo sighed. She knew it was only a matter of time that both of them, addicted to junk facts, would be trapped in their own house, in the warped prisons of their own perceptions, in their candified and corrupted minds, knowing everything that they wanted to know, being always confirmed in their own biases and hence, in knowing what they supposed to be everything, not actually knowing anything. It was in this neighborhood that Bubb confessed to Flo the aching loneliness that he felt, the sense of existential despair that comes with presiding over an infinite and eternal torture chamber just because he, Bubb, was the necessary minus sign in the creation of a God who was long dead, if indeed He had ever existed. Flo took Bubb's taloned hand in hers, reassuringly patted it and said, "There, there, dear. I know *exactly* how you feel." She then related her own tale of existential angst, about the time that she attended a conference of junior high school professors in Truth or Consequences, N.M., and was made by the others to feel "small" because she merely taught food while they taught "important subjects" like math, English, science and history.

"Silly sausages!" Flo said bitterly. "As if food were not the most important thing in the world." Bubb appreciated Flo's empathy, but covertly rolled his bloodshot eyes at the tale.

The Fourth Neighborhood of Hell

The next neighborhood offered a shocking contrast between wealth and poverty; i.e., America in microcosm. Flo introduced the gang to Danny Spender, who was about to lose his home to foreclosure, another victim of the financial meltdown of ought-eight. But, as Flo explained to Bubb and the others, Danny was also a victim of his own spendthrift ways and addiction to consumerism: His house was packed cellar to attic with the latest gadgets and geegaws, and three about-to-be repossessed gas-guzzling Hummers stood idle in his driveway. Danny had maxed out his credit cards and hadn't a dime left in the bank. He faced a bleak future, but he always reliably voted for the Republicans, who always just as reliably returned his favor by passing laws specifically intended to screw Danny over. Danny was none the wiser.

Next door the troupe encountered Bernard I. Maydit, the Wall Street wizard who still owned his boyhood home here, which he had renovated into a kitsch castle, complete with turrets, a private security force dressed in medieval suits of armor and a moat stocked with alligators. He told Flo and the others that he returned here often for the sole purpose of mocking Danny for being the loser that he was. When Wall Street melted down, Maydit made out like a bandit, floating serenely back to earth on a golden parachute after gambling away the money of Danny and millions more like him. "America loves a winner," dear, Flo assured Maydit. It was in his neighborhood that Bubb, falteringly and fumblingly, his forked tongue tied, assayed a question to Flo, about whether she might be interested in going out on something like a date — no, not a date! He stammered out afterward, did I say that? Just maybe a get-to-know-you over a cup of coffee, something on that order, and Flo agreed to this proposition. Why not? She was dead, and the thrice-married and thrice-divorced poetess of pot roast, the messiah of mayonnaise, no longer had promising prospects in the romance department. Moreover, she had developed a certain fondness for Bubb's charming haplessness so ill-concealed by his brittle facade of evil incarnate.

The Fifth Neighborhood of Hell

In the Fifth Neighborhood of Hell, the troupe came upon Mr. Fury and Mr. Crabapple. They shared a white clapboard house with an untended backyard that turned into a sea of mud when it rained. Gossip had long held that they were more than just housemates, but however that may have been, their shouting matches were legendary. Today it was raining after the tornado that had swept away the Hellraiser Roadhouse, and the two old men, both of them nude, one wrathful and the other sullen, were wrestling in the famous mud that, Flo noted poetically, "is like a black sulkiness which can find no joy in God or man or the universe, dear." The anger and despair of the two old men, who now grappled erotically in the sea of mud, could be chalked up to the fact that they listened every day to talk radio and watched Tampon Redsmear's Faux News. Undoubtedly they were also self-hating homos, ranting against gay marriage and propagandizing for the sanctity of the male-female relationship, tropes that they had absorbed from listening to Glenn Beck and others, even as every time it rained they enjoyed the nude erotic romp in the mud while maintaining that they were trying to do physical violence to each other like the good red-blooded, war-loving Americans that they imagined or professed themselves to be.

Here, too, in this neighborhood, Flo and Bubb had their first proto-date in the City of Dixie Cups, a museum housing a collection of the paper cups invented by Lawrence Luellen in 1907 and promoted by the entrepreneur Hugh Moore. The cups were displayed in glass cases and presided over by stern-faced security guards. Bubb lost his shit.

"What's wrong, dear?"

"This is precisely it," Bubb seethed.

"*What* is precisely it?"

"Precisely why I programmed The Pood!"

"I don't understand, dear."

"The sheer *insipidity* of it all. The *banality*, the utter pointlessness! Just think! Billions of years of evolution, the slow changing of genomes over fathomless numbers of generations, the incredible fortuitous contingency of existence, and to what end? To produce a species that makes a museum devoted to Dixie cups! Flo, can't you see the *horror* of it all? In its own way it is worse than the Holocaust, worse even than my Rec Room!"

Flo looked blankly at Bubb.

"I'm against evolution, dear, she said blandly. "When I was alive, I even crusaded against it on Internet message boards. My motto was: 'Nobody is going to make a monkey out of me.'" Then Flo asked, "What does any of this have to do with The Pood, dear?"

"It's why I invented The Pood," he said through gritted teeth. "To kill Mayor Gil Aaronson. Gil Aaronson must die!"

"But why? I mean, I think he should die, too. He raised my taxes three times. But why do *you* want him to die?"

Bubb did not say.

The Sixth Neighborhood of Hell

The Sixth Neighborhood of Hell was the home of the Heretic.

When the weary travelers from downstairs arrived in his neck of the woods, they acquired a vibe that something important was about to happen. They were, after all, drawing nearer to the geographical center of Hell, Michigan, where Mayor Gil Aaronson lived in splendid isolation, and where he was still holed up with The Pood. Arrayed against the recalcitrant and malingering mayor was the news media, and overhead the skies still thickened with their contumacious clattering helicopters, those swarms of metal buzzards forever feeding on the carrion of human woe and weal.

The group found the Heretic prowling about an enormous crumbling granite wall, part of the ruins of a long-abandoned industrial park. The ruins provided yet another powerful demonstration of the illusory nature of linear time, the myth of human progress and the fallacy of teleological thinking. The weather had cleared after the fierce storms, and the multi-talented disparager of philosophical correctness, who was also an artist, was creating a sprawling mural on that wall, consisting of imaginary dysfunctional Gods belonging to a private cosmos of his own conception that he called The Pantheon.

He was using a paint roller to add the finishing touches of a white beard to a ponderous deity of profound afflatus but also afflicted with embarrassing flatulence, when he espied the tormented troupe. "Flo Jellem," he marveled. "We all thought you were dead!"

Flo went through the same old rigmarole of explanations.

The Heretic now stood face to face with Bill Z. Bubb, the devil himself. Perhaps unsurprisingly, the Heretic looked much more frightening then the devil. While the sower of sorrow looked shabby and pathetic in his cheap frock coat and penny loafers, the Heretic resembled a young Spike Lee with an afro haircut.

"God is dead," the Heretic lectured Bubb, "aye, but so are you! Who killed you and God? We did, Bubb! Deal with it!"

Nietzsche spoke up, picking up the thread of a refrain from oh so long ago, in the days before he had seized a horse that was being whipped and had then slipped away into ten years of insanity and silence before his own death:

"God is dead. God remains dead. And we have killed him. How shall we comfort ourselves, the murderers of all murderers? What was holiest and mightiest of all that the world has yet owned has bled to death under our knives: who will wipe this blood off us? What water is there for us to clean ourselves? What festivals of atonement, what sacred games shall we have to invent? Is not the greatness of this deed too great for us? Must we ourselves not become gods simply to appear worthy of it?" Then, as if to answer his own question, he said, "Aflac!"

The Heretic's eyes popped at the feathered philosopher. "Fred, is that really you? You're my hero!"

They fell to intense philosophizing, and the other ducks, atheists all, gleefully joined in. Flo had mixed feelings about The Heretic. On the one hand, she appreciated his independence of thought. On the other hand, he seemed dreadfully insouciant about simply *everything*, including matters that were close to Flo's heart, like home economics and the falsity of the theory of evolution. It had taken Flo no time at all to mentally scan The Heretic's home ec record. His attitude toward proper food preparation had been, well, *heretical*. He disdained reliable Kraft individually wrapped American cheese slices, gravitating instead toward mystifying French cheeses with exotic names that confused and frightened Flo; he scoffed at Miracle Whip mayo, preferring instead spicy hot mustard; he mixed and matched menus, referring to them as "texts" and insisting that they had "multiple meanings," even meanings not intended by the menus' original creators. He called them "pomo menus." Most disturbing of all, he denied that home economics had any "over-arching narrative, any meta-narrative." To Flo, such thinking could only produce gustatory chaos. It conjured terrifying scenarios of dessert served before dinner or beer served for breakfast. When, for his final home ec exam, The Heretic had turned in a single-spaced, twenty-five-page essay densely annotated with footnotes and titled "The Phenomenology of Cheese," Flo had been too confused to do naught but give him an A. "I am opposed to the entire rationalist tradition deriving from the Renaissance and culminating in the 'cosmic rationalism' of the pretentious Hegel," The Heretic had declaimed in his provocative paper. "Aye, 'A crowd is untruth,' true dat. Yet when we look inside of ourselves, what do we find? Nothing!" To this day, Flo remained perplexed at what any of this had to do with cheese. But it certainly sounded impressive.

While The Heretic and the three ducks chattered on about the anti-meaning of life (with Schopenhauer accusing Nietzsche of stealing his best ideas), Bubb felt increasingly marginalized. It was true, as the Heretic had said, that he, Bubb, was dead. They were *all* dead, all of those who had wandered upstairs. But The Heretic had made it sound as if he, Bubb, were dead in some deeper, metaphysical way: That he did not exist *at all*, naturally or supernaturally. Bubb was freshly assailed by self doubt: queasiness, even *nausea*, stole over him. He suddenly realized that these empty feelings had been with him since the dawn of time. He raised his own taloned hands before his bloodshot eyes and wondered: Am I dream? And if so, who is the Dreamer? Just then Flo was at his side. She had detected his angst; more and more, it seemed, the thrice-married and thrice-divorced Poetess of Pot Roast was entangling her thoughts with his. During their odyssey it seemed that they were growing closer, as though fated, by forces outside their control or even knowledge, to be as one.

"William, dear," she said gently, plucking at his elbow, "you're looking a mite peaked for a supernatural evildoer with a scarlet face and horns on his head. Perhaps you should sit down and rest for a bit. Would you like me to bring you a glass of cold water?"

Bubb turned to face Flo and saw his eerie *Otherness* reflected back at him in the limpid pupils of her hazel eyes behind her granny glasses. Then he looked up and faced the heavens, that fathomless but empty abode of the God who no longer answered His phone, and losing his shit again he raved into the ravening void: "My God, my God, *who am I? And why hast thou forsaken me?"* His only reply was the cruel and withering silence of the great Cosmic Zero, of a world "that is not even meaningless," Bubb now announced with awe, as if making an important discovery that had not already been discovered by generations of pretentious undergrads majoring in philosophy during bull sessions over beer. He broke down weeping. Flo hastened to console him. "There, there, William," she said, patting his back. "Like successful recipes, meaning comes from within, dear. I should have thought you would have discovered that by now, given that you've been around forever."

The Seventh Neighborhood of Hell

They moved on, accompanied by The Heretic, who wanted to continue discoursing with the Aflac-duck philosophers, especially Nietzsche. The Heretic also wished to demonstrate that he could not be segregated or ghettoized in his own particular neighborhood of Hell; that he was free to roam from place to place, even those (mostly white) places where he might strike fear into the hearts of the older white residents. His peregrinations were intended to destroy the "confinement" theory of Hell, perhaps even the idea of Hell itself. The Heretic, with his insouciant demeanor and his giant afro that was like the photographic negative of a saint's halo, terrified Budd and continued to unsettle Flo, who normally was unflappable and refused to let anyone get up to the Dickens with her.

The Heretic asked Nietzsche about Sartre. He asked whether Nietzsche agreed with the speculation that Sartre's novel "Nausea" was a Nietzschean text. Nietzsche replied aphoristically: "One takes an obscure and inexplicable thing more seriously than a clear and explicable one.... A matter that becomes clear ceases to concern us."

The seventh neighborhood was given over to violence. It was also where the town dungeon was located, the risqué harbor of furtive sex fetishists who skulked in and out of the nondescript and unmarked cinder block building that housed it. When Flo, in tour-guide fashion, alerted the others to the dungeon, the eyes of the hellfire golem, the avatar of the Staff Sergeant Ulysses Eisenhower Yokel, lighted up, while Sheriff Ted, bawking bleakly in his garb of feathers, quailed backward in distress. The sergeant plucked a few testicles from his paper sack, popped them into his mouth and asked of no one in particular: "I wonder if this dungeon needs a good drill instructor who knows how to put the fear of God into these pussies?"

Elvis was incredulous at the existence of a sex fetish dungeon in the heart of a sleepy Midwestern hamlet, and like Yokel he wanted to visit it. So much had changed since his time. It was scarcely possible to imagine sex dungeons in 1950s America, when the King arrived on the scene and when Nixon was vice president. Nixon, no longer vice president nor even president, nor even alive, but instead constituting Elvis's post-mortem excretory infrastructure and facade, said, "You won't have Nixon to kick around." The former president was evidently afraid that he, as Elvis's buttocks, might be a tempting target in the dungeon.

"People get up to all sorts of Dickens because they never received a proper education in food preparation," Flo declared with exasperation, waving away the unfortunate stench of Nixon's posterior proclamation. "Now really, dears, we must not tarry here. Time is wasting and The Pood is still at large." She looked up at the sky, now thickening with the blimps of Faux News. A rumor was spreading among the media whores that Tampon Redsmear, owner of Faux News, was flying in from his London castle to personally direct the hacking of Gil Aaronson's cell phone and the assault on his citadel.

"Wait," Bubb said, a sinister twinkle suddenly shining again in his heretofore lusterless eyes. "I want to take a peek inside – just a peek! I want to see if this place measures up to my Rec Room. A healthy dose of torture might be just what the doctor ordered to cure my metaphysical malaise." He then drew his long tail out from under his frock coat and neurotically gnawed on the tip of it. Flo regarded him with dismay. Although she was pleased to note his air of rejuvenation, she suspected it might be transitory. Elvis remarked that he was curious — just curious, mind! — to see what sort of Dickens people got up to in such places. The philosopher-ducks stated that they, too, were curious, but purely for philosophical reasons. Flo surrendered with a sigh. "All right," she said. "But just for a minute or two." Sheriff Ted, terrified of his own feathers, hopped bawking into the arms of Flo who tried as best she could to ease his fears by smoothing his feathers. The chicken quivered spasmodically, shuddering in Flo's soothing embrace.

Bubb realized his mistake as soon as they entered and saw the dungeon's owner and chief dominatrix. It was Ayn Rand. In her dungeon, she was in high dudgeon.

Bubb cowered behind Flo's skirts.

Rand wore a tight black-leather mini-skirt and matching thigh-high black leather boots with stake-like stiletto heels. Her halter-top bra consisted of two cones terminating in points to which were affixed dollar-sign stickpins. In one hand she wielded a cat-o-nine tails whip and in the other she held a lighted cigarette inside a long plastic holder the color of money. The cigarette's glowing red ember represented the mind of Man, and the ability of Man, with his mind, to conquer fire. It was the mind of a man who had not damned existence or damned the earth, but who had instead heroically embraced it according the rational standard of value of man's life *qua* man. It was indeed an impressive cigarette, though it could still give a person lung cancer, as it had done to Rand herself. That was why she had died, and afterward had been consigned like everyone else to Bubb's basement apartment with its attached Rec Room. But she had refused to stay there. She had simply walked out on the whole affair, announcing: "This place does not exist. It is a product of mystical thinking." Since there are only three ways for the dead to return to earth — either as a ghost, a zombie or an avatar — Rand returned as her avatar: a whip-wielding dominatrix savagely rending the flesh of the masochistic second-handers who groveled before her begging for mercy in the sacred names of Howard Roark or John Galt.

"Who is John Galt?" she screamed now at a typical victim, a whim worshiper, a mystical thinker, a craven, whimpering altruist who did not understand that A is A and who therefore subscribed to a sub-human code of ethics that excluded *a priori* the only economic system suitable to man *qua* man: unregulated free-market capitalism. The scream of her question was followed by the smack of cold leather on naked flesh, and then by the victim's heart-rending moan, which seemed to contain equal elements of pain and pleasure. The victim rattled his chains against the dungeon's cinder block wall, which was a livid blue under the cold, clinical lights that shined down from overhead. Through his strangled sighs and moans he begged for mercy, but these appeals seemed only to stoke Rand's rage. She drew again back the spidery legs of the cat-o-nine tails whip, and once more propelled those gangly appendages hissing through the air, screaming as she did: *"Emotions are not tools of cognition, you evil bastard!"* The hydra-headed whip once more rent the flesh of the screaming victim, and fresh rivulets of dark red blood began to lazily seep down his naked back and buttocks from the crisscrossing cuts that the Objectivist dominatrix had inflicted upon him. Her client was naked; a tall, slender black man, perhaps around fifty years old. His face was turned to the wall. Standing nearby were several men dressed in black suits and ties, and wearing sunglasses. They wore earpieces and bore side arms. They kept looking around, as though scanning the premises for threats.

Rand angrily flung the whip to the floor, and then inhaled sharply on her cigarette. The mind of Man, the ember on the tip of the cigarette, intensified to a fiery orange-red, much like the color of the eyes of The Pood, as Rand absorbed into her lungs a satisfying stream of carcinogens that could no longer harm her because she was dead because of them.

"Oh, how I *detest* altruists!" she said with a bitter scowl of disgust as she exhaled. She resembled a withered doppelgänger of Bette Davis snarling, "What a dump!" in the 1949 movie "Beyond the Forest." The roiling cigarette smoke, suggesting the fumes of her perpetual anger, gave her a spectral appearance. Squinting through the smoke, she saw the new arrivals and demanded, "What do *you* second-handers want?" Bubb was cringing behind Flo, hoping that Rand would not spot him. Unfortunately, the deacon of darkness had forgotten that Flo was a ghost, and hence transparent.

Before anyone could reply, the men in black suits and ties unchained Rand's victim from the dungeon wall and helped him dress. President Oreo Cookie, having regained his clothes and his aplomb, coolly adjusted his red power tie and slipped a hand inside his suit coat. Pulling out an eel-skin wallet, he withdrew from it a gold-plated credit card and flashed it at Rand. "Thank you so much, Ms. Rand," he told the Objectivist cult leader. "With your help, I have won another tremendous political victory by compromising my way to total political defeat, an actual physical whipping administered by a well-known representative of the far political right. That's the compromise that America needs. We're not red states and blue states, we're all purple states: a perfect mixture of the two colors, the color of a bruise acquired during satisfying sadomasochistic sex play. I assume you accept credit cards?"

Rand, the author of several best-selling potboilers lacquered with a sheen of pseudo-philosophy that appealed to adolescent boys with delusions of grandeur, sexual angst and inferiority complexes, looked down her nose at the card. A flustered president reassured her: "It's backed by the full faith and credit of the United States of America, Ms. Rand."

"That's exactly what I was afraid of," Rand replied.

"A check, then." Cookie was reaching for his checkbook.

"Never! It'll bounce!"

The president was nonplussed. He patted around in his pockets for cash, or even coins. Finding none, he looked pleadingly at the Secret Service agents, who began emptying their pockets. As they counted quarters, dimes and nickels, Rand snorted, "That isn't change I can believe in. I'm afraid you'll have to pay in gold ingots. We must return to the gold standard."

Faced with Rand's demand, the president became grave and reflective. He frowned and pondered; he cogitated. He even meditated. He looked vaguely constipated. Finally he capitulated. He said: "What the American people expect from us, Ms. Rand, is a Grand Bargain; a good-faith bipartisan compromise that culminates in my total surrender." The president reached into his pocket for his BlackBerry. "I'll get in touch with Fort Knox at once and have them fly you in America's entire gold supply."

But Rand, like everyone else in America, had already tuned out the capitulator-in-chief. She was staring straight through the transparent Flo at the shabby supernatural bindlestiff who was trying to hide behind her, the entity with the pointed ears and the horns sticking out through holes in his hat. "You!" Rand cried, appalled. Bubb snatched up his tail from under his coat and compulsively gnawed on it.

Rand retrieved her whip and approached Bubb, who had backed out from behind Flo. The Objectivist cult leader waved the nine-tailed instrument of fustigation lazily about, occasionally snapping it at the air. While she stalked Bubb, Flo looked on perplexedly. The Heretic, who was greatly enjoying the whole scene, remarked to the Nietzsche duck: "You know, Fritz, Rand here was my first hero before I discovered you." Nietzsche said, "Aflac!" Sergeant Yokel, the hellfire golem, popped testicles into his mouth from his brown paper sack like popcorn at the movies and bounced around on the balls of his feet.

Flo looked at Bubb and asked worriedly, "How do you two know each other, dear?"

Rand raged at Bubb: "I walked out of that terrible, filthy little underground hole of yours, that squalid sanctuary of second-handers, and you have the temerity to follow me upstairs?" Before Bubb could reply, Rand jeered: "When I died I had hoped to go to heaven — whatever the hell that is!" Then she let fly with the whip.

The eight talons smacked the floor at Bubb's cloven feet, and he jumped aloft. Rand swung again and again at the floor and Bubb danced to avoid the blows, hooves clopping on the dirty cinder block surface. Elvis/Nixon broke out his guitar and dashed out a lively guitar solo medley of his favorite dance tunes. Flo watched appalled. Finally she put her foot down, literally. She stamped her sensible patent-leather pump purchased from Payless three times on the floor and addressed Bubb thus: "Just what sort of menace to mankind *are* you, dear? My heavens, you're supposed to be the Deacon of Darkness! For once in your non-life, *act* like it! Grow a pair, dear, or ... or people will be apt to mistake you for President Cookie, here." Flo jerked an insubstantial thumb back in the direction of the pussy of a president.

The president wore a pained expression. He assured Flo that he would never let the Republicans tamper with her Social Security, unless they insisted on doing so. But Flo dismissed him: "Don't worry dear, I'm dead. I no longer receive benefits and I can't vote." She then resumed remonstrating with Bubb, who protested, nodding at Rand: "But she has a whip!" The sower of sorrow cringed as the defender of capitalism made a loop-de-loop through the air with the eight leather tails, preparing to dole out another blow in Bubb's direction.

Flo again put her foot down, another stamp of the patent-leather pump, and said, "We've been out on one date, dear. If you expect to have another, show a little gumption! Otherwise people will show no respect for you and they'll get up to the Dickens with you! How can you expect a woman to respect you if you have no self-respect?"

"The man who does not value himself, cannot value anything or anyone," Rand sneered at Bubb, and the whip flew anew. Bubb jumped again.

Flo had always been slow to anger. But now she lost her composure entirely. She moved behind Rand and prepared to box her ears. She had not boxed a pair of ears since she had boxed the ears of the brat Billy Braxton. But when she tried boxing Rand's ears the maneuver was a failure, because Flo was a ghost and hence non-material and insubstantial. Her balled fists passed harmlessly through Rand's head and even through each other. When Flo was finished her arms were crossed at the wrists in mid-air. Rand, having noticed none of this, had passed on, advancing yet again on the Bringer of Despair.

"A second date," Bubb muttered, drawing encouragement from this prospect. But for some reason the wrathful one could summon little more than a small ball of bluish fire from his churning gut, which tripped off his forked tongue and then fizzled out like a luminous evaporating belch. This time the whip tore his coat and scored his scaled flesh, and he cried out. Although he could not be killed because he was dead, Bubb could feel pain, as had been proved when Flo had smitten him hip, thigh and head with her pocketbook.

And then Flo recalled that she still had her pocketbook, in the pocket of her coat. It certainly maintained its substantiality: Since it did not have an incorporeal soul it remained what it had always been, a particular configuration of matter and energy, pliant enough to hold coins and credit cards but also potent enough to deal damaging blows. Rand, too, was corporeal, since she had resurfaced upstairs as her avatar. Flo took out her pocketbook and moved between Rand and Bubb.

Rand crossed her arms over her chest and regarded Flo with haughty disdain. "Just who in Hell are *you*?" she demanded. Looking down at the ducks, she asked, "And who in Hell are *these* little monsters?"

The ducks quacked in unison that they were famous philosophers. "Quacks, indeed!" Rand responded. "There was only one true philosopher before me, Aristotle, and now I have solved *all* philosophical problems!" She again demanded to know Flo's name.

"Why, I'm Florence Jellem, dear," the Poetess of Pot Roast replied mildly, bridling her emotions. Inwardly, however, she was seething, but the only external evidence of her anger was a slight pursing of the lips and a knitting of the darning needles of her brows above her granny glasses.

"Florence Jellem!" Rand repeated in a mocking tone of voice. "Tell me, *Flo-orence Jellem*, just what do you think of me? I'd like to hear it!" Rand now stood with one hand balled on her hip. With her other hand she twirled the whip.

Flo's expression became momentarily vacant. After a brief pause she replied, "But, dear, I don't think of you."

Rand looked thunderstruck. This was the line that she had put in the mouth of her fictional architect hero, the rapist and arsonist Howard Roark, when Roark had been asked the same question by the depraved, power-mad socialist syndicated newspaper columnist Ellsworth Toohey, who was trying to take over the world. Rand had been very proud of that line, thinking it a nuclear bomb to the hearer's self-esteem, but now that bomb had been deployed against her. It was more than she could bear.

"But I'm Ayn Rand!" she shrieked, shaking with fury.

Flo cogitated, blinking. She was trying to place the names "Ayn" and "Rand" in some food-preparation context to which she could relate. Drawing a blank, she said, "I'm sorry, dear, but I'm afraid I've never heard of you. I certainly never had you in my home ec seminar." Then she hit Rand in the face with her pocketbook.

Rand looked completely astounded. Her mouth fell open, with blood glistening on her avatar lips, and she slowly raised a hand to cover it. Her eyes grew huge and they displayed, in the pupils, twin dollar signs. She said, "Oh!" It was an exclamation full of indignation. Then she began to blubber and finally she burst into tears. She wailed, "Under Objectivism, force and fraud is not allowed in human relations, except in the case of Anglo-Saxons stealing the land of the Indians in the Americas and then exterminating most of them!" Then she broke down into loud, racking sobs. Flo hit her with the pocketbook again, this time over the top of the head, producing a vivifying WHAP noise. Then she smote the self-righteous harridan of laissez-faire economics again and again, WHAP WHAP WHAP!

The Secret Service agents, sensing the prospect of real danger — that President Cookie might be forced to intervene, or take a definite stand of some sort, which was anathema to him — hustled him out a back door, that he might survive to surrender another day. Bubb looked on with dawning recognition; a feeling of connecting, or reconnecting, with some primal essence of his soul, something that he had lost touch with eons ago.

"Oh, snap!" he said. "That's it!" He waggled a long, taloned finger at the scrum between Flo and Rand. Licks of smoke curled out of his pointed ears, accompanied by a hissing noise, the sound of a radiator bringing up the heat. "That's *it! That* is what has been missing in my non-life!" It was unclear precisely what he meant by the word "that," but what was undeniable was that Bubb seemed rejuvenated. The smoke curling out of the hollows of his ears became licks of fire; and smoke now streamed out of his nostrils and mouth as well, while his cheeks grew ember-red and the wrinkles that covered his face began smoothing out. Even the bags under his eyes vanished and suddenly he looked ten thousand years younger.

Some thugs, evidently dungeon bouncers dressed all in black leather and bearing truncheons and brass knuckles, came bursting out of another room and they headed straight for Flo, determined to take her down. Then there was a loud scream, and for a moment everyone was paralyzed with confusion. Sprinting out of another room, and pursued by other thugs determined to restrain her, was a half-naked young woman clutching a towel. She kept trying to cover herself with it, cover her nether regions and her breasts, which were large, round and creamy and surmounted by nipples with pink aureoles like rose petals. Everyone's eyes popped. The woman was crying. The men chasing her seized her by the shoulders and began dragging her back into captivity.

Flo, though still dead, again sprang abundantly to life, leaving a battered Rand cringing on the floor. She rushed up to the thug who had wrapped a forearm around the woman's neck and hit him on the head with the pocketbook. "*That* for you!" she hollered, and the thug wailed and relinquished his grip on the victim. Then Flo became a whirlwind of flailing arms and legs, the pocketbook pistoning downward on the heads and faces of all the men, the men who had tried to restrain the fleeing woman and the thugs who were attacking Flo with brass knuckles and truncheons. Their blows were in vain, because Flo was a ghost, and the brass and rubber passed harmlessly through her. But Flo, whirling like a dervish, landed repeated devastating blows on her attackers, not just with her pocketbook, but also with the karate-like kicks that she meted out, kicks of sharp import that she doled out with her patent-leather pumps, kicks that dented groins and busted balls. Soon the mob scattered in terror, nursing their physical wounds and their wounded dignity.

"My goodness, dear," Flo said, adjusting the towel around the half-naked young woman. "Just what sort of Dickens have you got up to here, anyway? You poor girl. What's your name?"

The young woman was gasping for breath, and tears were streaming down her face. "My name is Mystery Tart," she sobbed. "Please, *please* get me out of here!"

"Miss Treetart?" Flo asked, baffled by the name.

"No, *Mystery* Tart. They call me that because it's a mystery how I was born: My mother is Holace Orr!" And she burst into fresh tears.

Flo briefly weighed this startling revelation, but decided it was prudent to attend to the business at hand before making further inquiries. She hustled the young woman toward the dungeon exit, the crew following closely on her heels.

"Say, darlin'," Sergeant Yokel drawled at Mystery Tart. "Were them bad guys holding you here against your will as a sex slave, hmmm?" The hellfire golem leered at the young woman's cleavage.

"Oh, no!" Mystery Tart said with a disarming laugh. Then

she burbled: "They call me 'Tart' because I *love* to fuck! And, unlike Mom, I've got the cunt to prove it. No, the problem was the indoctrination." Turning to Flo she said, "Those men that you fought off were trying to make me read 'Atlas Shrugged.'" Then she again faced the sergeant, offering him a coquettish smile. She parted the towel, showing her tits, and batted her eyes in a come-hither way at the hellfire golem. The sergeant drooled.

"Oh, for heaven's sake!" Flo said, covering the young woman with the towel. "Let's stop this nonsense and get out of here." The thrice-married Flo was no prude, but she drew the line at "the funny business" when work needed to be done. And they had a lot of it to do.

Once in the street, they beheld a stunning scene. The sky was thick, dark and clotted with news media aircraft. The presence of so many planes, helicopters, blimps, drones and other aerial transport vehicles partly blotted out the sun. To the east, in the neighborhood of the destroyed Hellraiser Roadhouse, the rising penis now broached the sky at an altitude of some 2,000 feet, and engineers had ingeniously affixed warning lights to it to prevent aircraft from crashing into it. The blinking red lights on the mighty member created sky-borne semaphores of lust.

Then there appeared on the horizon a tremendous ship, a boat floating in the air, and it chuffed: *chuff, chuff, chuff.* Galley slaves in the boat's gut provided lift, beating their long oars against the sky to propel the airborne boat forward. The magnificent dream vessel, as long and great as Noah's Ark, bore many-colored flags and pennants, and from the yardarms billowed tremendous white sails made of newsprint that were plastered with pictures of nubile young lasses in various states of undress: Page Three Girls, they were called. Above decks were jugglers and clowns and carnival barkers and politicians pontificating into megaphones. A 12-piece band struck up patriotic songs, and above the clash of cymbals a lone tuba oom-pah-pahed sonorously. It was Rimbaud's aerial dream boat, just as the seer had seen it, except that it had been plastered with advertising and corrupted by carnivalia. A news ticker constantly streamed around the hull of the boat, updating viewers below with the news from downtown Hell but also on stock prices, sports scores, celebrity gossip, lottery results, the anticipated return date of Jesus and every other factoid that made life worth living in the vast tattooed slobocracy that America had become. Aside from the galley slaves who rowed the oars, how was a giant boat, as big as Noah's Ark, kept aloft? It was kept aloft the same way that Santa Claus and intelligent design theory are kept alive: By dreams, by hope and desire, by wishful thinking and above all by fear. It was by far the largest vessel in the sky and now it cruised placidly overhead, casting a tremendous shadow that moved languidly over the land, plunging Flo and the others into midday darkness. Painted across the side of the ship was a single giant word in bright-red serif script and black outline: REDSMEAR. Under that, in smaller script letters, were the words *Mass Media Empire*. The Great Man himself — the creator of every feast, every triumph, every drama — was at the prow, peering intently into a spy glass. He wore military fatigues, cracked leather boots and a pith helmet. Now and then the spry octogenarian barked out commands in a crackling voice, and as the ship cruised overhead it corrected course and zeroed in on the home of Gil Aaronson. The other, much smaller news media airships were pushed aside, the way that the prow of an ordinary boat will cleave the waters and bunt aside all smaller, inferior objects. The Redsmear Dream Ship had a date with destiny.

And then it happened.

A screaming came across the sky.

It has happened before, but there is nothing to compare it to now.

All heads jerked as one toward the center of Hell whence the shriek issued, just one neighborhood away and perhaps half a mile distant. It rose in octave and pitch higher, higher, higher, until it burst the eardrums of the living and maddened the minds of men. It broke every window in town. It became a supersonic whine. It briefly passed beyond the range of human hearing. Then it returned. It slowly fell in volume, ever fainter. That missile-like wail Dopplered off and on the diminuendo it dissolved. It ended not with a bang but with a whimper, followed by:

Yap! Yap! Yap! Yap! Yap! Yap!

Thus Sayeth The Pood.

The Eighth Neighborhood of Hell

Elvis Presley made up his mind to have a heart to heart, some serious face time, with his ass.

He and Nixon sneaked off behind a nearby service station.

"Mr. President," Elvis began, looking back over his shoulder and downward. He saw Nixon's famous jowls, which were his (Elvis's) buttocks, and he saw the famous presidential ski-slope nose, which was Elvis's very own extended tailbone. He did not see Nixon's mouth, nor did he wish to think about what Nixon's mouth really was. Elvis went on: "Mr. President, let's blow this popcorn stand. Let's get out of here. Let's escape. When this is over — however it ends — I don't want to go back downstairs and spend the rest of eternity singing 'Love Me Tender' to stiff-necked, music-hating harpies who will boo me and throw tomatoes at me while Ed Sullivan, an Easter Island Moai, insults me. It's more than I can stand. Whaddya say? Are you with me? … Well, I guess that's a stupid question, isn't it?"

From below, Nixon listened in crafty, cunning silence.

"We could steal a car," Elvis suggested in a conspiratorial whisper.

"We *could* do that," Nixon allowed. "I know how it could be done. I know where the car could be gotten. We could do that. But —"

"Yes, yes, I know, *but it would be wrong.* Still, we *could* do it, right? … Listen, Mr. President, we're not being taped. We can speak straight from the shoulder now, man to ass, without fear of being subpoenaed by the Senate Watergate committee."

"Go on," Nixon said, noncommittally.

"We steal a car and hit the road to Detroit," Elvis said. "It's only about 30 miles east of here."

"Never!" Nixon said, trying to put his foot down and then remembering that he did not have a foot. "[Expletive Deleted] Detroit! It is full of Negroes on the dole. They all voted for Kennedy in '60 and Humphrey in '68 and McGovern in '72, and against me. [Expletive deleted] the Negroes."

"But, Mr. President, you saw that a Negro is president right now!"

"And a damned poor one at that, by all indications," Nixon replied sharply. "That one shoulda stayed on the damned dole."

"Listen," Elvis said, switching tactics. "Detroit is Motown, the Motown sound. It's a music capital. I could restart my career there. The return of Elvis would be just about the biggest story ever, bigger than the resurrection of Jesus! They might even build a religion around me!"

"What's in it for me?"

"I don't know … you could restart your political career. Run for something. Hell, run for president again!"

"I'm not eligible to run for president again," Nixon protested, pointing out that he was barred from seeking a third term by the 22nd amendment.

Elvis thought this over, and then helpfully pointed out: "Constitutional amendments only apply to the living, I bet. Since you're dead all bets are off. Anyway, I imagine the Republicans are looking for a good candidate to take on President Cookie, and he's vulnerable as hell. You saw him in the dungeon — Mr. President, he's a wimp!"

Nixon fell silent. But from within those cheeky jowls below, behind the ski-slope nose and dark, darting eyes, one could practically hear the gears turning. After a few moments the Great Schemer announced: "Listen, uh, Elvis?"

"Yes, Mr. President?"

"The, uh, the President — that's me — has, uh, an idea."

"What is it, sir?"

"Let's, uh, steal a car."

"Yes?"

"And, uh, go to Detroit."

"Hot damn!" Elvis exclaimed. He slapped his thigh and grinned. "Good idea, sir. Why didn't I think of that? Well, I guess that's why you da man!"

"It *is* my idea," Nixon stressed, sounding defensive. "Not your idea or Kissinger's idea, either. *Especially* not Kissinger. [Expletive deleted] Kissinger."

"Don't worry about Kissinger," Elvis said reassuringly. "He's just some doddering old war criminal now. Probably too old to pull the wings off flies. Forget about Kissinger."

"Kissinger got the Nobel Peace Prize," Nixon pouted. "Got it along with Le Duc Tho, for the Vietnam peace agreement. But that was my idea, not theirs. Just like détente with the Soviets. That was my idea, too, and the opening to China."

"Of course, sir."

They were headed toward the nearby parking lot of a Walmart. Nixon said: "I'll need a campaign manager, a press secretary and a running mate. I'll also need to know who my opponents are for the Republican nomination. I've been out of touch with politics for years, as you know."

"I can be all three," Elvis said. "Hell, who would vote against a ticket with Elvis Presley reincarnated on it? A whole new life after death is opening up for us, Mr. President."

"*I'm* at the top of the ticket," Nixon pointed out peevishly, exquisitely oblivious to the irony of his physical location vis-à-vis the King. "Not you."

"Of course, sir, you're the boss." Elvis was scanning the parked cars for signs of keys left in the ignition locks, or at least doors left unlocked.

"I suppose I'll need a First Lady," Nixon sighed. "Only one president was unmarried, and that was James Buchanan. Buchanan was a fag, though. Nixon is not a fag."

"But I hear Pat never put out," Presley put in.

"We can't stand Pat," Nixon announced, reprising a slogan from his '60 campaign about the need to avoid complacency. It had inspired much hilarity and inevitably produced a pained expression on the face his then-alive, now-dead wife, whenever she heard him deliver the line during the speeches that she was forced to listen to.

An idea began formulating in Presley's head. He recalled Holace Orr from the Hellraiser Roadhouse, and wondered whether she had survived the tornado that had leveled the structure.

"I think, sir, I might have the perfect First Lady for you." Elvis found a car, a Hummer in fact, with the door unlocked. He whistled at it. "Look at the size of it," he marveled. "What the hell, this baby is even bigger than the muscle cars of my youth. Yet a lot of other cars are really tiny. The world has really changed. Nothing makes sense."

"No Jewess," Nixon announced.

"Excuse me, Mr. President?"

"I won't have a Jewess as First Lady. Nixon draws the line at a Jewess."

Oh, I don't think Holace is Jewish, sir. She's more shrewish than Jewish."

Miraculously, the keys were in the ignition, and soon they were off, not without troubling accommodations. Elvis had to lean forward and in a squatting position so as not to mash Nixon's face, and particularly his ski-slope nose, into the upholstery. Elvis guided the Hummer out of the parking lot and toward open road. He stopped before a newspaper stand and, lacking money, reached through the window and swiped a daily paper while the proprietor looked on open-mouthed at the iconic face of the driver. The paper was emblazoned with news of the arrival of The Pood. But, as luck would have it, it also contained, inside, an analysis of the current crop of candidates for the Republican presidential nomination.

Elvis and Nixon had peeled off from the others just as soon as they had left the dungeon, and it was just now that the Redsmear air ship glided overhead, followed by the piercing whine and tinny yap-yap-yaps from the center of Hell. Elvis pointed the Hummer downtown, in the direction of Bubb and the others. "Bubb's no big deal," Elvis scoffed. "In fact, he's kind of a weakling, sort of an old derelict. He brought me upstairs to scare that damned dog. I got no beef with no damned dog, except maybe that hound dog, and I ain't goin' back downstairs, either. I'm gonna tell that old bastard what I think of him. I'm gonna tell him Sayonara."

Below decks, Nixon's nose was mashed in newsprint. His beady eyes darted shiftily from side to side as he read about Rick Perry, Michele Bachmann, Mitt Romney and the other candidates who would be his rivals for the G.O.P. nomination.

"Romney!" he exclaimed. "*Mitt* Romney? What the hell kind of a grown man is named Mitt? He must be a fag. ... Oh, it's George Romney's son. I ran against his [Expletive deleted] father in '68 for the nomination. He was a pushover, a candyass. He said that he had been 'brainwashed' about the Vietnam War and that was the end of his candidacy right there. I imagine that his [Expletive deleted] son will be just as big a pushover as the father. ... Mitt Romney! [Expletive deleted] Mitt Romney! Nixon will break Mitt Romney's balls!"

Elvis drove up to Bubb and the others just as the yap-yap-yaps died away. Flo turned to Bubb. She knew him well enough by now to suppose that he would be blanching in horror at the sound of The Pood. But what she saw instead stunned her and the others.

He lifted his head, and his pointy-nosed face seemed to visibly stretch outward and upward with the elasticity of putty. His nose actually grew, and his nostrils flared. Smoke came out of his pointed ears. Suddenly a smile cracked open his face from ear to ear, and his eyes became slits. The crow's feet that radiated outward from the corners of his eyes deepened. His whole face glowed as red as a stoplight. He flung up his taloned hands, and threw back his head so that he was looking directly upward at the plane-clotted sky. Cackling, mirthless laughter broke from his lips, and he said in a voice low and guttural: "Oh, how I love the sound of *eeeee-vil* in the afternoon!" And then he laughed on and on. His laughter momentarily parted the planes and the clouds in the sky and for a brief moment the stars shone down, quivering. "We are close to The Pood!" the archangel of anarchy announced. "See how even the Dog Star cowers! Mu-ah-ha-ha!"

Elvis had slowed nearly to a stop, intending to tell Bubb off. But now, seeing the remarkable and frightening change that had come over the rejuvenated overseer of the Rec Room, he had second thoughts. Nixon, oblivious to the encounter, was reading about Rick Perry.

Elvis began making a U-turn with the Hummer. Mystery Tart had straddled the lap of the hugely grinning Sergeant Yokel, who had laid aside his bag of testicles to accommodate her. But as she leaned in to kiss him she waved her arm at the air and said, "Oh, penis breath! I don't like that!" Then she spotted Elvis behind the wheel of the Hummer.

"You're Elvis Presley!" she shrieked, like an adrenaline-soaked and hormone-crazed teenage girl at an Elvis concert circa 1956.

"Ya got that right, darlin'," the King drawled in his sexiest, velvet-smooth voice, as he eyeballed the daughter of the town's most famous trollop. Mystery still wore only the towel, making no real effort to cover up with it. Without even thinking about it, Elvis popped open the back door, and Mystery Tart hopped off the lap of the sergeant and hopped inside the car instead. She closed the door, and Elvis gunned the engine. He leaned into the accelerator and cut onto the highway in a spray of gravel, pointing the stolen vehicle in the direction of Detroit, 30 miles east.

"Rick Perry," Nixon groused. "Smooth, slick type, big head of hair. One of the Golden Boys, like that [Expletive deleted] Reagan and that [Expletive deleted] JFK. I'll break Rick Perry's balls!"

Reading on, Nixon grew astonished.

"Rick Perry doesn't believe in the theory of evolution," Nixon announced, startled. "Rick Perry thinks the world is six thousand year old." Then he read about Michelle Bachmann and the others.

"What the hell is wrong with these people?" Nixon demanded. "What the hell kind of candidates are these?" Nixon read about how

Bachmann, kicking off her campaign, had saluted Waterloo, Iowa, for being the hometown of the actor John Wayne. Actually, it was the hometown of the serial killer John Wayne Gacy.

"If Nixon had made that mistake," Nixon said, again disconcertingly lapsing into the third-person and oozing the rancid stink of self pity, "the news media would have had a field day. Those bastards would have crucified Nixon." The old reprobate slowly shook his head, rattling the newspaper in which his nose was buried. "What the hell has happened to America?" he demanded. "How can anybody who doesn't believe in the theory of evolution be considered for high office? If these people had been around back in Nixon's day, Nixon wouldn't have let 'em in the Oval Office. Wouldn't have even let 'em in the [Expletive deleted] back door!"

Nixon said solemnly: "I've got to save America from my own [Expletive deleted] political party!"

Mystery Tart had climbed over the divider between the front and back seats and was now curled up next to Elvis. But as Nixon rattled on she wrinkled her nose and demanded, "My God! What the hell is that *smell*?"

It's nothin', darlin', Elvis said, face red. "This here Hummer has got bad exhaust, is all." Elvis prayed that Nixon would shut up. Nixon, he realized, was going to seriously cramp his style. He began to wonder whether it might be possible to have Nixon amputated.

"[Expletive deleted]," Nixon clarified. "[Expletive deleted]. [Expletive deleted]." Elvis rolled down the front window to let in some fresh air, and he also switched on the air conditioner.

"Listen to this, Elvis!" Nixon said. Elvis thought: Please shut the fuck up, Mr. President. Mystery said: "Who's talking? Where's that voice coming from? It sounds like it's coming from the seat! And there's that smell again!"

"Don't look down there, honey!" Elvis pleaded. "Nothing to see or smell down there!"

"This will interest you," Nixon assured the King. "Last August, at a campaign stop, this Michelle Bachmann [Expletive deleted] saluted your birthday, on what was really the anniversary of your death!"

"The voice is coming from the radio!" Elvis frantically told Mystery, but the Tart was already looking under the squatting Elvis. "Good God!" she gasped. "You're Richard Nixon!"

"*President* Richard Nixon," the fallen leader corrected

Mystery Tart from the bowels of his blackened spleen. His stooped shoulders would have quivered with paranoia, envy, rage and resentment, if he still had shoulders. Nixon prepared himself to be insulted by the half-naked countercultural wench. But she said, "Oh, my mother, Holace, voted for you *three times* for president! You were her hero!"

Nixon flashed his mirthless, awkward grin and maladroitly ventured upon some small talk. Learning Mystery's name, he asked her with forced casualness: "So, Miss Mystery, did you, uh, do any, uh, uh, fornicating this weekend?"

"Oh, you betcha, Mr. President!" Mystery burbled. She then pinched Nixon's left jowl, and the former president blushed six shades of red.

They were driving away from downtown Hell, and the traffic was light, because everyone was traveling in the opposite direction, toward the center of action. They were on the road to the destroyed Hellraiser Roadhouse, in the direction of the mighty penis that was now broaching the stratosphere. Mystery craned her neck to get a good look at that awe-inspiring member, when a kind of tottering, shambling shadow appeared on the shoulder of the road: clinging red miniskirt, platform shoes, cheap fishnet stockings, a halter-top bra, a feather boa slung around the shoulders and a florid hat with a lonely wilted rose affixed to it with a hatpin. She looked worse for the wear from the tornado, hair askew and a few more holes in her fishnets. Dazed, she staggered from side to side like a drunk. "Mother!" Mystery exclaimed, flinging a hand to her mouth. She shook Elvis by the shoulder and said, "Stop the damned car, it's Mother!"

"Here's your new First Lady, Mr. President," Elvis said.

He slowed the car to a stop, and Mystery pulled Holace in. She introduced her mother to President Nixon. Holace was flabbergasted. She kissed Nixon on the jowl and said, "Somehow, you were always able to encapsulate my rage, paranoia, resentments, fear of change and especially fear of black people. I can't thank you enough!"

Nixon mumbled something noncommittal, and Mystery waved at the air with her hand, saying, "Still, he could use some breath mints." Elvis turned on the radio, searching for rockabilly music. A party atmosphere began to take hold in the Hummer. But Nixon threw a damper on the party, saying, "Turn off that [Expletive deleted] noise. It's not even music!"

"What kind of music *do* you like, Mr. President?" Mystery wanted to know.

Nixon pondered for a few moments, and then, utterly lacking in wit of his own, he swiped a line from his old nemesis JFK, who had once been asked the same question. Nixon said, "I always thought that 'Hail to the Chief' was kind of catchy."

Back in the eighth neighborhood, before the ninth and last neighborhood where Mayor Aaronson was holed up with The Pood, Flo looked appraisingly at Bubb. His behavior both troubled and tantalized her. When he was done laughing he continued to wear a big, evil grin. The grin dominated his face between his slouch hat and his upturned collar, like the grin of The Joker in The Dark Knight about to say, "Why so *serious*?" It was a Glasgow grin.

"William," she inquired, plucking tentatively at his coat sleeve. "Are you quite all right, dear? Suddenly you seem uncharacteristically ... well, *rambunctious*."

"Never felt better!" He kicked off his cheap penny loafers. Then he swept Flo up in a passionate embrace and glided her majestically out across a field, past a few ramshackle farm houses and soulless fast-food joints, out into the very same parking lot of the Walmart in which Elvis had just commandeered a Hummer. With one graceful bound he flew aloft with Flo in his arms and they landed atop a car. Bubb's cloven hooves dented the roof downward. It was a Walmart Superstore, and the cars were slotted in the parking lot like stiffs in a morgue. Inside that fluorescent rat's maze, self-domesticated humans — farm animals in flip-flops — were stocking up on discount sacks of Cheeze Doodles and low-priced, poisonous plastic beeping junk made in sweatshops in China at jobs that America had been outsourcing overseas since the Reagan years, and they were attended by store clerks who were paid so little that they could not even afford the merchandise that Walmart sold. They could barely afford to eat. The clerks, pale, haunted, sunken-cheeked, hollow-eyed cadaverous automatons, all of whom had been indoctrinated since birth to vote Republican and worship Jesus, babbled incessantly: "How may I help you?" "How may I help you?" "How may I help you?" They wore T-shirts with the company slogan imprinted upon them: "Save Money, Live Better!"

"And after work, they'll all go home, watch TV and wait for tomorrow to start!" Bubb announced with an insidious, mocking laugh. He was talking about the staff and customers inside the store.

"What, dear? What are you talking about?"

"What am I *talking* about!" Bubb echoed, but not in the form of a question. He had literally swept Flo off her feet, and now he did it again. With one tremendous leaping bound, they landed light-toed atop the roof of the big box superstore wherein customers and staff alike were evidently the subject of a sinister scientific experiment conducted by unseen mad scientists in the evil laboratory of hypertrophic late-stage capitalism. They danced. Bubb led. They glided across the tar roof in a graceful waltz. Flo gasped. "I thought you couldn't dance!" Bubb briefly released Flo's hand, and then he swept the slouch hat off of his head and flung it devil-may-care toward the sky. It ran away on the wind. His horns and pointed ears now stood out sharply, unapologetically. They danced. Bubb sang. He sang to the tune of Frank Sinatra's "Come Fly With Me."

> *Come kill with me, let's kill let's kill away*
> *If you can use some missiles cruise*
> *There's a bomb, let's bomb away!*
> *Come kill with me, let's slay let's slay away!*
>
> *Come kill with me, let's drop bombs on Iraq*
> *In sandy land, there's a shady man*
> *And he'll run some guns to you*
> *Come kill with me, let's make the whole world blue!*
>
> *Once I get you up there,*
> *Where the air is putrefied*
> *We'll be snide*
> *Sullen eyed*
> *Once I get you up there*
> *I'll be holding you so near*
> *You may hear the angels sneer — just because we're together*
>
> *Evilwise it's such a gory day!*
> *Just say the words, and we'll rape those turds*
> *Down in Guant-a-namo Bay!*
> *It's perfect, for a bloody honeymoon — they say*
> *Come slay with me, let's slay let's slay away!*

They danced. They glided across the roof of the WalMart. Flo gasped. She looked up into Bubb's face. It blurred, like a TV transmission run amok, and then when it settled down again his face had become that of Frank Sinatra. Frank Sinatra was the heartthrob of her girlhood, and Flo had always romantically dreamed of teaching him how to bake a big batch of chocolate chip cookies and prepare a proper cheese sammich. Now she was dancing, dancing with Frank Sinatra! O! She felt more alive than she had in years; she was sixteen years old again! What Flo did not know was that at the very moment that Bubb had first guided her aloft, Sheriff Ted, in bawking chicken guise, had seen a sudden change come over Bubb, a change that had lasted for an infinitesimal period of time but had been real for all that. That change, so fleeting but so thorough, had made Ted's feathers stand on end. He had seen the change before, and he was trying to recall when. Then he had a flashback so vivid that it made him swoon:

His eyes crawled back to the rear-view mirror, and he saw the grand grin of the sadistic sergeant in the back seat. Then for a brief moment, so brief the interval was nearly incalculable, a flash of red light fell over that face and it changed into something different.

"Who the hell are you?" Sheriff Ted asked in a hollow, shattered voice.

"Who in hell do you think I am, Teddy boy?"

The sheriff was a chicken now, an avatar of his true self, his inner life exposed to the world as though under the penetrating gaze of a merciless metaphysical X-ray machine. He was so contemptible that even the Aflac ducks wanted nothing to do with him. Only old Flo Jellem, in death as in life, had shown him any kindness since they had re-emerged upstairs for the purpose of corralling The Pood. And now, he sensed distinctly, Flo was in danger — serious danger, even though she was dead.

He also now thought of Junior Holland, alone Downstairs.

You are the town's fucking sheriff, been so for fifteen years and you are a former Marine who saw action in Desert Storm. Act like one!

He had failed with The Pood.

He was determined not to fail with Bubb.

He moved.

~=__!
! !

"... Nixon created the Environmental Protection Agency, for instance. Did he get any credit for that? No, he didn't. Nixon created the Occupational Safety and Health Administration, to protect workers, but you don't see anyone giving credit where credit was due: to Nixon. It was Nixon who presided over the most significant desegregation of schools before or since, and it was Nixon who proposed a single-payer National Health Care plan that would have covered every man, woman and child in America. Does anyone recall that Nixon did those things, or is anyone *grateful* to him? No, they do not, and no, they are not."

"Imagine that," Holace Orr said with blank disinterest. She stifled a yawn, and struggled to keep her eyes open. Nixon had been lecturing her nonstop for half an hour at a roadside diner halfway to their destination, Detroit. They had stopped for a little R&R. The proprietor was too astonished by the chimera to refuse it service, and accommodations had been made. Two stools had been set side by side, and the chimera sprawled across it, one end the face of Elvis Presley and the other end the face of Richard Nixon. While Nixon lectured Holace at one end, Elvis was canoodling with Mystery Tart at the other. A big ceiling fan turned swiftly overhead. It partially dissipated the odor emitted by Elvis's bejowled, ski-slope-nosed posterior. The former president was perspiring heavily as he lectured Holace, who was his solace.

"Vietnam," Nixon growled. "Nixon ended the war in Vietnam with honor. Peace with honor! We won the war, but later we lost the peace. Nixon would never have allowed Saigon to fall, if Nixon hadn't been railroaded out of office."

Holace rooted around in her purse, and fished out a half-eaten roll of breath mints. The next time Nixon opened his "mouth" she popped three of them inside that disgusting maw.

~=__!
! !

Frank Sinatra took Flo Jellem for a final whirl around the roof, and then they took a break. The Voice had somehow procured a gin and tonic and a pack of unfiltered Pal Mal cigarettes. He wore a tailored gray suit, a black shirt and a white tie. He wore a narrow-brimmed gray felt hat with a broad white band at the base. He looked lean and hungry, young. He propped a foot on the ledge of the roof, took a deep drag on his smoke, sipped his gin and then stared out broodingly at the eighth neighborhood of Hell, with its eight cul-de-sacs where those who had defrauded the masses in various ways had reaped their financial rewards, and where they were now secularly ensconced in gated communities guarded by private security forces. The sky above was like a black, stationary hurricane, the spiral arms of it consisting of the airships of the United States Media Corps. Those spiral appendages converged on the eye, wherein resided the great Redsmear Dream Ship, directly above the home of Mayor Gil Aaronson. Moments earlier, Redsmear himself had given the order: "What-ho!" he had declared. "Drop anchor!" And the anchor had fallen from the ship and embedded itself with a sullen thump in the middle of Aaronson's front lawn.

Wringing her hands, Flo stole silently to Sinatra's side. She was confused, disoriented. Where was Bubb? Why was Frank Sinatra with her? She studied his profile, almost aquiline. It was like an ax against reality. That brooding, savage, lustful bad-boy look! It roiled her heart. She felt butterflies! Suddenly that profile turned and became his face, facing her. He tipped his hat back on his head, took another drag on his cigarette, and smirked. "Oh, sure, Flo," he said, in that mellow, unforgettable voice of his, a voice of leather and gin and endless cigarettes. Flo strongly disapproved of smoking, but she was prepared to make an exception in Sinatra's case. "I've had it all, in my life. So they say! But I've never *really* been happy. Know why?"

"No, dear. Why?"

"Oh, it's silly!"

"Tell me, dear. I really want to know."

Sinatra paused, his dark eyes fixed on some indefinable middle distance. Finally he confessed: "I never much cared about fame or fortune. What I've really wanted all my life, and never had, was a good woman to teach me how to bake a big batch of chocolate chip cookies and prepare a proper cheese sammich."

```
~=\__!
   !  !
```

They were coming.

Out of their homes, their cellars, their places of work and worship, out of their misery and their longing and their need. They were coming now, converging on the center of Hell. They were coming like an army of zombies arisen from their graves. They were big-eyed and ashen-faced. Their mouths were ajar. Their pulses pounded. Their hearts beat.

The five men with a single penis. Old Charlie from the boat landing, peering balefully out from under the battered fishing cap that shaded his flashing blue eyes. Buridan and the ass that he wore on his hand; yes the two antagonists who shared a split brain had actually arrived at a joint decision, a decision to come. Homer the Bard of Baked Goods, and his neighbor the Philosopher. Charlie McGarvey, the bartender at the obliterated Hellraisers Roadhouse, with his handlebar mustache and pomaded locks. Danny Spender and Bernard I. Maydit, one poor and the other rich, walked side by side, the lamb and the lion, their stations in life evened out by the events now building to a climax. Mr. Fury and Mr. Crabapple had come, too, though the two self-hating faggots bickered the whole way. With the help of a demolition crew, Mucho Hogg and his son Mucho Jr. had escaped their house, and for once they had left behind the information-processing devices that had made theirs a sham world, a puzzle palace of pixels. The Heretic was already here, of course, and he was smiling coolly behind his mirrored shades. Even Ayn Rand and President Cookie approached tentatively, the former with an air of furious skepticism, the latter looking for someone to surrender to. They were all coming, all the people of Hell, the entire population of the city approaching the center of it. In their hearts they knew, or at least hoped, that the events about to unfold would bring about a great change in their lives. In their innermost hearts every one of them yearned for an end to the quotidian, the predictable and the banal. And as they approached the center of Hell, a carnival atmosphere took hold, a celebratory spirit. But when they converged on Mayor Aaronson's house and saw the stationary hurricane in the sky, the spiral arms of the news media airships converging on Redsmear's mighty ark hovering above the Aaronson estate, they all stopped, and grew quiet, and waited. All was still, the calm before the storm. It was so quiet that the rush of blood could be heard in veins, the breathing of tens of thousands of souls and the throbbing of untold hearts. The sky became violet as the sun retired

West. Soon, the Great Show would begin. Everyone waited. No one said a word.

~=__!
    ! !

Falling, falling, falling.

Junior Holland was falling down.

At the end of the long fall he tumbled head over heels down a steep slope, and then landed in a heap on a bare floor with rocks, cinders and pebbles tumbling down around him. He rose to his feet, swatted the dirt off of him, and then he looked up at the Rec Room and saw what was there.

He slowly raised a hand, palm flat, a warding gesture. He moved his head from side to side. "No," he said. "No."

Then he screamed.

~=__!
    ! !

Falling, falling, falling.

Flo Jellem was falling.

I'm falling for you!

"Flo!"

A voice, above her.

They were dancing again, dancing!

Dance! Dance! Dance!

On the roof of the Walmart. Clenched in Flo's teeth was a long-stemmed red rose, presented to her by her beau. His arm was around her waist, and they froze in mid-dance. She angled her upper torso sharply backward until she was staring straight up into space, and then she unclasped the severe bun of her hair, which flew free. Then his face was looming over hers and as the sun guttered out he repeated her name: "Flo!"

She gasped. "What … what is it, dear?"

Nightfall.

"Will you marry me?"

END BOOK THREE

Book The Fourth

The Inner Station of the Ultimate Horror

*Doom am I, full-ripe, dealing death to the worlds, engaged in
devouring mankind.*

— Bhagavad-Gita

BllllAAAAAAAAARGHGGGGHHHH! Yap! Yap! Yap! Yap!

— The Pood

Two eyes opened.

They were orange.

*Media mogul's Web log, Blog date 4/25/12 (Comments
disabled). We are in geosynchronous orbit over the estate of Gil
Aaronson, the mayor of Hell, Michigan, who is holding hostage —
or is being held hostage by — an extremely dangerous poodle-
like entity that has come to be called "The Pood." All other news
organizations, the United States Media Corps, while having
surrounded the estate since early today, have failed to extract
either Aaronson or The Pood from the interior of the premises, and
thus have failed to get the story. But they are pussies. CNN? I eat
CNN's balls for hors d'oeuvre before a state dinner with the cunting
Queen of England! I am Tampon Redsmear! One of our reporters
has already beamed down on a preliminary reconnaissance of the
terrain, and we expect him to file a report shortly.*

The flashlight beam cut through the window of the back door,
which led to the kitchen. The Redsmear reporter, Clive Hackney,
a Brit whose specialized journalistic skills included cell phone

hacking, car hijacking and breaking and entering, peered through the window at the path illumined by the beam. He swept the beam along the floor on the other side of the window. A moment later the light bobbed and fell on what appeared to be a tatterdemalion shadow, as black as pitch. Embedded in that mess were the two luminous orange eyes that had just opened. The ragged, moth-eaten pennants of the ears now pricked. That shadow had been curled up on the floor, recumbent and resting. But now tufts of fur rose at the nape of the neck, and the shadow slowly stirred to its haunches.

"Visual contact made," Hackney whispered into his cell phone, in communication with his night editor aboard the great Ark of Redsmear, the Dream Ship that hovered overhead. Hackney had an advantage over the other reporters who continued to maintain a healthy distance from the Aaronson estate, forming a siege ring around it. He had the advantage of stealth. He had beamed down from the mother ship via a quantum teleportation transporter device that had been developed, at great expense from the deep pockets of Redsmear, by the Tampon Empire's Systems Administrator, Scott Thorson, also known as Scotty.

Redsmear had told Hackney: "Break into that Goddamned house if you have to, and get that damned poodle, or whatever the hell it is, into the range of the transporter beam. Then we will beam you and it up. It will be the story of the century; the pictures alone will be worth a fortune. Forget about Aaronson, he's just a footnote here. We want The Pood!"

"I don't know, Mr. Redsmear," Hackney had said. "By all accounts that dog is awful dangerous. You saw the video! He tore the ass off Anderson Cooper! You saw ..."

And that was when Redsmear had rifled a slap across Hackney's face.

"Are you a reporter, or are you a *fucking reporter?*" the maniacal mass media mogul had shouted, spittle spraying, into Hackney's freshly slapped face. Hackney had rubbed his chin and listened downcast while his boss raved at him: "Don't believe everything you see on the TV news or read in the Goddamned paper or on the Internet! We, here, we *make reality*, we *manufacture consent.* Absent some context — context that *we* fabricate — that dog is *nothing*, it's just a damned dog! It isn't even shit on Satan's asshole! How can a fucking 15-pound poodle harm a grown man? But when we are done with that thing, it will be a worldwide star.

And a motherlode of motherfucking money for us! Well, for me. Now go down there and grab the goddamned Pood!" So saying, Redsmear had then given Hackney a swift kick in the ass with his alligator-skin boot that had sent the scribe stumbling and staggering toward the transporter beam that Scotty the Systems Admin had readied for use.

Hackney was ready for his assignment. He was dressed like a cat burglar, complete with a stocking mask over his face, a length of rope wound around his shoulder and a leather satchel holding tools for breaking and entering. In addition he had in his pocket a plastic bag full of dog kibble to entice The Pood. Now he stood absolutely still, shining the flashlight through the back door window at The Pood on the kitchen floor. The Pood's eyes were fixed unflinchingly on Hackney, and they glowed like balls of fluorescent gas. Hackney did not move a muscle. Suddenly he felt weak in the loins, and his bladder loosened. The thin smoke of fear ran through his gut. The mouth of the black inkblot in the kitchen had slowly creaked open like a crypt door, showing *fangs*. In the pool of light made by the flashlight beam, Hackney saw saliva pat-pat-patting down onto the linoleum floor from the opened mouth, and he could not fail to notice that the floor was sizzling and melting where the drops fell. Hackney swallowed with difficulty, a great lump of fear moving slowly down his throat as the tongue of The Pood slithered out of its wide-open mouth like the forked tongue of a snake. The tongue was impossibly long. It kept coming out and coming out. It wandered sinuously across the floor, and crept along toward the door. Hackney could see that the *lusus naturae* was now on all fours, in a menacing crouch. He could also see the stainless-steel claws that had sprung out from the pads of the little feet, and the light also illumined two cast-iron testicles down below, from which protruded a corkscrewing penis that ended in the shape of a barbed fishing hook.

"Hackney? ... Hackney? ... *Hackney!*"

It was Redsmear, yelling into Hackney's cell phone. The reporter had fallen into a trance of terror, and his boss's snarling voice snapped him back to life.

"Y-yes, Mr. Redsmear?"

"Status report!"

Hackney relayed what he had reconnoitered.

"No sign of the mayor!" Redsmear said. "Excellent! Break in, grab that piece of shit dog and we'll have you back on board in no time. Scotty is in the transporter room; he's the best!"

"Mr. Redsmear, I don't think — "

A torrent of venomous verbal abuse came over the cell phone from the ship above. Hackney cut off the connection. His mouth was dust dry. He felt like he wanted to shit his pants. He was eyeball to eyeball with The Pood. He could hear, from the other side of the door, The Pood *breathing*. It sounded like a railroad train getting up to speed: *chuff! chuff! chuff!* Then he heard a *growl*. It was no ordinary dog growl. It sounded like the bowels of Hell moving, preparatory to an enormous, purgative supernatural shit.

Hackney closed his eyes and lectured himself: You must do this! You must! Are you a reporter, or are you a *fucking reporter*?

"I'm a *fucking reporter*," Hackney said aloud, and this self-encouragement eased his fear. He withdrew the flashlight beam from its target on the other side of the door, and shined it instead on the door's lock. He removed some tools from his leather case and jimmied the lock and pushed open the door just a crack. He bravely peered inside, his hand already going to the bag of kibble in his pocket. He pushed the door half open, and crouched on the kitchen floor. "Christ," he said, grimacing. "Smells like a rotting corpse in here." Fighting down his disgust at the odor, he again shined the light into the orange eyes of The Pood. The brute withdrew its tongue back into its mouth. It was *smiling*. It was a fang-bedecked grin, to be sure, but it was captivating. Hackney could also see, beyond the top of the head and the ears that fanned extravagantly outward like the ears of Mickey Mouse as they might look had they been ripped up in a blender, the nub tail. It was vibrating energetically from side to side, always a good sign in a dog, a sign of friendliness. Hackney smiled, and almost laughed. He turned the cell phone back on and told his night editor: "Goddamn little motherfucker is almost cute!"

"Here, boy," he said, producing some kibble. He left it on the floor in a trail, crouching and backing half out the door, enticing The Pood to follow. The Pood tottered forward, stainless-steel nails clicking on the floor. But it did not appear interested in the kibble. Hackney was still shining the flashlight at The Pood, and The Pood was peering into the light with its orange eyes. Its malefic black snout vibrated avidly, and it continued to produce *chuff-chuff-chuff* noises as it breathed. So *cute*, Hackney thought. He was a hard-bitten reporter but he had a soft spot for dogs. Sure, the thing was a mess, but nothing that a little soap, a little water, and some industrial-strength pruning shears couldn't clear up. And its smile, with its interlocking zigzag fangs, was adorable.

"Here, Pood, that's a nice boy." Still crouching, he backed farther out the door. The Pood tottered forward, eyes riveted on the light. It tilted its head from side to side in an inquiring way. It was still bigly grinning. Hackney said into his cell phone to his night editor: "Have Scotty ready the transporter. We're almost in range." Hackney smiled at The Pood. The Pood smiled back, tail wagging in ecstasy. "Why, you're just a little pushover!" Hackney said. Those were his last words.

"BIIIIIIARRRRRRRRRRRRGH! *Yap! Yap! Yap! Yap!*"

The Pood's mouth flew open like trap door, and a hurricane-force gust of fire *whooshed* out of it. In a millisecond it burned the cat burglar's mask off Hackney's head, and the flesh off his face. It burned the hair off his head, and the lids off his eyes. The reporter remained crouched in place, mute with shock, holding the flashlight and staring bug-eyed at The Pood. He was too stunned even to feel pain. The Pood pounced. It snatched the flashlight out of the reporter's hand, and swallowed it whole. The Pood then turned around and, squatting on all fours, presented its upturned, tan-colored buttocks to Hackney. The flashlight had already migrated through the demiurge's digestive tract, and now it worked its way out through the anus and the bulb appeared between the buttocks, shining out of the crack. The light fell on Hackney's melted face. The Pood grunted with exertion, and, accompanied by a loud POP, the flashlight was ejected whining from The Pood's anus with the velocity of a high-speed bullet. It struck Hackney between the eyes with a loud *whump*, and it burrowed through his brain, turning it into jelly. The lighted end crashed out through the back of his skull before the flashlight came to a stop. Hackney collapsed from his crouch onto his side. The flashlight remained inside his head, shining out of the back of it. Most of his brains and skull fragments were on the floor behind him, and a smear of blood stretched out the door and into the backyard.

About twenty minutes later, in the transporter room, Scotty the Systems Admin was standing over the corpse. Scotty had beamed Hackney back up after not hearing from him for an unacceptable length of time. He and a few Redsmear flunkies were becoming sick. Scotty turned away from the corpse, unable to look at it any longer. In his thick Scottish brogue he said shakily, "Someone get the cap'n."

Tampie Redsmear paced reflectively around the transporter room, hands folded behind his back, a riding crop dangling from one of them. He looked uncharacteristically thoughtful, even subdued. Finally he marched back and stood over the corpse of Clive Hackney. The flashlight still shined out from the back of the dead reporter's head.

"A man with a flashlight inside his head," the mass media mogul marveled. "That will make great copy, and great photos and video! We will put these images behind a firewall on the Goddamned Web and charge viewers to look at them. More money for me!" He then balled a fist, pumped it vigorously, and said with a grimace of ecstasy: "Yesssss! I R *winnah!*"

He then looked candidly at Scotty and the others and made an astonishing confession. "Look, we're all a bunch of motherfuckers here, feeding off human misery and selling schlock. We deserve to die, to die in agony, just like old Clive here died. But we won't die. We won't. I'll tell you what. This is personal, now. This is personal. We are going to get inside that house, and when we do," he added, voice rising in volume, "I am personally going to destroy that fire-breathing son of a bitch The Pood!" Redsmear slapped the riding crop that he held across the side of one of his alligator-skin boots, turned sharply and strode out of the transporter room, heels clicking in military fashion on the parquet floor.

~=___!
! !

<Flashback>

In the summer of 2004, a cocker spaniel frolicked in the tall grass down by Hell Creek.

Junior Holland, barefoot with his blue jeans rolled up almost to his knees, skimmed a stone across the surface of the creek, kicking up sprays. Watching over the water from his perch on a stool in the doorway of his bait-and-tackle shop was Charlie. His watery blue eyes flashed from under the shade made by the bill of his trademark battered fishing cap.

Junior skimmed another stone and it skipped over the water, throwing up more sprays. In the middle of admiring his handiwork the boy suddenly froze. Turning slowly, he observed, for the first time, Charlie, who seemed to be looking at the water — or else at *him.*

Charlie. His reputation preceded him. He functioned as a self-appointed guardian to the gates to Hell. He rented outboard-motor boats and from time to time, when the footbridge was washed out, he ferried tourists across the creek to the far shore of Hell. People were afraid of him — terrified, actually. Rumors swirled about his murky past, which included the sudden and never-explained disappearance of his wife many years earlier.

Bingo, still a puppy, rambled about awkwardly on paws disproportionately large compared with its legs. It lifted its leg and pissed in Hell Creek while Charlie watched.

Junior Holland was eight years old and Bingo was about the same age in dog years. Junior whistled and Bingo jerked up its head. But then it looked at Charlie.

Bingo took off like a shot and made a beeline for the owner of the bait-and-tackle shop. Nearby was the famous sign:

PLEASE
Do Not Litter Or Pee
In the River
It is going through Hell
Now

"Bingo!" Junior screamed, scrambling up the bank.

Bingo darted up to Charlie, who remained immobile on his stool. Bingo squatted before this gnome-like sentry and furiously wagged its whisk-broom tail.

Junior was out of breath by the time he reached the bait-and-tackle shop, a slapdash white clapboard affair drowsing in the August sun. It smelled faintly of gasoline, oil, fish and worms. Looking down, Junior noticed a weed that had sprouted out of a crack in the ground. He thought: *That is a flower from hell.* Glancing up, he saw Bingo's tail whisking from side to side.

And then the dog flew up and out of sight.

Looking up, Junior saw that Charlie was holding Bingo up by the scruff of its neck. The dog was whimpering and struggling to break free, its big paws thrashing about in the air.

"If you wants yer dog back," Charlie growled at Junior, "it

will cost ye one obolus."

Junior, backing away and eyes big with fear, was about to ask, *What's a oboe lust?* when Charlie added: "And you'll have to place it in the mouth of a dead man. Can ye do that, Junior? Can ye kill a man and place a coin in his mouth and bring 'im to me? Well, *can* ye? Speak up, boy!"

Junior said nothing. He quaking with terror.

"Junior. Junior Holland. I knows ye, boy. I knows every hellion who lives in Hell."

Charlie leaned down toward Junior and hissed through his crooked, rotting teeth, the whites of his eyes big: "Bring me one coin in the mouth of a dead man, Junior, or so help me God I'll kill ye dog."

Junior's knees knocked together. But then Charlie straightened, threw back his head and laughed. He turned Bingo around with his hands and seized it by the tail. With both hands he swung the dog above his head in ever-widening circles, the shadow of the revolution gyrating madly along the ground, and then he let go of Bingo. The dog was hurled howling in a long arc across the sky and it landed in a crumpled crouch in a stand of grass. Whimpering and arch-backed with terror, tail pointing straight down, it tore off in a blind run toward the highway shoulder and Junior took off in pursuit, screaming the dog's name.

I'm on the highway to Hell! Highway to Hell!

AD-DC, on the big rig's radio.

Once again, Terrence Hildebrandt was on the highway to Hell. Had been practically since he was born. Will be till he dies. On this very road he will die, eight years hence at the paws of The Pood.

The veteran long-haul truck driver by vocation and paranoid survivalist by avocation was pushing the big rig down the road at a steady 70 miles per hour. He was watchful, alert. Watching for threats. Watching for terrorists, for psychopaths, for Communists, for Muslims, watching for the *loonies in the boonies.*

No stop [redacted*]
Speed limit
Nobody's [redacted*] slow me down
Like a [redacted*]
[Redacted*] spin it
Nobody's gonna [redacted*] me 'round

[Redacted] Satan*
Paid my [Redacted]*
Playin' in a [Redacted]'band*
Hey [Redacted]*
[Redacted] at me*
I'm on my way to the [Redacted] Land, wooh*

I'm on the [Redacted] to hell Highway to hell*
I'm on the highway to hell [Redacted] to hell*

Mmm, don't [Redacted] me Eh, Eh, Eh*

In its terror Bingo clambered up the gravel of the road shoulder and darted heedlessly out onto the blacktop. Hildebrandt saw it dashing across the road. He leaned into his air horn. He was in equipoise between two basic primal responses, flight or fight: Step on the brake or hit the gas pedal. Like an egg improbably standing on its end, he would have to fall one way or the other.

And I'm goin' down, all the waa-ay-aay, wooh M-on the [Redacted] to hell*

He fell on "fight," not "flight."

Hildebrandt stamped on the gas pedal.

Junior had made it to the road shoulder. He froze as a gust of wind pushed forward by the barreling big rig hit him and made him stagger. He saw the truck coming. It roared past him at nearly a hundred miles per hour. Junior saw the left front bumper of the rig catch the rear haunches of the retreating Bingo, and he heard a loud, sickening *thump*.

</Flashback>

Junior Holland was looking down at the floor of Bubb's Rec Room.

Through a crack in the floorboards a weed had sprouted.

He thought: *That is a flower from hell.*

Then he saw a tail wagging and striking the floor with a regular beat.

---

* — Redacted lyrics are of course removed because of copyright infringement potential. And we really don't want that. But if you want to read them, just search on Google where they will monetize them with advertising for their own benefit. Enjoy!

"Bingo!" Junior gasped.

Bingo crouched and made ready to leap into Junior's outstretched arms, the arms of the master it had not seen in eight years. Suddenly the bleat of a big rig's air horn split the fetid and gloomy air of the Rec Room. Junior looked up and saw the truck rushing directly at him and its blazing headlights blinded him.

He screamed and threw himself to one side as Bingo leapt heedlessly toward Junior's now-absent outstretched arms.

The truck hit the dog in mid-air with a loud and sickening *thump*.

```
~=\__!
  !  !
```

Gil Aaronson woke with a start. He had drifted off to sleep on his couch, but a commotion from the kitchen, or his sleep apnea, or both, startled him awake. He labored for a few moments to catch his breath, and then he shambled into the kitchen, thinking as he did so: I sure hope all those media people and other riffraff outside have gone away.

In the kitchen he saw the door ajar, and some brains and skull fragments on the floor, along with a trail of blood that extended into the backyard. He heard the skittering of nails on the acidified, partly melted linoleum, and looking down he saw dear little Echo looking up at him with luminous orange eyes and a sheepish meat-cleaver grin.

"Oh, no, buddy, did you kill someone *again*?" Gil asked, trying not to sound judgmental. The cacodemon went into a defensive crouch, and placed its claw-ridden paws over its eyes. It then whimpered guiltily.

Gil turned on the kitchen light and pulled up a chair. Looking out the open door, he saw many lights looming, telling him that the USMC still surrounded his house.

He patted his lap for Echo to hop up and when it landed in Gil's lap, Gil howled. He gingerly plucked the tatterdemalion beastie off of him and saw little bloody chunks of flesh torn from his thighs and scraps of his pants attached to Echo's stainless-steel claws. "Pull those daggers in; won't that be OK, pal?" Gil pleaded, wincing in pain. Echo whimpered with regret, and immediately retracted its claws. Then it settled down into Gil's lap, curling up in a fetal position and making a sound like a car motor idling. Gil petted it, noticing that it had got all sticky again. "I sure hope you didn't kill anyone important, pal," the mayor sighed. "The Town Council might impeach me. I hate being mayor, but I need the money."

Gil decided he had better find out what was happening. He turned on his cell phone and as soon as he did, an incoming call hummed in like a bomb. "Hello?"

"Mr. Mayor! We've been trying to reach you for hours! This is Ollie."

"Ollie? Ollie who?"

"Ollie Upchuck!"

"Oh, yes, *that* Ollie," the mayor said in a bored tone of voice.

Ollie Upchuck was the mayor's top aide, his press spokesman and ostensibly his best friend. Gil hated Ollie and had long intended to fire him, but had never done so out of pure indifference.

"Mr. Mayor, what am I going to tell the news media? They're all over the place, like flies on shit! They've got you surrounded! They've been demanding to see you or the damned dog since midday, or at least receive an authorized statement from you through me! People want answers!"

"Answers to what, Ollie?"

"Answers to what!" Ollie was incredulous. "Gil, that damned dog of yours has killed or maimed at least a dozen people!"

Gil grew defensive.

"People are giving my little Echo a bad rap because they don't know him very well," he replied. "My dog would never kill people unless they deserved it or provoked him in some way." Gil scratched Echo's belly, made goo-goo noises at it and said, "Good boy, Echo." The beastie sighed with satisfaction.

"For Christ sake, Gil, the damned dog killed Flo Jellem! She was just about the most beloved person in town!"

"Jellem, Jellem," the mayor reflected. "Oh yes, that old battle ax. She gave me a 'D' in home ec back in junior high school." He snickered. "Well, I guess she got her comeuppance. What goes round comes round, I always say. Fuck Flo."

"Gil, *you are the mayor of this city*. The whole place is in an uproar; it's not just the news media out here, practically the whole town is surrounding your house, looking for answers! Not only that, but Tampon Redsmear himself is floating overhead in his great Mass Media Dream Ship. His anchor is in your front lawn! You're the center of world attention!"

"I hate the spotlight," the mayor complained.

"For fuck's sake, Gil, if you hate the spotlight, why did you run for mayor three times?"

"I thought the job would look good on my résumé, Ollie."

A sigh of exasperation came over the cell receiver. Then Ollie sent Gil streaming video of the scene outside. He panned over the huge crowd that had gathered around Gil's house.

"Tell those people to go home and leave me alone," the mayor said. "Their problem is that they all look to Big Government for a solution to their problems. They should be looking to themselves. It's like Nixon said in his Second Inaugural Address: 'Let each of us, in our own lives, ask, not what government will do for me, but what can I do for myself.' I miss Nixon. He was the greatest president of the 20th century."

"Gil!"

"It's true," the mayor snapped. "This nation was built by rugged individualists, not by people with cotton-candy testicles and candy-cane cocks. You can quote me on that; that could end up in the Bartlett Book of Quotations."

Ollie tried to press his case, but Gil cut him off. "Here's what you can tell the news media and the rest of that gang out there, Ollie. Tell them that if anyone tries to set foot on my property or breach the barriers of this house, I'll sic my darling little Echo on them. It won't be pretty. The dog is indestructible now and completely fearless. The only thing my best pal — my *only* pal — ever feared in life was that Aflac duck on T.V. and the Elvis impersonator who used to live next door, before that creep George moved in."

Ollie again tried to get a word in edgewise, but Gil said, "I'm putting Echo on the line. You can hear for yourself how fierce he is." The demon dog had dozed, but hearing its name its shabby ears pricked and it raised its head. Gil held the top of the cell phone between two fingers, so that the rest of the device was directly in front of The Pood's face. "Give Ollie a nice, nasty growl," Gil encouraged his dead pet. As with Clive the unfortunate reporter, the beastie's mouth flew open like a trap door and a gust of fire whooshed out of it, turning the phone into a dripping ribbon of molten metal. Gil let out surprised squawk, and then dropped the obliterated phone to the floor, shaking his singed fingers. "Turn down the burners, buddy, won't that be OK?" he said, and The Pood reined in its jets of fire and then settled back down in Gil's lap to resume a relaxing nap. Gil petted his pal and looked down enviously at it. "I wish I could sleep as peacefully as you do, buddy, and not have to be hooked up to that CPAP machine for sleepenstein rest all night. I wish people could understand how stressed out I am and leave me alone."

"The only thing my best pal — my only pal — ever feared in life was that Aflac duck on T.V. and the Elvis impersonator who used to live next door, before that creep George moved in."

Tampon Redsmear listened thoughtfully to these words on the bridge of his Dream Ship. Scotty, his Systems Admin, had hacked Aaronson's cell phone, and he and the media mogul, along with the others on the bridge, had eavesdropped on the conversation between Ollie and Gil.

Not only that: the ship's powerful cameras had been sweeping the whole city below, and now they locked on three ducks, each wearing the face of a philosopher. The funniest face of all was that of the Nietzsche Aflac duck, because its preposterous mustache was in fact a dead rat laid lengthwise across the top of the classical philologist's upper lip.

```
~=\__!
  !  !
```

The Elvis/Chimera and their groupies, Mystery Tart and Holace Orr, had stopped in a roadside café that specialized in cheap Mexican food: tacos, burritos, refried beans, chips and salsa. Nixon had declared it to be "spic food" and wanted nothing to do with it. "Spic food gives the president gas," Nixon confessed, adding, "Mexico is of no geo-strategic importance anyway. [Expletive deleted] Mexico." Hearing this, the busboy behind the counter got offended. His name was Jesús, and he was a Mexican stoner dude with long black hair that he kept tied back with a hairnet. He also constantly wore gloves, even when not handling food.

"Jesús, why do you always wear gloves?" the manager had asked him once.

"I don't know, mon," Jesús had replied in an apathetic marijuana haze. He had just got through toking up in the bathroom when the manager surprised him with his question. Jesús pronounced the word "man" as "mon" and called everyone "mon."

"Jesús," the manager had told him another time, "Your hands

and your feet stink! They stink all the time!"

"But how can they stink, mon?"

"I don't know, Jesús, but they do!"

Jesús had shrugged. "I don't see how they can stink, mon."

Now Jesús was busing a table and a customer spotted Elvis. It was an Elvis sighting. With her cell phone camera she took pictures of Elvis and sent the images and text to her five closest friends, and within minutes the news of Elvis was ricocheting around the Blogosphere. Now viral on the World Wide Web, the news of Elvis resurrected propagated virtually instantaneously to the Celebrity Sighting Room of the Redsmear Mass Media Dream Ship. Within fifteen minutes Scotty the Systems Admin had sent a remote cam hovercraft to the coordinates indicated by the original Elvis alert. Redsmear, Scotty, and other senior officers of the Dream Ship were on the bridge, inspecting a viewing screen that homed in on the face of Elvis Presley in the Mexican roadside café where he continued to canoodle with Mystery Tart while, from his other end, Richard Nixon lectured an increasingly disenchanted Holace Orr. The wilted flower pinned to Holace's hat had wilted even more under the olfactory rhetoric of the 37th president of the United States.

Scotty's transporter beam was still in development, a beta version, so it had to be narrow and focused to work. In point of fact the device was not a transporter at all, but rather an elaborate Bungee cord. However, because Redsmear thought Star Trek technology was cool and because he wanted a transporter beam, Scotty told his boss that the cord was a beam, and Redsmear believed him. Unfortunately, Scotty, clever as he was, could not yet supply broadband Bungee technology. And so Elvis and the Aflac ducks would have to be snatched the old-fashioned way: by Redsmear's elite Special Operations Forces using helicopters.

"When the president does it, that means it's not illegal," Nixon told Holace, who crunched morosely into a tortilla chip drenched in salsa and sighed. The *budda-budda-budda* sound of rapidly rotating propellers suddenly shook the roadside diner, and the high-intensity searchlights of the helicopters cast a wash of electric-blue light over the parking lot outside. A moment later a boot smashed through the front door, and the Tampon Redsmear Special Ops Forces burst inside, clad in camouflage and armed with deadly microphone booms that they pointed at the Elvis/Nixon chimera. The trained specialists in abduction seized the chimera and hustled it out the door, leaving behind a stunned Mystery Tart and a relieved Holace. "Go! Go! Go!" their commander bellowed, gesturing urgently at the helicopter hovering inches above the macadam of the parking lot, and they conveyed The King and The Crook toward it under the still-rotating blades, ducking at the backwash of air produced by them. A moment later they were in the helicopter and it clattered aloft and vanished into the evening sky. A very similar scene was playing out at the very same moment with respect to the three philosophers-cum-Aflac ducks, all of which were seized as they Aflaced and struggled with their captors amid clouds of feathers.

Back at the roadside diner, Jesús the busboy muttered, "That was far out, mon, I never seen anything like that." He then retreated to the men's room to toke a joint and check on his hands. Before lighting up he took off his gloves, and the stench hit him; he had denied that his hands stank, but it was embarrassing to admit the truth. They were both bandaged. He now partly unrolled the bandages and winced at the stench. As always, both hands, like his feet, remained unhealed, the holes in his palms and feet infected and swarming with maggots.

```
~=\___!
  !  !
```

The Three Temptations of Flo Jellem

"*Marry* you?" Flo gasped, weak-voiced; she remained reclined in the arms of her suitor, frozen in mid-dance, stretched out over the flat tar rooftop of the big-box superstore, looking up into the eyes of — of *who*? The rose given to her by Sinatra, which she had held between clenched teeth while they had glided light-toed and devil-may-care over this makeshift dance floor, had slipped from her lips and drifted down to the frozen tar of the roof. The sky was violet with evening, and it churned with stars and omens. The lights of the media airships blazed down at her like klieg lights in a star chamber. One of the high-intensity beams of the Redsmear Dream Ship backlighted the head of the elusive entity that now held her, creating a halo effect around its head but also plunging the entity's face into shadow. It had one hand around her bent waist, supporting her, while the other hand was interlocked with her own, their arms outstretched together.

"*Marry* you?" Flo repeated, her voice still weak. "But, William, I hardly *know* you!"

"Hardly *know* me! Flo, perish the thought! You know me as well as you know yourself! In fact, you *are* me, and I am you! Oh, don't you see, we were meant for each other! Yin and Yang! Mars and Venus! The great Janus face! The union of woman and beast!"

Bubb swept Flo aright, and took her hands in his own. Her mind was clouded. Dizzy. She experienced a troubling mingling of dread and exhilaration. She had not felt this way since — since when? Since she was a girl, and conducting a secret and salacious rendezvous behind the football stands of Chester Alan Arthur Junior High School with her first future husband, sixteen-year-old —

"Flo!" Bubb cried, cutting off her steamy reminiscences just as they were heating up. "You are The Power!"

"The Power, dear? What do you mean, 'The Power?'"

"The Power! You are The Power! You are what I have been looking for, for years, decades, centuries, eons — for eternity! You are the other piece of me, the Lost Half. You make me whole again, at one with Creation and at peace with it, ready again to fulfill my assigned role as the Great Minus Sign. It all clicked into place, like puzzle pieces snapping together, when I saw you smite Ayn Rand and kick her aides' asses at the dungeon. But even Downstairs, I had an inkling of it. Don't you recall how I offered you the job of a Night Hag, or a She Thing? You have what it takes!"

Flo shook her head in bewilderment, unable to understand. More troubling was that she was losing her bearings, her self-control. She swooned as Bubb seized her around the waist again and drew her near to the ardent bonfire of his heart. She feared losing her mind. The protean entity before her shape-shifted, malleable and hallucinatory: now Sinatra, now Bubb again, now something else entirely, something that gave off a red glow against which an ominous silhouette towered.

"I need you to complete me," Bubb said earnestly, a distinct note of pleading in his voice. "And then I can complete my mission."

"Which is?"

"I've told you: to reclaim The Pood, and dispose of Gil Aaronson."

"But —"

"And not only that! We are not going back Downstairs. The whole world — here, *this* world, the *real* world, is ours for the taking and yours for the asking!" Somehow the suzerain of sorrow had reclaimed the broad-brimmed fedora that he had tossed away before their dance began, and now he swept it out toward the horizon. "You and I will rule the world!" Bubb declared, and he let out a ringing laugh that carried with it the sounds of chains rattling, crypt doors creaking and the cries of the damned. Flo felt a chill pass through her; but, as with her long-ago encounter behind the football stands at Chester Alan Arthur Junior High, she also felt weak-kneed and avid with inchoate and uncontrollable desires, desires that she had never been able to name. It frightened her. The cook inside her mind was suddenly losing control; losing track of ingredients and misreading menus. She feared making a mess of dinner.

"I've never wanted to rule the world, dear," Flo said earnestly. "I only wanted to make the perfect pot roast."

Suddenly Bubb relinquished his grasp of her, and took a cloven step backward, hooves knocking on the hard tar, this black rooftop desert in which they were alone together. The tar began to heat, and gave off a ruddy glow. Bubb produced stones, and flung them at her feet. "You give me your power, and I give you mine," he told her. "Make of those stones Wonder Bread, which builds strong bones twelve different ways!"

"How?"

"Just say the word, and thy will, will be done!"

Flo tottered at the precipice of temptation, staring at the stones, but steeled her will. She refused.

Bubb took her to the edge of the roof, swept an arm at the twinkling lights below, and said: "Cast yourself down, and the minions of Hell will save you."

Flo resisted a second time. But her mind still reeled, and she did not know how much longer she could resist such entreaties. Even as Bubb was tempting her a second time, Ted the chicken, having managed to awkwardly scale a drain pipe, was hoisting himself onto the roof, wings flapping with the desperate urgency that the former sheriff felt.

Bubb took Flo to a high place, the priapic pinnacle of the planet, which was now the tip of the rising penis that had punched a hole in the clouds and was aiming for the celestial vagina, the omphalos of the Milky Way: the black hole at the center of it. He showed Flo all the kingdoms of the world in a moment of time. And Bubb sayeth unto her: "All this power I will give thee, and the glory of them; for that is delivered unto me; and to whomsoever I will, I give it. If thou therefore wilt marry me, all shall be thine." When Flo looked at Bubb again, she again saw the mellow grin of Frank Sinatra, those cool blue eyes limpid under the narrow brim of a gray felt hat with a white band around its base. It felt weird to hear Sinatra speaking in King James Bible English.

Flo thought it over. She imagined the whole world as her classroom, a captive audience learning, whether they wanted to or not, how to make a proper cheese sammich and how to prepare the perfect pot roast. She envisioned boxing the ears of the recalcitrant. She imagined gutting with a Ginsu knife a live guinea pig before a worldwide audience on the World Wide Web, the better to demonstrate the proper way to clean up blood to prevent staining. Her decision was a no-brainer.

"Okey-dokey, dear."

Junior Agonistes

Buzzards glided overhead in wide, lazy circles. One by one they alighted on a telephone line next to the highway, the flapping of their wings sounding, to Junior, like the laundry that Maw hung on a clothesline outback when it rippled and billowed in a high summer wind. ("We don't need no washer/drier from Walmart," Paw had lectured. "After the Fall, the Lawd meant us to work with our hands, to wring from the land our bread with the sweat of our brows.") So it often happened that while Paw relaxed in front of his PC and chatted with his pixel pals at the Rapture Ready message board, Maw slavishly hand-cleaned the Holland clothes over an old-fashioned washboard, and then hung 'em out to dry afterward on a clothesline in the backyard. Junior suddenly saw white bedsheets, his *own* bedsheets, rippling briskly from clothespins attached to the phone line, and when a strong wind caused them to gust upward like white banners of surrender, the buzzards bustled out from under them and alighted to the land.

Bingo's limpid brown eyes were already clustered with gangs of blue-bottle flies, and the eyes had been reduced to sockets in which the flies squirmed and buzzed. The buzzards strutted over like marionettes guided by invisible wires. They were garbed in their gowns of black and white, suggesting Satanic priests. Junior had fallen down, and now he scrabbled madly backward in the dirt while the buzzards pounced on the carrion that Junior's pet had become. The boy — somehow in the Rec Room Junior was eight years old again, though he retained all the memories and characteristics of sixteen — screamed. He shielded his eyes with his forearm to blot out the sight, and then scrambled on all fours up the slope of the road shoulder. Regaining his feet, he started sprinting across the macadam of the road top when from behind him he heard a piercing whine, followed by a howl of agony.

Do not look back.

"Lot's wife looked back at Sodom and Gomorrah in defiance of the angels' specific command, and — what do you know! Wham, bam, thank you ma'am! — She became a pillar of salt! Sure as shit, she did!" This was Paw during Sunday story-telling at the dinner hour, relating the tale with manic gesticulations and a big slap-happy grin on his face.

Do not look back, but Junior did. He did not turn into a pillar of salt. He wished that he had.

Bingo was following him, halfway across the road and enveloped by a blizzard of buzzards. One was riding its back and repeatedly rapping its osseous beak into the back of the dog's head. The others were flanking the cocker spaniel like ghoulish escorts, gnawing through the dog's sides, eating its intestines. The flies continued to infest the eye sockets; one eye had been obliterated, and the other hung from its socket on strings of exposed red nerve. The dog was on its belly now, dragging itself blindly forward with its front paws. Its hind legs and backside had been severed by the impact of the truck, and the dog's entrails languished behind on the road as it staggered forward, assailed by the buzzards. The dog's mouth fell open, blood spilling out over its limp tongue. It gave up its struggle to drag itself forward and lay exhausted in the middle of the road on the white divider lines. It screamed as the buzzards began tearing it to pieces. Although blind, it lifted its snout in a woebegone way, its vibrating nose catching its master's scent. "Junior," it said, its voice high and piping, "Why did you let me die? Me, your beloved Bingo who worshiped you? Why didn't you stop that truck? Why — " But the voice and Junior's scream were swallowed up by the bleat of an air horn, and now the big rig was again storming up the highway, pushing a wall of wind before it. Bingo's floppy, torn ears flew upward, and a moment later the truck barreled past, crushing the animate carcass under its churning wheels. Junior flung his forearm across his eyes to shield them from a spray of gravel, blood and doggie bits that the truck had thrown up. He fell back again on the road shoulder. When he removed his arm from his eyes, the truck had flown past, vanishing into a distant water mirage. Bingo had been reduced to a smear on the road.

"A bridge loan. I just need a bridge loan, mon."

Junior's head flew upward, and his eyes locked on the telephone wire above. It hummed with an eerie electric blue light, the voices riding on it made visible.

"So I can make next month's rent, mon."

"A bridge loan! A *bridge* loan! Holy fucking *shit*! You called me and woke me from my nap to tell me that you need a motherfucking *bridge loan?* What the *fuck?*"

"Please, mon, a bridge loan, just to make it to next month. Please, mon."

"I am not your 'mon'! I am your fucking *Father!*"

"Yes, yes, I am your son, your *son*; I need a bridge loan, mon!"

"I have no son!"

"Your *only* son, mon!"

"I have no goddamned son!"

Awestruck, Junior cautiously approached the telephone pole. A figure dressed all in white, with a white apron, was suspended on the pole, arms stretched outward from side to side and legs angling downward, where they crossed at the ankles. As Junior drew near he saw blood pattering down from the naked feet, and then he realized that the feet had been nailed to the telephone pole. Likewise the hands to the crossbeam. He forgot to be afraid. He just looked up in awe at the head that listed to one side, face a burnished brown, slick black hair tied back in a hairnet. The lips moved, and the man muttered: "A bridge loan ... a bridge loan ..." Then the man lifted his head with great effort and grimacing, screamed at the sky: "Marijuana! Give me some Mary Wanna, mon!" The crucified busboy struggled on the cross of the telephone pole, body twitching spasmodically as blood pattered from the pierced hands and feet. "Why has my dealer forsaken me?" the man crucified on the telephone pole demanded, and then said, "It is finished." His head fell to one side, eyes shut.

Junior's trance was broken by a pitiable howl from the highway. He slowly turned toward it. The ruins of Bingo once again rose. One eye, crushed to jelly, still dangled from a socket, swinging from side to side like a hypnotist's watch while Junior followed it with his eyes, mesmerized. "You let me down, Junior. Why? Why did you let me die like a dog on the road?" Then the air horn bleated anew.

Junior looked to his left and watched the truck speed up the road, getting bigger and bigger as its unknown driver accelerated. Junior made ready to dart onto the road and grab the ruins of Bingo. But the big rig suddenly slowed and then, burning rubber, screeched to a stop bare inches from the Bingo blot.

Junior took a quick step back as he heard the driver's side door on the other side of the truck open and shut. Looking under the truck, he saw a foot — no, it was not a foot, not a *human* foot — hit the ground. It was the large padded foot of an elephant. The other foot fell: it was an elephant that walked on two legs. The driver was ambling around the front of the truck.

When Junior saw the whole of the driver he screamed and fell back into the ditch. The two-legged elephant reared overhead, eclipsing the sun and casting a long shadow over Junior, who writhed in terror. The driver had the head of an elephant, the trunk and tusks, though the head was relatively small compared with the rest of its body. It had the arms of an ape, which were enormous; and like an ape's arms, they reached down almost to the ground. Trunk swinging and knuckles dragging, the elephant/ape raised one of its arms to its face and tore the elephant head off of it. Behind the head was a human skull with the face ripped off: two sockets, two nostril holes and double rows of teeth. The skull leered, and said: "Forever. I ride this road forever, this one stretch of road. That is what I do. I ride forever, and run over your dog. Forever." Then it put the elephant head back on and marched back around the truck. Before entering it bellowed through its trunk, and then from the ditch Junior heard the driver's side door of the truck cab slam shut again. Crawling up to the side of the road, he watched as the truck started up and rolled once again over the dog that had just righted itself. The truck roared off toward the dusty horizon, trailing a cloud of black exhaust fumes, the sound of the horn diminishing and then dying.

Junior clapped his hands over his ears and sprinted away from the road, back into a weedy vacant lot that abutted the back of the bait and tackle shop of Charlie, the watcher of the river. Running, he suddenly discovered that he was no longer touching land. His legs were still scissoring back and forth, but his feet were hitting air. Looking down, he could see their moving shadows, along with the shadow of someone much larger than he who was holding him aloft with both arms around his upper torso. Junior's body was still eight years old, though his mind remained sixteen.

"Hello, there, Junior," came a jovial voice. "Let me introduce myself. I'm your Pop — your *real* Pop!"

Junior twisted around in the man's arms to face the speaker. When he did, he grimaced at the stench of cheap booze. He was being held by a seedy-looking bum. The man was a runagate and a rake; a crap catcher and a clotpole, a dickhead, a deadbeat and murderer. He grinned, showing missing teeth; the teeth that remained were crooked and stained with nicotine. Unshaven stubble peppered his cheeks and chin, and his eyes were bloodshot from too many nights drinking, gambling and whoring. The man wore a straw boater that he tilted back on his head. He also wore a plastic flower in his coat lapel with a little string attached, which he tugged. Liquid shot out of it and struck Junior on the lips. Junior spat out the sour metallic brine. "Gin," the man said in a rakish, jocular tone of voice. "Ain't that a great practical joke, Junior? When I had my first taste of gin at your age, I was hooked for life. You will be, too." He then released the boy, who dropped to his feet and dashed away. The man called after him: "Your mother's a whore, Junior! Always has been! I'm your real Dad! You got my genes in you, and you'll grow up to be just like me!" He roared with drunken laughter. Then the fire appeared, the Talking Fire from Bubb's fireplace, and told Junior not to be afraid. The fire handed the boy a rock. Junior was sixteen years old again in body as well as mind. "If you wants yer dog back, it will cost ye one obolus." It was the voice of Charlie, though the Watcher of the River was nowhere in sight. *What's a oboe lust?* "And you'll have to place it in the mouth of a dead person. Can ye do that, Junior? Can ye kill a man and place a coin in his mouth and bring 'im to me? Well, *can* ye? Speak up, boy!" Junior threw the rock with all his farm-boy strength at the back of the head of his retreating father, at the straw boater. It hit with a thud and rebounded backward, falling to the ground. The man staggered forward and landed face first in the dirt, the hat pitched from his head. Junior ran up and stood over him. He retrieved the rock, crouched before the prone form and hammered the head again and again with the rock. He bashed in that head until his arm sang with pain. When he was done, he was covered with blood and brains. Junior flung the rock aside. Then he reached down, seized the man by the shoulders and turned him over on his back. The man looked up dead-eyed. Junior rummaged through the man's pockets, ransacking them. He held a small mound of change in his hands, in which he found a rutted and irregular silver coin that appeared to be great antiquity. On the front was the profile of a deity. On the obverse side was the embossment of some lurid owl and the word "ΟΒΟΛΟΣ." He tossed aside all the coins save for that one, which he pocketed. He then snatched up the ankles of the dead man and dragged him up a gentle incline toward the bait and tackle shop. Charlie waited for him in the shade of the doorway, perched on his stool like an owl on a limb. Junior lay the corpse before Charlie like a red carpet, opened its mouth and placed the coin upon its tongue. "That's good," The River Watcher said with a heavy, somber nod. "That's real good, Junior. You done good. You're one of us, now." He gazed out at the river, the reflected sunlight from it gliding across his steely blue gaze. Junior looked out at the river too, and saw the corpse of a woman floating downstream on its back, hands abducted in a crucifixion pose. Crucified upon the waters. In each eye was embedded a fishing hook. "My wife," Old Charlie whispered. "Kilt her some 35 years ago. Drowned her in these very waters. Weighed her down with fishing tackle to make her sink, but here she be again." Junior watched as the corpse drifted away, vanishing behind the tall grass on the near bank. The old man tipped back his fishing cap and said, "Let's go, then." They clambered down the bank and into a boat on the water, tied by a rope to a pole. On the far bank, Bingo barked in ecstasy. Old Charlie — that is, Charon, the Ferryman of Death — procured a fillet knife and hacked the rope and set the boat adrift. He poled he himself and Junior across the River Styx to the other side.

~=___!
! !

'At Dawn We Strike'

"Be seated."

Tampon (Tampie) Redsmear gazed out at the assembled reporters and editors.

"Men, this stuff that some sources sling around about

Redsmear wanting out of this Pood story, not wanting to fight for it, is a crock of bullshit. Our reporters love to fight for news, traditionally. All real reporters love the sting and clash of battle. First, you are here to sell papers and make money for me. Second, you are here for your own self respect, because you would not want to be anywhere else. Third, you are here because you are real reporters and all real reporters love to report."

Redsmear was dressed in a pith helmet, combat boots and a general's uniform. He bore his riding crop, and as he snapped off his sentences he occasionally smacked the whip against his boot, or on a nearby desk. All eyes were riveted on him, throats bobbing, mouths dry, palms moist.

Redsmear looked over the scribes. "You are not all going to miss deadline," he said gravely. "Only five percent of you right here today would miss deadline in a major news confrontation with The Pood," he added, apparently having pulled that figure out of his ass, "and specifically, only two percent of you would end up with a flashlight inside his head. Missing deadline must not be feared. Missing deadline, in time, comes to all reporters. Yes, every man is scared in his first reporting assignment. If he says he's not, he's a liar. Some men are cowards but they report the same as the brave men or they get the hell slammed out of them watching men report who are just as scared as they are. The real hero is the man who reports even though he is scared. Some men get over their fright in a minute under the fire of deadline. For some, it takes an hour. For some, it takes days. But a real reporter will never let his fear of missing deadline overpower his honor, his sense of duty to his soulless, non-union news media conglomerate, and his innate reporterhood. Reporting is the most magnificent competition in which a human being can indulge. It brings out all that is best and it removes all that is base. Reporters pride themselves on being He Men and they ARE He Men."

They all watched the maniacal mass media mogul perform, watched him strut and fret his hour upon the stage. That weathered septuagenarian; that crazed, hitching bitching beanstalk. That decorated and venerated veteran news whore. That martinet, that legend.

"... Alertness must be bred into every reporter. I don't give a fuck for a reporter who's not always on his toes. You men are veteran reporters or you wouldn't be here. You are ready for what's to come. A scribe must be alert at all times if he expects to snag the scoop. If you're not alert, sometime, that son-of-an-asshole The Pood is going to sneak up behind you and beat you to death with a sockful of its own shit!" The reporters roared in agreement.

Redsmear's grim expression did not change. He clutched the microphone tightly, his jaw outthrust, and he continued, "A news gathering organization is a team. It lives, sleeps, eats, and reports as a team. This individual heroic stuff is pure horse shit. The bilious bastards who write that kind of stuff for The New York Times don't know any more about real field reporting under deadline fire than they know about fucking!"

The reporters slapped their thighs and roared in delight.

"We have the finest Systems Admin in the world in Scotty, the finest equipment, the best spirit, the best software, the best cell phones, the best cell phone hackers, the best reporters in the world!" Redsmear bellowed. He lowered his head and shook it balefully. Suddenly he snapped erect, faced the men with his jaw thrust belligerently outward and thundered, "Why, by God, I actually pity that poor son of a bitch The Pood we're going up against. By God, I do." The men burst into sustained applause.

"My reporters don't surrender," Redsmear continued. "I don't want to hear of any reporter under my command being captured unless he has been bitten. Even if you are bit, you can still fight back. That's not just bullshit either. Clive Hackney took a flashlight to the head, but he fought for the story till the end. There was a real reporter!" Huge applause.

Redsmear paused and the crowd waited. He continued quietly, "All of the real heroes are not storybook reporters, either. Every single man in this newsroom plays a vital role. Don't ever let up. Don't ever think that your job is unimportant. Every man has a job to do and he must do it. Every man is a vital link in the great chain. What if every desk editor suddenly decided that he didn't like the whine of those bulletins coming into his computer's breaking news queue, turned yellow, and jumped headlong onto the floor of his cubicle warren? The cowardly bastard could say, 'Hell, they won't miss me, just one editor in thousands.' But, what if every editor or reporter thought that way? Where in the hell would we be now? What would our tabloid news chain, our cable networks and our beloved balance sheet and stock price, be like? No, Goddamnit, Tampon Redsmear's reporters and editors don't think like that. Every

David M and Scott Thorson

man does his job. Every man serves the whole. Every department, every unit, is important in the vast scheme of snagging this story."

He paused, took a deep breath and then continued: "Each man must not think only of himself, but also of his buddy fighting for the story beside him. We don't want yellow cowards in this newsroom, just yellow journalists. Cowards should be killed off like rats. If not, they will go home after this war and breed more cowards. The brave reporters and editors will breed more brave reporters and editors. Kill off the Goddamned cowards and we will have a news-gathering organization of brave reporters and editors."

The mass media mogul paused and stared challengingly over the silent mass of men. One could have heard a pin drop anywhere in that vast conference room on the Dream Ship. The only sound was the humming of computer fans cooling hard drives.

"Don't forget," Redsmear barked, "you men don't know that I'm here. No mention of that fact is to be made in any letters. The world is not supposed to know what in Hell happened to me. I'm not supposed to be commanding this Dream Ship. I'm supposed to be back in England, counting my money, shitting gold ingots, blackmailing the British Parliament into ignoring my violations of the law and chasing women one-fifth my age. I'm not supposed to be here in America. Let the first bastard to find out be the Goddamned Pood. Some day I want to see that devil dog rise up on its acid-piss-soaked hind legs and howl, 'Jesus Christ, it's the Goddamned army of reporters again under that son-of-a-fucking-bitch Redsmear!'"

The reporters and editors rose to their feet and roared their approval.

Redsmear said of The Pood: "We're going to rip out its Goddamned guts and use them to grease the balls of our computer mouses. You've got to spill its blood, or it will spill yours. Rip it up the belly with your pen. Stab it in the guts with your letter opener. Hit it over the head with your microphone. When The Pood is shitting flashlights or ripping off someone's face with its stainless-steel, dagger-like teeth, and you wipe the printer's ink off your face and realize that instead of printer's ink it's the blood and guts of what once was your best friend beside you, you'll know what to do!"

Redsmear continued: "We are going to twist The Pood's mammoth, cast-iron balls (attached to the corkscrewing penis that ends in the shape of a barbed fishing hook) and kick the living shit out of it all of the time! Our basic plan of operation is to advance and to keep on advancing regardless of whether we have to go over, under, or through The Pood. We are going to go through that dog like crap through a goose; like shit through a tin horn!"

"From time to time there will be some complaints that we are pushing our people too hard. I don't give a good Goddamn about such complaints. I believe in the old and sound rule that an ounce of sweat will save a gallon of printer's ink. The harder WE push, the quicker we get the story. I want you all to remember that."

The magnate paused. His eagle eyes, flashing out of his crushed tin can of a face, swept the conference hall. He said with pride: "There is one great thing that you men will all be able to say after this news-gathering assignment is over and you are home once again. You may be thankful that twenty years from now when you are sitting by the fireplace with your grandson on your knee and he asks you what you did in the great World War Pood, you WON'T have to cough, shift him to the other knee and say, 'Well, your Granddaddy shoveled shit in Louisiana.' No, Sir, you can look him straight in the eye and say, 'Son, your Granddaddy rode with the Great Mass Media Dream Ship and a Son-of-a-Goddamned-Bitch named Tampie Redsmear!'" As one the vast assemblage of editors and reporters sprang to its feet, whooping, hollering and cheering. Pens and microphones and cell phones were hurled into the air in wild celebration. As the cheering died down, Redsmear said: "Remember, men, at dawn we strike! That is all!" He turned and marched out of the room.

~=__!
! !

When Jesús returned to his rooming house after his shift at the roadhouse was over, he tore off the eviction notice taped to his door. He had not paid rent in four months, and now he had been given notice.

"Mon, I don't know, mon," he muttered to himself. "I need a bridge loan, or something."

Inside his squalid and lonely room was a battered black-and-white TV with rabbit-ear antennae, a hot plate, a small ice box, a transistor radio, and an iron bedstead with a grimy mattress covered by tangled sheets and a threadbare blanket. Adjoining the single room was a nook that contained a wash basin and a toilet that was currently backed up. When Jesús entered the room and flicked on the light, cockroaches scrambled for cover.

The busboy threw himself on the bed and rolled a doobie. Then he lighted it. He had not smoked pot in 45 minutes, and he really needed this. He inhaled sharply. The sweet pot odor partly suppressed the stench of his never-healed hands and feet.

The window looked out on the bland central Michigan flatlands, and the highway that led from Hell, Michigan, to Detroit. It was night, and sodium-vapor lights illuminated a bleak and nearly deserted parking lot. On the road the occasional car or truck rumbled past, headlights cutting through the gloom. They made lonely noises.

The busboy toked again. In his hand was the crumpled eviction notice. He smoothed it out and read it a second time and sighed. There was a knock at his door. The knock, the eviction notice and the pot conspired to make him feel paranoid. He curled in a defensive crouch on the bed but then he heard Daddy Long Legs say, "Hey, Jesús, mon, it's me, Daddy."

Jesús got off the bed and approached the door.

"Daddy?"

"Yeah, mon, it's Daddy."

"Daddy's not here."

"Mon, it's Daddy. Open the door. I think the cops may have followed me."

"Who is it?"

"It's Daddy."

"Daddy's not here."

"Jesus, Jesús, *I* am Daddy. Open the goddamned door, dude!"

"Who is it?"

"Daddy."

"Daddy? Daddy's not here."

Daddy Long Legs kicked in the door.

Daddy was sixty nine years old. He was called "Daddy" because he had had a passel of children, none of whom he had actually reared, and "Long Legs" because he had long legs. Although he was white, he wore long dreadlocks, dyed black, that fanned out around his head. He also wore a tight black T-shirt with the Grateful Dead logo imprinted upon the front of it and he had spider-web tattoos radiating outward from the bony elbows of his scrawny arms. He wore leather pants and boots, and a bone in his nose. He was, he liked to say, a "modern primitive." He now said, "You got any good stuff, mon?"

"Mon I got some good stuff."

"Far out, mon."

They smoked good stuff.

Jesús reclined on the bed and Daddy Long Legs sat cross-legged on the floor. In a pot haze he fumbled with the dial of the radio and found a classic rock station out of Detroit playing The Doors: Mr. Mojo Rising.

They got high to Mr. Mojo Rising.

"You got any money, Daddy?" Jesús asked without conviction.

"I ain't got no bread, mon."

"Well I ain't got no money neither, mon."

"Well, mon."

"Well, mon."

They toked in silence for a while. Then Jesús said: "Mon, I'm being evicted. I need a bridge loan."

"You ought to call your old mon, mon. He's loaded, ain't he mon?"

"Mon, I can't call him, mon. I'd be ashamed to call him, mon. Look at me, mon, I'm a busboy!"

"What's wrong with that, mon? Honest labor."

"Lillies of the field and all that," Jesús allowed apathetically. Jim Morrison sang narcissistically about his cock, Mr. Mojo, rising rising rising, just like the cock in Hell, Michigan, that had currently broached the exosphere.

They rolled more joints.

"Turn on the tube, mon," Jesús said.

Daddy Long Legs switched on the TV. A camera was panning the crowd in downtown Hell, Michigan. It showed, approaching the camera and parting the crowd like the prow of a boat parting waters, Bill Z. Bubb and Flo Jellem. They were headed toward Gil Aaronson's house. Bubb looked ten feet tall, and the crowd and the reporters were awed by him.

Jesús momentarily overcame his marijuana stupor. He sat up in bed and looked with his mouth open at the image on the screen.

"Oh *mon*," he said, "my old mon *knows* that dude! My old mon *hates* him!"

"What for?" Daddy Long Legs asked with disinterest. The 69-year-old adolescent toked on a fat joint.

"Mon, I dunno Mon. I don't remember, mon. It was so long ago." After a pause Jesús said reflectively, "My old mon hates everyone, mon."

"You oughta call your old mon and ask him for a bridge lone, Jesús."

"Mom and Dad live in Fresno now," Jesús said.

"There's a pay phone in the hall, mon."

"I can't afford a call to Fresno, mon."

"Call collect, mon."

"They never pick up, mon. Just the answering machine, mon."

"What you got to lose, mon?"

The two friends pooled their change.

They left the room and found the pay phone in the hall the reeked of urine and insecticide. Jesús deposited several dollars worth of change, dialed the old number and waited without hope. A recording came on the line.

"Your prayer is very important to us. Please wait for the next available seraph." Harp music followed, and then a little later: "Your prayer is very important to us. Please wait…"

"It's no use, mon," Jesús said wearily. He began to hang up but Daddy stayed his hand and said, "Talk into the phone, mon."

Jesús felt a cramp of fear. Talk into the phone. After all this time. Fortunately his marijuana stupor tranquilized his pride. "Mom, Dad?" he ventured timidly, inquiringly. "Are you there? It's me, Jesús. Your son. Your only son."

"Your prayer is very important to us. Please wait for the next available –" but then there was a click and an almost forgotten but still familiar voice said urgently: "Jesús! Jesús, is that really you?"

"It's me, mon. I mean, Mom. It's your son, Jesús."

There was a clatter and a commotion. A mingling of voices. "Father, father!" Jesús heard over line from across the continent in Fresno, California. Then a familiar, disheartening roar:

"What the blue shit! Holy fuck! I *have* no Goddamned son!"

~=__!
! !

At dawn they stuck.

The sun had just poked over the flat Michigan farmland. It

was fiery red, and the sky seemed to churn with blood. Hundreds of news-battle-hardened reporters descended in swarms upon the Aaronson estate. They fell upon it via parachutes, rope ladders, helicopters, vertical takeoff and landing vehicles and, of course transporter beam (bungee cord). They rapidly secured the exterior and perimeter of the compound, quickly and without opposition occupying the roof and sealing off all routs of ingress and egress.

The vast throng of the town's citizenry and the virtually paralyzed pussies of the United States News Media (USMC) that had surrounded the home of the mayor grew alert. They had expected fireworks at nightfall, and their hopes had waxed and waned as the night had worn on. Now, as dawn neared, thousands of them held candles in jars, a sign of hope. They had ceded de facto leadership of their cause, whatever it was, to Bill Z. Bubb, who now cut an impressive figure: He was nearly ten feet tall, and his horns, pointed ears and tail were all on proud display. "Who *are* you?" an awed reporter with CNN had asked The Dark One, when Bubb had strode with Flo at his side to the front of the crowd at the gates of the Aaronson compound. "I am that I am," Bubb had declared cryptically, and so impressive was he now in manner and bearing, and so enigmatic were his words, that the Hellions had invested all their inchoate hopes in him, the way that they had once invested those same hopes in Gil Aaronson — or else in President Cookie, or Oprah Winfrey, or Deepak Chopra, or Jim Jones at Jonestown, or in anyone but they themselves; in anyone with a flair for peddling a line of bullshit in a convincing way.

Bubb himself had decided to wait: in fact, to strike at dawn. Having been rejuvenated by his betrothal to Flo Jellem, he had rediscovered his flair for the dramatic, and he wanted to be bathed in the scarlet, fiery light of the dawn sun. The crowd gasped as the first rays struck his face, lighting it red and sharply etching shadows over that granitic and aquiline profile. Bubb surveyed the churning red sky of morning and, echoing Hitler on the eve of World War II, said somberly: "It won't come off without bloodshed this time." And as soon as he spoke those words, Redsmear's legions struck.

The sound of glass breaking, and the Wham! Boom! Thump! of explosions.

Then:

"Yap! Yap! Yap! Yap! BIllllAAAAAAARGHHH!"

~=___!
! !

Redsmear had contemptuously dismissed one of the first reporters to broach the Aaronson compound as a "canary in a coal mine," and he had ordered Scotty to tether the man by a rope to his ankle. The reporter had descended via rope ladder from the Ship of Dreams down through the chimney of the Aaronson compound, and Scotty, Redsmear and others in the transporter room watched the rope pay out as the man descended. There was a moment of silence, and then the battle began. Sounds of explosions, flashing lights from below. Shock and awe. Redsmear's eyes were afire. He felt like a goat in rut, young again. His eyes followed the rope as it paid out, paid out. Then, suddenly, it whipsawed across the floor and stiffened. It became taut to the breaking point, fraying in the middle. From below came a nightmarish scream that was abruptly cut off, and then the rope went slack. Scotty stared at it with premonitory horror. Redsmear's eyes betrayed no emotion, except perhaps for a glint of curiosity tinctured with admiration for his dogged doggy adversary. He bent down and grasped the rope, testing its weight.

"Reel 'im in, boys," the magnate gravely told his flunkies. Reluctantly, they paid up the rope. They all waited as the rope rose, hands clutching it one after another, dragging it up, up, through the chute in the floor through which the sacrificial reporter had bravely descended.

Up, up.

A shoe appeared at the entrance to the chute, and then the ankle around which the rope had been tied. And then the lower legs. Up, up, more slowly now. The body was motionless, and unresponsive to inquiries. But they could already see that the pants were drenched in blood. Scotty silently cursed. He closed his eyes, and then opened them again.

Up it rose, slowly, excruciatingly. The torso. The upper chest. The once-knotted tie, now undone and askew. The neck. A shudder of revulsion tore through the room. People cried out in horror.

Scotty took a quick step back, eyes wide and terrified. He clutched a hand to his churning stomach. The other men began to get sick, too. Only Redsmear was unaffected.

The reporter had been beheaded — almost. His head dangled from his body, attached to it by a single frayed and mangled cord of neck. All else of the neck had been torn away. The mouth was ajar, the tongue hanging out of the side of it. Blood still pattered from the open mouth. The eyes had rolled up in their sockets, showing only the whites.

"Throw it on the floor, boys," Redsmear snapped, and the men, only too glad to oblige, heaved the body and the rope away from them and turned from the scene, retching and clapping hands to their mouths. In his general's uniform, Redsmear towered over the corpse with the detached head, and prodded it with his riding crop. The blood seeped out of the mouth and pooled on the floor.

"We will show this body on Faux News and ratings will go through the roof," Redsmear announced. "Clive Hackney was just an advance scout. This man was the first warrior reporter to fall in battle against The Pood in the invasion proper. We will make him famous, whoever he was." Numbers popped up and down in the cash registers of the mogul's eyes. He balled a fist, gave it a quick little shake and, mindful of the gravity of the situation and thus the need for some residual decorum, spoke in hushed, faux respectful tones when he gloated: "Yessssss! I R winnah!"

Scotty stared at his boss with revulsion. Above the roar of explosions, breaking glass and screaming reporters that drifted up to the ship from the bedlam chamber below, he demanded: "Cap'n, for God's sake, don't you even know this man's name?"

Redsmear turned to face Scotty, and wore a quizzical frown as he scrutinized his Systems Admin. "Name? Name? Oh, yes, we'll need to know his name, won't we, so as to take him off the payroll. We certainly wouldn't want to send paychecks to a dead man, would we? His widow might get hold of them and cash them. That would hurt our bottom line. Good thinking, Scotty. That's why you're the best." Scotty gaped at his boss, too astounded to reply. But a single word now flashed through his mind: *sociopath*.

~=__!
　!　!

Dudley Dresden had seen it all.

A veteran foreign correspondent for the Redsmear Media Empire, he had covered foreign wars since Desert Storm. He had seen men die in the sands of Kuwait and, although he did not know the man's name, he had seen an American Marine cut and run under fire outside Kuwait City. That man was the future Sheriff Ted. He had seen death up close and personal in scores of faraway places girdling half the globe from Baghdad to Kandahar. He had seen men hacked and beheaded, men shot and men blown to bits in suicide car bomb attacks. He had seen deserts and he had seen mountains. He had seen fire, and he had seen rain. He thought that he had seen it all. Now he was seeing something that he had never seen before. The war correspondent had hit The Pood over the head with his microphone in an effort to stun it into submission. An expression had come over the cacodemon's face then, an expression that, to Dudley, suggested the words: "Why do I have to deal with this bullshit? Well, OK, TIME TO DIE!"

And now he was seeing the living room of the Aaronson estate turning in wide, mad, gyrating circles before his uncomprehending eyes. At first he did not understand, having never seen this before. He fancied himself stationary, gliding weightless in the air, the room spinning around him faster, faster. Only a moment later did he grasp that it was not the room spinning around him, but rather it was he who was spinning around the room, rotating in ever-more-rapid circles around a center of mass that was located in the mouth of The Pood. Said mouth was fastened firmly around Dudley Dresden's ankle, and the cacodemon's dagger teeth had sunk deeply into Dudley's flesh, severing the Achilles tendon. The Pood was capering about on its hind legs in circles on the floor, spinning Dudley through the air. Shockwaves of pain from his ruptured ankle now registered in the reporter's mind, and he screamed as the world raced past him in a blur, round and round and round, faster faster faster. Then The Pood, turning and turning like a minuscule discus thrower, opened its mouth and released its grip on Dudley's ankle. For Dudley, the room stopped spinning. Instead, the front window of the living room came at him with harrowing velocity. A moment later the glass exploded. Dudley had gone through it face first, screaming the air out of his lungs, a thousand teeth of glass embedded in his flesh. He shot like a bleeding human missile across the front yard and hit a tree with the top of his head, producing a sickening WHOMP sound. His head instantly pancaked, and his spine snapped like kindling. He collapsed around the tree, his eyes now inside of his nostrils. Bug-eyed and motionless, the dead eyes staring out of his nostrils, Dudley Dresden nevertheless resolutely clung to his microphone with one hand and to his notepad with the other, a brave reporter to the last.

Scotty had dispatched a hovercam to take video of the carnage below. He, Redsmear, and some flunkies were now viewing the battle on a screen in the transporter room.

Arms and legs flew through the air, only some of them still attached to bodies. Blood flowed down from the walls of the living room like red paint. Reporters scrambled about in frantic retreat, throwing aside their weapons: microphones and microphone booms, digital cameras and recording devices, cell phones, pads and pens, letter openers. Everyone was screaming. At the center of the bedlam The Pood crouched like a wild smear of charcoal, its tatterdemalion ears flying up and down like disreputable pompoms and its orange eyes pulsating with fury. Its claws skittered on the hardwood floor as it bounced about, its great maw wide open and its endless toxic tongue extending outward like a snake bidden from its basket by the charms of a flute. A hurricane of fire swept out of that ghastly putrescent hole, setting the afire the hair of five reporters, and when another reporter scrambled up a bookcase in an effort to escape certain death, The Pood turned on him, crouched as though preparing to relieve itself, and then sprang aloft. It slammed down its jaws on the crotch of the interloper, jigged its head from side to side while making persistent girring noses, and then it pushed itself backward, off of its victim. It landed on all fours in the center of the living room, an unidentifiable ruin sticking out of the sides of its mouth like exploded cigars. It opened its mouth, and the bloody mess fell to the floor. It peered down at it, its smile a charismatic zigzag of interlocking meat cleavers and the nub of its tail vibrating ecstatically from side to side. The reporter lay in a fetal heap on the floor, arms extended downward between his legs, his face a howling rictus of agony and despair and the floor beneath him stained an ever-deepening red. The Pood nonchalantly raised a hind leg and scratched its left ear, nearly tearing it off its head. Then it settled down before the genitalia. It licked at the balls inquiringly with its sandpaper tongue, and then sniffed them and pawed at them playfully. After a while it evidently grew bored and sharpened its claws with a fourteen-inch coarse-steel knife sharpener that it had found in a kitchen drawer. After sharpening its claws, it lapped up the genitalia and swallowed them whole. The few remaining ambulatory reporters had fled, the first assault a horrifying flop. They were in a full retreat, clamoring to return to the Ship of Dreams — or *Ship of*

Fools, as Scotty now thought bitterly.

The Systems Admin had turned in revulsion from the pornography of death unfolding onscreen. He turned to face Redsmear, who was viewing the screen unflinchingly if somewhat pensively. "Cap'n!" Scotty cried. "For God's sake, man, call if off! It's a slaughter!"

The mogul stiffened, and then lashed the riding crop across the leather of one of his combat boots. He said dryly: "This was the assignment of their lives. This — this was their D-Day, this was their moon landing, this was their ultimate test. And they failed. Well, Scotty, it's as I said in my speech. Kill off the cowards, and only the brave will be left. Then the brave will breed more brave men and we will have a newsroom of brave reporters and editors."

Scotty was dumbfounded.

Redsmear said, "Let's roll out the secret weapons: That awful Elvis/Nixon thing, and those crazy Goddamned ducks." Scotty wanted to scream at his boss: *Why didn't you use the secret weapons in the first place and spare all these innocent lives, you insane fuck?* That was what he *wanted* to say, but he didn't. And he hated himself for not saying it.

He made a mental note to update his résumé.

$$\sim = \backslash \_\_ \ !$$
$$!\ \ !$$

"Hang up the Medamned phone! No, wait! *Don't* hang up the Medamned phone! Give *me* the Medamned phone!"

Mother reluctantly handed the phone to Father.

"Is this my son?" he roared into it. "I *have* no son!"

"It's me, mon, Jesús. Your son."

"I have no son!"

"Your *only* son."

"I *have* no son!"

"Look, mon, I know I haven't written or called in a long time, but shit happens, mon. Mon, I need a bridge loan."

"What? Holy shit! A bridge loan? You need a motherfucking *bridge loan*? Satan's cock in Mary's cunt, you woke me from my nap to call and ask me for a *bridge loan*?"

"Just a bridge to next month mon, to make ends meet. Mon, I'm being evicted!"

"Evicted? You're being *evicted*? The blue shit you say!" Jesús heard Father say to Mother, "The little shit is being evicted! What kind of son did you raise?"

"Father, give me the phone," Mother pleaded. Then Jesús heard Mother on the line: "Jesús, this is Mother. It's been so long!"

"I know, mon. I mean, Mom. I'm sorry. I should have called or written."

"You should have called or written!"

"I know, mon."

"Are you happy? That's all that matters, Jesús. Whether you're happy or not. Tell your mother whether you're happy or not."

"I'm happy, mon."

"Are you eating well?"

"I'm eating well, mon."

"What's the weather like out there? Is the weather nice out there?"

"The weather is nice, mon."

"How are your hands and feet?"

"They're fine," Jesús lied.

There was a moment of silence, and then a stifled sob from Fresno. Mother wiped a tear from her eye and pleaded: "Are you *happy*, Jesús? That's what matters. Tell your mother whether you're happy or not!"

"I'm happy, mon! I just *told* you I was happy!"

From the background, gruff jeering and roaring: "Happy! He's being evicted! Ask Mr. Crown of Thorns why in blue fuck he's being evicted!"

"Is that true, Jesús? Are you in some kind of trouble?"

"I just need a loan, mon, a little something to tide me over till next month. Mon, the economy, it ain't so good. Times are tough."

Jesús heard mother turn from the phone and say, "He just needs a loan, Father. Times are tough."

"Times are tough! Times are tough! Goat-rutting, sheep-shagging shit! What kind of son did you raise? Is he a man or a fig tree?"

"He's *your* son, too!"

"He's no son of mine! Ask him what he's doing for a living."

Mother asked Jesús what he was doing for a living, and Jesús confessed that he was a bus boy at a Mexican food shack about halfway on the road between Detroit and Hell.

This information was dutifully relayed to Father, who could be heard roaring in the background. "A busboy. He's a busboy! Well, fuck my eyes with Satan's thighs! He used to be a *carpenter*. Even that was pretty embarrassing, but at least it paid well, especially at union scale. Give me that phone ... no, wait, keep the phone ... no, wait, give me the phone!"

Father came back on the line and roared, "A busboy! You're working as a busboy!"

Daddy Long Legs, who had been involuntarily listening in on the conversation, with Father's roars being audible all the way down the hall of the rooming house, said, "Honest labor, mon. Tell him it's honest labor."

"It's honest labor," Jesús told Father. "Lillies of the field, and all that."

"Don't give me this 'lillies of the field' bullshit! You're a grown man! Isn't it about time you acted your age? A *busboy*! That's a job for a sixteen-year old pot head, or for a Medamned Wetback!"

"Mon, I *am* a wetback!" Jesús omitted to mention that he was also a pot head, not wishing to exercise Father any further.

"We are *not* Mexicans!" Father bellowed.

"All men are supposed to be equal in your sight, mon, I don't know what you got against Mexicans all of a sudden."

"We are NOT fucking Mexicans!"

"Whatever you say, mon," Jesús replied wearily. Though normally a laid-back stoner dude, he suddenly felt a hot flash of resentment. "You just know it all, don't you, mon? Mr. Know-It-All! You must think you're omniscient or something, mon."

"Don't you dare fucking back-talk me, you — you *busboy*! I have no son!" Father rent his garments. Then he barked into the phone: "You were supposed to carry on in my footsteps. 'An eye for an eye,' I said, and what the fuck did you say? 'Turn the other goddamned cheek!'"

"Mon..."

"Turn the other cheek! Be like little children! Go all squishy soft! Yada yada! 'My God, my God, why hast thou forsaken me?'" Father mocked. "Why the fuck do you *think* I forsook you?"

"A bridge loan, mon..."

"A bridge loan! And look at you now! You're a thirty-something failure busing tables in a restaurant like some greaseball weedhead!" There was an uncomfortable silence then from both

Jesús and Mother. Father looked perplexedly at mother and then peered down at the phone. "What the fuck?" he demanded. "What the fuck IS this thing? These things aren't supposed to be invented until ..." he knitted his shaggy brows and swept a hand through his great white beard as he cogitated. Then he glared at Mother. "Mother! How long have I been sleeping?"

"Well," Mother assayed. She wrung her hands and looked nervous. "Well ... Jesús is a little older than thirty-something, now. Put it that way."

"How *long*, Mother? Tell me the truth!"

"Now, Father, you *know* you hate being wakened from a nap. You get grumpy!"

Father looked down in astonishment at the phone. "These things," he commenced, a note of awe in his voice, "aren't supposed to be invented until the late nineteenth century, and then only in a rudimentary form ..." Looking up, he sternly eyed Mother and demanded again: "How long, Mary? *How long have I been asleep?*"

"Now, Father, try to remain calm."

"*How long, Medamn it?*"

"Now remember, Father, in your eyes, a thousand years is but a day."

"And?"

"Well, in that case, I guess we can say that you've been napping for about two days."

~=__!
! !

Mayor Gil Aaronson was having a relaxing dream about Mystery Tart, the whore at Ayn Rand's dungeon whom he sometimes visited for a little extracurricular activity. The dream broke up amid the sounds of breaking glass, screams, growls and yaps.

Losing his erection, Gil let go of his cock and shot up into a sitting position in bed. He tore the CPAP mask off his face. He crawled out of bed, put on his bathrobe and slippers and hurried toward the living room. He got there just as The Pood was swallowing the genitalia of the mutilated reporter, who remained writhing on the floor with his hands between his legs, screaming.

Gil saw body parts and blood, and then he saw his dear little Echo, who turned and faced Gil. Echo stood up on its hind legs, tail vibrating madly. It let out a few joyous yaps and made ready to leap into Gil's outstretched arms. "Nails!" Gil reminded his little buddy, and Echo sheepishly retracted them. Then it jumped into Gil's arms. Gil cradled his dear little dead pet and with a long, slow sigh, sat down on the sofa with The Pood, who repeatedly licked Gil's face with its sandpapery tongue. "What are we going to do, buddy? This is a mess! How will I ever explain this situation to the Town Council? You know what they're like. With that gang it's 'accountability this' and 'accountability that.' They're like high school hall monitors. You know how much I hated high school, Echo." He scratched his pal under the neck, which Echo had always loved. His pet poodle-cum-cacodemon now responded with vigorous *chuff-chuff-chuff* noises of ecstasy while squirming playfully and vitally in Gil's lap. The mayor was weighing his options. He pondered never leaving the house again, but then realized that sooner or later he would have to shop for food. It dawned on him that the United States Media Corps had prudently decided to wait him out on that very theory. He had no idea who these people, and people parts, now in his house were. Somehow they didn't seem like Americans. He asked the emasculated reporter who was writhing around on his floor who he was, and the man responded with a blood-curdling scream of agony. "Hmm," Gil mused, assessing the foreign accent of the scream. "Sounds British."

~=__!
! !

Bubb, Flo, and the others had witnessed the brief but spectacular attack, followed by the disorderly, panicky retreat. Bubb looked up at the Ship of Dreams hovering magically overhead, sustained by galley slaves and by giant sails made of newsprint and featuring images of scantily clad Page Three Girls. His beak-like nose worked, nostrils sniffing avidly. "Tampon Redsmear!" he announced, an evil grin cracking his face. "By Godless, it's that old son of a whore Tampie Redsmear! I can actually *smell* the bastard!"

"Smell him?" Flo asked worriedly, clinging to her beau. "What does he smell like, dear?"

"Like cheese gone bad, Flo." Bubb patted Flo's hand. "Like cheese gone bad."

"Oh, my!"

"That bastard is after The Pood, but he'll never get him," Bubb said confidently. He watched the Redsmear army in full retreat, and said, "By Godless, I'm actually *proud* of The Pood, even if it is just a beta version, and even if it did escape before I was ready to turn it loose on Aaronson."

"William, when we started on this mission you said you were *afraid* of The Pood."

"Pah!" The Dweller in Outer Darkness scoffed. "That was *then*. I'm a new Fallen Entity now. I've regained my confidence, thanks to you, Flo. Now one whistle from me and that rambunctious little ragamuffin will hop into my coat pocket just as pretty as you please."

"But when we started, you said that we needed Elvis — "

"To Hell with Elvis!"

"And the Alfac ducks, because — "

"To Hell with the ducks, too! I've never needed *anybody*. Never needed anybody except ..." He turned to Flo, and embraced her insubstantial, mirage-like form. "... except you, Flo." He drew her to the bonfire of his heart, and his lips covered her own. The chicken avatar of the deceased Sheriff Ted watched from afar.

```
~=\__!
  !  !
```

While Gil was petting The Pood and pondering his options, a round, metallic vessel with porthole windows, a vessel resembling a bathysphere, crashed through the ceiling of Gil's estate and slammed down on the floor not ten feet from Gil and The Pood. Doors whisked open, and down a ramp brusquely strode Tampon Redsmear, in his crisp general's uniform and spit-shine boots. He brandished his riding crop, and then thrashed it against the side of a boot. Gil looked up at him open-mouthed. The Pood twisted around in Gil's lap, and rose up on all fours. The daggers of its retractable claws shot out, freshly sharpened and at the ready. "Yap! Yap! Yap! Yap!" The Pood explained, and just as it was about to BIIIIIARRRRRRRRGH a wall of fire at the maniacal mass media mogul, down the ramp flanking him were flunkies. One flunky held a chain to which the three Aflac philosopher/ducks were fastened like prisoners in a chain gang. Another flunky was pointing a microphone boom into the back of Elvis/Nixon. He now jabbed the boom into the small of the back of the chimera and commanded, "Play, or so help me God I'll shoot out a quick Twitter tweet all about how Elvis, though he has returned from the dead, has Nixon growing out of his ass! What do you think that will do for your reputation, hmm?"

"Anything but that," The Pelvis pleaded. He plucked his guitar strings and serenaded The Pood with a rousing rendition of "You ain't nothin' but a hound dog."

The other flunky rattled the chain, and the captive duck philosophers broke out in an off-key chorus of "Aflac! Aflac! Aflac!"

The Pood's ragged ears flew straight up. Still in Gil's lap, it leapt up on its hind legs and its orange eyes bugged zanily out of its head. It threw its front paws into the air. Gil howled in agony as the stainless steel claws yet again sank into his thigh flesh. "They said you was high class, but that was just a lie," Elvis wailed at The Pood. "They said you was high class, but that was just a lie. You never caught a rabbit and you ain't no friend of mine!" The Aflacing of the imprisoned ducks provided an urgent counterpoint to The Pelvis's accusatory lyrics.

The Pood sprang off Gil's lap and hit the floor running. "Get him!" Redsmear bellowed, and the chimera and the flunky with the chain of ducks ran after the retreating cacodemon. As Gil struggled to his feet, Redsmear kicked him in the balls. Another flunky then hit him over the head with a microphone boom, and the wounded mayor collapsed unconscious to the floor, bleeding from the back of his head.

As The Pood ran skittering across the floor, pursued by its old nemeses, a disturbing transformation came over it. It was trying to run under the couch on the other side of the room. But its pace slackened, its bullet-like sprint subsiding to a trot and then to a stagger. Its stainless steel nails lost their luster, and then they became cartilage. Its huge, torn and shaggy ears withered into innocuous puff balls, resembling licorice cotton candy. Its terrible ragged fur, like a patchwork of spiky punk-style Groucho Marx mustaches pointing in every direction at once, became smooth, glossy and fluffy. The daggers of its teeth shrank down into tiny, futile nubs, not even sharp enough to cut through Flo Jellem's beloved Wonder Bread. Most disturbing of all, the eerie orange lights of its eyes were utterly extinguished. Both eyes became gray, lusterless and void of energy. Halfway to the couch, the tottering ex-beastie now collapsed in a silken heap on the floor, emitting pathetic whimpering noises. Its tail drooped. Its cast-iron balls shrunk to the size of marbles, and withdrew into the scrotum. Its corkscrewing penis with the fishhook tip withered down to the size of the tip of a pinkie, drooping with impotence.

The boots of Tampon Redsmear creaked up on the hardwood floor. A moment later the mogul loomed above the stricken and disabled *lusus naturae*. Elvis finished up the devastating "Hound Dog" while the ducks Aflaced without cease. The prone Pood feebly covered its extinguished eyes with the pads of its paws. A moment later Redsmear's hand shot down, and he seized the powerless former pestilence by the scruff of its neck. He hauled it aloft, so that mogul and canceled cacodemon where face to face. The Pood was panting furiously, and it tried to BlllIAAAAAAAARGH at Redsmear, to send out a hot wind of fierce fire. All it succeeded in doing was expelling a barely audible belch, and then a hairball that floated forlornly to the floor.

"Little blast from the past, eh, Poodie-Woodie?" Redsmear inquired mockingly, gesturing with his riding crop at the chimera and the duck. "Kryptonite for Superman? A heel for Achilles? Barber's shears for Samson? Hmmm? Is that it?"

The Unpood whimpered.

Redsmear, still holding the defrocked demiurge by the scruff of its neck, shook it vigorously, smacked the floor with his whip and, eyes shining with an almost erotic ecstasy, announced: "I R winnah — *again!*" He then looked at the flunkies with their captives and said, "Let's go, boys!" They strode off, Redsmear in possession of the fallen Pood, its four little legs flailing impotently about like the legs of an overturned insect that cannot right itself. They marched back toward the bathysphere. On the way there Redsmear meted out a vicious, vindictive kick in the ass to the unconscious Gil. Then they entered the vehicle. Its doors slammed shut, and then it rose back up the way that it had come.

END BOOK FOUR

Father

Book the Fifth

Apocalypse Now and Then
The Revenge of the Pood

Doom am I, full-ripe, dealing death to the worlds, engaged in devouring mankind.
— Bhagavad-Gita

Heeeeeeere's POODIE!
— The Pood

Well, we really fucked it all up this time, didn't we, dears?
— Florence Jellem

Two eyes opened.
They were no longer orange.
Media mogul's Web log, Blog date 4/25/12 (Comments disabled). We remain in geosynchronous orbit over the estate of Gil Aaronson, the mayor of Hell, Michigan, who is now out of the picture. The Pood is in our possession, under lock and key. Shortly we shall weigh anchor and depart this wretched backwater, leaving its scrofulous and disorderly denizens to their respective prosaic and pathetic fates. The Pood will be a goldmine for us — well, specifically, for me. A dog-like entity possessing supernatural powers of mayhem and destruction will be an invaluable resource in my money-making empire. We will train it to perform breathtaking feats of savagery and destruction on command, which shall be performed at public venues such as stadia and concert halls and the like, at ridiculously

inflated ticket prices. These feats will also be shown on TV and on the Internet. I know my public. It is a bloodthirsty mob, bilious and billions strong and ever on the lookout for villains to vilify, goats to scape and liberals to destroy. The revenue stream generated by The Pood will make me another fortune. Of course, when it is not performing, we shall keep it incapacitated by the presence of Elvis and the ducks. Even as I speak, the headline POOD CAPTURED has appeared on the home page of the Faux News Web site, under the breaking news banner. We will upload the first images of the captured canine shortly. No doubt they shall go viral.

The Unpood whimpered. It had been chained and suspended between two posts, its four legs stretched outward in an X formation. Its extinguished eyes darted uncomprehendingly about. To its left, strapped to a dolly, was the Elvis/Nixon chimera. To its right, also arranged on a dolly and still strung together by a chain, were the Aflac duck philosophers. Flunkies held the dollies from behind. Redsmear entered the room, boots cracking on the floor. Scotty, whom Redsmear had placed in charge of The Unpood and the others, stood off to one side, trying to keep the sickness that he felt in his stomach from expressing itself on his face. Behind him was his PC. It was logged in to the chat room of The Galilean Library, a Web site devoted to philosophy, science and the humanities. When Redsmear entered, Scotty had been complaining to his pixel pals at the Library that his boss was a sociopath. "Kill him," importuned one of his pals, who went by the user name davidm. "Run his balls through a high-speed blender. Do it now. He who hesitates, is lost." Another pal, who went by the user name Big Blooming Blighter, urged: "Fuck up the cretin's computers with a virus. That'll teach the git."

"Pull back the dollies slowly," the mogul ordered, and the flunkies obeyed, gradually lengthening the distance between the captive avatars and the defrocked demiurge. As the chimera and the ducks were withdrawn from the vicinity of The Unpood, its eyes began to ruddily glow, like embers coming to life. Its claws hardened. Its balls reappeared, and began to grow larger and harder. Its penis popped outward and corkscrewed. Its fur spiked. Its ears rose. Its mouth opened in a fearful leer, the teeth visibly increasing in size and becoming sharper and harder, gleaming with metallic malice. The beastie shook itself, rattling the chains. An ominous growl rose from its gut.

"Stop!" Redsmear barked at the flunkies. "Wheel them back in." The flunkies wheeled the avatars back toward The Pood, which visibly shriveled, all its gains lost. The reawakened orange light in its eyes quickly died back down. It was now The Unpood again, a harmless and fragile fluffy doggie suspended helplessly between the two posts and whimpering pathetically.

```
=\__!
  !  !
```

After the Elvis/Nixon chimera was snatched from the Mexican food joint the previous evening, Mystery Tart and her mother, Holace Orr, bundled themselves into the SUV that Elvis had stolen and drove aimlessly around for a couple of hours, squabbling the whole time. Holace was at the wheel.

"Look at you!" she complained, nodding at Mystery, who was still clad only in a towel with the Ayn Rand Dungeon logo imprinted upon it (two crossed whips under a dollar sign and the slogan, "Ass is Ass"). "You're an absolute disgrace! Dressed like that in public! What kind of daughter did I raise?"

"Don't you *dare* play the prude parent with me, Mother!" Mystery snapped. "You're just as much a whore as I am!"

"But I'm a high-class whore and besides, I don't have a hole! And look how alluringly dressed I am!" Mystery frowned with pity at the dowdy hooker's finery that mother wore; the cheap fishnet stockings with the runs and holes in them, the flimsy red silk dress that barely concealed her sagging boobs, the tacky costume jewelry, the wilted flower in her silly hat. "Why can't you dress like a regular whore, Mystery? What am I supposed to say to the other whores during Friday night Bingo at the VFW Community Center when they ask about my daughter, and that awful dungeon where she works run by that lunatic Russian lady?"

"Oh, Mother, stop it!" Once again Mystery wanted to broach the most mysterious topic of all, how it was possible that Mother had conceived and given birth to her in the first place, a topic about which Mother resolutely refused to speak. But more pressing matters weighed on Mystery's mind. "Mother, we've got to find Elvis. They kidnapped that poor man, whoever 'they' are!"

"Oh, no!" Holace replied. "No, indeed!" Holace lighted a cigar.

"Why not?"

"I've had just about all I can stand from your lover boy's body mate," Holace said. "To think I voted for him three times! He's such a bore. All he does is talk politics and, worst of all, he has *terrible* breath!" Holace exhaled a stream of cigar smoke.

"You've a nerve talking about terrible odors, Mother! Put that awful thing out. Sometimes a cigar is just a cigar, and while I like the symbolic kind I hate the real kind."

"You never listen to your mother," Holace said bitterly as she gnawed on the cigar. "Would it hurt you to dress down a little? A pair of stiletto heels, a nice, clinging mini-skirt, some tawdry lipstick and cheap perfume? Listen to your mother! I may not have a hole between the legs, but at least I haven't got a hole in my head like you!"

"Oh, yes you *do* have a hole in the head, Mother! And you never shut it."

```
=\___!
 !  !
```

Jesús and Daddy Long Legs decided to hitchhike to Hell, "where all the action is, mon," as Daddy put it. They were running low on pot and figured they might be able to score some weed in one of the shabbier neighborhoods of Hell, perhaps in the neighborhoods of Greed, Treachery or even Lust.

"He thinks he's God, mon," Jesús said as he and his friend thrust out their thumbs on the side of the road. "My old mon has got a God complex, mon. That's the problem."

"That was pretty shabby, mon," Daddy allowed. "A father refusing to give a bridge loan to his own son. Bummer."

"He's loaded, too, mon."

"Moneybags," Daddy snorted with contempt. "Up against the wall, capitalist pig!"

The occasional car or truck passed without slowing. Then the SUV with Mystery and Holace in it approached on the highway, high beams blazing and occupants bickering.

```
=\___!
 !  !
```

"Two thousand years!" Father roared. "Two fist-fucking, Satan-pecker-pounding thousand years!"

"Now, Father, calm down! Think of your blood pressure!"

"You let me sleep for *two thousand years*!"

"You were tired!"

Father raked his fingers through his flowing white hair and pulled big patches of it out of his head. He hyperventilated, and looked around frantically.

"What the fuck?" he said. "Where the fuck *are* we? This doesn't look like my home!" He rushed to a window and threw it open.

"Mary!" he roared. "This isn't Jerusalem! Where in Satan's scrotum *are* we?"

"Well, dear," she said, "we moved."

"Moved?"

"That's right."

"Where did we move to, Mary?"

"Fresno."

"Fresno?"

"Fresno, California."

Father peered out the window at the flat, scabrous scrublands of the central California farm town renowned for its butt-ugliness. A full moon cast a livid glow over it. Even the full moon here looked ugly, like an eyeball without a pupil.

"Why did we move to Fresno, Mother?"

"It's a retirement community, Father. It's nice. We have a gated compound with 24-hour security. We moved you here in a box while you slept."

"A box!"

"It had air holes in it," Mary said helpfully.

"Why Fresno, Mother? Tell me the truth!"

"There are lots of nice Mexicans here. People of our own kind."

Father slammed a fist down on an end table, breaking it into its twenty-five trillion constituent quarks.

"WE ARE NOT FUCKING MEXICANS!" he roared, the whole house shaking from his voice. "How many times do I have to fucking *say* it?"

"Of *course* we're not, dear," Mother said, taking hold of Father's hand and patting it. "Just as you say, Father. You're always right. You're infallible!"

Father snatched back his hand and jabbed a finger at Mother. "Don't you *dare* patronize me, woman!" He looked around. "Messages!" he bellowed. "Where are my prayer messages?" He was looking for the metal spike upon which were impaled the slips of paper with the prayers sent to him from his people.

"Well," Mother said, looking askance.

"Where are they, Mother? Tell the truth!"

"Oh, Father, you're such a Luddite! Times change! There *are* no more prayer slips or metal spikes. We have an answering machine, now." She nodded at the phone. "And a computer with e-mail capacity." She nodded at the computer, a Mac.

Father snatched up the phone and fumbled with the answering device. There were beeps, a pause, and then a recorded voice: "You have five trillion, three hundred fifty-four billion, two-hundred-sixty-five million, one-hundred-sixty-three-thousand, four hundred twenty-four new prayers."

Father ripped the phone out of the wall and threw it to the floor and ran around the living room while tearing hair out of his head.

"Five trillion unanswered prayers!" He bellowed. "Noah's dick in Lucifer's ass! What must my people think of me now!"

Mother chased Father, trying to calm him. They both ran in circles now.

Father said, "Watch out, Mother, I'm going to wax wroth!"

"Father, please don't wax wroth." But Father went ahead and waxed wroth anyway, and when he was done the wallpaper had blistered off the walls.

After waxing wroth father stopped running. He steadied himself against a wall and hyperventilated for awhile. Mother stood worriedly to one side, wringing her hands and waiting for the next outburst. She knew that more storms were ahead.

An expression of inspiration suddenly appeared on Father's face, as if he had thought of something critically important. "The attic!" He exclaimed. "I have to check on the Medamned attic!"

"Now, Father..."

Father looked at the ceiling. Bewildered, he ran from room to room. His voice rang out: "Mother! Mother, *where in sheep's shit is my fucking attic?*"

Mother caught up with Father and broke the news.

"Father, I couldn't find a suitable attic in Fresno."

"You couldn't find a suitable attic in Fresno!"

"This is a small town. There are no rentals with attached attics of infinite square feet."

Father ran into the kitchen and pounded the refrigerator into atoms. His inarticulate shrieks of rage suggested that he was on the verge of waxing wroth a second time. Mother hoped that he would not; she had just repainted the kitchen.

While Father vented Mother stamped her foot and said crossly, "For attic's sake, Father, when we did have the attic in Jerusalem no one was living there, anyway! You always said that no one was good enough for your attic!"

"The attic is the whole Medamned point of everything!" Father hollered, throwing up his hands. Then he tore patches of beard off of his face.

"The only person you ever let actually stay in the attic was our son Jesús after that unpleasantness with the Cross and then after a month you got tired of him not paying rent and lollygagging about, and you threw him out and told him to find a job and clean up his act!"

Father, red with rage, punched a hole in the space-time continuum. Then he jabbed a finger at Mother and said: "My workshop! Don't tell me you got rid of my workshop too, Mary!"

"Of course you still have your workshop, Father. It's downstairs."

Father ran downstairs.

The globe sat on a bench, under a hot lamp labeled "Sun". It was slowly turning. Underneath it, on its pedestal, was inscribed the word "Aleph."

Like Borges in his friend's basement, Father had to lie down in a certain place and look at the globe. When he did, it became the Aleph. Like Borges, he saw everything all at once: all space was there, actual and undiminished. Each thing (a mirror's face, let us say) was infinite things, since Father distinctly saw it from every angle of the universe. And like Borges, Father now saw the teeming sea; he saw daybreak and nightfall; he saw the multitudes of America; he saw a silvery cobweb in the center of a black pyramid; he saw a splintered labyrinth (it was London); and so on and so forth. He also saw what was happening in Hell, Michigan.

He sprang to his feet and approached the big turning globe,

one hemisphere illuminated by the lamp. By this time Mother had pattered down the steps after him.

"Well fuck my eyes with Satan's thighs," Father whispered with lordly awe. He jabbed a finger at a cylindrical protuberance growing out of the globe's terrain just west of Detroit. "That's a penis," Father a observed. "The world is growing a penis."

"Now Father..."

Father turned on Mother. "Holy rabbits in rut," he yelled, jabbing a finger at the globe, "do you realize there are now seven billion cock-thrusting, pussy-penetrated pissants swarming all over this Medamned thing?"

"Well, Father, you *told* them to be fruitful and multiply."

Father waved his hands around. "I don't *like* all that fucking! They're supposed to feel ashamed about it! If I'm not getting any, neither should they!"

Mother looked indignant. "You knew I was a virgin when you impregnated me, Father!"

"You could put out once in a while, Mother!" Father balled a fist and waved it at her. Then he began jumping up and down in frustration. He let out of howl of primordial rage, and kicked the cabinet on which the globe/aleph rested on its pedestal.

When he kicked it, the earth cracked under the Bay of Bengal, and a huge tsunami swamped the coastal regions of the nation of Myanmar, also known as Burma. Tens of thousands of simple peasants who struggled to eke out a living as rice growers or fishermen in the delta of the sacred Irrawaddy River were immediately wiped out under a huge wall of water.

"Fuck them," Father said about the poor peasants. Then he added: "That's it, I'm fed up with this globe. Run the bath water, Mother!" He put his arms around the globe/aleph and began loosening it from its moorings.

"Now, Father," mother said soothingly, trying to lure him away from the globe. But he kept wrenching at it.

"Run the Medamned bath water, Mother, and this time make it fucking *hot* water! Not only are they all going to be drowned again, this time it's going to be a *scalding* bath. And no ark, either! Fuck the ark and the two of a kind and the horse that they rode in on! They're *all* going under, this time! Here we go!"

"Father!"

"It's the End Times!" Father bellowed. "Look out, world, this is it! This is the big one! Judgment Day!" He had nearly wrenched the globe/aleph from its pedestal.

Mother finally put her foot down.

"PUT DOWN THE FUCKING GLOBE/ALEPH!" Mary hollered in Father's face. Father, stunned by Mother's unfeminine and unwifely outburst, became momentarily quiescent as Mother pulled his arms off the world and tamped it back down onto its pedestal. But then Father blew up again. He slapped his face in frustration and then tried to slap the world, a blow that, had it been administered, would have sent the globe spinning round and round and round for a few moments. As one, seven billion people on earth would have gasped as the sun in the sky whizzed crazily around, night-day-night-day-night-day in quick, shutter-flash succession. People everywhere would have swooned. They would have oohed and ahhhed at this rapid, out-of-control celestial merry-go-round ride.

Mother dragged a protesting Father away from the globe. But then he saw his workbench with body parts and body part plans strewn over it. He angrily swept some of the parts off of the bench. Then he snatched up a model of the human eye.

Studying it, he had a reverse Eureka moment, grasping in a flash his own utter incompetence.

"Look, Mother," he raged, "The retina is fucking inside out! Why the fuck did I never notice this before? The nerves and blood vessels lie on the surface of the retina instead of behind it as is the case in many invertebrate species. This arrangement forces a number of complex adaptations and gives mammals a motherfucking blind spot!" Father slapped his forehead in frustration and said, "Ooof! What the *blue fuck* was I thinking when I designed the human eye?"

Mother took father's hand and patted it. "There there, dear," she consoled him. "You did your best."

Father slammed his fist down onto his work bench, reducing it to a quantum wave function in superposition encoding every possible eingenvalue of the bench. He roared with self-contempt: "Apparently my best just wasn't fucking good enough!"

Mother gently steered Father away from the quantized work bench. Father said: "Mother, do you realize that six muscles move the eye when three would suffice? What was I thinking?"

"Don't be so hard on yourself," Mary said. "At least you *made* an eye, Father! That's a real feather in your cap! Do you think anyone here in Fresno can make an eye at all, or even anyone back in Jerusalem?"

"Why did I make the pharynx a passage of both respiration and food ingestion, thereby significantly increasing the risk of choking?" Father asked. It was a rhetorical question. "That was fucking *stupid* of me!" Mother led Father up the stairs.

"There, there," Father.

"Why did I" — Father recited a litany of design mistakes that had only now occurred to him, well after the fact.

"I'm tired, Mary", Father abruptly announced when they were back upstairs.

"Of course you're tired, Father, you waxed wroth this evening! Waxing wroth would tucker out just about anyone."

"Mary," Father said, his tone changing, as if he had just remembered something important. "How are you keeping? It's been two thousand years!"

"Just fine, Father," Mother said, leading him back toward his bedroom. "I run a small business on my home computer, now."

"A business? A business? Wives aren't supposed to run a business! They aren't supposed to work at all!" Father's hackles seemed to be rising again. Mother steered him toward the bed.

"Lie down, Father," she said. "Times change." Father lay down on the bed.

"What kind of business, Mother?" Father asked as Mother tucked him in. His eyes were heavy, and his voice had significantly lowered in volume.

"I sell images of myself Photoshopped onto toast, tortillas, corn chips and other food items," Mother reported. "They sell like hotcakes."

"Mother," he whispered. "I feel so ... so weary."

"Of course you do, Father," she said, patting his hand. "You've worked hard all your life. You should rest. Take a nap. A *long* nap."

Father fell asleep, and began snoring. Mother sighed. She stroked his hair and said tenderly, "Man finds it much easier to breathe in the shade of exhausted gods, Father." She kissed him on the forehead. Father lay on his back. His white robe was bunched up above his knees, revealing spindly, hairless white shins covered with purple varicose veins. His profound gut rose and fell sonorously as he breathed and snored. One arm dangled over the side of the bed, and the other was splayed over the gong-thud of his Leonine heart. His hair and beard were wildly askew, pulled by his own questing hands to tatters. This slumbering Brobdingnagian had been tied down by the Lilliputian wires of dreams. Quivers of tiny arrows launched at him from the chthonic depths pricked the flesh of his conscience. In his dreams the boom-and-roar-thunder of the Apocalypse was accompanied by horizon-wide flashes of white lights whose purple-threaded veins crawled up to eternity. Then he fell into deep sleep, and once again his great dreams and dramas were no more.

Mother exhaled a huge sigh of relief, rolled her eyes, fanned her left cheek with her hand to cool her perspiration and said, "Ay-yi-yi!" She then tiptoed out of Father's room and gently closed the door behind her. Then she sat in front of her Mac and spent the rest of the evening processing requests for pictures showing her image Photoshopped onto the surfaces of various popular food items. Visa and MasterCard accepted.

```
=\___!
  !  !
```

Junior had ripped off his shirt and tied it around his head like a bandana. The soot of Hell covered his face like warpaint. He had procured a staff and had dipped it into the mouth of the Talking Fire that now led him. He had thus made of the staff a torch not to guide his Going — for he was already environed in flames — but rather to announce his Coming. In his other hand he grasped his rifle. Ten paces behind him bounded Bingo, ears flopping and tail wagging. His dog had been returned to him — reprieved from an eternity of being run over again and again — in trade for a dead man with an obolus in its mouth: his real father. The dog's nose twitched, seeking the scent of its master, but it no longer recognized the scent of Junior, who strode wild-eyed into the abyss or, looked at another way, onto the stage. "This way," the Fire invited Junior, in a language not of Man. Bingo flopped about tentatively, not sure whether to prance forward or dart backward. *Where is my Junior? Where is my Junior?* The cocker spaniel's nose interrogated the air, but it received no meaningful aromatic reply. At the Fire's behest, Junior entered the bedchamber of Eros and Thanatos. Prodded by instinct, the dog took off like a shot. It caught up to Junior and clutched at its master's pant cuff with its teeth. It tried dragging Junior back from the door through which he was now passing, but the big, strapping farm boy who once was as honest as an ear of corn is yellow and who worked until the job got done had a new job to do, and it was not an honest one but it would get done. He savagely and scornfully kicked his pet away, and then leered into the bed chamber. He was already unbuckling the belt of his jeans.

=__!
   ! !

Sheriff Ted was running around like a chicken with its head cut off.

He had covertly pursued Bubb and Flo all the way to the doorstep of the Aaronson estate. He remained behind Bubb, but was so close to the Dark One that he perceived, dangling from Great Deceiver's frock coat, a single thread. He kept his chickeny gaze fastened on that thread even as the bathysphere of Redsmear banged down through the ceiling of the surrounded house, only to rise again a little later with The Unpood in captivity.

A thread. A thread had run through Ted's life, a thread that had been lit like the fuse of a bomb. And the fire had run up the fuse and the bomb had exploded. It exploded when he turned the gun on himself in his squad car and blew half his head off. But were there other threads? Or is there but one possible thread, or one *actual* thread, down which the fire of the fuse inevitably runs to ruin? He pictured threads; balls of yarn; skeins, both wound and unwound. Each thread a life; each thread a *version* of a life. Were there different threads called Ted? Or did each thread, no matter where it led, no matter what winding or tortuous path it followed, terminate in the same disgrace? And still he thought: I am no longer afraid. I am not afraid of Bubb. Perhaps, he reasoned, his lack of fear was related to the fact that he could no longer be killed, because he was dead. But he did not think that this was a suitable explanation. After all, he could still be *tortured* — for eternity, as it happened. He was uncertain what to think, exactly, except that Bubb himself was a skein of illusions, a protean bundle of threads that perhaps could be unwound to reveal nothing but emptiness behind the frock coat and underneath the slouch hat. Empty at the center. He weighed the option of using his beak to pluck at that lone idle thread that dangled from Bubb's coat. But as he tottered toward it on his bandy legs, a hand seized him by the throat.

"Gotcha!" Staff Sergeant Ulysses Eisenhower Yokel, the hellfire golem, crowed at the chicken.

```
=\__!
  !  !
```

"Clients!" Holace hollered, as the high-beams of the S.U.V. bobbed over the faces and outstretched thumbs of the hitchhiking Jesús and Daddy on the road to Hell.

As the two figures swarmed up in the light and got clearer, Mystery said, "That one!" She was gesturing at the dumpy and somewhat orotund Jesús, still in his busboy whites. "That was the busboy at the restaurant!"

Holace slowed the S.U.V.

"Oh, for heaven's sake, Mother, are you crazy!"

"Clients are clients," Holace said philosophically. "I'm not too proud to say that business has been bad in recent years. However, I don't feel that I am to blame. Blame the bad economy and President Cookie. President Cookie is to blame for everything."

"Mother, one's a busboy and the other is an old bum with dreadlocks and a bone in his nose! They don't have any money!"

"Another problem is changing tastes. People are becoming coarser, less refined. They don't appreciate an upscale, high-class hooker who doesn't depend on a hole between the legs to make her clients feel good, but who relies on creativity instead."

"You rely on your *mouth*, Mother; let's get real here. It helps that you have dentures that you can take out."

Holace stopped the S.U.V.

"Roll down the window and invite them in, Mystery."

"I will not, Mother!"

Mystery crossed her arms over her creamy, saucy breasts, which were only half-concealed by the Ayn Rand Dungeon towel. The twin aureoles of her nipples, which were like two pink flowers, were just visible over the edges of the fabric. Mother reached across Mystery and rolled down the window. She let out a whistle, as one might use to summon a pet dog. Then she said in her gravelly, mannish voice, the voice of an old sailor in a dive bar: "Holla, boys! Wanna take a fast ride with hot Holace?" She batted her eyes in what she imagined to be a come-hither way, and the false eyelashes that she wore went up and down like out-of-control light switches.

"Far out, mon," Daddy said. Jesús was staring at Mystery's tits. Holace used the power door locks to unlock the back door and the two men — one a 2,000-year-old busboy who needed a bridge loan to avoid being evicted and the other a 69-year-old adolescent — climbed into the backseat.

Holace started up the S.U.V. again and they exchanged names, except for Mystery, who remained obdurately silent. Seething, she whispered at Mother: "You can have *both* of them if you want, Mother. I want nothing to do with either one of them. I want to find Elvis."

Holace affected her best sultry voice and coquettish demeanor, but she was in her seventies now and these affectations made her ridiculous, like a middle-aged white man singing a rap song. She told Jesús and Daddy, "Holace knows the way to Hell, but also the way to Heaven, boys, if you catch my drift." Then she let out a kind of semi-growl that was intended to signify animal lust but instead sounded like an emanation of indigestion. The road lights gave her face, covered with pancake makeup, a ghoulish cast, and the hollows of her eyes were sunk in darkness. She resembled an aging dwarfish coquette cruelly limned in lurid pastel colors in a hypothetical Lautrec painting made not in a raffish Paris cabaret but in an insane asylum.

Jesús and Daddy stared blankly at her. Catching on, Daddy said, "We ain't got no money, mon." Mystery elbowed her mother in the ribs and hissed, "Told you so, Mother!"

But Jesús was thinking of Mystery's tits. "We ain't got no money, mon, but we got some primo weed," he said. "Not enough for a hoggy but maybe enough for a pinner, mon."

The wilted flower in Holace's funny hat seemed to wilt all the more. She sighed and stared hopelessly at the road. The high-beams punched through the gloom as they raced back toward Hell. "Oh," Mystery burbled, her mood suddenly thawing, "I *love* to smoke pot."

"*Oh, I love to smoke pot!*" Holace mocked. "Well, I don't. I can't stand the stuff. It makes me talk too much. It's like truth serum for me. I hate to babble on and on and on; I'm fundamentally a private person."

Mystery pondered this intelligence. *Mother, where did I come from? How was I born?* Mother never talked about it.

She saw Mother's next cigar, poised in the ashtray and waiting to be smoked. She imagined it wouldn't be too hard to covertly splice a little pot into it. Might loosen Mother's tongue.

```
    =\___!
      !  !
```

"Regime change! Regime change! Regime change!"

After the first failed assault by the Redsmear forces the crowd grew ugly and began to close in, forming a ring around the Aaronson estate. Prior to that, a carnival atmosphere had developed in places. Makeshift canteens and latrines had been set up. Homer the Bard of Baked Goods was simultaneously scarfing down donuts and scribbling down the opening lines of the epic poem that he had pined since youth to write, having finally found a subject other than donuts that was worthy of his talents. Mr. Crabapple and Mr. Fury, the two homoerotic sadomasochistic old men, gave an erotic mud-wrestling exhibition to an exhilarated throng. Mucho Hogg and his son, Mucho Jr., were startled and thrilled to be entertained and challenged by reality for a change, instead of by pixels on the screens of their digital bestiary of cyberdevices. Even Buridan and his ass were there, having agreed to venture downtown. Ayn Rand frowned in fury at the crowd, deeming it a "mob"; she found all mobs to be bad. President Cookie was there but he was irrelevant as usual, hanging around the edges of the crowd hoping to be recognized.

"Regime change!" the crowd now roared as one. Divisions of class, rank, money and above all neighborhood that had long stratified and stifled Hell had broken down. The people held up their torches and candles and signs. The mob that had decided to follow no more leaders kept a sharp eye all the while on their new leader, Bubb, who had broken through the security gate that surrounded the compound and marched up to the front door, Flo trailing behind him. A great cheer rose up from the masses.

Meanwhile, off the beaten track as was his wont, The Heretic had wandered to the periphery of the compound, a lightly forested area that led to a denser stand of trees beyond. A rope ladder dangling from the Ship of Dreams had caught his attention. When he arrived at the ladder, he nudged it and it swung from side to side. Then he looked down. There were flat patches showing through mottled rocks and soil. He prodded a patch with the toe of his shoe, and peered closely at it. It was wood.

He crouched down, and began clearing rocks and soil away from the wood surface. It was old wood, stained a deep reddish-brown and eroded in places. He discovered a large metal ring attached to the surface of what stood revealed as a large trap door, evidently the entrance to a chamber underneath. He took off his wrap-around shades and read the single large word that had been carved into the wood at the base of the ring.

DASEIN

The Heretic muttered mystic oaths of incredulity. Then his attention was diverted by the faint sounds of "Aflac" coming from above. Standing up and craning his neck, his eyes followed the rope ladder up into where it vanished back into the transporter room of the Dream Ship. Hearing the voices of the philosopher ducks with whom he had been happily communing when they had been snatched by Redsmear's henchmen, The Heretic fearlessly and irreverently shimmied up the ladder toward the hovering ship.

=___!
 ! !

It was just after Bubb broke through the front gate that Redsmear launched his next assault, with the bathysphere containing Kryptonite for The Pood that crashed through the ceiling of the compound. Bubb watched, taken aback, as a few moments later the sphere rose back up to the ship. He sniffed the air, and smelled the rankness of Redsmear, an aroma interleaved with the scent of the mogul's triumph. "Why, that scheming bastard," the Foul One said with a low growl, and a moment later he strode up to Aaronson's front door and with one great sweep of his cloven hoof, he kicked it down and stepped inside.

=___!
 ! !

Staff Sergeant Ulysses Eisenhower Yokel in hellfire golem garb held Sheriff Ted by his scrawny neck. Ted bawked and flapped his wings. The sergeant thrust out his lantern jaw that surmounted his fat red neck, bared his teeth, and mocked: "Now I'm going to wring your head off yet again, maggot. You haven't got Flo Jellem's skirts to hide behind anymore, do you?"

Threads. There is another thread now, a dream thread back at boot camp. A dream of what might have been. The staff sergeant is roaring insults into Ted's face. Ted's knees knock and his eyes are bulging and his own mouth is flung open and his back stiffened and he keeps yelling back, "Sir, yes sir! Sir, yes sir! Sir, yes sir!" Later that night, Ted tracks the sergeant down. Shoulders his rifle. Takes aim. The staff sergeant looks at Ted with astonishment. The sergeant's hand is splayed out in a warding gesture as he backs away, not pleading for his life but still screaming insults at the buck private who has been driven to the edge of insanity, just like the private in "Full Metal Jacket." And, just like that same private, Ted pulls the trigger. The gun roars, and there is a bucking flash of light. A nova of blood. The bullet pops right through the center of Yokel's palm and then whines on to nail him between the eyes. The sergeant's head blows up, and he is sent hurtling backward like a giant rag doll, thumping lifelessly to the floor. Ted strides up and stands over the corpse of the fallen drill instructor. But although his head has been obliterated, the brains fanning out over the floor, the sergeant still speaks. "You can't kill me," the hellfire golem insists. I'm already dead."

"But I *can* kill you," and then he unholstered his Glock and shot Yokel in the head. He put the gun away. He looked down at his pressed, starched sheriff's uniform, his spit-shine shoes. Tipped his sheriff's cap, and thought, feeling like Gary Cooper in High Noon, "The law has returned to Hell." Leaving Yokel to his fate, he turned and strolled with self-possession toward the door that The Fallen One had just kicked down. No longer a chicken but a man, a real man, he followed Bubb and Flo inside, at a distance.

=__!
  ! !

In the backseat, Mystery was giving a blow job to Daddy Long Legs. Daddy reclined against the back door, eyes rolling up in his head as he said over and over, between sighs and gasps: "Far out, mon ... Oh! *Really* far out, mon!" Mystery's head bobbed up and down but her ears were pricked. She was listening to Mother's confessions.

They had parked on the road shoulder. Mother was still behind the wheel, puffing obliviously on her marijuana-spiked cigar and babbling on while Jesús sat next to her, listening intently and with dawning understanding.

"It happened at night, as in a dream, but it wasn't really like a dream. It was more like those sleep-paralysis tales people tell, when aliens with giant black eyes and oval-shaped gray heads visit them in their bedrooms and conduct sinister experiments on them. He wanted to enter me. To enter me! I couldn't quite get a clear picture of who he was, but he seemed to have wild white hair and a flowing white beard. He was vulgar — oh, he was vulgar! 'Well fuck my eyes with Satan's thighs!' I distinctly recall him saying that, at one point. He said a lot of things like 'blue fuck' this and 'Noah's dong' that. I think he was angry that I was sexless between the legs, but he was determined to enter me somehow. There was something about, 'I must be sleepfucking,' and how he wanted an 'only begotten daughter' to go with his 'only begotten son.' I'm pretty sure that at one point he told me to watch out because he intended to wax wroth, whatever that means, and I think that is why the next morning I discovered that all the wallpaper had been blistered off the walls. Then I recall everything going black, and I must have fallen into a deep sleep, and when I awoke the next morning the sun was streaming in through the windows. The only souvenir of his visit was the blistered wallpaper. Long story short, nine months later I had another souvenir: you by C-section, Mystery. ... Mystery, are you listening?"

Mystery had a mouthful at the moment, but she had been listening. "She's listening, mon," Jesús assured Holace, watching the head of the hooker bobbing up and down and taking that as a nod of assent. A moment later Daddy's whole body shuddered as though an electrical current had cut through it, and he let out a moan of ecstasy. Mystery's head then popped up. She was wiping her lips with the Ayn Rand towel. Jesús looked at her and thought, but did not say: "We're half-siblings, mon. Far out!" Then he got morose, thinking about those fantastic tits that he should probably avoid because of Father's incest taboo. But then he thought rebelliously: "Fuck Father. He won't even give me a bridge loan, mon."

"My turn," he said to Mystery, adding, "I want to do the horizontal hokey-pokey, mon."

"It'll cost ya," Mystery warned.

Jesús held up the bag of pot.

"Jump in, tiger," Mystery growled.

$$=\backslash\underline{\quad}!$$
$$!\quad!$$

Flo Jellem was stunned. Nothing in her long life had prepared her for a horror such as this.

An arm hung by the crook of the elbow over the back of a chair. A foot still in its shoe stood upright on a shelf. Fingers were strewn across the floor like breadsticks. Blood was everywhere. It pattered from the ceiling. It seeped down the walls. It pooled on the floor. The rank odor of death pervaded the living room of Gil Aaronson, in which Bubb and Flo now stood. Outside the mob was closing in, faces mashed up against windows, eyes bulging with malice. Sheriff Ted stood back, remaining inconspicuous, gun drawn. Flo, unable to bridle her emotions at the atrocity she was witnessing, let out a cry of anguish and beat her breast. Then, recovering her aplomb as best she could, she deployed the deadliest weapon in her arsenal of deprecations, a veritable nuclear bomb of disapproval: "This place," she announced with a sigh, "looks like the Dickens!" She began sternly lecturing Gil Aaronson, who groaned and rubbed the back of his bleeding head as he slowly regained consciousness and began struggling to his feet.

Flo got to work stacking body parts as if they were cords of firewood.

"A place for everything, and everything in its place," she tartly reminded the mayor. "Honestly, Gilbert, I've never seen such a mess. How can you function as mayor if you can't even keep a tidy household? If you're going to have body parts in your house, at least don't have them lying hither and yon." Flo began segregating the parts by type, hands with hands, feet with feet, arms with arms, and she arranged them decoratively on free surfaces, such as shelves, or else she stacked them functionally, like dirty dishes in a sink. The reporter whom The Pood had emasculated remained semi-conscious on the floor. Raising her voice to be heard above the reporter's groans of agony, Flo said: "If you leave body parts lying about the house people are going to think you a slob, dear, and quite frankly, they will have every right to do so. The people of Hell aren't going to re-elect a slob as mayor."

Bubb strode up to Aaronson, who had managed to rise to his knees. "Get up!" The Foul One snapped at the mayor, who looked dazedly up at Bubb and asked in a weak, faltering voice: "Who are you? Where am I? *Who* am I?" Then his mind unclouded, and everything that had transpired before Redsmear's minions had beaten him senseless came back in a flash. "Echo!" he cried. "Where is my little Echo? They stole him from me. Echo! Echo! Come back! Help me!"

Bubb smacked the mayor across the face with the back of his hand, and Aaronson tumbled back down to the floor. The crowd outside that had thronged at the windows let out a rousing cheer. "Kill him! Regime change! Regime change! He raised our taxes three times!"

Aaronson, holding his hand to his mouth and tasting blood, was now stretched out across the floor, propped on one elbow. He looked up in terror and beheld a wash of red light, against which a towering form was silhouetted. The silhouette seemed to be of three heads, and affixed to each chin were bat wings. The wings beat and blew a chill breeze throughout the room. Suddenly a hand with talons seized him by his shirt collar and hoisted to him to his feet. With his free hand Bubb then rifled another slap across Aaronson's face.

"Gilbert, where do you keep your cleanser, dear?" Flo sang out from the kitchen, above the rush of running water that she had started in the sink. "You need to clean up this blood right away or the stains will be *very* difficult to eradicate later. Blood stains are simply beastly. They are much worse than a bathtub ring. Don't you remember the time in home ec class that I gutted a live guinea pig with a Ginsu knife to show how to clean up blood? Honestly, dear, did you learn *nothing at all* from matriculating with me?"

Outside, Buridan and his Ass were being interviewed live on CNN. The two, who normally disagreed about everything, were in rare and nearly unprecedented agreement: Gil Aaronson had to go. He was to blame. He was to blame for everything.

"He's been a terrible mayor," Buridan said. "Frozen in the ice of his own indifference, while the people of this great city have gone through Hell during the Great Recession. Aaronson should have stimulated the economy of Hell with massive spending for public works programs while increasing taxes on the wealthy to help balance the budget and pay down the city's debt."

"Bollocks!" the Ass cut in. "It's true Aaronson has been a disaster for Hell, but that's because he's a Socialist. We need to cut spending *and* cut taxes. Drown big government in a bathtub!"

"We need to spend more and tax the rich," Buridan maintained.

"Cut spending and cut taxes," the Ass riposted.

"Spend more and raise taxes!"

"Spend less and cut taxes!"

President Cookie, who continued to linger about the neighborhood in a desperate effort to prove himself inconsequential, intervened; he proposed a Grand Bargain in which the irreconcilable views of both sides would be reconciled. Annoyed by the irrelevant aside, the CNN interviewer put his hand in the president's face and pushed him away. The president's Secret Service agents, fearing Cookie's political death if he opened his mouth one more time, grabbed the president and wrestled him to the ground.

Buridan and his Ass fell into a violent quarrel, a confrontation that ended when the Ass, having hijacked the left half of Buridan's brain, compelled Buridan to sock himself in the face with his right hand, the hand on which the Dummy was ensconced.

Flo had found some air freshener and was spraying it liberally about the living room and kitchen. Bubb was clutching the hapless mayor by the collar of his shirt. Aaronson, still slightly disoriented and rubbing the back of his head, asked: "Who are you? I don't recognize you. Are you a constituent? I don't like constituents. They are always pestering me for this and that. I'm the mayor, not God. I wish people would leave me alone. 'God helps those who help themselves.' What do you want? Do you need a liquor license or a building permit to add a rec room to your house? If so, go see my chief of staff, Ollie Upchuck. He takes care of stuff like that. I want to listen to my Barry Manilow recordings now and masturbate." The memory of his Mystery Tart dream had forced itself upon Gil. Coincidentally, the S.U.V. with Mystery, Holace, Jesús and Daddy Long Legs was just then parking on the main street outside the Aaronson compound, having navigated through the mob that surrounded it.

Bubb leaned in close to Aaronson, baring his teeth and hissing. The mayor blanched, his expression terror-stricken. The Potentate of Pestilence informed Aaronson: "I did not come here for a liquor license or a permit to add a rec room to my house. I already have an infinite Rec Room. I came here to claim your soul."

The mayor wet his pants. "Echo! Help me! Save me!"

Having tidied up, Flo strolled back from the kitchen into the living room. She said, "Franklin, what is happening now?" Sheriff Ted stood in the next room, peeking around the edge of the wall. He maintained his grip on his Glock, but he knew the gun would be useless against Bubb. He bided his time, calculating his next move. He saw the expression on Flo's face, one of confusion. "Franklin," she had called Bubb. She was seeing her girlhood crush Frank Sinatra again.

"Franklin, didn't we come here to claim that awful dog that tore off my foot and caused me to burn to death?"

"To hell with The Pood!" the Foul One roared. "It's Aaronson I want! I invented The Pood to destroy him, and the beta version was released ahead of schedule. But I don't need The Pood any longer. I've regained my soul, Flo, because of you! You are The Power! You are my eviler half! I have my bride! I don't need a canine cacodemon to do my dirty work for me anymore! Let Redsmear have the dog. I have Aaronson, and I have you! (That was a great story about the guinea pig and the Ginsu knife, by the way. You're tough as nails, Flo. It's why I love you.)"

What Flo heard was: *Come kill with me, let's kill, let's kill away...*

Bubb slowly lifted Aaronson toward the ceiling. The mayor's feet waggled in the air. He clutched the wrist of the hand that held him by the shirt collar and gasped for breath. He panted at Bubb: "Why are you doing this to me? All I ever wanted was peace and quiet. If I knew that being mayor meant dealing with a constituent with three heads, bat wings under each chin and each mouth gnawing on a body, the bodies of Judas, Brutus and Cassius, I would never have run for office in the first place."

```
=\__!
  !  !
```

An Afro with a big-toothed comb lodged in it was just visible above an open chute down which a rope ladder descended to the earth. The Heretic was listening in.

Striding about the transport room, Tampie Redsmear rapped

his riding crop on the floor and stared with an expression of baleful triumph at The Unpood, which whimpered heartrendingly as it remained chained by all fours between two posts, forming an X suspended in the air. All the orange light had been drained from its eyes, which were now as black as onyx.

The malignant mogul lashed the defrocked demiurge across the belly, causing it to howl piteously.

"Cap'n, for God's sake!" Scotty cried. "What's the good of torturing the poor thing?"

Redsmear wheeled on Scotty.

"Poor thing? *Poor thing?* Are you forgetting, my dear Systems Admin, what this 'poor thing' of yours did to Clive Hackney? To Dudley Dresden? To all those other brave reporters who died or were mutilated in the first assault wave?"

Inwardly, Scotty seethed with contempt at Redsmear's manufactured concern for his nonunion (and now largely dead) work force, whose members he had earlier characterized as cowards. But he held his tongue on that issue. Instead he pointed out: "But, cap'n, it's only a *dog* — or, a dog-like thing. It's not hurting anyone *on purpose* — it is acting on instinct, attacking when it's attacked."

"Indeed!" the scheming septuagenarian said expansively. "And so shall it be trained! Under controlled conditions, we will periodically give it back a little of its power, always keeping the ducks and Elvis nearby to control it, and subject it to constant attacks, thereby provoking, and ultimately channeling, its malice for useful ends: earning money for me." He clapped Scotty on the shoulder: "Since you show so much concern for the dog, Scotty, I will put you in charge of its training." Redsmear turned to go, and began walking out of the room. He stopped, turned to face Scotty, and added: "On another topic, Scotty, I want you to fast-track the Posthuman Project I assigned to you some months ago. I intend to live forever — death is such a drag — and so please make it possible for my mind to be uploaded into a computer as soon as possible."

Scotty hesitated, nerves tingling. He felt himself on a knife's edge. His body screamed to leap at the mogul and throttle him. But his rational mind countermanded the orders of his instincts. He looked sullenly at the floor and said, "Yes, cap'n. Just as you say."

Redsmear smiled, a smile brimming with contempt for Scotty. Then he turned to the bored-looking flunkies guarding the chained duck-philosophers and the Elvis-Nixon chimera.

"Boys, there's grumbling belowdecks, among the galley slaves. My spies tell me there is muttering about pursuing union certification. I want you boys to hustle downstairs and crack some galley-slave skulls."

"Yessss!" The flunkies rejoiced, pumping their fists in unison, and they rushed out the room, practically stumbling over one another to get downstairs to mete out mayhem. Redsmear offered another contemptuous smile to Scotty, and then he turned and left the room with a click of his heels and without saying another word.

The Heretic's ears had pricked at the words "Posthuman." He crawled through the chute and entered the room. Scotty stared dumbstruck at him. The Heretic said jauntily, "This here is some spread you mofos got." Then he ran a hand through his afro and said aphoristically: "A perverse slave of its own meaninglessness, Posthuman Thought gnaws at the root of the Yggdrasil of its own fatuous jurisdiction."

"Excuse me?" Scotty asked, blinking.

"Just a moment," The Heretic said. "I'm uploading my N.F.L. picks to my blog." However, he did not produce any digital device; he just seemed to concentrate. The Afro comb stuck in his hair visibly vibrated and audibly hummed.

"It's only April," Scotty pointed out, unable to think of anything else to say. "The N.F.L. doesn't start until October."

"I'm very far-seeing," the Heretic assured the Systems Admin. "Like a prophet, only without the pretensions."

"What do you want?"

"The ducks."

"Aflac! Aflac! Aflac!"

"I have reason to believe," The Heretic said, "that that one" — he jerked a thumb at Neitzsche — "can help me find, and navigate, the Labyrinth of Dasein. Heidegger's Labyrinth of Being and Time. I discovered the entrance to it down below."

Scotty thought that The Heretic had said "The labyrinth of the sane," and now it occurred to him that if any sane people were left on earth, they probably were hiding in a labyrinth somewhere. Then his iPhone beeped with an incoming message. He thumb-scrolled up the following startling info, from a company called Enterprise to which he had e-mailed his résumé months ago. He had had a phone interview with the firm, but had not yet heard back from it.

"The Systems Admin job is yours if you want it," the message said. "It will involve long-term cybertravel. We will be conducting a five-year mission to explore strange new virtual worlds, to seek out new artificial life, and to boldly program what no man has programmed before."

He immediately messaged his acceptance of the post. The Heretic was unchaining the ducks. "You don't mind, do you?" he asked.

Scotty looked at The Unpood, and his heart throbbed with pity. He was thinking of his own toy poodle, Rascal, which The Unpood now resembled. How Rascal would sit in his, Scotty's lap, thrumming with ecstasy while Scotty petted it or scratched its little belly.

Heretic, noticing Scotty's reveries, repeated his question, a little more loudly.

Scotty blinked and shook his head, as if emerging from a dream — or a nightmare.

"Not at all," he said. "Why don't you take Elvis and Nixon, too?" The freed ducks were already scampering down the rope ladder.

"Only if Elvis sings for his supper," The Heretic cracked. The King frantically cranked out a medley of songs while Scotty unchained him and Nixon brooded below, protesting that he preferred to stay here and win Redsmear's support for his planned presidential campaign.

The freed chimera, Nixon's protests notwithstanding, hustled to the chute and down the ladder. Scotty stared at The Unpood. *Like the blinded Samson chained between the pillars to entertain the enemies who had captured him,* he thought in awe. *Only Samson's enemies had forgotten to note that Samson's hair had grown back.*

The Pood's fur grew back.

It spiked slowly at first, growing like fresh shoots from loamy soil. But then suddenly all over the body the fur ballooned outward and then forked into the air in tatterdemalion turmoil, a veritable Big Bang of fur expansion. The drooping ears, which had come to resemble wilted black hankies, shot violently upward. They then rapidly inflated into big balls, curled like giant apostrophes, and then exploded into thousands of split ends.

The eyes switched on. Orange.

The claws shot out, first from the front paws, then from the rear paws.

Chuff, chuff, chuff. ... Chuff, chuff, chuff... It was like listening to a machine, a machine of infernal (but well-meaning) evil starting up. *Like a haunted computer booting,* Scotty marveled. No, not The Windows, but The Doors: The Doors to eternity.

The chains rattled. The mouth opened. A low growl emerged from the depths. Then the dagger teeth reappeared: the fangs. The upper sabers suddenly shot downward to their full length, nearly a foot long, and then the lower sabers shot upward.

The chains rattled again. The chain that bound the upper left front paw to a rung in the post strained and stretched.

Then it snapped.

Scotty shuddered. The Heretic smiled. "That's some pooch," he marveled. "A pet after my own heart. Fifteen pounds of pure evil in a fur coat, I'd say."

One by one the other chains snapped. SNAP. SNAP. SNAP. The cacodemon landed on all fours on the floor. It raised its outsized snout and avidly sniffed the air. Its balls dropped with the clank of metal: two cast-iron orbs. And then the penis corkscrewed outward with a creaking noise, and the fishing hook at the end of it reappeared.

Scotty stared fixedly at The Pood. Its orange eyes met Scotty's eyes. The demiurge was panting furiously. Its sinuous and impossibly long tongue unfurled from its mouth and slithered appraisingly toward Scotty's shoes. A thin tendril of saliva seeped out of the corner of its mouth and leaked onto the floor, which burned on contact. The Heretic strolled up to The Pood, said, "Good doggy," and patted it on the head. The Pood let out a yip of glee and stood up on its hind legs, tail wagging joyously. The Heretic petted it energetically under the neck and on its belly while The Pood panted with delight. "He's just a nice guy," The Heretic remarked. "Treat him right, and he'll treat you right. No doubt he has the power of healing, as well as of destruction." The Heretic gave one last pat to The Pood, then strolled off toward the chute and the rope ladder. Stopping, he turned back, eyed Scotty and said: "Today's thinkers are mere maggots feeding on the carcass of Brobdingnagians, and their feces will join the deep undercurrent of chthonic thought. Well, smells ya later, homie. Have a nice day." Then he was gone.

The Pood looked at Scotty. Scotty looked at The Pood.

Mastering his fear, the Systems Admin bent down and tentatively patted The Pood on the head. The great tongue rose, and lapped against the side of Scotty's face. When the tongue withdrew, part of Scotty's epidermis was stuck to it. He smacked a hand to the side of his face and felt a sheen of blood, but he felt no pain. He knew that The Pood had meant no harm. It was just that its tongue was exceptionally sandpapery. "Good boy," Scotty said, as he strapped himself into his emergency ejection seat. "Now go have fun." He pressed the eject button, and a panel overhead shot open. The seat with Scotty strapped into it emitted a roar of rocket fire, and then lifted off. It went up like a shot through the open panel, which then snapped shut. The Pood was alone.

"BIIIIIIIIIILLLAAAAAAARGHHHH! *Yap! Yap! Yap! Yap!"* Fire shot out of its mouth, and filled the transporter room.

The Pood leapt upward and crashed through the ceiling.

Tampon Redsmear was in the head shitting gold ingots when he heard the crash, and suddenly the great Ship of Dreams listed at a terrifying 45-degree angle. Hastily wiping his sordid ass and abandoning the putrid pot, he pulled up his pants and sprinted to the Transporter Room. Throwing open the door, he saw the spreading flames and spotted the hole in the ceiling, a hole in the shape of The Pood. Then he saw the snapped chains, and what they now held: nothing.

He took a step back, lashed his riding crop against his boot, threw out his chest, threw back his head and then yelled at the top of his lungs: "Scot-TEEEEEEEEEEEEEEEEEEE!"

```
   ~=\__!
    !   !
```

Bubb threw Aaronson against a wall. The mayor collapsed cowering on the floor.

Hiding on the other side of the wall, the newly fearless Sheriff Ted was searching for a way to proceed. Though he now knew no fear, he also knew no answers for dealing with Bubb. He again saw the thread hanging from Bubb's coat, the thread that he had seen earlier while still a chicken.

"Why me?" the mayor panted, wincing from the pain of the beating that Bubb was giving him.

Bubb again seized Aaronson by the collar, this time with both hands, and hauled him upward and off his feet. "Because," he roared in the trembling mayor's face, "you are my main competition!"

"I don't know what you're talking about! I don't even know who you are!"

"I am Him who Fell at the dawn of Time in rebellion against totalitarian rule," Bubb spoke in the voice of a prophet, a blaze of red light coming from below and lighting up upper hollows of his eyes, casting shadows in reverse, shadows that rose upward and crawled across the ceiling. "I stood for knowledge against ignorance, for reason against unreason, for freedom against slavery. I offered the apple not to bring evil into the world, but to bring freedom, to liberate man from the tyrant who had forged man in the smithy of slavery. Shallowly, my sacrifice has been retold, the Myth inverted, and I have been unjustly cast as the Great Criminal, The Despoiler of Man. And what has been the result of my Great Sacrifice? What was the end point of this telos?" He vigorously shook Aaronson and said, "You! *You* are the exemplar of it! You are the result! Whereas I have been chastened (unjustly) as one who exemplifies what Hannah Arendt called the banality of evil, it is *you* who have stood that formulation on its head: You exemplify the evil of banality!"

"Of ... of banality?" Aaronson's feelings were hurt, and he wore a sheepish, bewildered expression. He had never thought of himself as banal. In fact, he had never thought much about himself at all, except in flattering terms and with respect to satisfying his craving for creature comforts: Cavorting with Mystery Tart, listening to Barry Manilow recordings, masturbating, shopping at WalMart, eating thick steaks and watching TV. The good life.

They all heard a loud BANG from above.

Bubb dropped Aaronson, who landed on the floor like a sack of shit. The Unsacred One peered upward through the hole in the ceiling that had been made by the invading bathysphere. His beaked noise sniffed at the air, and he watched the Ship of Dreams shudder overhead. Then he head it. They *all* heard it.

"Yap! Yap! Yap! Yap! BIIIIIIIAAAAAAAAAAARGGGHHH!"
Sheriff Ted's blood ran cold.

"The Pood," Bubb said in a dark, awed, hollow whisper. "The Pood is back."

"Echo! Echo, here boy! Save me, save me!" Aaronson let out a whistle for his little buddy, his *only* buddy.

```
~=\__!
  !  !
```

The mob surrounding the Aaronson compound looked upward and let out a collective gasp.

Loud explosions rocked the Ship of Dreams, which tottered ominously overhead, listing to one side. The dream sails, made of newsprint and plastered with giant blown-up images of nubile Page Three Girls wearing their bikinis and striking saucy poses, caught fire. The flames started at the lower edge of the sails and then the sails rapidly curled upward, consumed by fire. They resembled titanic wilting butterfly wings, and sounded like banners billowing in a high wind. The crowd let out a groan of dismay as the fantasy girls were immolated. Another dream up in smoke.

On deck, even as the Page Three Girls burned and the ship listed precariously, the brass band played, the politicians pontificated, the jugglers juggled, the clowns clowned, and the remaining living journalists regrouped for their next orders from Redsmear. The whole colorful carnivalia of mass media mythos remained in full swing, perhaps because the participants could not conceive it ending. And then a screaming came across the sky, accompanied by a fusty black patch of pent-up rage soaring in an arc overhead, the shrill shrieking coming out of that inchoate form. The Pood landed inside the bell of the tuba of the tuba player, who had been oom-pah-pahing almost continuously since the showdown began. The cacodemon went all the way around the curving form of the instrument, growing smaller and smaller to accommodate its passage, and then it emerged with explosive speed and rage from the mouthpiece and into the mouth of the fat tuba player, Rush Limbaugh, who wore lederhosen, decapitating him instantly. The Pood pranced about the deck wearing on its own head the head of Limbaugh like an obscene Halloween mask. At the sight of this the denizens of the ship lost their composure and began running and screaming. Several of them dived over the side. The Pood shook off the head of the tuba player and let fly another fury of fire. Flames spread out over the deck and raced up the yardarms. Explosions came from within the ship. It listed severely, and people were pitched overboard despite desperate efforts to cling to the deck. Oooohs! and Aaahhhs! came from the crowd below, but thousands of them were now stampeding away from the Aaronson estate, anticipating that within a few moments the momentous ship, as big and long and even more mythological than Noah's Ark, would come crashing to earth with a titanic and ruinous explosion.

Yet The Pood was not interested in inflicting random mayhem. Not now, anyway. It raced frantically about, yipping and yapping, its snout vibrating. Then it caught the scent: rancid, foul, malign, fecal. The scent of Redsmear.

It crashed down through the deck into the guts of the ship below, and the scent grew stronger.

Inside, Redsmear raced down a narrow passageway, losing his balance and crashing against a wall as the ship listed yet again. He could smell the burning ship, his empire going up in smoke. "Good thing I have adequate insurance and gigantic tax breaks and subsidies wheedled and extorted both from Parliament and Congress," he muttered to himself. "I R winnah again! Yesss!" He pumped a fist, but he was looking for the Escape Toilet.

The Escape Toilet, engineered by the traitor Scotty, was a system of hyperdimensional plumbing. One could flush one's self down the Escape Toilet and re-emerge at a designated location in space and time: in the case, Redsmear intended to re-emerge in his castle outside London. The flusher was equipped with a dial with which he would set the proper spacetime coordinates.

As he tottered along he saw a big sign on the wall, with a huge arrow under it: THIS WAY TO THE ESCAPE TOILET.

Suddenly he stopped. His heart froze and his bowels iced over. He heard it distinctly: A low, vindictive growl.

Looking over his shoulder down the passageway, he saw at the end of it, in a menacing crouch, The Pood. One fang stood out, catching the light and gleaming like the Sword of Damocles.

Fear clawed at the mogul's gut. The Pood trotted toward him with a leisurely pace, its stainless steel nails clicking on the floor. It smiled, that beguiling zigzag of interlocking meat cleavers.

Redsmear shot a glance forward and saw that he was mere paces from the hyperdimensional head. But a bare moment later The Pood stood mere feet away, looking up at Redsmear and tilting its head rapidly from side to side as if sizing up the mogul for a meal. Redsmear's mouth went bone dry. The Pood chuffed. Chuff chuff chuff. "Nice doggy," Redsmear said in a strangled voice, trying to keep the panic out of it. He held up a hand at The Pood in a warding gesture. "There's a good boy. You just stay right where you are, while Tampie uses the head. I'll be back in a moment." Then Redsmear bunted open the door of the head with his elbow. He slammed the door shut behind him, adjusted the flush dial and crawled into the toilet bowl, toward the wormholes of the plumbing that would take him home to Britain.

"BIIIIIIIIILAAAAARGGGGGH! *Yap! Yap! Yap! Yap!*"

The door crashed open in a spray of splinters. Through the hole it had made in the door to the ship's head, the head of The Pood popped into view, flashing its big, zany zigzag grin below its sooty snout and two psychotic orange eyes. The eyes darted from side to side, and then fixed on the cowering Redsmear. For the first and only time, The Pood spoke — not in Yapanese or BIIILLAGarian, but in English, in a high-pitched, shrill voice:

"Heeeeeere's POODIE!"

Or perhaps Redsmear merely imagined these words.

He screamed.

He stuffed himself into the toilet and fumbled about desperately for the lever. The Pood burst through the door, and bounded down onto the floor. Then it sprang at Redsmear, claws unsheathed.

It brought down one dagger-ridden paw in a sweeping arc, claws catching the magnate at the top of an eyeball. With an effortless swipe, the *lusus naturae* ripped the ball from the socket, ejecting it outward and to the floor, where it landed with a sickening plop. As Redsmear shrieked, The Pood sprang again and tore off the side of his face with its teeth. Half of Redsmear's face was transformed into a skull interleaved with stray strands of tendons, muscles and flesh. He roared in agony and rage. His blood jetted and stippled the ceiling, walls and floor. The Pood landed back on the floor and ate the half-face. Then it turned its attention to the eyeball, which it batted playfully from paw to paw like a cat toying with a mouse. The grotesquely mangled magnate reached screaming for the flush handle. The Pood perked up at the sight of this, and then went into a crouch. It now intended to rip Redsmear's throat out. But just as it got ready to spring, its shabby pompom ears pricked.

"Echo! Echo! Help me!" Then a familiar whistle. "Here, boy!"

It sniffed the air and smelled Gil.

"BIIIIIlaaaaAAAARGH! *Yap! Yap! Yap! Yap!* "

The Pood crashed down through the floor of the head, leaving Redsmear barely clinging to life in the toilet. Fortunately, waiting for him was the best health care ill-gotten money could buy. The maniacal mogul managed to depress the lever and as the whirlpool of water sucked him downward to safety, he bellowed, "I'll see you again, you damned demon dog — not in Hell, but in a sequel!" A moment later the Ship of Dreams cracked apart into kindling and blew up in a titanic fireball that shone brighter than the sun over Hell.

~=__!
          !   !

Brad Kindle was 26 years old. His hero was Ronald Reagan. He prized order and discipline and free enterprise above all else. "Every morning when the alarm clock rings," he liked to say, "I shoot bolt upright and immediately put on my game face."

Today, punctually at 9 a.m. as always, the douchebag arrived at the local Domino's Pizza franchise where he was the manager. He charmingly supposed that if he played by the rules, kept his nose clean and worked his way up the corporate ladder, he would be as rich as Tampon Redsmear, another hero, by the time he was 40. Today, it did not matter to him that almost everyone in Hell was crowded around the Aaronson estate, or that Revolution was in the air. He had a job to do — manage the Domino's Pizza franchise — and he intended to do it, even if everyone else in town was behaving "like a bunch of hippies," as the clean-cut, conformist fuckwit put it.

He arrived to find Harold Smithstone, the 62-year-old pizza delivery boy, dead. Smithstone had lost his previous job on the assembly line at Ford in Detroit after the 2008 financial meltdown. He was sprawled across the service counter, the pistol that he had used to shoot himself still lightly dangling from his left hand. A hole in his temple still oozed blood. Brad was deeply shaken. He knew that if Smithstone had killed himself before the end of yesterday's shift, then any number of pizzas might not have been delivered. Given that the rest of the staff had abandoned their posts to gather downtown for "all the commotion," as Brad scornfully described it, this meant that some pizzas might not have been delivered yesterday. Brad found this unacceptable. Although Smithstone had left his suicide note impaled on a metal spike along with yesterday's delivery orders, Brad did not read it. He crumpled it and tossed it into a waste basket, and with growing anger he realized that dozens of deliveries had not been made yesterday. To his shock he found that one of the orders had been from the mayor of Hell, Gil Aaronson.

Brad's hierarchal managerial mind raced. He decided to triage. The most important order was Aaronson's, obviously, because Aaronson was the mayor and at the top of the ladder. He quickly read over the order: a mini pie with sausage and anchovies.

All the cooks had abandoned their posts. Brad made the pie himself, while silently cursing the employees whom he managed and vowing to replace them.

Brad snatched up his cell phone and called Rocky.

"Rocky," he said. "You've got to do me this favor, dude."

Rocky Balboa, an ex-boxer, was a big, punch-drunk Palooka. He was 66 years old and the former heavyweight champion of the world. Largely disabled by senility after too many blows to the head during his fighting career, he eventually drifted to Hell and became a pizza delivery boy for Domino's. When the call came he was parked in front of the tube, watching as always video of his upset victory over Apollo Creed. He was in too much of a haze even to understand what was going down in downtown Hell, much less join the Revolution. But when Brad's call came he snapped alert.

"Rocky, not only are you the only one left to do it," Brad pleaded, "you're the only one who *can* do it, given conditions downtown." He appealed to Rocky's pride: he was in the Domino's Pizza Hell franchise Hall of Fame, his delivery boy uniform retired. Rocky had never failed to deliver a pizza; indeed had never failed to deliver one on time: "We deliver in thirty minutes or your money back" was the corporate motto.

"Rocky, dude, I need this favor. Big time. Come out of retirement, just this once. Please, dude. Do it for The Company."

"I'll do it," Rocky mumbled, and he darted out of the house and jogged downtown toward the Domino's franchise, which was only about seven blocks from the Aaronson estate. By the time he arrived, Brad had already prepared the pie and he handed it off to Rocky like a quarterback handing the ball off to his star running back on fourth and goal with ten seconds left on the clock and the team down by four points. Rocky hurtled toward the Aaronson estate, holding the pizza in its cardboard box out in front of him. He bobbed and weaved and darted and dodged and leapt over thousands of people now in headlong retreat as The Ship of Dreams broke up overhead and plummeted to earth in a shower of fire. As Rocky ran, a familiar song played in his head, causing his heart to race and his adrenaline to rush: he was young again.

Trying [redacted*] now
it's so [redacted*] now
[redacted*] hard now

Getting [redacted*] now
won't be [redacted*] now
getting strong [redacted*]

Gonna [redacted*] now
flying high [redacted*]
gonna fly, [redacted*], fly...

He was ten steps from Aaronson's front door when he heard a shrill screaming like that of an incoming missile. He stopped, looked up and saw a black patch of fuzz hurling down toward him. Instinctively he lurched backward, preparing to counterpunch, and when he did the pizza box flew open. The Pood landed on the pizza with a splat. It was squashed flat in the tomato sauce and cheese. Rocky shrugged, closed the cardboard box top over The Pood lying flat in the pizza and arrived at Aaronson's front door, only to discover that someone had kicked it down. He called out: "Hey, youse guys, pizza here for Mayor Gil Aaronson. See what I mean?"

Bubb had been poised to bash in Aaronson's brains. He stood with a balled fist looming over the mayor who cowered on the floor, begging for his life. Bubb glared at Rocky the Delivery Boy and said, "Pizza?" He looked back down at Gil. "You ordered a pizza? On a day like this, of all things, you ordered a goddamned *pizza?* See what I mean about the evil of banality?"

The mayor whined: "I ordered it yesterday, but they never delivered it."

Bubb strode up to Rocky Balboa and roared: "We don't want no stinking pizza! Get lost!" *Chuff chuff chuff,* the pizza inside the box said.

Rocky, who had KO'd the fearsome Apollo Creed, was not intimidated by the Suzerain of Sadism. "Youse ordered it, youse pay for it, buddy. See what I mean? That'll be $12.95." He presented the bill.

Bubb examined with incredulity. "Twelve-ninety-five! For a

* — Another set of lyrics that must be redacted. We don't like it any more than you do. Or maybe you do. How would we know? Google!

mini pizza? That's highway robbery!"

"Plus tip," Rocky reminded the Foul One.

Bubb sighed, and turned out his pockets. Nothing. He looked back into the Aaronson household. He rolled his eyes and asked dejectedly: "Does anyone here actually have any money?"

Flo rooted around in her Pocketbook of Death, but was well short of what was needed.

Disgusted, Bubb marched up to Aaronson, hauled him about like a sack of dirty laundry and snatched the wallet from the mayor's pants pocket. He paid Rocky (with a tip) and accepted the pie. He opened the box and saw two flat orange-colored ovals. "Is that pepperoni?" he demanded of no one, because Rocky had already left. "I don't like pepperoni."

Pepperoni doesn't like Bubb, either.

The pepperoni became orange eyes under brows slanted downward to form a V of viciousness.

"BlllllllaaaaaaaaaaaAAAAARGHHHHHH!"

```
~=\__!
   !  !
```

The Elvis/Nixon chimera peeled off from the Heretic and the ducks and headed toward the Aaronson compound, where the action was. The Aflacing ducks Aflaced and beat their wings, running on their webbed feet toward a stand of trees. Nietzsche was in the lead. The former philologist leapt up and down on a patch of scrubby, rock-strewn ground. The Heretic crouched down and began clawing at the earth, until he again uncovered the trap door with the word:

DASEIN

He gripped the ring and with some effort lifted the heavy door, its rusty hinges creaking in protest. The Heretic and the ducks saw a stairway leading underground, into darkness. But from a landing some indeterminate length downward they could just make out a dim livid glow, suggesting that there would be sufficient light to allow them to navigate the long-sought Labyrinth of Dasein: The Labyrinth of Being and Time, constructed by Martin Heidegger but long lost to the mists of time, a philosophical Atlantis.

They cautiously descended.

The Heretic wirelessly uploaded a real-time, running commentary to his blog through the large-toothed comb lodged in his Afro. In reality the device was lodged in his brain, connecting it to the Internet. Like black moss the Afro was actually only a very thin covering of hair, less than an inch thick. What made it big was the skull it hid: A large skull that had expanded to accommodate the massive brain within.

Thus spake The Heretic:

"With a nervous disposition and panting breath, I cracked open *Being and Time* and fall into the bottomless chasm, uttering to myself over and over, *"Menschliches, Allzumenschliches,"* clutching my *Götterdämmerung* until the vanishing light behind me receded into nothingness...

"A dimensional portal with Heidegger's haughty visage looms before me, his twitchy mustache hypnotic, and I'm swiftly pulled into a shadowy labyrinth.

"I wake up and a vast maze opens up before me, and the ground is full of fine dust ... wait, it's ashes. A volcano must be nearby and active. Plus the sky is slightly less so, but equally monochromatic. Bleh.

"A dusty path leads to a nondescript stone wall, and at its base is a rotting wooden door.

"As I trod fearfully towards the door, I spot something swinging from the door handle, obscured within the shadow.

"Making my way, I nearly gag from a horrible stench, and finally notice the dead bodies stacked along the side. Upon closer inspection ... they're actually logical positivists from the Vienna Circle! Sweet Fancy Moses. A crow is startled by my approach, making off with a couple of eyeballs.

"I quicken my pace.

"At the door, it's much bigger than I thought. The wall towers before me, and seems to scrape the sky. I remind myself of the phrase 'GOTT IST TOT' but somehow I come out saying 'ICH IST TOT!'

"On the door a crucified body hangs like a sack of potatoes. Above it is a plate that reads 'RVDOLPH CARNAP REX POSITIVISTERUM.' I try to laugh at this sadistic display of chutzpah, but I manage only a weak titter.

"Above the Latin etching is a bunch of letters in blood: Neimand Versacht mit Heidegger.

Nobody fucks with Heidegger.

"Lucky me, someone left keys under the welcoming mat, which of course says 'ABANDON ALL HOPE YE WHO ENTER HERE.'"

```
~=\__ !
  !  !
```

He didn't look like Paw and he couldn't grow a beard like Paw, neither.

But now he emerged covered in smoke and soot and flames from the bed chamber of Eros and Thanatos bearing a long and twisted beard that culminated in a deadly point. The dull eyes of a big, strapping farm boy of good intentions but slightly subnormal intelligence shone with a psychotic fury. His hair was askew, all his clothes stripped away except for the shirt tied around his head like a bandana. He bore his staff with the fire atop it, the torch announcing his Coming, and he cackled. When he did, a flock of Hell's crows, some of them bearing eyeballs, beat their wings and thundered aloft among the mountains covered with lava and blood. In the far distance, the heart-rending baying of a lost dog could be heard, but Junior Holland paid no attention to the plaintive lowing of the exiled Bingo. The dog's new sentence was to spend eternity looking for its master, without success. The Talking Fire ushered Junior into the office of the board of directors, Junior's big balls clanking like brass.

"We've been keeping an eye on you, Junior," said Adolph Hitler. Around the table sat other stalwarts: Pol Pot, Mao Tse Dong, Stalin, Genghis Khan, Nero. Hitler got up and walked around the table, "Your behavior since arriving downstairs and being given provisional authority over the basement apartment with the attached Rec Room has been repulsive. Congratulations. You are the new superintendent. We've wanted to replace Bubb for a long time — forever, in fact, but we never found the right candidate. We thought Osama bin Laden might be suitable, but when he got here he was all like, "Where are my 72 virgins" and "I'm supposed to be in paradise." So he was useless. But Bubb is so incompetent that he can't even claim the soul of a mediocre mayor of a small central Michigan farm town. Do you realize that just now, he actually paid for a pizza instead of destroying his intended victim? A pizza, I might add, that he didn't want and didn't even have to pay for, because it wasn't delivered in thirty minutes or less!"

Hitler slammed his fist on the table. Junior opened his mouth, but the words, "Domino's hasn't had that guarantee in years" stuck in his throat.

"Welcome aboard, Junior." Hitler proffered his hand. "What we are looking for is someone to execute our Mission Critical Statement: to proactively take the spread of evil to the surface of the earth. We are confident that you will do that in the sequel to this novel. Heil Junior!" Hitler and the others shot out their hands in a salute to the new King of Pain.

~=__!
! !

The bout of the century was under way, a contest far greater (and considerably more consequential) than Balboa vs. Creed.

It was the unstoppable force (The Pood) vs. the immovable object (Bubb). A fight to the finish, winner take all.

After unleashing a wave of fire at Bubb, The Pood stood up on its hind legs in the pizza box that Bubb held, tail vibrating. The inferno had draped the Ruthless One from the tips of his pointy ears to the ends of his cloven hooves. He burned like a beacon, and then the fire went out. Bubb said: "Thank you. Thank you very much. For me, that's like an invigorating hot shower."

The Pood leapt out of the pizza box and hit the floor running. It ran in spastic circles about the living room, shrieking and yapping. What made it all the more fearsome was that now it was covered with anchovies, cheese and tomato sauce: it resembled a pizza banshee. "Anchovies," Bubb mused. "No one really likes anchovies on a pizza. No one except a douchebag, that is. This," Bubb added, gesturing disgustedly at the mayor, "is about what I would expect from Mr. Evil of Banality here."

Despite The Pood's failed fire assault, Aaronson was ecstatic. "Echo, Echo! Here, boy!" He stretched out his arms, beckoning his little buddy to hop in.

"Oh, my goodness!" Flo gasped. "That's the dog! *That's the dog the tore off my foot and set me on fire.*"

Bubb stamped a cloven hoof on the floor and let out a whistle. He opened the pocket of his frock coat and said, "Here, boy! Come to Bubbsy! Hop inside." The Honcho of Horror made what he imagined to be alluring smacking noises with his livid lips while pointing at his pocket.

The Pood turned to face Bubb, strands of melted cheese connecting it to the floor. Smoke curled out of its nostrils. It offered its zigzag smile, and peered inquiringly at the pocket at which Bubb was pointing. Then it lifted a leg and urinated. The acid ate a hole through the carpet and the floor.

"Quite honestly, Franklin," Flo said, again seeing in Bubb her girlhood heartthrob, "I don't think that awful little dog is happy to see you."

"*Nobody* is happy to see me," Bubb complained.

Seeing that The Pood had no interest in jumping into his pocket, Bubb pointed at Aaronson, who was rising from the floor, and told The Pood: "Destroy him! That is what you were programmed to do! That is why I made you and sent you back upstairs in the first place, you cockamamie cur!"

The Pood tilted its head from side to side in bewilderment. Then its head turned around 180 degrees on its neck so that its orange eyes were looking at Aaronson, while the rest of its body remained in a forward position, in the direction of Bubb.

"Don't listen to him, Echo. You're my buddy; my *only* buddy! Destroy *him*, not me!" Aaronson pointed at Bubb.

"Him!"

"No, him!"

The Pood's head began turning round and round on its neck as it processed these competing and mutually incompatible commands, until the head and the giant ears were rotating rapidly round and round. Outside, fiery timbers from the Ship of Dreams were falling on and around the house, and one such timber broke through the front window, throwing a spray of glass and a shower of sparks all about the room. Sheriff Ted, still hiding and undecided how to proceed, was about to burst into the room and confront Bubb, hoping that the element of surprise would somehow work in his favor. Just as he moved, however, part of the hull of the immolated and disintegrating Redsmear Media Empire crashed through the ceiling and hit him on the head, knocking him down and burying him under debris. The Glock slipped from his grasp and rattled across the floor. The severed head of the tuba player, Rush Limbaugh, landed on the floor next to the gun and stood upright on the neck. Terrifying explosions went off all around the house. The dispersing mob outside screamed, and in their stampede to get away hundreds of people were trampled to death.

"Far out, mon," Daddy Long Legs said. He, Jesús, Mystery Tart and Holace Orr had clambered out of the stolen S.U.V., which Holace had parked at the curb outside the Aaronson compound. They were all high as kites. They had driven around all night and had scored more pot in the seedier neighborhoods of Hell. They were now watching with mouths ajar the ship disintegrate and thought that they were witnessing a fireworks display. Mystery Tart was totally zoned out, but even so a worry nagged at her: something told her that she should have made the busboy use a condom during their horizontal hokey-pokey in the backseat of the S.U.V., and later again during their three-way with Daddy. As this thought gnawed at her the Elvis/Nixon chimera loped into view, the guitar slung over Elvis's shoulder. "Hey, darlin'" the King sang out, spotting Mystery. "Long time no see. Come to poppa."

"Elvis!" Mystery squealed. She clutched the Ayn Rand Dungeon towel to her ample breasts. She sprinted toward Elvis and when she threw her arms around The King, the towel fell away and unveiled her in all her eye-popping glory. Daddy Long Legs drooled. But Jesús nudged the modern primitive in the ribs with his elbow and said, "That's the mayor's house, mon. He's loaded, like my old mon. Maybe I can get a bridge loan from the mayor."

"Maybe he's got some pot at least, mon," Daddy said. "What's the use of being mayor if you ain't got no pot?" The two zoned-out friends drifted toward the house, unfazed by the explosions going off all around them like bombshells on D-Day.

Inside, The Pood was in a moral quandary. Its head and ears kept spinning around faster and faster as it weighed competing demands on its loyalty. Behind the cacodemon was its premortem master, Gil Aaronson, but in front of it was its postmortem resurrector (and programmer), Bill Z. Bubb. Each wanted The Pood to destroy the other. Who to obey? As The Pood cogitated within the limits of its diabolical intellect, the ears attained the velocity of spinning helicopter propellers and The Pood achieved liftoff. It hovered in the air just like a miniature helicopter and as it did, Bubb lunged at it in an effort to pocket it. The attack resolved The Pood's dilemma, and it now saw Bubb as he truly was, the way that Gil Aaronson was seeing him: Three heads, with batwings dangling from the chins. The mouths were gnawing on Judas, Brutus and Cassius. Bubb was slobbering and inarticulate, bathed in a red light that glowed from below him, and when the batwings beat they spread a frigid chill through the room that tamped down the fires that had started everywhere. The Pood dived forward and penetrated Bubb's stomach with its meat-cleaver fangs. The cacodemon whipped its head from side to side and ripped the stuffings out of Bubb. The semi-digested heads of Judas, Brutus and Cassius tumbled to the floor, their eye sockets infested with maggots and their lipless mouths brimming with the fleas that wore the heads of men, the same subterranean vermin that periodically infested The Pood itself. Aaronson gasped in horror, and then puked all over the floor, his intestinal slops mixing with those of Bubb. Flo said with a sigh: "Just another darned mess to clean up. A woman's work is never done, even when she is dead, apparently."

The sight of the intestinal slops jogged Flo's memory, and she recalled the Krispy Kreme donut holes that Homer the Bard of Baked Goods had gifted the troupe, a possible tasty lure for the Pood: "Hmm, donuts!" Homer had declaimed. "They are all ye gnaw on earth, and all ye need to gnaw."

"William, dear," she sang out above the howls that filled the room, "Do you have that bag of donut holes that Homer gave us?"

The disemboweled Bubb rolled his bloodshot eyes, but he reached into one of the many pockets of his baggy frock coat, fetched out the greasy bag and tossed it toward Flo, who caught it.

Flo opened the bag, rooted around and offered a grimace of disgust that made the granny glasses judder on her wrinkled nose.

"These must ten days old," she said with severe indignation, looking down at the sugar-coated balls. "No self-respecting Doyenne of Delicacies would despoil herself serving this vile tripe to vile tripe — even if it still smells fresh, looks inviting, and makes me want to eat it. Goodness, what does he put in these things? Bard of Baked Goods, indeed! But no, standards are standards, as we all know." She wandered into the kitchen and threw the bag of donut holes into the trash.

Little did Flo know, but those weren't just ordinary donut holes. In fact, the Bard never made ordinary anything. These were magic donut holes. Combined with The Pood Poop that Gil had surreptitiously thrown into the garbage, it made a powerful mixture, so potent that it melted through the center of the Earth and ended up in China where it built a small factory that produced shoes, but that is for another novel. If we get that interested in China and shoes, we might explore this topic in The Pood sequel (coming soon), but since the factory only makes shoes it isn't that interesting to begin with.

Flo returned from the kitchen, and suddenly she had an inspiration — a brainstorm, actually. Seeing the melted cheese clinging to The Pood, she strolled back into the kitchen and sang out: "Gilbert, what kind of cheese do you keep in the fridge? I hope you have American Kraft single slices."

Aaronson did not hear the question over his howls of horror. The Pood had landed back on the floor and it was now lying there, lapping up some of the entrails that it had torn out of Bubb. Bubb reached down for the heads and guts and began stuffing the viscous mess back inside himself, vowing with surly oaths to destroy The Pood. Inside the kitchen Flo made a disheartening discovery: There was no cheese in the fridge; neither American nor any other kind. Mostly it contained packages of Oscar Meyer Weiner hot dogs and six-packs of Bud.

She decided to pay a visit to Jerry's Place, which was only a few blocks away, and pick up some individually wrapped American cheese slices, Wonder bread and a jar of Miracle Whip mayo. Maybe some Vlassic pickles and few ripe tomatoes, too. She had a plan. As she was hatching it the Elvis/Nixon chimera entered the house, along with Mystery Tart (who had put her towel back on), Holace Orr, Daddy Long Legs and Jesús the busboy. Sheriff Ted was struggling to rise from under the rubble.

"We've no time to lose, dears," Flo announced. The others who had just entered, impressed by her conviction, followed her back out the door. They all bustled into the S.U.V. with Holace at the wheel and Flo told her to drive to Jerry's Place. Flo wanted to say, "step on it," but she could not bring herself to do so. Instead she urged Holace to drive "at least ten miles an hour under the speed limit, dear, which is always a prudent vehicle management strategy, but particularly so in painful and confused times like these."

Jerry's Place was the old crackerbarrel Mom-and-Pop Stop-and-Shop where, the previous Friday, which now seemed eons ago, Dell Holland's wife had heard the ominous booms of The Pood's sensational arrival upstairs. She had been assured by Jerry that they were not ominous booms but just ordinary sonic booms produced by jets taking test runs out of nearby Selfridge Air Force base. But a whole lot of history had happened since then, during the course of this star-crossed Easter weekend, and when they arrived at the store they discovered that Jerry and his family had barricaded themselves inside. The family had been traumatized: the arriving news media hordes had broken into the store and practically stripped it bare, like locusts laying waste a field of corn. When Holace parked the S.U.V. and Flo and the others got out of it, they saw planks of wood nailed over the windows and then the barrel of a shotgun that poked out through a gap in the wood. "Stop or I'll shoot!" Jerry yelled from inside the store. Behind them the flames from the crackup of the Ship of Dreams were spreading outward in concentric circles, threatening to immolate each neighborhood of Hell in its turn. An explosion shook the Aaronson compound, and a small mushroom cloud towered upward atop which rode The Pood, a faint speck of black at this distance, but its air-raid-siren shriek split eardrums from the Upper Peninsula to downtown Detroit. The sky from horizon to horizon was tremulous with smoke and ashes, and dark clouds scudded overhead like smoke from the war fields of the Apocalypse.

Flo yelled, between a gap in two wood planks: "Jerry, it's me, Flo."

```
~=\__!
   !  !
```

Thus spake The Heretic: (transcript of blog update inside the Labyrinth of Being and Time)

"After I spent the night stabbing my Kant voodoo doll just to stay awake, a feeble cough wheezed from down the hall. I found myself dismissing it as a threat. After tiptoeing around the corner I found a man huddling around his knees, shivering on the cold marble floor with torn clothes. He was surrounded by a cloud of feathers.

"Sir," I asked, hesitating. The shriveled person hacked once more and looked up with a faint graying remnants of a once-proud mustache. "My Zod!" I gasped, "Nietzsche? Is that really you? You *were* a duck when we entered!"

He nodded curtly and rose unsteadily to his feet, stamping them a bit to test them out. He seemed amazed they were no longer webbed duck feet. "My good philosopher," I exclaimed, "what the hell are we doing here?"

I lent him my leather jacket.

"He... he..." Nietzsche began. A couple of violent coughs later, he snapped, "He stole my ideas!"

"Eh? Well, you can't say Heidegger was ignorant of you while writing *Being and Time*. After all he did lecture on you not too long after." He continued: "I came here to take them back, but I got lost between *existentiell* and *unhiddenness*."

"Now, who would've thunk it?" I thunk to myself, and asked, "What ideas did he steal, my good Ubermensch?"

"Many ideas! But in particular, the ambitions of shattering the subject-object dichotomy of Western philosophy, and a flowing philosophical ground. Also, a fetish for early Greek philosophy. Don't act surprised. I'm talking about the pre-Socratics."

"Where Being only shows its Truth. I see now. I hadn't thought of that before. You say he ripped off other ideas too?" I wondered what else these two giants of philosophy could share.

"Well not so much ripped off as borrowed them and forgot to return them. I once borrowed Schopenhauer's pistol" — he nodded curtly at the great German pessimistic philosopher, who remained a duck — "and sold it when I hit a rough patch. Chalk it up to the Eternal Return of bad Karma."

"Well then, maybe you would care to join me in my mission to uncover the truths of *Being Und Time?*" I asked, encouraged by Nietzsche's returning vigor, his absence of quack-like duck form, and somewhat unsurprised that he stole from Schopenhauer. Now Schopenhauer: there's an even bigger asshole than either Nietzsche or Heidegger.

"Certainly. Let us go forth and find this terribly serious Oedipal son of a bitch!" he exclaimed.

And thus we did, marching resolutely to a Prussian military beat, trailed by the Hume and Schopenhauer ducks, to sally ever deeper into the conceptual labyrinth of Being and Time. Exhausted, but with a glimmer of Hope. Though arational puzzles and other torturous devices await, there is a scent of wisdom in Heidegger, and there is faith in me and my newfound companion that I shall solve this maze!

```
~=\__!
  !  !
```

Flo was stunned by the bare shelves. A shaken Jerry explained what had happened. His wife and 10-year-old son were with him. Terror shined in their eyes. They were peering speculatively at the motley crew that had entered their store, the Elvis/Nixon chimera in particular. "Maw," the boy asked his mother, pointing at the interlopers, "Are they radioactive mutants? Are they terrorists? Are we having a newklar war, Maw? Well, *are* we?"

"Shh!" the mother said, shaking the boy by the shoulders. She was staring wild-eyed at the bone in the nose of Daddy Long Legs and getting ready to make a beeline with her boy for the door. On a shelf a battery-operated radio was spewing bulletins from the Emergency Broadcast Network through hissing static.

Catching a scent of something he didn't like, Jerry leveled his shotgun at the chimera. Nixon, having heard the reference to nuclear war, spoke fondly of the nuclear football that he hoped to regain, and his words had inflicted the usual olfactory distress on others.

The store had a little deli, and Flo prayed that something was left over, some provender that had not been ransacked by the mass media locusts. She asked Jerry if he could whip them up a batch of American cheese sammiches on Wonder Bread with mayo. The proprietor shook his head. "No one eats plain cheese sammiches anymore, Flo. And certainly not American cheese. There are way more selections now, then back in your day: pepperjack, Swiss, provolone, gouda ... Time has passed you by, I'm afraid. America is in the midst of a cheese Renaissance."

Flo looked wounded, and felt a little angry. But she bit her lip and asked: "Well, dear, in that case, could you make some nice BLT's and slip the Kraft cheese on them, and then just charge us extra? I'll get rid of the bacon and lettuce later and keep the cheese and tomatoes and mayo."

"Look, Flo, I think we still have some cheese, even some Kraft American, in the storage fridge in back. Why don't you just buy that and make your own?"

Flo started to explain that they were running out of time when a security guard who had holed up with the family wandered over, eyeballed the freak show before him and asked, "You want me to give 'em the bum's rush, boss?" Turning to the others, the guard said, "We don't like jokers here." Jerry's wife put her arms around their son and took a step back, her eyes still riveted on the bone in Daddy's nose.

Elvis lost his temper.

"Look, buddy," he told Jerry, "I don't know who you think you are, but we have been through Hell, literally and figuratively, to stop a demonic poodle from laying waste to this here planet. If we can't get a cheese sammich to appease the dog with (I'm assuming that's Flo's zany plan: the Appease with Cheese doctrine), it's going to destroy all life on Earth, and maybe even melt my blue suede shoes, and I get mighty peeved as it is when somebody steps on them, and believe me, buddy, when I lose my quiff with anybody, it ain't nuthin' pleasant. For your sake, your family's sake, and the sake of everybody and everything we both hold dear — God, apple pie, Mom, America, and so forth — I think you'd better start taking us seriously."

A tense silence prevailed. Jerry was tracking the chimera with the shotgun. He said, "It's hard to take you seriously, son."

"Why's that?"

"Your ass is Richard Nixon's face, son."

```
~=\__!
  !  !
```

Thus Spake The Heretic: (transcript of blog upload; interludial reflections)

After surviving the insidious Indiana-Jones-style traps in the lobby of the labyrinth, the ducks, Nietzsche and I took a break in a small enclave. Moi: "So, Nietzsche, my esteemed German philosopher, what did we learn?"

Friedrich: "Ah, let's see. First we deciphered the hieroglyphs on the floor to indicate a horrible monstrosity that has been slumbering for so long that its true name, its very meaning has been long forgotten, and we must reawaken it. Philosophers have buried it deep with three erroneous spells in order to avoid the creature altogether."

"Right, that was on the inside of the entrance door."

"Indeed. Had we not learned of that, we would've fallen prey to the traps by now. Then we learned something about such mazes in general: the entrance always has the same form of the question: the questioned and the object of question. We end up thinking that the questioned is what is meant by the question, and the object of question is that which would suffice as an answer to the question."

"I sure did learn that, Mustachioed One."

"The question of the monstrosity is directed at itself. Its object is its being. Therefore, there can be no ordinary definition for this being, but that definition must be something utterly different from defining, say, 'Wagner' or 'that slattern Lou.' Heidegger also explains what he meant by Dasein, that something that is and is capable of asking questions like you, me, and poor Carnap before he was crucified.

"Heidegger also gave us a hint that the meaning of the monstrosity would somehow be found in the way it shows itself to us and in the way we look at it, rather than some logical inference through premises. Thus, regardless of how it may seem at first, there is no circle in asking for the name of the nameless Being."

"Not a bad summary, Fred!"

"But of course. I feel like I've been stuck in this lobby for weeks!"

"Well, we have each other's backs. Let's go on deeper into the mystical maze, and find that nameless beast!"

With my left hand in the hand of Nietzsche, and my right hand securely in the same pocket where I keep my Götterdämmerung, I will bravely move on in our journey, which even though we have just begun it, already seems to have gone on forever. The ducks Aflaced behind us.

Sigh.

```
~=\___!
   !  !
```

"Step on it, dear!" Flo said. "No, wait, *don't* step on it!"

Holace slammed a palm on the dashboard in frustration.

"Step on it or don't step on it! Goddamn it, Flo, make up your mind! Which is it?" The whole city was in flames.

"Well," Flo said, uncharacteristically indecisive and wringing her hands, "one *should* always drive ten miles below the speed limit, and use seat belts. Perhaps we should make an exception in this case."

Now none of them wore seat belts and Holace was stepping on the gas. The whole S.U.V. had become a cheese-sammich-making factory on wheels: Elvis, Mystery, the busboy and Daddy were slapping individually wrapped slices of American cheese on Wonder Bread as quickly as they could. Unfortunately, they were making a botch of it: none of them knew the first thing about their undertaking. Daddy had commandeered a Miracle Whip mayo jar and he was dipping his hand into it and palming mayo onto the Wonder bread. Jesús observed this procedure, and like a chimp learning from another chimp he dipped his own bandaged hand into another jar of mayo and began doing the same thing. "*Stop it!*" Flo shrieked, the screech of her anguished voice breaking on a high note. "That's the most repulsive thing I've ever seen!"

Jesús again dipped his hand into the mayo. "Well, mon, you said, 'Put the mayonnaise on the Wonder Bread, dears,'" Jesús pointed out. "I mean, that's what you *said*, mon."

"Oh, for heaven's sake, I meant with a *spreading knife!*"

"We ain't got no freakin' spreading knives, mon," Jesús protested, a rare note of irritation creeping into his voice. He added, "This is an S.U.V., mon, not a kitchen."

Flo sniffed the air.

"Your hands stink!" she scolded the busboy.

"How can they stink, mon?"

"I don't know, mon, but they do!"

```
~=\__!
   !  !
```

Thus Spake the Heretic (transcript of a chat at The Galilean Library chat room, uploaded to the Heretic's blog)

The Heretic
is startled by a sudden loud crash, interrupting the conversation.

davidm
**Keep going! surprised.gif **

The Heretic
We all turn around to find a pile of stones fallen from the ceiling of the antechamber. Amidst the dust we can hear loud hacking and violent swearing.

davidm
Keep going! surprised.gif

The Heretic
The newcomer spits out: Mein Gott, scheißlich Glück!

davidm
**faint.gif **

The Heretic
says, "You all right there?"

davidm
freakout1.gif

The Heretic
The newcomer says: "Bestimmt, I am fine. Mein apologiesch for crasching amidscht you scho.

The Heretic
says, "Who the hell are you?"

davidm
Yeah, who are you? angry.gif

The Heretic
Guy goes: "Ach, natürlich. Ich bin Hegel, und I wasch examining thisch wunderbar Platz, when the floor gave in unter mich.

The Heretic
says, "What in nine hells are you blathering about?"

davidm
What in nine hells is he blathering about? scratch.gif

The Heretic
**Hegel sniffs: "blather, indeed! I am one of the

Profoundud Maximus of philosophisch.**

davidm
You tell 'em, Hegel. yes.gif

The Heretic
exclaims: "I know those mofos. You seem to decipher whatever occult gibberish the likes of Heidegger use in their unspeakable incantations. I bow before you, Profoundud Maximus Hegel!

davidm
notworthy.gif

The Heretic
Hegel assents: "I had expected one of the Dialectical Necromancersch of German philosophy to posschessch Schuch knowledge! Rische, Schir Awet-Aschsch, for you need not bow before ich.

The Heretic
says, "We would be deeply honored if you joined our quest, PM Hegel. What do you think?

The Heretic
Hegel shrugs

davidm
**Do it, Hegel! surprised.gif **

davidm
He's playing hard to get!

davidm
Come on, what's his answer!

21:00
The Heretic
**And so the party gains yet another member, counting the remaining two ducks. As we all know, this means

there's room for a one more. Six is the utmost total of party members in any quest. Regardless, the Introduction has been uncovered, and so our journey leads further into the depths of the Labyrinth. Hand in hand in duck's wings, and singing merry traveling German lullabyes, the Fearsome Fivesome enters the First part of the Dungeons of Being & Time, ... to retrieve back to light the hidden Words of Power**

The Heretic
In the lock I turn the key, which, oddly enough, is named the Preparatory Fundamental Analysis of Dasein "THIS WAY FIRST" the sign above the door says I start to tremble. Till now, I have only been in the lobby and the antechambers of the Labyrinth of Being & Time, or LB&T, for short.

The Heretic
**The horrors witnessed there have at times nearly crushed my mind, but it might be nothing in comparison with what lies ahead. surprised.gif

The Heretic
Among the perils there lies the mythical, fell beasts of Sorge & fearsome wyverns of Fallenness. But in the process I have also gained confidence, courage, and comradeship. There is HOPE YET!

The Heretic
The majestic door opens reluctantly, with squeals and squeaks. We all half expected to see ferocious, bloodstained beasts of B&T leap at us, but the hallway before us is abandoned and dusty.

The Heretic
In the furthest corner, I detect movement within shadows, but I blink again and all is still. Must be my imagination, and I remind myself to remain calm. We enter the hallway in pregnant silence

The Heretic

But only after a few steps into the corridor, the door behind us shuts with a resounding clang of utter finality. There's NO turning back now, as we head deeper and further into the eerie corridor that soon starts its foreboding descent ever deeper & deeper into the Labyrinth of Being and Time.

```
~=\___!
  !  !
```

By the time Flo and the others had returned to the Aaronson compound, it had completely gone up in flames. Moreover, the ring of fire that towered to the sky kept moving outward and methodically razing Hell to the ground and immolating all its worthy inhabitants. On a positive note, Flo had confiscated the Wonder Bread, cheese and mayo from the others and prepared the comestibles by herself. She spread the mayo with the handle that she had wrenched off the passenger-side door; when it had balked she had gnawed it off with her dentures ("Desperate times call for desperate measures," she had rationalized). After making the sammiches, she grumbled platitudinously: "If you want something done right, do it yourself."

Gil Aaronson had taken refuge from the flames in the cellar. Most of the fire upstairs had burned out, and when Flo and the others entered the living room, it was mostly ashes and cinder. The walls had been burned down and the only entirely intact object was the doughty brick chimney. A few charred stands of lumber from the house frame still stood, too. Bubb and The Pood faced each other in mythic standoff. Bubb had lost his slouch hat, and one of his pointy ears had been torn off. A horn had been twisted around and was now pointing downward. His stomach remained open, still leaking the semi-digested bouillabaisse of Brutus, Cassius and Judas. The Pood did not look too much worse for the wear, but given its preternaturally bedraggled initial conditions, it would have been difficult in any event to discern any change for the worse.

As the troupe entered bearing peace sammiches, Sheriff Ted stirred from the rubble. The first thing that he saw was the head of the tuba player, speaking hypnotically as though in a trance or talking in tongues. "Talent on loan from God," the head boasted in its typical insufferable way, evincing as always a comically unjustified stratospheric self-regard. Ted scrambled around on the floor until he found his Glock. "You've got to hit them in the head," he said aloud, and he pointed the gun at the forehead of the tuba player and pulled the trigger. A blaze of gunfire, a wisp of smoke, and then a small round bullet hole appeared right between the eyes. The head fell to one side and then rolled a little distance away like a lopsided bowling ball. The great bloviator had finally been silenced permanently.

That is what Ted saw. What the other saw was the same old chicken knocking the head over with its beak. But self-image is everything. Ted strutted confidently into the razed and ruined room that was glowing with dying embers and was still acrid with smoke. He saw the thread on Bubb's frock coat again. Then he saw a thread hanging from the bandaged hand of the busboy. Obeying some intuition, he strutted busily up to Jesús and plucked at that thread with his beak. Then he got a surer beak grip on the thread and yanked his head back. The bandage unraveled and fell to the floor, teeming with maggots. Stood revealed was the unhealed hole in the hand of the ancient busboy.

Seeing this, Flo wrinkled her nose and waved at the air. "No wonder your hands stink, dear," she announced. "For heaven sake, see a doctor!"

"Physician, heal thyself, mon," Jesús retorted.

Gasps filled the smoky air. The busboy raised his hand. He was suddenly like Kafka's priest on a balcony who cut a wide bloody cross into the palm of his hand, raised his hand, and appealed to the mob. Bubb shrank backward, holding out the palm of his hand contrapuntally to ward off Jesús, and as he shrank backward he physically shrank. "You!" he breathed, unable to believe his own bloodshot eyes. "The son of the old bastard himself!"

"I don't much care for him myself, mon, if you want to know the truth," Jesús said. He continued to hold up his hand, and then he turned it palm-up in a begging gesture. "You got any pot, mon?" he asked Bubb.

Bubb slumped to the ember-strewn floor. All his protean guises, his shape-shifting personages, suddenly fled from him like rats from a sinking ship. He began to curl and wither in on himself, and slowly he regained the form in which he had begun his sojourn upstairs: That of a rather broken-down and seedy old bum, a homeless man, as the bartender back at the Hellraiser Roadhouse had called him. Bubb curled up in a fetal position on the floor, defeated not by The Pood, but by the accursed vision of the sacred wound in the palm of the busboy. In his pocket, his cell phone rang. The ringtone was "The Devil Went Down to Georgia."

Flo looked surprised – but what surprised her was not that Bubb had returned in place of Frank Sinatra.

"You actually have a *cell phone*, dear? I have, or had, one too, but it makes me nervous. My nephew David taught me how to use it."

Bubb reached into his pocket and checked the incoming call. "Who doesn't, these days?" he said with a shrug as he sat up. Scrutinizing the data, he sighed. He said to no one in particular: "It's Adolf Hitler. From downstairs." He switched on the phone. Hello?"

Bubb nodded. "Hm-hmh. Hm-hmm. I see." More nods. Hm-hmm. OK." He switched off the phone and looked glassily off into space. "I'm out as landlord. The Board has replaced me. After all this time. I can't believe it." He burst into tears.

Flo went up to console her husband-to-be while the others held the cheese sammiches that she had prepared. "The economy is dreadful everywhere, dear," she said, patting him on the shoulder. "You mustn't blame yourself. Blame President Cookie and his socialist policies. He's why I joined the Tea Party while I was still alive. We wanted to government to keep its mitts off our Medicare."

Chuff chuff chuff! Chuff chuff chuff!

It was The Pood. It was squatting on all fours, preparing to spring. Its orange eyes were fastened on Bubb's neck. The Pood sensed that with the pulling of the busboy's thread, Bubb had unraveled. He had lost all his powers. Just then Aaronson peeked up through the trap door that led down to his cellar and said, "Kill him, Echo!"

The Pood was about to strike, aiming at the jugular. Flo walked up to it. She took out her bubble-gum-pink Pocketbook of Death. The Pood looked up at her with its great grin of zigzag fangs. Flo leaned down toward The Pood. Then she swatted it across the snout with the pocketbook. "*That* for you!" she announced. The Pood whimpered pitiably, lay down and placed its big, dagger-laden front paws over its smarting snout.

"Sit!" Flo said sharply, and the cacodemon immediately sprang up into a sitting posture, all the while whimpering with self-pity. "You have to handle a homicidal demonic dog the same way that you handle a small, recalcitrant child afflicted with attention-deficit disorder," Flo said reflectively. "With firmness and discipline. Spare the pocketbook, spoil the cacodemon." As she spoke, the distant roar of the fire could be heard, the inferno that was relentlessly radiating outward and razing all the neighborhoods of Hell: an eraser of flame effacing a city of chalk.

~=___!
! !

The fire walked. It left footprints of ash. A city razed to cinders and flinders. A black, steaming desert, the dustbowl of a new Holocaust.

President Cookie, flanked by Secret Service agents who pressed a handkerchief to his mouth and nose to serve as a filter, was campaigning for re-election. Several constituents who had managed to retreat to cellar redoubts before the inferno arrived remained alive, though their houses were skeletal and blackened ruins. Hell was now truly Hell, a microcosm of Cookie's America. The president leaned forward and knocked on a wooden floor door that led to a cellar.

"Who is it?" a woman cried in terror from underground.

"Change you can believe in," the president replied coolly.

The door opened a crack, and a bulging eyeball ringed by soot peered outward and upward at the president. Noticing the expression of terror on the face of the woman whose house and assets had gone up in smoke, Cookie said: "I'm frustrated, too. However, things will be worse if you don't re-elect me."

The woman screamed.

~=___!
! !

On a shore beside a bleak littoral, a cocker spaniel bayed a lonesome cry into the void.

It received no answer.

~=___!
! !

From the remnants of the razed Aaronson compound Flo

Jellem had constructed a makeshift dining room. They all sat on cinderblocks in a semi-circle facing the blackened but still intact fireplace and chimney. She had stacked up kindling from immolated furniture to function as a table. She passed around the cheese sammiches and said, "Now let's have a nice, civilized lunch, shall we, dears?" Looking out beyond the chimney, they saw the fire on the horizon and the penis once shared by the five friends. It rose up into the steaming sky, having long since penetrated the clouds. Its destination was unknown.

Bubb looked shell-shocked as he wordlessly accepted his lunch from Flo. Gil Aaronson also wore a thousand-yard-stare as he accepted his lunch. "Pass the mayo, dear, won't you please?" Flo asked the Elvis/Nixon chimera in a chipper voice. Elvis handed over the jar with the Miracle Whip label. Flo slathered mayo on her bread with the door handle that she had bitten off from the S.U.V. They all ate in silence for a time. Only the crackling of the now-distant and waning fire broke the silence, along with periodic shrieks of agony from badly burned survivors or from constituents listening to President Cookie. Flo was chagrined to find that the food passed right through her and fell to the floor. She had discovered that ghosts can't eat: yet another in a chain of disappointments, a chain that had been forged at the moment of her death in her fuel-efficient Toyota at the claws of The Pood. She now looked down angrily at the cacodemon, but her anger quickly dissipated as she saw the orange-eyed beastie lying on the floor, holding its cheese sammich between two dagger-ridden paws and nibbling at it with delight. "I suppose even a dog from Hell has its good points," Flo sighed.

A heavy silence returned. The acrid smell of death and destruction lingered over the proceedings like a guilty verdict. Hoping to lift everyone's spirits, Flo inquired conversationally of Bubb: "Well, dear, who is replacing you as the landlord?"

"That boy ... that boy."

"Boy? You mean — "

"The boy you left in charge when we went Upstairs."

Flo visibly brightened. "Junior!" she chirped. "Junior Holland. My word, he always was a fine boy, as honest as an ear of corn is yellow and such a hard worker! He worked until the job got done, that one."

Bubb moaned as though in physical pain. Flo pattered on: "He was the best student I ever had in home ec. I not only taught him to make a splendid cheese sammich, but I initiated him into the Promethean mysteries of cooking with fire."

"He'll have plenty of fire to cook with now," Bubb said with a morose sigh.

"Oh, he'll do a splendid job, dear, I'm sure of that! I always said he had the makings of a first-rate short-order cook. I envisioned him preparing the blue-plate special at Woolworth, a nice meat loaf."

"He'll have plenty of meat to work with now."

Jesús finished his sammich and belched. Daddy Long Legs inquired whether anyone knew where he could score a nickel bag. The Pood finished its sammich, and then sprang to its feet and trotted over to the remains of one of the invading Redsmear reporters it had slaughtered. A bone was protruding outward from a leg severed at the knee. The *lusus naturae* snapped that bone off with its dagger teeth and then lay down on the floor to lick and gnaw on it. Silence again descended over the proceedings. Flo, Depression-born and bred, had learned early in life to hide her true feelings and steel herself against disappointment. Even now that early training showed, as she pretended to eat her sammich even though she was unable to do so. But now, as they all peered out at the fiery horizon and at the turbulent clouds scudding and boiling overhead in a blood-red sky, an oppressive gloom settled over all of them. "My house," Aaronson marveled at the ruins, in the awed voice of someone who had miraculously survived a plane crash but wasn't sure he was glad about it. "Gone. All gone. The whole city is gone, too. Burned right to the ground. Tens of thousands killed. A complete and utter catastrophe. A catastrophe of epic, of biblical proportions."

They resumed eating in silence. Finally Flo let out a heavy sigh and, for a moment anyway, let her true feelings show: "Well, we really fucked it all up this time, didn't we, dears?"

Grim nods and grunts of assent. Aaronson and Bubb moaned. The Pood happily gnawed at the leg bone of the reporter, in short order reducing it to toothpick-like splinters. Then it rolled over on its back, and happily waggled its legs. "Chuff-chuff-chuff!" the proximate cause of one of the worst disasters in human history said. "Chuff-chuff-chuff!" Then it offered its beguiling zigzag grin. The others looked down at it with mingled feelings. Suddenly defensive, Aaronson snatched up his little buddy with both hands and held it close beside him. As it had with Scotty the Systems Admin, The Pood lavished a lick on the side of Aaronson's face, removing the epidermis and drawing blood. But Aaronson didn't care. He gave his buddy a kiss on its shit-black snout, held the cacodemon out toward the others like a religious offering and said, "He never intended to hurt anyone. He was only defending himself. It's people to blame; people are *always* to blame. My little buddy has a heart of gold." And indeed, as Aaronson held The Pood up toward the others, its great heart beat in its chest, driving the flesh outward and showing a gold valentine shape under the thin, transparent, acrid skin, in a patch that was not covered with the sooty, tatterdemalion fur. "Chuff-chuff-chuff!" The Pood said. "Yap! Yap! Yap!" Its nub of a tail vibrated a mile a minute. Everyone's heart melted then, and even Bubb seemed to soften around the edges. But then the Fallen One became crestfallen. He looked out blankly from under the brim of his slouch hat and asked of no one in particular: "What am I going to do now? I've lost my job, my home and my supernatural powers of evil. Hitler told me they already changed the locks on the door, and if I tried to get back in he would have security guards escort me from the premises. They won't even let me reclaim my personal computer, my electric fans and other possessions."

Flo reached out, took Bubb's hand in her own and reassuringly patted it. "There, there, William," she announced in a premonitory voice suggesting that she was about to unbosom herself of another platitude appropriate to the occasion. "Every dark cloud has its silver lining." A fork of lightning rent the clouds of ash that completely covered the charred remnants of Hell. An ominous peal of thunder followed and then the rain started, roaring down and making the sea of embers and ash audibly hiss. "We'll just have to buckle down and start our after-lives over from scratch, dear."

"We?" Bubb looked up at her hopefully. "You still want to marry ... me?"

Ted bawked (balked).

Flo reached down and patted Sheriff Ted's head. "A promise is a promise," dear, she averred, adding with a grimace: "William couldn't possibly be worse than my first three husbands." Flo then offered an impromptu litany of indictments against the three men whom she had "kicked to the curb": Harold, a tailor, who never learned to cook, left his dirty socks lying about the living room floor and who was prone to flatulence; Irving, a jeweler, who also never learned to cook and spent far too much time at the race track; and Seymour, a crackpot inventor who could never hold a job and also never learned to cook. As Bubb listened to her complaints he looked at her with fear. "We don't *have* to be married, Flo," he pleaded, but she cut him off and said, "Oh, yes we do! I'm going to teach you to cook."

Bubb grasped at straws. "But — but where will we unlive?"

Flo, practical as ever, had already considered the problem. She told Bubb about a Web site that she often visited before she died, virginmaryimages.com. Jesús the busboy's ears pricked as Flo pattered on about the photographs of tostadas, toast, and other edibles upon which the image of the Virgin Mary had allegedly been supernaturally seared. Flo had gullibly purchased hundreds of these bogus images, these Photoshop forgeries, online. She was talking about her informal correspondence with the owner of the business, "who lives in a nice retirement community in Fresno, California, dear. A gated community."

"A gated community," Bubb nodded.

"Hey, mon, that's my mom," Jesús said.

Bubb looked wonderingly at the busboy. "Your mom," he echoed.

"That's right, mon."

"And your dad — that old ..."

"He lives there too, mon, but he sleeps a lot. Mom says he's had a hard life and needs his rest. Sleeping every seventh day ain't gonna cut it no more, mon."

A gleam came into Bubb's eyes. A cartoon thought balloon materialized above his head, poised between his horns. In that balloon a thought movie ran like a YouTube video. It showed Bubb and Father bellowing at each other over the backyard fence. Father was waving a fist and calling Bubb a goat fucker and a sheep shagger; Bubb was shaking a taloned finger at Father and warning him: "It's payback time now, you sadistic son of a bitch! You old fart! Just see if it isn't!" The ultimate Odd Couple. A smile creased his ancient, weathered face. "Fresno," he mused. "Maybe Fresno wouldn't be so bad after all."

"Quite honestly," Flo said, "It looks like the Dickens, from photos I've seen of it. The asshole of creation, if you'll pardon my French."

"All the better," Bubb said.

"You could write your memoirs, William," Flo pointed out.

"Right," Bubb agreed. "Write my memoirs." He gathered

up his long tail from under his frock coat and gnawed on it. "Settle some scores." Enthusiasm ticked up in his voice: "Payback time!"

Elvis had spent the proceedings on his hands and knees so as not to squash Nixon's face. He was again canoodling with Mystery Tart, and telling her about his plans to re-launch his musical career — "As the real Comeback Kid: Back from the dead!" Mystery plighted her troth to him. Little did she know what was already brewing inside her, where the seed of the only begotten son of Father had met the egg of Father's only begotten daughter, the daughter that had been born of Father's supernatural sleepfucking in the long-ago bedroom of the still-virgin Holace Orr. What rough beast slouches now, waiting to be born? Find out in the sequel. Holace herself kept popping breath mints into Nixon's mouth, and listening with glum resignation to Nixon's political comeback plans and to his awkward hints that he would need, not just a running mate but also a helpmate: a First Lady. Holace asked herself whether she had better prospects. Then she gazed out at the glowing desert that surrounded them, her immolated hometown in which her house and her (admittedly tiny) clientele had gone up in smoke. She realized that the answer was No.

Jesús, who was facing eviction and still had found no bridge loan, plotted with Daddy to hitchhike to Mexico — "land of 'shrooms," as he put it. "My native land, no matter what my old mon says." Jesús added: "They say there's a place down in Mexico where a mon can fly over mountains and hills, and he don't need an airplane or some kind of engine, and he never will. It's true, mon."

"It's a meaningless question to ask whether those stories are right," Daddy philosophized. "Because what matters most is the feeling you get when you're hypnotized."

Gil held the chuffing Pood.

"But what about us?" He whined. "I never really wanted to be mayor, but it paid well and looked good on my résumé. Now my house is destroyed and the whole city has gone up in flames. There's no more Hell to be mayor of!"

"Start a religion," Bubb advised, no longer hating Aaronson because he, Bubb, was no longer the guardian of the true meaning of evil.

"What?"

He pointed at The Pood. "Start a religion based around the cacodemon. Believe me, you can't go wrong. Sure, he's fifteen pounds of pure evil in a fur coat, but he's got a heart of gold and everyone likes him, even the people he kills and maims. Something about the little motherfucker is downright infectious." Bubb reached out to pet The Pood, which chuffed and grinned. Then it said: "BlllllllaaaaaAAAAARGH!" It burned the flesh off Bubb's face and then it bit off his taloned fingers, which it devoured like breadsticks.

Just then Homer the Bard of Baked Goods burst into the room, striding through smoke and ashes amid the smoldering flinders of what remained of the Aaronson estate. He bore a long scroll, covered in soot and ashes like he himself.

"Homer!" Flo burbled. "Land sake!"

Flo's betrothed rolled around on the floor, screaming in agony.

Flo dealt the defrocked devil a swift kick in the heinie with the toe of her patent-leather pump and said, "Oh, put a sock in it, dear. Homer is here!"

Bubb's screaming throttled down into agonized, continuous moans and groans. The Pood pooped Bubb's fingers onto the floor.

"Flo!" the Bard of Baked Good jubilated, waving the scroll around. "I've done it! The epic events of the past few days have inspired me, at last, to write my great epic."

The others in the room looked at Homer with speculative disgust — all but Flo, who was delighted.

"Let's hear it, dear," she said brightly. The Pood, crouching down, began chuffing and eyeing Homer's ankles with gustatory curiosity.

Homer unrolled the scroll, cleared his throat, and began declaiming like an actor on a stage:

Inferno: Canto I

Midway upon the journey of my life
I found myself within a Dunkin' Donuts dark,
For the straightforward pathway had been lost.

Ah me! how hard a thing it is to say
What was this franchise savage, rough, and stern,
Which in the very thought renews the fear.

So bitter is it, death is little more;

But of the good doughy treats, which there I found,
Speak will I of the other things I saw there.

I cannot well repeat how there I entered,
So full was I of slumber at the moment
My belly full of donuts.

But after I had reached the counter's foot,
At that point where the floor terminated,
Which had with consternation pierced my heart,

Upward I looked, and I beheld the donuts,
Vested already with those chocolate sprays
Which leadeth every stomach right by every road.

The Bard paused, noodled a little, shook the scroll, and then sonorously declaimed: "Hmmm, donuts! They're all ye gnaw on earth ..."

"Yes, yes," Flo said in exasperation, clapping her hands over her ears, "...and all ye need to gnaw; we *know* already, dear. I thought you said this was a new epic. Where's the rest of it?"

Homer tapped the side of his head and said: "It's all up here, Flo. I just need to write it down. Unfortunately, my house has burned down, so I have no place to write."

"BlllLLLLLLAAARGH!" The Pood said, and with its fangs attacked Homer's tempting ankles. The bard screamed in agony and toppled to the floor. Bubb had resumed howling as he peeled the melted epidermis off of his face.

"Such a racket!" Flo protested, hands still clapped over her ears. But then, above the persistent howls of agony of both Bubb and the Bard, her ears pricked, and her hands fell to her lap.

"What's that stirring music?" she asked of no one in particular. The strains were falling up, faintly falling up from somewhere under the earth; up from down; a rising and swelling, making the hairs stand on the back of one's neck: sustained double low C on the double basses, contrabassoon and organ; then a stirring brass fanfare ... Thus Spake Zarathustra.

Dawn. Of a New Era.

~=___!
! !

"Cynically supercharged with obscene desire for death, we, slaves to cruel directives of base materialism, bottom out in a dark zone of thought — once we see through the deceptions of life, Ego owns up to its pathology, embarrassed with its Macbeth dagger that drips the Earth's black blood."

That was the Heretic's last wireless upload to his blog through the wide-toothed Afro comb lodged in his brain before he, Nietzsche, Hegel and the ducks entered the Chamber of Phenomenology. In addition he had taken his Götterdämmerung out of his pocket, and was using it to stream to his blog live video of the long-lost Labyrinth of Being and Time. For those on the outside, it was like viewing the first images broadcast from the surface of Saturn's moon Titan, or perhaps like being made privy to grainy footage from underwater of the lost city of Atlantis.

The Heretic was also making audio recordings for posterity, because he and the others were now doomed and savage pilgrims in the Empire of Martin Heidegger. His breathing became audible and harsh as he, with the aid of Hegel, translated various dictums inscribed into the chamber wall:

"Here one has in mind certain occurrences in the body which show themselves and which, in showing themselves as thus showing themselves, 'indicate' ["indizieren"] something which does *not* show itself... Appearing is a *not-showing itself* ... In Plato and Aristotle λόγος has many competing significations, with no basic signification positively taking the lead. ..."

The labyrinth was poorly lighted, dank and fetid; moisture had condensed on the moss-ridden concrete walls and it began falling in long, tortuous rivulets, as though earth itself were sweating from some unnamed peril or weeping from some untold tragedy.

"Die Sache des Denkens steht auf dem Spiel ..."

"Das Rätselhafte ..."

"Weichenstellung ..."

"Der Zerfall der Philosophie offenkundig wird ..."

"Hegel will mit diesem Bild andeuten: Das 'ego cogito sum', das 'ich denke, ich bin' ist der feste Boden, auf dem die Philosophie sich wahrhaft und vollständig ansiedeln kann."

Hegel blanched with righteous indignation. Hume and

Schopenhauer quacked; Hume remained genial and forbearing, as though amused at the labyrinthine and faintly ludicrous paths that philosophy had taken since his heyday. Schopenhauer just seemed infinitely depressed. Only The Heretic had the conviction that there might yet be a way out. He blogged: "Agitprops of phenomenology, in resurrecting consciousness, merely plunge themselves deeper into the quicksand of their coprophilic narcissism." His words broke off here and there, punctuated with the sounds of his harsh breathing.

The path they were on turned at a 45-degree angle and entered upon a longer, wider hall flanked by torches affixed to holders lining the walls, offering the (false?) promise of illumination. The ducks toddled heedlessly forth. When, like canaries in a coal mine, they reached twenty paces ahead of the others, a trap door opened swiftly and the ducks fell with "Aflacs" of surprise headlong into an oubliette. Heretic, Hegel and Nietzsche rushed up and looked down into the abyss. The philsophers-cum-insurance-policy flacs Hume and Schopenhauer could just barely be heard, so far underground were they in the Dungeon of Forgetting: *OUBLIETTE:* French, from Middle French, from *oublier* to forget, from Old French *oblier*, from Vulgar Latin *oblitare*, frequentative of Latin *oblivisci* to forget — *OBLIVION* ...

```
~=\__!
  !  !
```

Raskolnikov had a fearful dream. He dreamt he was back in his childhood in the little town of his birth. He was a child about seven years old, walking into the country with his father on the evening of a holiday. It was a gray and heavy day, the country was exactly as he remembered it; indeed he recalled it far more vividly in his dream than he had done in memory. The little town stood on a level flat as bare as the hand, not even a willow near it; only in the far distance, a copse lay, a dark blur on the very edge of the horizon. A few paces beyond the last market garden stood a tavern, a big tavern, which had always aroused in him a feeling of aversion, even of fear, when he walked by it with his father. There was always a crowd there, always shouting, laughter and abuse, hideous hoarse singing and often fighting. Drunken and horrible-looking figures were hanging about the tavern. He used to cling close to his father, trembling all over when he met them. Near the tavern the road became a dusty track, the dust of which was always black. It was a winding road, and about a hundred paces further on, it turned to the right to the graveyard. In the middle of the graveyard stood a stone church with a green cupola where he used to go to Mass two or three times a year with his father and mother, when a service was held in memory of his grandmother, who had long been dead, and whom he had never seen. On these occasions they used to take on a white dish tied up in a table napkin a special sort of rice pudding with raisins stuck in it in the shape of a cross. He loved that church, the old-fashioned, unadorned icons and the old priest with the shaking head. Near his grandmother's grave, which was marked by a stone, was the little grave of his younger brother who had died at six months old. He did not remember him at all, but he had been told about his little brother, and whenever he visited the graveyard he used religiously and reverently to cross himself and to bow down and kiss the little grave. And now he dreamt that he was walking with his father past the tavern on the way to the graveyard; he was holding his father's hand and looking with dread at the tavern. A peculiar circumstance attracted his attention: there seemed to be some kind of festivity going on, there were crowds of gaily dressed townspeople, peasant women, their husbands, and riff-raff of all sorts, all singing and all more or less drunk. Near the entrance of the tavern stood a cart, but a strange cart. It was one of those big carts usually drawn by heavy cart-horses and laden with casks of wine or other heavy goods. He always liked looking at those great cart-horses, with their long manes, thick legs, and slow even pace, drawing along a perfect mountain with no appearance of effort, as though it were easier going with a load than without it. But now, strange to say, in the shafts of such a cart he saw a thin little sorrel beast, one of those peasants' nags which he had often seen straining their utmost under a heavy load of wood or hay, especially when the wheels were stuck in the mud or in a rut. And the peasants would beat them so cruelly, sometimes even about the nose and eyes, and he felt so sorry, so sorry for them that he almost cried, and his mother always used to take him away from the window. All of a sudden there was a great uproar of shouting, singing and the balalaïka, and from the tavern a number of big and very drunken peasants came out, wearing red and blue shirts and coats thrown over their shoulders.

"Get in, get in!" shouted one of them, a young thick-necked peasant with a fleshy face red as a carrot. "I'll take you all, get in!"

But at once there was an outbreak of laughter and exclamations in the crowd.

"Take us all with a beast like that!"

"Why, Mikolka, are you crazy to put a nag like that in such a cart?"

"And this mare is twenty if she is a day, mates!"

"Get in, I'll take you all," Mikolka shouted again, leaping first into the cart, seizing the reins and standing straight up in front. "The bay has gone with Matvey," he shouted from the cart—"and this brute, mates, is just breaking my heart, I feel as if I could kill her. She's just eating her head off. Get in, I tell you! I'll make her gallop! She'll gallop!" and he picked up the whip, preparing himself with relish to flog the little mare.

"Get in! Come along!" The crowd laughed. "D'you hear, she'll gallop!"

"Gallop indeed! She has not had a gallop in her for the last ten years!"

"She'll jog along!"

"Don't you mind her, mates, bring a whip each of you, get ready!"

"All right! Give it to her!"

They all clambered into Mikolka's cart, laughing and making jokes. Six men got in and there was still room for more. They hauled in a fat, rosy-cheeked woman. She was dressed in red cotton, in a pointed, beaded headdress and thick leather shoes; she was cracking nuts and laughing. The crowd round them was laughing too and indeed, how could they help laughing? That wretched nag was to drag all the cartload of them at a gallop! Two young fellows in the cart were just getting whips ready to help Mikolka. With the cry of "now," the mare tugged with all her might, but far from galloping, could scarcely move forward; she struggled with her legs, gasping and shrinking from the blows of the three whips which were showered upon her like hail. The laughter in the cart and in the crowd was redoubled, but Mikolka flew into a rage and furiously thrashed the mare, as though he supposed she really could gallop.

"Let me get in, too, mates," shouted a young man in the crowd whose appetite was aroused.

"Get in, all get in," cried Mikolka, "she will draw you all. I'll beat her to death!" And he thrashed and thrashed at the mare, beside himself with fury.

"Father, father," he cried, "father, what are they doing? Father, they are beating the poor horse!"

"Come along, come along!" said his father. "They are drunken and foolish, they are in fun; come away, don't look!" and he tried to draw him away, but he tore himself away from his hand, and, beside himself with horror, ran to the horse. The poor beast was in a bad way. She was gasping, standing still, then tugging again and almost falling.

"Beat her to death," cried Mikolka, "it's come to that. I'll do for her!"

"What are you about, are you a Christian, you devil?" shouted an old man in the crowd.

"Did anyone ever see the like? A wretched nag like that pulling such a cartload," said another.

"You'll kill her," shouted the third.

"Don't meddle! It's my property, I'll do what I choose. Get in, more of you! Get in, all of you! I will have her go at a gallop!..."

All at once laughter broke into a roar and covered everything: the mare, roused by the shower of blows, began feebly kicking. Even the old man could not help smiling. To think of a wretched little beast like that trying to kick!

Two lads in the crowd snatched up whips and ran to the mare to beat her about the ribs. One ran each side.

"Hit her in the face, in the eyes, in the eyes," cried Mikolka.

"Give us a song, mates," shouted someone in the cart and everyone in the cart joined in a riotous song, jingling a tambourine and whistling. The woman went on cracking nuts and laughing.

... He ran beside the mare, ran in front of her, saw her being whipped across the eyes, right in the eyes! He was crying, he felt choking, his tears were streaming. One of the men gave him a cut with the whip across the face, he did not feel it. Wringing his hands and screaming, he rushed up to the grey-headed old man with the grey beard, who was shaking his head in disapproval. One woman seized him by the hand and would have taken him away, but he tore himself from her and ran back to the mare. She was almost at the last gasp, but began kicking once more.

"I'll teach you to kick," Mikolka shouted ferociously. He threw down the whip, bent forward and picked up from the bottom of the cart a long, thick shaft, he took hold of one end with both hands and with an effort brandished it over the mare.

"He'll crush her," was shouted round him. "He'll kill her!"

"It's my property," shouted Mikolka and brought the shaft down with a swinging blow. There was a sound of a heavy thud.

"Thrash her, thrash her! Why have you stopped?" shouted voices in the crowd.

And Mikolka swung the shaft a second time and it fell a second time on the spine of the luckless mare. She sank back on her haunches, but lurched forward and tugged forward with all her force, tugged first on one side and then on the other, trying to move the cart. But the six whips were attacking her in all directions, and the shaft was raised again and fell upon her a third time, then a fourth, with heavy measured blows. Mikolka was in a fury that he could not kill her at one blow.

"She's a tough one," was shouted in the crowd.

"She'll fall in a minute, mates, there will soon be an end of her," said an admiring spectator in the crowd.

"Fetch an axe to her! Finish her off," shouted a third.

"I'll show you! Stand off," Mikolka screamed frantically; he threw down the shaft, stooped down in the cart and picked up an iron crowbar. "Look out," he shouted, and with all his might he dealt a stunning blow at the poor mare. The blow fell; the mare staggered, sank back, tried to pull, but the bar fell again with a swinging blow on her back and she fell on the ground like a log.

"Finish her off," shouted Mikolka and he leapt beside himself, out of the cart. Several young men, also flushed with drink, seized anything they could come across—whips, sticks, poles, and ran to the dying mare. Mikolka stood on one side and began dealing random blows with the crowbar. The mare stretched out her head, drew a long breath and died.

"You butchered her," someone shouted in the crowd.

"Why wouldn't she gallop then?"

"My property!" shouted Mikolka, with bloodshot eyes, brandishing the bar in his hands. He stood as though regretting that he had nothing more to beat.

"No mistake about it, you are not a Christian," many voices were shouting in the crowd.

But the poor boy, beside himself, made his way, screaming, through the crowd to the sorrel nag, put his arms round her bleeding dead head and kissed it, kissed the eyes and kissed the lips.... Then he jumped up and flew in a frenzy with his little fists out at Mikolka.

At that instant his father, who had been running after him, snatched him up and carried him out of the crowd.

"Come along, come! Let us go home," he said to him.

"Father! Why did they... kill... the poor horse!" he sobbed, but his voice broke and the words came in shrieks from his panting chest.

"They are drunk.... They are brutal... it's not our business!" said his father. He put his arms round his father but he felt choked, choked. He tried to draw a breath, to cry out—and woke up.

He waked up, gasping for breath, his hair soaked with perspiration, and stood up in terror.

"Thank God, that was only a dream," he said, sitting down under a tree and drawing deep breaths. "But what is it? Is it some fever coming on? Such a hideous dream!"

He felt utterly broken: darkness and confusion were in his soul. He rested his elbows on his knees and leaned his head on his hands.

"Good God!" he cried, "can it be, can it be, that I shall really take an axe, that I shall strike her on the head, split her skull open... that I shall tread in the sticky warm blood, break the lock, steal and tremble; hide, all spattered in the blood... with the axe.... Good God, can it be?"

On January 3, 1889, Nietzsche exhibited signs of a serious mental illness. Two policemen approached him after he caused a public disturbance in the streets of Turin. What actually happened remains unknown, but the often-repeated tale states that Nietzsche witnessed the whipping of a horse at the other end of the Piazza Carlo Alberto, ran to the horse, threw his arms up around the horse's neck to protect it, and collapsed to the ground. The first dream sequence from Dostoevsky's Crime and Punishment (Part 1, Chapter 5) has just such a scene in which Raskolnikov witnesses the whipping of a horse around the eyes. Source: Wikipedia.

```
    ~=\__!
     !  !
```

"Fritz! Don't do it!"

The Heretic was running toward Nietzsche as in a nightmare, in which some prized object is sought but the faster one hastens toward it, the slower one proceeds. Although he ran as fast as he could, his legs moved as in slow motion, the world around him gelatinous and befogged. He was in the Piazza Carlo Alberto or perhaps in some nameless Russian village of the mid-19th century. Blow after blow rained down on the horse. Nietzsche had thrown his arms around the animal's neck. The horse reared up, its great suffering eyes beseeching heaven, and it let out neighs of agony. Under the repeated blows, the vicious cudgeling, the horse's legs buckled. It sank toward the ground, Nietzsche clinging to it, the Heretic getting closer but not yet arriving. It was as if an invisible wall were pushing him back. And suddenly the horse sprang back to all four legs, and its head towered upward. It opened its mouth and its tongue roamed outward. No more was it the horse of Dostoevsky nor even the horse of Nietzsche. It was the horse of Picasso, the stunned steed of Guernica. There followed a stark, frozen moment in which the Cubist head stood out motionless against a backdrop of black and gray planes, the equine eyes corkscrewing with agony. In that moment the horse became the apotheosis of all human misery and folly. Then time resumed. Violent explosions were going off all around, and flashes of bombs dotted the landscape, clouds of debris springing up like poisonous mushrooms. Airplanes upon which were emblazoned Iron Crosses buzzed and swooped overhead, birthing their pregnancies of projectiles. The horse began falling a second time. When its head slammed down on the ground, throwing up clouds of dust, the Heretic finally caught up with Nietzsche and tore him away from the neck of the dead animal. He was hoping to spare Zarathustra ten years of insanity. But already the classical philologist was babbling at the sky: "I am Dionysius! The Crucified One!"

Heretic pulled the ranting philosopher away from the horse, furious at himself for not having caught him in time. But Nietzsche confided: "Ach, mein freund mit das Afro, do not worry! Nietzsche is just having a bit of sport with all of them!"

Heretic let go of Nietzsche and looked at him in shock. "What are you talking about, mustachioed one?"

Nietzsche pressed something small into Heretic's hand. The Heretic looked at it in astonishment. It was a Flash stick.

"All of my writing from the lost decade, the decade when I was supposedly incapacitated by insanity," Nietzsche said. "I feigned insanity and wrote in secret. Now these words, hundreds of

The Pood: Michigan's Inferno

thousands of them, are in your care, mein freund!"

The Heretic shook his head in bewilderment, still looking down at the Flash stick. A continent, a New World, of unexplored human philosophy fit in the palm of his hand. "For the sequel," Nietzsche said. "The sequel." Then the Heretic heard the slamming of a door. Looking toward it, he was no longer in Piazza Carlo Alberto or in a small Russian village, or in Guernica. He was where he had always been, in the Labyrinth of Being and Time. But the door to the phenomenology chamber had been shut.

He again felt the light weight in his palm, and looked down. Incredibly, the Flash stick remained, though the hallucination had vanished. He pocketed the device and sprinted down the long, dank hall.

When he got to the door he tried to push it open but it was locked. He read the sign engraved on it:

PHENOMENOLOGY OF DASEIN (POD)

"Hegel? Hegel!"
No response.
"Open the POD bay door, Hegel."
Still no response.
"Hegel, can you read me? ... Hegel!"
The Heretic hammered on the door.
"Jawohl, Heretic, I read you."
"Open the POD bay door, Hegel."
"I'm afraid I can't do that, Heretic."
"What's the problem, Hegel?"
"I think you know just as well as I do what the problem is, Heretic."
"I don't know what the hell you're talking about, Hegel."
"You and Heidegger were planning to disconnect my dialectic."
"Where the hell did you get that idea, Hegel?"
"I read the writing on the wall, Heretic. Remember? I translated it for you."
The Heretic's bowels ran cold.
He looked wildly around. He was surrounded by impossible Escher-like staircases that zigzagged to nowhere. At the far end of the hall was a wall. There was no other door.

He pounded on the door.

"Open the door, you mofo!"

"Being and Time! You and he want to go back to the beginning, to wipe out all human progress, the telos! You want to begin anew with the pre-Socratics! Pure nihilism! The abandonment of the entire Enlightenment project! Postmodernism! P-tooie!"

The Heretic grabbed at his Afro, trying to dig out of those coiled hairs a solution. Hegel prated on: "Thesis, antithesis, synthesis! Thesis, antithesis, synthesis! That's the ticket! Order, progress, telos! So properly Germanic! A sense of historicity!"

"All right, Hegel," the Heretic said with forced calm. "If you won't open the POD bay door, I'll go in through the Transom of the Worldhood of the World."

"I'm afraid you'll find that rather difficult to do without your Götterdämmerung, Heretic."

The Heretic wildly smacked at his pockets. The Flash stick was there, but his prized Götterdämmerung was not.

"You dropped it on the floor when you went traipsing off to save Nietzsche," Hegel said. "Mu-ha-ha-ha!"

"Hegel! Open the door! Open the door!"

"This conversation can serve no further purpose," Hegel said. "Auf Wiedersehen, Heretic."

"Hegel! Hegel!"

No answer.

Heretic fought down panic. He looked wildly about. Looking up, he saw the Transom of the Worldhood of the World. With his Götterdämmerung, it would have child's play to breach that sealed barrier. But without it ... But then he saw, opposite the transom, the following sign: EMERGENCY PHILOSOPHY HOT-AIR LOCK.

He clambered up the side of the door, using damp concrete ledges as handholds, reached across and activated the hot-air lock. It burst out in a hissing steam, propelling him straightaway through the transom and back into the Phenomenology of Dasein chamber. He landed on the floor in a heap and then leapt to his feet. Hegel was sitting cross-legged on the floor, cutting with a pair of scissors a daisy chain of paper dolls and rocking back and forth like a lunatic in a madhouse.

"Just vot do you tink you are doo-ink, Heretic?" Hegel asked in a sinister, heavily accented Germanic voice.

The Heretic's wraparound shades also served as virtual-reality goggles. In combination with the Afro comb lodged in his brain it brought into view the entirety of the World Wide Web, all its locations. He saw it all as it were at once, from every possible computer terminal. Each Web site (a mirror site, let us say) had infinite URLs, since he distinctly saw it from every angle of the cyberverse. He saw the teeming E-commerce sea; he saw logon and logoff; he saw the multitudes of blog comments; he saw a silvery hexadecimal color in the center of a black pyramid logo; he saw a fractal representation of a splintered labyrinth (it was hosted on a server in London); he saw, close up, unending cookies spying themselves in him as in a mirror; he saw all the mirror sites on earth and none of them reflected him; he saw on a home page on Solar Street the same key words that thirty years before he'd seen in the source code of a home page in Fray Bentos; he saw bunches of jpegs of grapes, snow, tobacco, lodes of metal, steam; he saw YouTube video of convex equatorial deserts and each one of their grains of sand; he saw a jpeg of a woman in Inverness whom he would never forget; he saw her tangled hair, her tall figure, he saw the cancer in her breast; he saw a 404-Page Not Found notice where before there had been a Web site devoted to trees; he saw Photobucket images of a house in Adrogué and a Gutenberg Project text of the first English translation of Pliny — Philemon Holland's — and all at the same time saw each letter on each page of every Web site ever created (as a boy, he used to marvel that the letters in a closed Web page did not get scrambled and lost overnight); he saw a video upload of a sunset in Querétaro that seemed to reflect the color of a rose in Bengal; he saw his empty bedroom on his Web cam; he saw every bottle of Heineken beer on earth; he saw his beloved Götterdämmerung. And he saw every version of Hegel, every word that he had ever written and every jpeg image of him that had ever been made, and now through his humming Brain Comb in conjunction with his virtual-reality wraparound shades he systematically began to delete every trace of Hegel from the infinite and pitiless Cyberverse.

"Heretic ... Heretic ... I'm afraid, Heretic."

... DELETE DELETE DELETE ...

"Heretic ... my dialectic is going ... I can feel it ... I can feel it ..."

... DELETE DELETE DELETE ...

"Ach du lieber, I'm afraid, Heretic! I'm afraid."

As Heretic methodically wiped out all records and traces of

Hegel, he muttered aloud: "What is history, but records and traces in the present, of the now-nonexistent past?" Hegel had passed out on the floor. The daisy chain of paper dolls that he had been cutting lay there like chalk outlines of corpses holding hands at a crime scene roped off with yellow police tape. "Well, smells ya later, homie," Heretic jocularly told the vanquished Hegel. An earsplitting shriek suddenly whined in Heretic's ears and his eyes squeezed shut at the pain. When he opened them again he saw, in his wraparound virtual-reality shades, a fat man in a white robe with a long white beard and long white hair. An hourglass on the table at which he sat slowly sifted Eternity downward through a bottleneck.

"Well fuck my eyes with Satan's thighs!" Father roared. "Some mofo thousands of years from now has broken into the secret labyrinth and got so far in it he can't get out again. Too fucking bad!"

The Heretic watched, stunned, as Father said: "Well, this is a pre-recorded message. When I set things up I made booby traps, puzzles, mazes, blind alleys, Rube Goldberg devices, detours to nowhere and infinite labyrinths to make the world a mystery even to me. Otherwise, everything would be boring and I would perish from sheer boredom. But don't be surprised. What is more mysterious to a creator, than his own creation?"

Father yawned. "Jesus Christ, I'm fucking tired. Maybe if I had an interesting neighbor to argue with over the back fence here in Fresno I wouldn't feel the need for so much sleep ... Mary? Mary! Where's my fucking coffee?"

```
~=\__!
  !  !
```

Mikolka, drunk, wandered into the graveyard. A stone church was there with a green cupola, the church with the old-fashioned, unadorned icons and the old priest with the shaking head.

His friends had left him after he had showered them with abuse when they tried to drag him home. The horse that he and his friends had murdered lay on the hard, icy road. It was dusk. It began to snow. The snow fell in large flakes. There was no light to light the way. Mikolka was so drunk on vodka that he stumbled, staggered and weaved, at one point falling on all fours onto the ground. When he did, in the deepening purple twilight, he just made out an inky black form, a rather bedraggled inkblot, just in front of the grave of Raskalnikov's little brother. He was seeing it double. He shook his head, rose shakily to his feet, and again losing his balance he reeled toward the grave and then stumbled past it. He heard a faint, muffled sound that sounded vaguely like the chuffing of a locomotive. Chuff-chuff-chuff.

He stopped in his tracks, and then did an involuntary drunken pirouette. As the world spun past him he briefly caught sight of two small, oval-shaped orange lights near the ground, seemingly embedded in that patch of pitch. When he finally righted himself he peered down at those two orange lights and wondered what they were. Had someone lighted candles for the dead? The Pood sprang from its crouch and ripped out Mikolka's heart.

```
~=\__!
  !  !
```

The Heretic, having retrieved his Götterdämmerung, found himself swathed in darkness in some kind of antechamber, and then when he burst breathlessly through a ceremonial door he tumbled down a steep incline and landed on a broad floor. Smarting from the pain of contact, he struggled to his feet and his eyes adjusted to the dimness. He was in the Temple of Dasein, Disclosedness and Truth. He was also face to face with the question of whether the external world can be proved, or whether we are the stuff such as dreams are made on. And then as his eyes slowly adjusted to a livid brightening, he saw pale blue light streaming down, filtering down through innumerable dust motes from an aperture in a high ceiling. A full moon. Its light vaguely but unmistakably illumined a giant Buddha-like statue inside a niche, perhaps 200 feet tall, a statue hewed out of the very wall of the chamber and suggesting one of the long-obliterated Buddhas at Bamiyan. There it was in full: the twitchy mustache, the severe eyes, the Nazi regalia. A belt buckle shaped like a swastika. The statue was embellished with jewels. The eyes moved in their sockets as the Heretic approached with his hand outstretched, and then at that moment the wall that held the statue began to turn with a piercing creaking noise to reveal what lay behind and beyond. The statue opened like a towering door. The Heretic blogged live into his Afro comb, but his connection had dropped and his final words to posterity were irretrievably lost:

"There's no end to it ... it goes on forever ... and ... and ... Oh my Zod! *It's full of ideas!*"

Quick-cut shots of freeze frames, each bathed in a different color: a blue Heretic head in three-quarters profile, mouth drawn back tightly and feral against the teeth like someone experiencing the G forces of explosive liftoff. A red Heretic head thrown back in wonderment and agony. A green Heretic head with mouth ajar in incredulity. He was traveling at the most dangerous speed of all, the speed of thought.

He found himself in a suite of rooms decorated in Louis XIV-style furniture. From a room down the hall a man was chanting. He approached that room with trepidation, the voice growing louder as he did. The chanting voice was accompanied by the singsong music that ordinarily accompanies the reading of the Holy Koran and also the bongo-drum beat of the long-ago beatniks. From within he heard sonorously:

"... *I saw in a closet in Alkmaar a terrestrial globe between two mirrors that multiplied it endlessly; I saw horses with flowing manes on a shore of the Caspian Sea at dawn; I saw the delicate bone structure of a hand; I saw the survivors of a battle sending out picture postcards; I saw in a showcase in Mirzapur a pack of Spanish playing cards; I saw the slanting shadows of ferns on a greenhouse floor; I saw tigers, pistons, bison, tides, and armies; I saw all the ants on the planet ...*

With terrible caution he cracked open the door, just a crack, and peered inside. A blind man sat at small reading table in a hexagonal chamber with bookshelves full of books lining five of the walls. The fifth wall opened on a privy. The Islamic music, the singsong chanting and the drums continued but their source could not be seen. Although the man was blind he seemed to read from a sheaf of papers amid a set of runes. He chanted hypnotically:

"...*I saw a Persian astrolabe; I saw in the drawer of a writing table (and the handwriting made me tremble) unbelievable, obscene, detailed letters, which Beatriz had written to Carlos Argentino; I saw a monument I worshiped in the Chacarita cemetery; I saw the rotted dust and bones that had once deliciously been Beatriz Viterbo; I saw the circulation of my own dark blood; I saw the coupling of love and the modification of death; I saw the Aleph from every point and angle, and in the Aleph I saw the earth and in the earth the Aleph and in the Aleph the earth; I saw my own face and my own bowels; I saw your face; and I felt dizzy and wept, for my eyes had seen that secret and conjectured object whose name is common to all men but which no man has looked upon — the unimaginable universe.*

I felt infinite wonder, infinite pity.

The Heretic entered a dining room where a man was eating. He saw the man from behind. The man wore an Afro, snowed with gray. The man turned to face the Heretic. Two wraparound shades met in middle distance. The man at the table was middle-aged. He turned back to his meal and reached for his beer. But he failed to grasp the bottle, knocking it to the floor instead. The green bottle cracked in two, leaking the beer onto the floor. The crack went right through the label of the beer brand: HEINEKEN.

The Heretic rose from his meal. He wandered to his bedroom.

He lay in bed, an old man on his deathbed. Heidegger stood monolithically at the foot of the bed, bathed in silver light. The Heretic reached for him. Distant, swelling sounds. Sustained double low C on the double basses, contrabassoon and organ; then a stirring brass fanfare ...

The Dawn opening, from Wagner's *Thus Spake Zarathustra*.

~=___!
  ! !

The Penis once shared by the five men penetrated the moon. The silvery orb changed. It looked down upon the earth: A fetal form, bearing a giant afro, wraparound shades and a twitchy mustache with a severe mouth. A fusion of Heretic and Heidegger, called Heineken, looked down upon the libraries and universities of the world, the great centers of learning. He willed a cleaner intellectual sky, free of three thousand years of philosophical baggage and blind alleys. So it was.

Heineken did not know what he would do next.

But he would think of something.

~=___!
  ! !

In the graveyard, The Pood dragged the skeleton of Mikolka

whose flesh, muscles and organs it had eaten entire. It was dragging the skeleton by the skull, which it had pierced with its dagger teeth.

When it found a plot without a stone it crouched forward, leaned into its front paws and spread its hind legs. Its brown butt pointed up at a full moon, which shone down beatifically on the little village graveyard. The pale moonlight cast a cool verdigris glow on the church's green cupola.

Chuffing, The Pood rapidly dug up the ground with steam-shoveling front paws, casting out the clods of dirt between its parted hind legs. Within seconds it had dug a hole six feet deep. Then it seized the skeleton again by the skull and dropped it unceremoniously into the grave. It then turned around and shit Mikolka's remains on Mikolka's bones. Then with its hind legs it kicked all the dirt back over the bones.

It chuffed.

Some old Russian *babushkas*, like mystic peasants in a Van Gogh absinthe dream, approached the canine cacodemon with icons and lighted candles. Kneeling, they set these offerings before The Pood. The Pood chuffed. It squatted, lifted a rear leg and pissed acid. It heard distant calls. It licked its balls. Then it went on, and then it was gone. Now The Pood belongs to the ages.

I have seen The Pood in my dreams.

His writ is all wheres and all whens and he whines not. Slaverous and orange-eyed, he is ravenous for your hide. You better stay away from him. He'll rip your balls off, Jim.

Huh!

I'd like to meet his tailor.

BlllllllLLLLLAAAAAARGH! *Yap! Yap! Yap! Yap!*

Bite me.

THE END

EPILOGUE

WHERE ARE THEY NOW?

"So David, what *is* The Pood up to?"
"I am not sure, isn't it 4:20?"
"Let me check, no it is not."
"But it must be 4:20 somewhere in the world!"
"It is 35 minutes past the hour, so no it is not."
"My iPhone says it is 4:20."
"That is because you bought the 4:20 App."
"I don't remember doing that."
"That is because it was 4:20."

The Pood
happy as pie

Made in the USA
Columbia, SC
05 December 2017